The Book of Generations
Book I: The Calling – Out of Her Mind

The Calling: Out of Her Mind

Marta J. Luzim

First Printing: 2014

ISBN 978-0-9886522-1-7

www.martaluzim.com

Contents

Acknowledgements

To my dearest and nearest who gave me their hearts, commitment and undying love so that the first book of the Book of Generations, *The Calling - Out of Her Mind* could be birthed.

To my husband Ron, who is my soulmate. He has never left my side and has always encouraged me to find my bliss. His strength of heart and compassion endures eternally. My daughter Lara, who is the spirit of all I create and the wings beneath my feet. She is from my tribe in this life and many lives; an everlasting love beyond words. Her wisdom and creative genius inspired my creative work. Evelyn Park, my spiritual daughter. Her dedication, devotion and love kept me on the path. She is the example of a true warrior.

To Deborah Seidman, Elaine Forney and Martha Alderson, who I cherish as friends, coaches and soul-sisters and are part of an ancient circle of women: courage, compassion, and creative passion; they are my midwives.

To my deceased lineage of women: grandmother Sarah, my mother Ray and my sister Carla who live in me as the heartbeat of this story. Their untold stories, their heartache and pain, and yearning for love that eluded them awakened me to my purpose. I miss them and hope to mend the brokenness through this book and the books to follow.

To the memory of my first Jungian therapist, Dr. Schulman, who ignited my dreams, art and writing. At age sixteen Dr. Schulman validated my pain, named the abuse I suffered, set fire to my soul and opened my psyche to the mysteries of knowing myself. He pointed the way inward and started my spiritual journey.

A special thanks to Shelley Lieber, coach, friend and cheerleader for getting my book out there now. She helped me to find the courage to just do it! Thanks to Joanne O'Sullivan for her proofreading and encouragement, and Janet Aiossa for her beautiful cover design.

Preface

My horoscope by Rob Brezsny
When he was 21, the Capricorn writer Jack London set off to prospect for gold in the 1897 Klondike Gold Rush. He had a rough time. Malnourished, he suffered from scurvy. To make matters worse, he didn't find much gold and returned home broke. On the other hand, he met scores of adventure seekers who told him stories of their travels. These tales served as material for his novel The Call of the Wild, published in 1903 and regarded as his masterpiece. I'm guessing you will begin a similar trajectory, Capricorn.

Capricorn knows that sacrifice and personal responsibility are the building blocks of true love and realizes the goal with a special grace and maturity. This is a huge invitation at the depth at the suffering you create around love and is particularly suited for healing old emotional wounds. This is the full moon of tough love, facing the reality of love lost or denied.

It all matters
I am a Capricorn. January 1st is my birthday. To be born on the first day of the year is a religious experience for me. I am drawn inward to re-evaluate, atone and promise to change my ways. No balloons, party hats or 'yippee' for me. Just being close to the people I love, maybe seeing a movie and wondering what the next year will bring for me. The depth of living my birthday is like Yom Kippur, the holiest Jewish holiday, where you self-examine, forgive and atone. At first, this reflection brings up confusion, chaos and my impending mortality. That revelation always humbles me, and wakes me up like a cold splash of water to meet my demons and release my angels.

I've been writing this novel, *The Calling*, since the moment I was conceived. When I was sixteen I set out to find gold. Not gold coins, but the gold of consciousness, healing and love. While on my journey I met my demons: borderline personality, child abuse, eating addictions and the fear of my own female body. I realized I had multiple personalities that had no voice. At the age of 54, while working with a shaman in the hills of Taos, I developed the chronic illness gastroparesis. This monster of an illness forced me to face my demons in a way only G-d could have planned. That is when I decided to complete the millionth re-write of *The Calling*, and began to slash, edit and find the true story, and shape the trilogy that was screaming to be released.

Like Jack, I have met scores of soul seekers and mastered the gift of being a healer. I worked with hundreds upon hundreds of women that helped me write *The Calling*. I saw my protagonist, Ruby, in every woman I guided, and mostly in myself. Ruby Goldsmith's need to uncover the secrets of her family legacy is her holy grail, and every woman's search to know herself. Naomi Goldenberg states in her book, *Changing of the Gods*, "Every woman's story is biblical." My search for those stories became a passionate obsession.

The mission to find the truth in my body and soul was a terrifying surrender. I had to erase everything I was taught about being a woman, being Jewish and being alive. I quantum leaped into my soul and channeled, screaming from the onset, "I'm not good enough! Not me!" But, why not me? Why not me!

Ruby Goldsmith is a reluctant shaman. She resists her calling. She is a power to be reckoned with. The forces of angels, demons and the Creator are stronger than her petty ego, and throws her to her knees to let this story flow out of her belly.

It has taken twenty-plus years to weave this story. It crosses spans of time, from the ancient to modern civilization.

It made a woman out of me.

Life: messy, juicy, mysterious, exciting, sorrowful and joyful. Read on and on…maybe you will see, feel, hear and free yourself, or maybe you won't. This is up to you.

This is Ruby's time. It is your time. It is now.

Prologue

1986 Westfall Residential Healing Center, California

Ruby clung to the sheets soaked from her perspiration. She swatted invisible forces and screamed. "No! Damn, no, noo!" Her body shook, struggling with schizophrenia, could it be bi-polar disorder, borderline, or was it an awakening? Her hands trembled as she reached toward the gray light. Was it her dark night of the soul? This was her last chance. Her last chance to ground the visions and voices. She clasped her hands over her ears and whispered, "I can't." Shook her head, "I can!"

A silky summer breeze blew through the patio doors as nightfall quickened. She rolled out of the bed and slipped into the bathroom, turned on the light. The walls were painted blues and greens to calm her nerves. But nothing soothed the anxiety that kept her underweight and fatigued. She turned the knob on the sink. Cold water splattered as she slapped it on her face and over her naked body.

For years, she had downed a myriad of medications to block the depression, hallucinations, and self-hatred that pounded her feelings into putty. Now after two drug-free years in Westfall, the images were random, fierce, at times muddled, but vivid; her emotions sharp and raw.

Tired onyx eyes stared back at her from the mirror. Was that their true color? She flinched. Black curls, disheveled; face pale; full lips; sunken cheekbones: her face intrigued her. She vaguely remembered that she had turned thirty-six the previous January. The hit song "Walk Like an Egyptian" rippled through her mind. She hummed a few notes of the kooky song and whispered the verse, *"All the old paintings on the*

tombs. They do the sand dance don't you know, Walk like an Egyptian."
Ruby bobbed her head from side to side. She smiled, imagined herself
wrapped in veils. She swirled around, her hands dancing above her
head. Dizzy, she swayed and stopped.

The pounding of running water snapped her back. She turned the
faucet off, wobbled back into the room and tumbled into the bed. It
seemed like an eternity since she had flown from Florida to California.
She remembered how each cloud embraced the bluest sky and held
the promise that she could, would resurrect her fragmented mind and
piece her life together.

At that moment a flashback tore through her. Eyes teary and tight,
she trembled as images hit her dead on. "Surrender, surrender." She
pounded her chest. A shiver, a flood of warm fluids, her mother's angry
cry splashed in her DNA. Bright wings of angels sipped her infant
soul. The small beings dragged her spirit down from the heavens and
pushed her into her mother's womb. Tiny whispers in her ear: *Come
in. Come in.* She dropped like steel into her mother's fluids. Ruby
squirmed, grabbed her head, moaned, "I hurt, Mama, I hurt."

The flashback retreated. Gone as fast as it came. She slipped out
of the bed to the floor. Exhausted, she spread-eagled and sighed. She
gazed at the wall she had painted red. A few days before, a surge of
creativity had snapped her into action. Paintings lined up one after
the other. The dark, ancient women; ecstatic faces of men and women
copulating under red suns clothed in golden sand. Most unfinished.
But it was a relief that once again the primal impulse to create poured
through her. *Yes!* She raised her arms in victory.

She stood up and ambled over to the desk. Papers and books
scattered about like forgotten mail. She stared out through the patio
doors. Lush mountains framed her view. Bold green oaks, pines,
and wild blue flowers brushed up against each other as if posed for a
snapshot on a postcard.

At once, another apparition pulsed. The ache, the push-pull
resistance vibrated through her muscles. *Steady. Steady, now. Move
with it.* Ruby grabbed a red pen, placed it firmly against the pad, wrote:
A waking experience. A voice in her head.—*Write now.* Her hand
moved on automatic pilot.

Marianne is here. I touch her hem.

"*No.*" *Marianne slaps my hand away.*

"Please, Marianne, tell me about my life."

Marianne's gutsy laugh moistens me. She twirls her crimson dress in the wind. "You have to live your life in order for me to teach you."

I stroke Marianne's twisted auburn hair, "Then why did you come to me as a child?"

Marianne's eyes tear, "Don't you remember?"

I fall at Marianne's feet, "My life is a mess, flawed, unsalvageable. I am in a forest. Smells of lavender and pine. Moist heat on my skin. Wind sings. I am tingling with sex. I long for Joel. I hunger for Steve. No! This is unbearable."

Marianne waves for me to follow. "Take in your life. What do you find?"

So hot here. Body shaking. "I find no...nothing. I'm wicked."

"Nothing!" Marianne stops, walks toward me, her dark-tiger eyes ravage through me. "Your grandmother crossed an ocean in a pickle barrel, left her family behind to burn in ovens. She gave birth to your mother, your mother to you. You carry the legacy of your ancestors. I am your ancestor. Your battle between husband and lover is the road to a deeper calling. Isn't that enough?"

"I don't know how to be a woman."

Marianne wedges my face into her palms. Your grandmother, mother, and sister, lost their way. The Shekinah buried alive in their vaginas. She waits for release in your body."

"I'm no seer! Marianne, I'm shamed by your words. My body heats up with sex and lust."

"Stop being so small. Sex is the feminine voice of God. It is primal and creative. The senses and the earth. Wake up!"

Marianne's eyes, oh my god her eyes, hurt my heart. "I'm not you, Marianne. I feel like shit."

Marianne steps back. "I'm an unmothered prostitute to the world. This is not an awakening, it's a reckoning!"

Ruby felt around the room, the light darkened. "I can't see you. Marianne!" Who was talking? *Is it me or Marianne?* Everything was mixed up. Ruby cried out. "I don't know the true story."

"Just write! It doesn't matter what comes first, middle, or last. Tell the story. Even if no one thinks it is true. All the mad women, the crazy women, the dark women, the holy prostitutes, the outcasts of society... these women are the legends of your freedom."

Ruby squirmed, her face knotted. "Marianne?" She was gone. Ruby's hands shook. She fiddled with the pen, breathed, closed her eyes, and wrote:

Sarah watches her mother raped by Cossacks, her grandfather shot in the back, and her father hung. The soldiers spot her. Her sisters and brothers scatter out of sight. She runs; crawls on her belly into the dark, dead forest. She hears men's growls, pounding hooves. She hides in the underbrush; the grass turns blood-green. Smoke and fire soak into her lungs. Sarah holds her breath, prays she is invisible to the demons approaching.

Ruby dropped the pen, shuddered. Placed her hand across her pounding chest. A young girl's face flashed in the window. The image caught in her mind. It was the face of six-year-old Ruby. She was about to fly off a roof.

Chapter 1: January 1, 1956 – Brooklyn Fly Away

When Ruby Goldsmith turned six, she decided she was old enough to fly. So, on the day of her birthday, she stood on the rooftop of her home at Claren Gardens apartments and flapped her arms. Plaid woolen coat buttoned tight to her neck, hands warmed in pink mittens, she imagined stepping off the ledge, diving into the magical blue Brooklyn sky and soaring through the cold sunny clouds. To Ruby, Kingsborough was the universe and the Milky Way revolved around it. She believed that if she closed her eyes and imagined pretty things,—pink bows, chocolate ice cream, rainbows and bubble gum—like Peter Pan, she'd fly high like a bluebird to Never Never Land. She giggled, her cheeks red from winter's brisk touch, her eyes glistening with adventure.

The winter winds swept her curly black hair across her round, cheeky face. The howling winds blew through the big oaks that lined the winding paths of the sixteen-unit complex. Dead branches shivered as the frosty air pressed against their trunks. The aromas of chicken soup and fried onions filled the hallways and danced their way up to the open air around Ruby's curious eyes, and into her nostrils. The smells made her stomach feel warm and full. She quivered with excitement. A sudden burst of energy made Ruby tighten the scarf around her neck. She breathed and spat out, "I will fly away and never come back."

Ruby trembled at the sound of her own command. A familiar fear ate away at her stomach. She grabbed her belly, coughed, then gagged a few times and vomited. She wiped her runny nose and sticky mouth and spat out the sour taste. Her heart pounded from the sick nausea. She gazed up and spread her arms out, one foot inching toward the edge. She'd do anything to escape from her family.

As she leaned over the bricks, a soft, yet stern, voice ripped through her mind and shook her body. *Stop! Stop! No! You're not to fly. Go home now!*

Ruby turned her head every which way, searching, trembling. "What? Mommy?" Silence greeted her question. Ruby stepped back, squeezed her eyes. A heavy, choppy breath shook her body. "Wha... who..who are you? Come out!"

The voice screamed. *Go home! I will tell you when.*

Ruby's right eye twitched and she backed away from the ledge. "I don't want to go home." She tripped over a loose lace from her sneaker and fell slam-dunk on her tush onto the tar roof.

Go home! Ruby! It's not safe yet.

Her mouth trembled and she crawled toward the open door, her jeans sticky against the tar. She hated the small apartment and the bedroom she shared with her older sister, Leah. She didn't want to speak to her mommy or daddy. She wanted to fly and leave them behind.

NO, NO, NO! This time the voice felt like a pressure inside her gut and pushed her farther toward the door.

Ruby twisted and squealed, "Okay. Just stop. Stop screaming." She held her ears as she jumped up and hurried off the roof, down the steps, back to the two-bedroom apartment on the third floor.

Chapter 2: Mama Committed

That night, Ruby burrowed under the covers in a restless battle between the sheets. It was a stormy evening. In her agitated sleep, Ruby heard the door slam. Footsteps pounded against the steps leading to the roof. She shot up. Startled, she stared at the shadows hunched in the corners of the ceiling. Leah wheezed in short spurts, sleeping. She heard her mother's scream echo from afar. Her father's shout. "Stop, Claire!" Her neck stretched toward the sounds. What was happening? A few minutes passed and another scream reverberated from outside her window. Ruby ran to her closet, threw her coat over her cotton flowered pajamas, and slipped her feet into her sneakers. For a moment, she stood and stared at Leah, watched her sleep. Her sister now purred like a dove. Her face smooth and pale, her body graceful, her blonde curls innocent upon the pillow. She was quiet, dreaming, oblivious to the surrounding drama. Ruby reached toward her, wanted to wake Leah, but changed her mind. She stepped back and tiptoed to the front door, opened it, and rushed up the steps.

The door to the rooftop was ajar. Ruby peeked out. Her eyes pierced through the dark. She hiccupped. She did that sometimes when she was really afraid. She clutched her chest; her heart raced, until she saw the outline of figures scrambling. Ruby squinted. She shivered as the freeze wrapped around her. A bit closer, she opened the door and saw her mother clad in a flimsy white nightgown, wailing like a crippled animal, "Take me now. Take me, God. The angels are waiting for me. They'll love me." Claire's bony arms and legs weakened her stance. Rain drummed down onto the street, made the bricks shine in the watery moonlight and silhouetted her parents. Her father grabbed her mother by the waist. Claire scratched and kicked. Her mother's mangled yelp turned into a high-pitched squeal, "I hate you, Morty, I hate everyone."

Ruby rubbed her puffed red eyes and thought: *she isn't really my mother. My real mother lives in the sky.* After all, Ruby's black 'twisted curls from hell,' as her mother described her furry locks, had no resemblance to her mother and older sister's gorgeous golden hair. Every time her mother brushed her uncooperative tresses, she'd say, "You looked like a monkey with a perm when you were born. Not like Leah, who was just a little angel face." Needless to say, when she examined herself in the mirror she felt nauseatingly ugly. Disgusted with her jumbled jungle of broken bumps of hair that only a strong steel brush could whack. Nausea swept down into her cells every time her mother bobby-pinned a lock of her hair. A gross feeling dug into her body. She gagged. A sudden crunch against the roof alerted Ruby that her parents were on the move.

Morty picked Claire up, balanced her over his shoulder, and carried her toward the exit. Claire beat her father's back but failed to get away. Ruby ran. She stumbled down the steps, back into the apartment. She cowered behind the television in the living room. The door slammed. Her mother screamed, "Bastard. You whoremonger." Her father dropped her onto the dark green carpet. Claire crawled like a snake into the spotless, white-tiled kitchen. She reappeared holding a knife. She stood, wobbled, and knocked over the fringed lamp on the oriental end table. Without warning, with one quick slice, she stabbed herself in the thigh. Blood trickled down her calf in a pool of gravy mush. Claire howled, "No one loves me. No one loves me."

Ruby leapt, screamed. She froze, unable to run. Hiccups jumped through her body. She tried to talk. "Ma...ma...*hic*...ma..*hic*...Daddy!"

Her father pointed at Ruby, "Stay there, Ruby. Don't move."

Then, like a wounded lion struck by a spear Claire limped toward Ruby, the knife clutched in her hand, "I'll get you, too." Disheveled, soaked with blood and rain, her platinum hair a straggled mess, she inched forward, knife in her palm.

Ruby tightened, clutched her throat, her eyes rolled back. That stopped her hiccups. Before her mother got a smidgen closer, her father tackled Claire, downed her to the floor, and smacked the knife out of her hand. "You're out of your motherfucking mind."

Claire curled up into a white ball. Blood and snot dripped all over the place.

At that moment, Leah appeared. Startled at the blood blotched on her mother's nightgown, she watched in terror as her parents struggled with the knife. Astonished, she flung her arms in the air, ran to the bathroom and locked the door.

Ruby plopped behind the television. She heaved and trembled. Her legs stiffened, paralyzed. A loud pop resounded in her ears. The sound shot through her body. In a flash, without effort, she floated up, above her immobilized body. Ruby was suspended in space, hovering over her own head like a balloon. She looked down; her back was straight and stiff against the wall, but she was not in her body. Huffing and pushing as hard as she could, she bore down, pulled, and growled. The harder she tried, the more she lifted away.

A voice rattled in her ears. *Now. Now. Fly! I will protect you.*

Ruby winged her arms and flew.

An angel of light guided her. *Now you can fly.*

A glaring light blinded Ruby. She cried out, "My eyes, my eyes. They hurt. Help." She levitated through mist, stars, and moon-glow.

Then light shaped into a woman. "My name is Marianne." Auburn ringlets tumbled down to her ankles. Wrinkles around her mouth and eyes were dotted with sand. Her skin smooth and dark, her long fingers graced in space. The angel chanted *"Schma Isroyael Adoni Elohenyou, Adoni Echard."* Her voice was silky cream. "Tell the story with your third eye. The one that sees me. I love you."

Ruby's feet dangled and circled in the vapor. Then, realizing she was far away, with a stranger, Ruby squealed. "Let me go!"

"When the light appears sometimes you think it's part of your nightmare, but it's not. I'm not," the angel whispered.

Her father's voice exploded and Ruby catapulted back into her body. Wet, shaky, and disoriented, a muddled breath, then a cold sweat shook her. She grasped the top of the television. Looked up. Down. Up, down. Scanned her hands over her belly, arms, legs. "Oh. No! Oh no. Oh no! Daddy! Help."

He was busy tending to her mother. "Claire, you're a stupid idiot."

Claire fainted.

Morty felt Claire's pulse and piled her into his arms, laying her on the green embroidered couch. He turned to Ruby. "What are you doin'? Watch your mother. I gotta get people to take care of her. Just come here, Ruby."

Ruby shook her head. A rapid shake. *No, no, no.*

"Okay, okay. Calm down. If she moves or does anything, just scream. I've got to make the call to the hospital. I've got to get an ambulance, quick." He glanced at his wristwatch. "And I've got to get your grandma over here. Right now."

Ruby begged, "Don't go. Don't go."

"Whose gonna make the calls? I gotta. It will be a minute. I promise. Nothing's gonna happen." He ran out.

Stunned and stiff, Ruby waited for her father to return. Time shivered in chopped hiccups through her body. She eyed her mother, eyed for her father's return.

Soon, Morty was back. He edged next to Claire, wiped her forehead with a cloth. "Okay, they're coming. And your grandma, so I can go to the hospital when they come."

Ruby quivered and hiccupped, "Who…who..*hic*…who else is coming, Daddy… *hic*?"

"Hold your breath and count to ten. Your hiccups will go away."

Ruby slid down the wall. Curled into a ball. She counted her fingers over and over. She let her breath go. Waited. Daddy was right. They were gone.

Twenty minutes passed while Ruby counted and held her breath, counted, held her breath, just to be sure. The bell rang. Her father ran to the door. Two stocky men with hairy arms charged into the living room. Ruby wobbled to her feet.

One of the men was fat, the other short. They placed a long tube with a needle into Claire's arm and a plastic mask over her nose and mouth. They examined her leg."Good tourniquet." They tended to the wound with thick gauze.

Ruby's mother was strapped into a bed on wheels. As the white-uniformed men pushed Claire away on the gurney, she lifted her head, muffled through the oxygen mask, "Only the angels will save me. Everyone hates me."

Ruby watched her mother fade into oblivion. The door slammed. Her husky grandmother arrived as they left. Cigarette dangling from her mouth, she buried herself in the armchair, stern and crumpled.

Ruby ran to her bedroom, knotted herself into the blanket. Her body jerked in tears. She clutched her stomach. She needed her father to stroke her head before he left. That never happened. The father void was familiar; no bedtime stories or being tucked in; no father's kiss upon her forehead; no goodnight wishes. Her father was hardly home. The deli business kept him going around the clock, kept her mother subdued with money to buy expensive couches and Chanel bags.

Ruby would run after him with a drawing, a pretty rock, or a broken toy, anything to get his attention. Her father's vacant, sad, green eyes would stare down at her. His tousled ebony hair fell over his forehead and he would command, "Stop doing stupid things. Learn your ABCs."

One day, one day, he'd say, "Everything is okay. Ruby. You're a good girl."

But, Ruby guessed, he'd never comfort her with those words because he knew they were lies.

It was not the first time her mother had gone crazy, and she knew it wouldn't be the last.

Chapter 3: Grandma Sarah's Blintzes and Schnapps

Sarah—Ruby's only living grandparent, her mother's mother—swooped over the household that night with her firm and efficient orderliness. She crawled into Ruby's bed and cuddled her into her breasts. Leah joined the two, crawled inside the circle of embrace. To Ruby, it felt like a family. But, it never happened again. Only that night.

Ruby woke the next morning, shaky from nightmares about snakes and witches. Ruby saw Marianne fly around in her dream. Confused and disoriented, she tumbled out of bed. Her cotton jammies stuck to her tush as she wandered into the kitchen. Leah was quiet and slumped over, eating Cheerios. Her grandmother complained above the clink, clang of dishes and pots, "Crazy *meshuganah*, your mama. Crazy, crazy, crazy." Chubby, squat grandma Sarah had a face covered with indented lines that looked like the map of some forgotten city. Her arthritic fingers showcased frosty white polish and a sapphire pinky ring. Grandma Sarah had the callused hands of a seamstress, of a mother who scrubbed floors, and yellow fingers from inhaling packs of unfiltered cigarettes. Today her hands delicately rolled the dough to make blintzes. "Come here, *mamala*. Roll. Make." Grandma wiped her hands on her red flowered apron.

Ruby stood on the tips of her toes, watched her grandma sprinkle baking powder and water to soften the dough and make it thin. Grandma's meticulous kneading and rolling made Ruby forget the night before, forget her mother, just for a moment. "You make it better, Grandma, not me. I just want to eat them." Ruby stuffed her hands into the mushy mixture.

Leah slid out from the chair, "I'm going over to Paula's."

Grandma sniffed, took a shot of whiskey from a tiny bottle on the counter. "Be back lunchtime."

Leah shuffled from the kitchen, "Yeah, Grandma."

Sarah slapped the ball of dough onto the wooden board and handed Ruby a rolling pin. "Here. Roll back and forth. If you eat, you make."

The potatoes boiled in the pot while Ruby flattened the dough. She liked how the pin slid across the dough, stretching it into a slim pancake. She felt like she was skidding along the counter like a swan on a lake as she swayed to and fro with each stroke. The smell of sweet heat warmed her. Ruby's mouth watered.

Grandma drained the potatoes, ran cold water over them, and dumped them into an orange bowl. She threw in a wad of butter, a half-cup of milk and a pinch of salt, pepper, and garlic; pounded and mashed them until creamy smooth.

"Grandma, please give me some."

"Such a hurry. Roll, then eat. No cheating. Make perfect beautiful blintz. Nothing like fried potato blintz with a big heap of sour cream. Huh, *Bubbalah*?"

Ruby stopped rolling. "Grandma. No fair. I'm hungry."

"Fair. What's fair in life? Nothing fair." Sarah took another slug of liquor.

Ruby frowned. Grandma was right. What was fair? Her mother didn't treat her fair. Sarah didn't even treat her own daughter fair, always screaming at Claire. Ruby hated the two women fighting, hated her grandma pushing and smacking Claire, yelling, "You don't know what it is to run from Cossacks and Nazis. You think you a movie star. *Feh!*"

With big blobby sobs, her mother stuttered in a kind of baby talk, "Ma...ma, ma..ma, I...I love you."

Her grandmother held an emotional iron rod over her mother's head and her mother grabbed it like a rattle from her crib.

Ruby didn't understand how her grandmother cradled her into her large bosoms, stroked her hair and sang "*bubbalah, shaynamadala*," but was mean to her mother. In some ways, it made Ruby happy to think that her grandma didn't like her mother. Liked her better.

"Grandma, what about your mama?"

Sarah never spoke of her family. Never showed a picture or any remnant from her past. Sarah threw her hands up. "Cut the dough into four strips!" She handed Ruby a dull knife.

Ruby hesitated before taking the knife. "I'm afraid." She held the knife down away from her body. "I don't like knives."

Grandma Sarah placed her hand on top of Ruby's wrist. "Here I'll guide you. This knife is to make food, not make you a scared girl." She held the knife and placed it in Ruby's palm. "Forget your mama. She can't hurt you now. You become a woman when you learn to cook."

Ruby peeked up at her grandmother, "I don't want to be a woman." She shook while her grandma guided her hand.

"You have no choice. Before you know it, God will make a woman from you. Better to know that now than later." Grandma wrapped her fingers around Ruby's hand. "Now cut nice. Make good blintz. Ones that I'll be proud of. Ones that will make you know you've done something bigger than being six. Then you'll grow up. Not like your mother."

Ruby cut the dough and sighed in relief. Her grandmother threw the knife into the sink.

"Grandma? Am I like mommy?" Ruby took a spoon and filled each square of dough with the soft potato and folded. "Grandma?" Careful with her next words, she peeked up with a shy stare, "Grandma, do angels live here?"

"Forget your mama. And what do you talk of angels? Forget things that are foolish. What man will want you if you don't cook? Quiet. Fold." Sarah sat down on the stool and drank.

Ruby threw her arms up, "Okay, but…" She sighed, wanted to get Grandma to talk more. "Did Grandpa eat blintzes?" Ruby squeezed the ends of the luscious delicacy, licked her fingers.

"He's dead. Don't talk of the dead." Sarah kept drinking.

Ruby stared at her grandmother, her hands lifeless on top of her lap, the bottle tipped from her hand.

"He hated blintz." The liquor bottle toppled to her lap. Sarah grabbed it, slid it across her mouth and took another slug. She wobbled off the chair, stuck the bottle into her apron pocket, pulled out a big frying pan, and crashed it onto the stove. Oil, butter, and fire smoked up the kitchen as Sarah dropped each blintz into the bubbling fat. "Get the plate."

Ruby obeyed her grandmother. She watched the first blintz fall onto the plate in her hand.

"Go. *Eshen*. Eat. Forget for now. Better to forget." Sarah scooped a spoonful of sour cream and gave it to Ruby.

Ruby sat on the floor, fingered the cream on the blintz. Her eyes hung on every move her grandma made. For a moment she thought she saw Grandma's eyes fill up wet. But Grandma never cried. Ruby knew to stop talking. She wondered about the grandfather she never saw. Ruby could only imagine a grandpa. Dark shiny hair, big bold eyes, and flappy lips. She wished she knew him.

"Grandma, I'm finished." Grease and sour cream spotted Ruby's face.

Sarah nodded, her eyes droopy. "Go. Go play in your room." Her grandma waved her arm. "Stop. Wait." She rummaged through her apron pocket. "Here. I forget. For you. Wear it."

Her grandmother handed her a Star of David. It had small rubies etched at the edge of each point. Ruby stared at it. "Is this yours, Grandma?"

"Take it. Go away."

Ruby had seen that sleepy frown on her grandma's face. It meant she was done cooking, cleaning, and being Grandma. "Okay, Grandma. Thank you."

She ran to her room and threw the spiritual trinket into a small, white ballerina-adorned jewelry box stashed on a shelf in her closet. Inside it, there were other fake bracelets, clips, and ribbons. Things she didn't pay much attention to. Stuffed from the food and in need of a bath, Ruby jumped into her bed and under the covers.

She thought about her mommy all messed up and crazy. It was easier to breathe with her mother gone, easier to sleep, easier. Although Ruby was relieved the men took her mother away, as she flipped side to side in bed, she missed her mother's morning ritual. *Strange*, she thought. Before the house got busy, Ruby would watch her mother apply mascara and lipstick. With a quick twist, Claire would pencil a beauty mark by the side of her curvy red lips. She'd turn, and say "Ruby lips," smile and smack her voluptuous mouth with a tissue. Each time, Ruby grabbed the used tissue before it was lost among discarded boxes and papers in the trashcan. She would press her lips against her mother's lipstick mark. "Ruby lips," she'd whisper.

Chapter 4: Synagogue, Ruby's Third Eye

The next day, Ruby's father woke her to attend Monday morning services.

"We're going to *shul*. I want you to come," Morty ordered.

The house was quiet and warmed with the smell of french toast.

"Eat and dress." Her father yelled from her parent's bedroom.

Ruby chose a blue sweater and blue skirt. Brushed her hair into a frenzy and slouched into the kitchen. She shoveled down the crisp, moist, syrupy breakfast, gulped the milk Sarah had left for her. She ran back to her bedroom, rummaged through her drawers, pulled out purple tights. She called out to her father, "Leah coming, Daddy?"

"No, Grandma is taking her to school."

"But, why?"

"Cause. I want you with me today. I think it best."

"But, why?"

"Stop asking questions."

Ruby felt odd and queasy, out of sorts. She finished dressing and threw her coat, mittens and boots on. She ran out. "Ready, Daddy."

Dressed in a black coat, Morty took her hand. "Let's go."

They strolled through the mashed-up snow and chilly winds. The synagogue was in a basement down the street, a left turn at the corner. When they arrived, a tall woman with a lace shawl covering her head took their coats. They clanked down the steps into rectangular room transformed into a holy space. Ruby held her nose. "It smells in here."

"Sit." Her father commanded.

They sat in the front row.

The chairs creaked as men stood, then sat, with each prayer. Each verse strummed against her heart. Ruby yawned. The men's chanting eased her. Chills edged her closer to her father to warm up. He paid no attention to her.

"Schma Isroyeal, Adoni Eloyhenyu Adoni Echart." Her father sang along with the congregation.

The sight of her father bowing, praying, and singing was new for Ruby. The shiny white shawl with small, blue Stars of David lined along the tassels crumpled in ripples across his shoulders. She wished he gave her the attention he gave to his bowing. The humming, droning sound of the prayer made Ruby drowsy. Sleepy, she asked, "Daddy what does the *Schma* song mean?"

"Means God is love and is everywhere and in everything."

Ruby tilted her head, rolled her eyes. She clenched her fist, "If that's true, why is Mommy so mean?"

"Only God knows."

"That stinks." Ruby folded her arms and curled her lips.

"Sit up. Listen." He pulled at her sweater. "You need God and you need to listen to what he says. I took you here so you can listen. Because you saw your mother… and well…maybe God will make it all go away for you."

Ruby felt a huge ball of fire tighten her chest. She held her breath and clenched down. Her face turned red. "How will God do that? How?"

"Quiet, Ruby. Just listen. Listen to the rabbi."

Ruby thought old Rabbi Herschowitz's white beard that straggled across his chest looked stupid. He stood between his two sons, who were also rabbis. *Where are the girls?* Ruby thought. Maybe standing behind the curtain? "Why aren't there girls up there, Daddy?"

"It's the way it is. It's called tradition."

"Why?"

"Ruby. No more questions."

The elder rabbi childishly danced and then, without warning dropped to the floor, feet and arms stiff like a dead starfish.

Ruby gasped. What happened? The congregation moaned, their prayers silenced. Between wisps of air, Ruby squinted and pointed. She saw it. "Ghost. I see it, Daddy!" She saw it. She knew she did. The ghost came out of the old man's body. His soul flew out through the ceiling into a soft light. Then the angel Marianne appeared, waved, and vanished.

Ruby cried out. "Daddy! Daddy! She's here. She's here."

A shrill cry ripped from the crowd. "Call an ambulance. Call a doctor. Anyone here a doctor? Help!"

Ruby leaned over and whispered to her father. "The rabbi is in the light, Daddy, with the fairy angel lady."

Her father gave her a hard look. "I just don't know what to do with you. You can't just say these things. It's wrong." Specks of dust ran through his wavy black hair. "How do you know where the rabbi went?" He grabbed her shoulders and tightened. "We gotta go. I don't want you around this."

"You're hurting me, Daddy."

Morty loosened his grip, grabbed her hand, and led her outside. They stood in the light rain. "Button up." He pulled her hood over her head, flipped up his collar. Moisture left a cold wet mask on both their faces. "You lie, Ruby. You didn't see the rabbi go into any light. Why do you keep lying? Only great people like Moses sees things like that."

Ruby squashed down a big cry. She rubbed her arm. She wanted her daddy to love her. "I don't know, Daddy. I make it up." She folded her arms in defiance. "I won't ever go to temple. Ever."

"You don't have to." He tapped her head. "I can't be worrying about you, Ruby. You want to be crazy like your mother? Just stop doin' it. Talk about little girl things. Like dolls."

"Mommy saw angels. I heard her say it."

"No. Your mother didn't see anything. She didn't know what she was saying. Just stop, Ruby. Stop. Don't mention it again. Do you hear me?"

"Why?" She looked up at him as if he were a god.

Morty softened. "Just don't. You want your mother to get better? Then don't talk about any of it. Any of it. You understand? You promise?"

Ruby teared up. "Yes, Daddy."

Her father patted her shoulder, "You want a malted and pretzel?"

She wiped her eyes. A bright bounce of glee lit up her eyes. "Yes, Daddy."

***

Ruby stared out of her window that night. The big oak spun moonlight through its branches. She frittered away the time in her room, drawing pictures of flowers and angels. Then she picked up a black crayon. Darkness and dust spread across the page. She cried. Tore it up. She couldn't tell her daddy. No one must know. But, she wanted to tell someone, or she felt she'd bust.

Chapter 5: September, 1956 – Marianne's Face, Kindergarten

Away for eight weeks, Ruby's mother returned home from the hospital in March. Ruby buried her fear of Claire's stiff, slurred, cold demeanor by being as quiet as she could. Always watching her mother through the corner of her eye, numb to her presence, she was still mesmerized when her mother drank dark, unsweetened coffee, ate English muffins with a smear of butter, and downed at least five pills every day. Once again, Ruby leaned against the bathroom door and watched her mother's morning make-up ritual. *Ruby lips.*

Nothing major occurred over the next five months. Her father went to work, squashing his stocky body into the smallest jet-blue car Ruby had ever seen. Claire went to the beauty parlor and shopped for Chanel bags and perfume, and held up her prizes for Ruby to see. Sarah cooked, swept, and mopped, never without a cigarette hanging from her lips. Once in a while, Claire shouted, "Shut up. I'll hit you," when Leah and Ruby played loudly in their room. Her mother's threats were ice against Ruby's tongue. She'd freeze up and ignore them. It was like that. Quiet fear before the storm.

The shattered chaos fell into cracked normalcy. The summer trees danced, the Goldsmiths folded into the months along with the squirrels and clouds. It was all the same again in Ruby's eyes.

***

The Tuesday after Labor Day, Claire led Ruby to her first day of kindergarten. Ruby wiggled from her mommy's firm grip as they scurried down Utica Avenue. "I don't want to go to kindergarten."

The coolness of the day matched her mother's mood. Ruby whined and kicked up her mommy's anger, "I'll squeeze harder if you don't walk faster." Her mother puffed her chin out. "Next time you'll take the bus with your sister."

"Mommy...I..." Her head sank down. "I don't want to go with Leah. She hits me."

"Oh, please." Her mother jerked Ruby's hand. "I missed my beauty parlor appointment this morning."

The crooked streets of Brooklyn were slotted between strips of tar. Ruby skipped over the cracks. Heat rose from the highway as they hurried across the thick yellow-and- white crosswalk. Ruby yearned to dive into the fat yellow strip; vanish like a mermaid in the yellow crosswalk ocean. Horns and tires screeched. An orange-dotted ladybug landed on her dress; a rare flutter of a blue-kaleidoscope butterfly flapped its wings toward the clouds. Along the way, they passed through aromas of greasy french fries and hamburgers, sweet cherry ices, mixed in with fresh baked breads. Green and black awnings flipped their edges, tossed by the wind. Storeowners were out window washing, sweeping dust from their entrances. Short bald men, grey-haired ladies, and young, dark boys took quick puffs on cigarettes as they rolled in stinky garbage cans. Brooklyn, with its loud noises and smorgasbord of sights, was Ruby's soul food. She opened her mouth and sucked in. The air tasted like a cool watermelon. Ruby squinted as the sun caught her eyes and warmed the fall day.

Her mother's fat bouffant captured the light rays like a fly in a spider's web.

"Mommy, your head takes up the sun."

"Do you want me to take my head off?" She huffed.

Ruby lowered her eyes. "Sorry." Ruby daydreamed as her eyes flitted along with her mother's red scarf blowing in the wind. Her pearls circled her neck, neat and prim. Waves of red and white dots swarmed in her eyes. Between the elusive images, Ruby caught glimpses of Marianne's warm face. Ruby reached, attempted to touch her, but she'd vanish.

With her free hand, Ruby tugged her fluffy sweater closer to her shoulders. Her starched, polka dot skirt irritated her knees. She hit the hem to stop the scratching.

"Fix your hair." Claire tugged at Ruby's dark strands of black waves that popped out like cotton balls.

"Ouch." She pushed her mother's hand away. Even with all the pills she took, Ruby knew her mother was as mean as ever. Every week a tall, hippy, flat-faced woman came to talk to Claire. When the woman left her mother would spit, "Idiot."

Ruby squealed as her mother pulled at her to quicken her pace.

"Keep this up and I'll tell your father and you'll get an even harder slap." A fierce glare crossed her mother's face.

"Daddy doesn't hit. You do." Ruby squeezed her eyes. She mumbled under her breath.

Their brisk walk came to a halt. Her mother turned. Ruby cringed as her mother's fireball stare ripped into Ruby's heart. "What did you say?"

Ruby shook and covered her face with her hands, recognizing that mommy-kill look. She peeped through her fingers.

"You mean child. Ungrateful! If we were home…" She tugged her daughter's arm. "Stand up straight. Look at me."

Ruby directed her head toward the sky. She couldn't believe her mommy heard. Stupid her.

"I said, look at me!" Her mother tapped her foot.

Ruby whirled her head in circles. "Nothing. Nothing, Mommy!"

"Uhh! Uhh! Better be nothing. And stop shaking. Just stop, stop. I can't stand it." Her mommy squatted and drew Ruby close to her. She dug her bright red polished nails into Ruby's forearms. They carved half-moon dents in her arms. Her mommy's jaw tightened, "If you ever, ever…" Her nails dug deeper. Her mother was about to pinch her cheek, then stopped.

Several groups of parents and children sprinted by. Claire threw a quick smile and stood up, releasing her daughter's arm.

A big sigh rushed through Ruby. She rubbed her arm. Tears of relief swarmed down her cheeks. She wiped them quick so her mommy wouldn't see.

Her mother waited for the passerby to be gone. "See what you did? You made me look horrid."

She peeked up at her mommy and shuddered. Mommy. Perfect movie star face. If she had the nerve, she'd hit her mommy back. Just once.

"Behave." Gray clouds slid through the sky as her mother crunched Ruby's fingers in her hand.

Straight ahead was the big, brown brick school building, P.S. 211. Students of all shapes and sizes scrambled up its steps, some shouting, some quiet, and some crying.

Ruby stumbled up the school steps and scraped her knee. She squawked, "Ouch. Ouch!" She sat down, held her knee.

"You're fine," Her mother yanked Ruby up each step like a monkey on a leash.

One last time, Ruby turned and soaked in the sun and trees. She prayed. *If you're there, creepy old God that Daddy talks to, save me.* She waited. Rolled her eyes up, down. No reply. *Daddy says you're everywhere. Be here God. Now!* Then, she heard the voice, the lady's voice, *Remember Ruby. You have your third eye. I know you're mad and scared. I'm here. Just remember you're not alone."*

"I am mad. Don't play hide and seek." Ruby screamed.

"What did you say?"

Ruby tightened her lips. "Nothing." Yes, her third eye. The lady put her voice in Ruby's head and made her see things that her daddy called stupid. Maybe he was right. She was stupid.

A tough drag up the steps and they were both inside the building. The lime green hallway smelled of fresh paint. She followed her mommy through the garbled crowd.

"It's supposed to be the one down there to the left." Like a chicken, her mother pecked her head in and out of open doorways, "Here it is. Here. This one."

Ruby glanced into the classroom. Children raced in every direction. The room was packed with wooden desks. Canvases leaned on top of spotted easels. Posters of the four major food groups, good and bad manners boards, and pictures of policemen and milkmen randomly hung on the walls. Rolled up, navy blue knotty blankets and cushy black mats were shoved off to the side of the room.

The children's screams could have cracked a thousand glasses. Ruby covered her ears. A paper cup hit Ruby in the head. These kids were bad bees, badder than her. She wondered, watched, and twirled her hair. What kind of school was this? Was it somewhere that kids could be stupid?

"What a mess!" Her mother shouted over the noise.

A lady with short, curly red hair and big red lips rustled toward them. She bent over, smoothed her brightly printed dress, and grinned. "Oh, my, hello! I'm your teacher. Miss Paula." She tripped over a chair. "Oh, my." She caught her balance. Miss Paula blushed. "My first year. But I'll get the hang of it."

"Well, get the hang of it soon. You're not too smart if you don't."

"I beg your pardon. It, it…it is only the first day. And they are only children." Her dark brown eyes were splattered with yellow spots like pimples ready to pop.

Ruby eyes widened. She was brave to talk back to her mommy.

"First day, my foot! Just give them a good jerk down in their seats. That's all."

Ruby thought the teacher would be pretty if it weren't for the bumps and holes in her cheeks, like birds had nipped at them. She tried to cover the face scars with pounds of powder.

The teacher flinched, then turned her attention to Ruby. "So, you're Ruby." The teacher offered her hand. "Let's shake, Ruby. What a pretty name. A red jewel. A Ruby."

"Ruby lips." Ruby shook her head.

Her mother frowned. "What did you say? Oh. You're mimicking me? Can you see how awful she is?"

"I need to ask you to leave, now." The teacher placed her hand on Ruby's shoulder.

"I'm sharing a mother's advice!"

Oh, no. Ruby knew. Her mommy hated Miss Paula. That's big trouble. Ruby hid her face in her hands.

Claire stroked her pearls like piano keys, "Don't let her get away with this kind of stuff." She huffed. "I'm going."

Through the corner of her eye, Ruby watched her mommy shrink away. No goodbye hug or kisses. Still shaky, she wanted to touch her private place to calm down. But she only did that when no one could see. So she squeezed her legs together. Her face turned pink.

"Do you need to go to the bathroom?" Miss Paula tilted her head.

She glanced toward the door to see if her mommy was lurking somewhere. "No!"

"What do you want?" Miss Paula whisked a strand of hair that hung over Ruby's eye.

What did she want? Ruby squinted. She scratched her head where her hair was pulled the tightest in her ponytail. What did she want? She scanned the room and focused clearly on the easels.

"I wa…wa.. want to make a painting." Oh, no. She had to count to ten to make her words better.

She closed her eyes, took a deep breath, and counted on her fingers.

"Are you alright, Ruby?"

Ruby nodded her head and let out a big breath. "Yes." Ah, they were gone.

Miss Paula led the way through the jungle of cannibal children eating crayons and spitting up water. Miss Paula pointed at a blank canvas. "Finger paints. It'll wash off. You'll be clean by the time you go home." She opened the jar of red paint and guided Ruby's pointer finger slowly into the jar. "Have fun."

Ruby stared at her red fingertip. She pushed her fist into the jar and rammed her knuckles all over the easel. Then she went to the blue, slipping, sliding, slapping. Then green, pumping, dripping, spurting, yellow, blue, purple and orange, until the easel was juicy and alive. Between the chaos of colors she drew a sloppy face.

The slabs, globs, and slashes of paint mirrored in Ruby's eyes, dripped down her pupils like droplets of blood.

"That's good, Ruby." Miss Paula applauded and stared closer at the painting. "Whose face is that?"

Ruby wiped the paints across her face and skirt. "No one."

"She has wings, Ruby."

"I can't tell you." Ruby kicked the easel. The canvas flopped with a thud.

Children gathered around. They started to cheer as Ruby destroyed the canvas.

"No. Ruby. No. Don't." The teacher grabbed her by the shoulders, rubbed her arms.

Miss Paula waved her hands like fans, "Hush, children, hush."

The students kept roaring.

"Look children, I'm a bird. Everyone make like a bird and find a nest to sit in. If you do, you'll get a surprise." She snapped her fingers. "Cookies. Cookies. Hush and you'll all get a cookie." Miss Paula placed her finger over her mouth.

Each student modeled the young teacher and put their finger over their lips.

From the shadows, Miss Paula's freckle-faced assistant jumped out and handed them each a cookie.

The boys and girls nibbled on their chocolate chip cookies like little squirrels.

"What happened to you, Ruby?" Ms. Paula held Ruby by the chin.

Ruby plunged down on the floor. With harsh and repeated strokes on her stained skirt, she sobbed. "I got to get the paint off. My mommy, she gets mad."

Ms. Paula whispered, "Sometimes, Ruby, when I'm afraid, I talk to angels."

Ruby's eyes widened. How did she know? Did she have a third eye too? She cuffed both hands around Miss Paula's skinny ankles. "Why don't they save me and Mommy?"

"I'm not sure Ruby. I think we have to save ourselves."

Chapter 6: June, 1959 – Family Move

Utica Avenue was a half hour away from East Flatbush, forty-five minutes if there was traffic. Ruby didn't know why they had to move. After all, her daddy's big deli and catering business enabled him to "reserve" a bed for Claire in a special treatment home that pampered the "mentally exhausted", as her daddy put it; the Summit Home, located in Baldwin Harbor, Long Island. What was the difference where they lived? But, it was done. In the summer, they'd all move. More than ever, her drawings were her only safe place.

From kindergarten on, Ruby's paintings of angels and stars had become a type of morning madness. She painted Marianne's face over and over until the faces of other dark women started to show up. Then moons, deserts, and circles of color and light that played around flowers and trees. She painted whatever her third eye saw. Another world, another place existed for Ruby. One day she'd go there forever. "Marianne, take me away. Please, I don't want to live here." And at times, when Marianne didn't show herself clearly, Ruby would get mad, throw crayons, and books. Stop eating, eat dirt, spit out her milk. "I hate you. I hate everyone."

That winter, Claire woke up during a snowstorm, turned the gas on in the oven, sat herself down in one of the leather kitchen chairs and waited until she'd faint from the fumes. If it weren't for the fact that her daddy got up every morning at three o'clock to gulp down a glass of seltzer, the Goldsmiths would have been a tragic memory. Ruby coughed and puked from the smell of skunk, the cold night, the trembling. The call. Then, the men in white coats. Her mother's last words: "Who'd miss me?"

Ruby overheard her father ask Claire as they carted her away, "Didn't you realize you could've killed all of us?"

"Yes. The angels told me to do it."

Ruby twisted and turned inside hearing her mother's words. Her mouth jelly, her tears clasped in her heart. What did she mean? *The angels made her do it.* What did that mean? Would Marianne make her do something horrible, too? Ruby ran into her bedroom and stared at paintings of Marianne. "Will you make me to terrible things?" Something deep in her belly, shook, shouted. "No. I will watch over you. I will protect you." Ruby sighed, only mildly relieved.

Claire was gone for four months. Sarah took over the household. Always over the stove cooking chicken, smoking, drinking. Ruby never understood how cold her grandma was about her mother. Never saw her flinch. "The medicine doesn't make her better Grandma, does it?"

"Your father should leave her at that nut house."

Ruby cried.

"Stop crying, *mamala*. I'm here."

Sarah hugged her to her cushy breasts. Ruby fell into the fleshy warmth, "Why don't you love mommy?"

Sarah pushed Ruby away. "Shush! Go! Go!"

Ruby went further away. Viewed her family as aliens. Watched them from afar. One day, Marianne would save her.

As planned, they moved into a new neighborhood with a custom-built townhouse.

To Ruby the two-story townhouse—with a small rectangular plot of land in both the front and back—was a castle compared to their apartment. Most of the development was still dumped in swampland and mud, and Ruby loved to watch the bulldozers dig up the earth. But her mother still had complaints. "Disgusting. Irish, Italians. Lower class. You couldn't get me into a better neighborhood?"

Her mother got a new diamond ring. It was bigger than a star in the sky. Ruby didn't understand why her father gave her presents for being so bad.

The family arrived at East 55th and Avenue K with a surprise. A bronze-skinned beauty from Jamaica named Rosetta moved in with the family.

Ruby heard her mother and father fight about the woman in new blue-and-white bedroom. "I got Mama. I don't need this whore woman in my house."

Her father yelled back. "She stays, Claire. That's that. And you know why."

Ruby followed her Rosetta around, listening to her sing jazzy melodies.

Claire screamed at Rosetta daily, "Damn. Get out of my house, you. You'll steal from me. I know you will." Ruby smiled because Rosetta never cared what her mother said. The exotic woman would harden her chin, turn up her nose, and hand her mother the pills with a cup of orange juice.

On the other hand, Claire loved Madame Charlotte, her interior designer. Ruby thought she looked like a skinny penguin. The madame wore fancy suits, her eyes outlined with dark liner, her lips red and pouty. She smoked a cigarette through a long holder and inhaled tiny puffs every other second. Claire crooned "Yes, Madame Charlotte. No, Madame Charlotte." Ruby thought she looked plastic and smelled of coffee stains. She said *voila*, and *merci bou coo*, or something weird all the time.

One morning, Claire and Madame ordered Ruby and Leah into the living room. "You can never sit on the couches when the plastic is off," Claire declared.

Ruby laughed. Leah hit Ruby's thigh.

"You better listen." Her mother eyes tightened into an *I'll kill you* scowl.

Ruby settled into the new plastic-wrapped home. At night, Ruby heard neighborhood mamas scream in Italian, Irish, and Yiddish for their children to come home. But Ruby knew her real home was somewhere else.

Chapter 7: 1959 – The Family Sabbath

Before Sabbath dinner, Claire plucked Sarah's brushy eyebrows and penciled them in dark. Crunched over at the edge of the bathtub, Ruby watched as Sarah wiggled in Claire's blue vanity chair.

"Sit still, Mama. I can't do this if you squirm."

With care and focus, Claire applied dark red lipstick; tried to hide the fact that Sarah preferred plain and simple, like the immigrant she was. "See Mama. Now you're beautiful for the Sabbath."

Sarah's Yiddish accent betrayed Claire's efforts to make her mother a modern American woman. "*Feh.* Beauty. *Feh.* It's not important." Sarah lit up a Chesterfield.

Claire's eyes glazed over into that cold distant look that scared Ruby. She threw the tweezers; chucked the lipstick into the sink. "Fine." She stormed out of the room.

Before the meal, Sarah, Claire, Leah, and Ruby lit candles planted in silver candelabras. A gentle flicker of flames softened her mother and grandmother. Heads covered in lace, they waved their hands over the candles. Her father wore his yarmulke and stood in the center. Sarah ended the prayer saying, "God does what God grants to us."

Those fleeting moments drenched in fiery warmth ignited Ruby. Her eyes closed, she saw Marianne bent over, surrounded by others, crooning, dancing, swaying to the desert moon and stars. This became Ruby's vision of the Sabbath light. But the serenity never lasted. The reverie split the moment the lace coverings came off everyone's heads.

Sarah served roasted chicken with potato pancakes and string beans for the sacred dinner. Rosetta learned to season Sarah's chicken with paprika, pepper, and salt. "Put a little ginger in it, Sarah," Rosetta would say.

Sarah hated her advice. "I don't need you here."

Rosetta ignored Sarah and washed the dishes and brewed the coffee.

As on every Friday, her grandmother sprouted the same rhetoric from the old country. "Remember, girls, Leah, Ruby, listen to me. Remember where you come from. Not this fancy stuff with fancy maids."

Claire resented Sarah's rejection. "You want me to live in the ghetto or the desert, Mama?"

Ruby perked up, "What ghetto? What desert, Grandma? Where do we come from?"

"We come from slaves and pogroms and…and don't ask." Sarah ran to the bathroom with her pocketbook wrapped around her wrist. She returned slurring her words. "*Rubalah.* Remember."

Leah laughed. "You come from a toilet, Ruby."

"No I don't," Ruby yelled.

"Be stronger, Ruby. Your sister is just kidding you." Morty held his hands up in the air. "Enough with you two."

"Shut up, both of you!" Claire screamed.

Rosetta intervened, saving the day with a scrumptious chocolate desert with flaky buttery crust. It quieted the family.

Sarah squinted at Rosetta with scorn. "Why don't you go home to your colored people?"

"I'm not colored. I'm Jamaican."

"Vhats the difference. Huh?"

"Mama, stop it." Claire pounded the table.

Morty balked, "Not tonight again. Let's leave it alone. Sarah, Rosetta has to be here."

"After dessert, go to bed." Claire licked the last bit of chocolate off the spoon. "Take them to bed, Rosetta."

"Yes ma'am." Rosetta grabbed both Ruby and Leah.

Sarah yelled. "I'll take them. Who needs her?"

Claire threw the spoon down, "You sit, Mama. We pay her. You can have some leisure."

Sarah crossed her arms. Her double chin sank into her chest. "Leisure, smeisure." Again she grabbed her pocketbook and slugged down a drink from the small liquor bottle that she kept inside. "Let's go, girls. I'll take you to bed."

Ruby got up. "Grandma. Aren't we supposed to dance for the Sabbath?"

Her grandma scoffed, eyes dropping, "Only if you're holy. What's holy around here?"

"Isn't everyone holy?" Ruby swayed.

"No." Grandma Sarah crushed her pocketbook to her chest.

Ruby prayed that night like the old men in temple. After Rosetta tucked her into bed, Ruby reached deep into her heart. She mumbled to God. She prayed to Marianne. "Please make everyone feel good. Please." Sometimes the angel would show up for Ruby, and sometimes she didn't. Ruby never knew.

But, whether she saw her or not, Marianne was in Ruby's cellular rhythms.

Chapter 8: Marianne's Sabbath

Marianne gathered the women. Dressed for the Sabbath in bright reds, blues, greens, and golds, veils covered their strong, supple bodies and ancient sand-swept faces. A reverberating howl poured from Marianne's throat, her lips quivered. "*Schmaaaaaaaaaa*, ya, ya, ho, ho, *schmaaaaaaaa, Shekinah, Adonai, Hashem,* YAAAAAAAAAAA."

Dance, song, cheers, and guttural yelps swung through each woman's voice. Hands touched, feet kicked up sand, and the full moon lit a translucent embrace that circled the women's eyes and feet. Drums beat, rattles shook, tambourines jingled, the prayer of their soul to *Aserah*, the goddess part of the tribe of the *Shekinah*, reached to the stars out to the galaxies. Hours of reverie passed through the camp of women. It was a celebration of the feminine, the *Shekinah* whose dark womb birthed the light.

The ebony body sweat of the women filled the air with lavender, sage, ash, and fire. They woke the spirits—the ancient ones, Sarah, Rebecca, and Leah—and filled a cup of wine for each of them.

Marianne's hypnotic stare caught a glimpse of moonlight. "We will live. We won't let your teachings die. We are the earth, sun, moon, and rivers. We drink your life."

In the chaos of revelation, they built a small altar with wood, sage, and fish bones that they had brought from their homes. A random display of the gentle white zygophyllum flower was tossed among the palms that sheltered the altar.

Marianne held a small knife and pricked her finger, then passed it to each woman. One by one they followed, and together they dripped their blood into a small silver cup.

"We are one!" Marianne buried the chalice in the dunes. "Now we go into the cities to heal the sick, the poor, and the lonely. We pass on the legacy. Awaken the body, vibrate to heal. Arouse the sexual transformation that is created from the center of the earth.

She pulled the water bag that hung from her body and drank from it. She held the wet pouch up towards the moon. "Thank you for this water. Thank you for the earth. Thank you for my body. Thank you for pushing out the vaginal void into the light. I pray. I pray. I pray this moment lives forever."

The women huddled around Marianne. A deep cry, a sacred union folded them into each other's arms.

Chapter 9: Rosetta

"I can't sleep. Stop talking to yourself." Leah flipped onto her side, threw off the puffy blanket and watched. Her yellow jammies were hiked up between her thighs.

"I'm praying." Ruby continued, head bowed, tiny hands in prayer pose at her heart.

"To who?" Leah picked her nose. "And for what?"

"God. To keep Rosetta and for Mommy to take her medicine." Through the corner of her half-closed eyes she saw Marianne. Ruby didn't blink or make a move. She didn't want Leah to know anything. That's what she did when Marianne popped in. Pretended she wasn't there. Ruby heard Marianne whisper in her prayer, *"God listens. You have to hear, Ruby. God does it Her way. Not your way."* Her third eye opened. "Shut up, Leah."

"Oh yeah? You shut up." Leah turned over and went to sleep.

Ruby prayed harder. If not for Rosetta to stay, at least for a friend to talk to. A sudden urge caused her to dance and spin around. She twirled and spun, repeating in a sing song way, *"Schma, schma, schma, Shekinah, Shekinah."*

Leah shot up. "Shut up already!"

Ruby crawled back into bed, breathless. "That was fun."

***

Only two months into the move, as Rosetta was combing Claire's hair, Claire smacked Rosetta across the face and threw the comb across the bathroom. It pinged against the tile floor.

Claire screamed. "Stop treating me like I'm two years old. If I take the pills, I take them. If I don't, I don't!"

Ruby ran to protect Rosetta. Stood in front of her. "Don't hit her."

"It's okay, child. Your mama doesn't know better." Rosetta moved in front of Ruby.

Claire turned on Ruby, stumbled to push her. "Don't you save her."

Rosetta blocked Claire's arm.

Ruby clutched Rosetta. "I swear Mommy. I swear. I'll hit you back if you ever hit me or Rosetta again."

"Why you little…" Claire leapt up, made a fist. Her bobby pins dropped out from her straggly hair.

And with that, she did it. Ruby hit her mother right across her arm.

Claire slumped back into the vanity chair, downed a pill. "Get out of here. Both of you. Get out, you bitches. I don't need any of you. Get out! Make that little snot her dinner. Just get out of here. Both of you."

Ruby and Rosetta scurried out and into the kitchen. Rosetta cooked up Ruby's favorite meal. Fried onions mixed with ketchup, hot sauce, franks, and beans. It had the sweetest, spiciest taste.

After Ruby smacked her lips with the last bite, Rosetta broke the news, "I'm going to be leaving, girl."

"No." Ruby hugged her, crying.

Rosetta patted Ruby on the head. "I have to. This place is no good for my soul." She washed out the pots. "But you, you got a heart, Ruby girl." She dropped the pot, wiped the suds across her skirt and took Ruby by the hand. "Come."

She guided Ruby into the back bedroom where Rosetta slept. The room was dark, with navy curtains covering the window and a checkered bedspread swerved across the edge of the mattress. Rosetta opened her closet door and pulled out a trunk. A small key unlocked it. Rosetta rummaged through a stack of colorful drawings of naked women, circles, and different animals with large magical eyes. Rosetta took out a small medallion of a beautiful woman plated in gold. Rosetta lit a candle, then placed her hand on Ruby's heart, "Beloved Goddess, grant this child healing and life. Give her eyes, give her song, and give her strength to carry the burden of her legacy. Let her rise with the oneness of God and all HIS angels. Amen." She tapped Ruby on the head, "Say amen." She gave the medallion to Ruby. "This is Mary Magdalena. She'll protect you."

"Amen." Ruby stared at the face of the saint. It couldn't be. The carved face resembled Marianne. She held the gold charm to her heart. "I love you."

Suddenly, a murderous yelp ended the epiphany. "Get the hell out of my house, you pagan shit whore! How dare you. We're Jewish. How dare you." Claire raised her hand.

Rosetta jumped and blew out the candle. She stood in front of Ruby, her body strong and impenetrable. "Be still. Be still."

Disheveled, hair every which way, housecoat open exposing her breast, Claire was an ugly sight. "Just get the hell out of my house. Now!" Her shoulders slumped. Then her eyes locked with Ruby's. "You're disgusting."

"No. No. No." Ruby held tight to the medallion and slid under the bed. She peeked out like a cat. She blinked in the darkness.

Claire stomped away. "You better stay there and don't come out."

As soon as Claire marched away, Rosetta lifted the bed skirt. "Come, girl. Give me Mary. She did her job."

Ruby crawled out from under and handed the delicate gold piece to her. "Don't go, Rosetta. Don't."

She kissed her on the head. "You know I have to."

The next morning, Rosetta left. Something inside nudged Ruby to wander to the nursemaid's room. She lifted one of the pillows. Rosetta's sweet coconut perfume lingered on the pillowcase. Suddenly, Ruby noticed: Rosetta had left the medallion of Mary and a string of black beads underneath the pillow. Ruby cradled the gifts in her hand and ran back to her own bedroom. The tiny jewelry box hidden under her panties in the top drawer waited for a treasure. She opened it. Inside laid the gold Jewish star on a chain, her grandmother's gift. Ruby never wore it through the years, thought it creepy and old. Now, it seemed silly that she didn't like the religious symbol. She took the medallion and slid it down the chain alongside the Star of David, then fastened it around her neck. They felt right together. She kissed the necklace. "Are you Marianne? Do you dance for God?"

Chapter 10: 1959 – The Goldsmiths and The Simons

It was a surprise to Ruby when Mitzi and Leo Simon moved next door at the end of June with their children, Joel and Pam. Pam was twelve years old like Leah. Joel had just turned ten. The entire summer, Leo and Morty played poker and bought new Cadillacs—Morty's pink, Leo's black.

Sunday Chinese food became a ritual for the two families. It was rainy that Labor Day weekend. The eight of them were cozy, sitting around a red booth at the Royal China Inn. Shiny red and gold lanterns and bright green dragons made the restaurant's ceiling and walls sparkle. Ruby leaned into the squishiness of sitting close. The two couples chatted, clinked glasses, and celebrated, Morty and Leo chirping, "We're going big!"

Ruby watched, listening to the jabber from the adults. Mitzi—round hipped, slinky-eyed, lashes long and curled—wore big jewelry and smoked Marlboros, popping them in and out of her mouth like mints. Mitzi was tan down to the follicles of her french knot, to her red toenails. Ruby was curious if she was one of the dark ladies in her painting. Mesmerized, Ruby followed Mitzi with her eyes as she tucked the cigarette between her middle and pointer finger and blew smoke circles, laughing in a hyena way. Ruby loved this.

Leo was bald, tall, and slouched over as if he were carrying a trunk on his back. Ruby thought his big toothy smile, thick moustache, and shiny skin made him look like some sort of magician. He leaned over and grinned at Ruby. "Hyareya." It sounded like he was saying *Hawaii*.

Pam was chubby and wore tiny ribbons in her big brown-haired bouffant. And then there was Joel. Devilish, cute, blonde Joel. Ruby never knew what Joel would do to her. He was constantly in Ruby's face with dirty remarks: *shit, fuck, boobs,* taunting her with pinches and jabs to her ribcage, tickling her until she'd scream out, *"Stop it!"* Sometimes, she'd start to stutter, and she'd cry. *"I.. I.. I..te, tell!"*

Joel didn't care. "You're such a girl. Yeah, go tell mommy and daddy."

She hated him for that, but secretly liked that he bothered her so much.

Ruby crunched on a fried wonton. "What's happening?" she asked Joel, who was sitting next to her.

"They're going to be partners in a catering hall."

"Really?" Ruby wondered why she didn't know and Joel did. She smudged a spot of mustard into the white tablecloth. Obsessed with every blink of Joel's blue eyes and flick of his fingers, she wiggled closer to him. His messed-up blonde waves twisted and turned.

"What class are you in?" Ruby asked.

"I'm in the smart class, 5-1. The 'ones' mean you're smart." Joel sniffed a piece of chicken and threw it back onto his plate.

"Me, too. I used to be in the gifted class. I hated it. I was the youngest one." Ruby forked a piece of pork.

"How old are you?"

"Nine." Her cheeks turned pink.

"How'd you get into my class? You're nine."

"I skipped third grade," Ruby said.

"So, you think you're smarter than me?" Joel glared at her and smashed an egg roll with his spoon.

"No. It's just…it's weird that's…I hate it."

Joel picked out small pieces of shrimp from the egg roll filling and ate them. "You're weird."

Ruby watched the way his mouth rotated as he ate. Watched the way his fingers sought out the little shrimps. Watched the way his cheekbones caved around his face. "No, you're weird."

They pointed a finger in each other's face, and in unison said, "You're weird."

Together they were fire and water.

Chapter 11: Summer, 1961

Before Ruby knew it, she had sprouted breasts and gotten her first period. This time when Claire smacked her across the face, she had a solid reason. It was good luck, a Jewish ritual. Bullshit. It was all bullshit, Ruby thought after her mother smugly left her red handprint on Ruby's cheek. Why was smacking your daughter for her first menstruation good luck? Ruby stuck her middle finger out at her mother as she walked away, ran into her bedroom and stared at the ceiling.

For Ruby, the arrival of her period meant that she could get pregnant. At least that's what the rumor was, when the girls gossiped at lunch to one another about their boy crushes. Pregnant at eleven. That seemed even more absurd. You'd have to do the dirty to get pregnant. A week after her first period she had a dream. Marianne cut a lock of her hair, which was dipped in Ruby's menstrual blood. They prayed. "Now you're a woman." Ruby awoke startled. She crimped through her hair. All intact. What? What? How? Be a woman? She didn't know what that meant. Her grandmother once told her that to be a woman was to cook. A woman. Joel made her feel like she was a woman? Something awakened wet between her legs when she was with Joel, watching television on his bed. Made her feel like more than a little girl. She touched her vagina. *No. No,* she thought. That was wrong. She didn't want to think about it. No. Something was awakened. A presence that vibrated in her vagina.

Ruby wasn't sure what these feeling were that made her hot and tingly around Joel. She just knew she couldn't get enough of him.

Chapter 12: Marianne, Circle of Women

Marianne called the women to the circle. They were fierce, young and filled with sex. Sheer colors of red, blue, and purple wrapped in transparent linen flowed from the thick and strong bodies of the tribe. Stars dripped into the moon's glow. Rich gems dripped from Marianne's ears and neck: amethyst, onyx, tiger's eye, ruby, and pearl adorned her. Tiny bells jingled around her ankles as she spun in the shadowy light cast across the animal-skin tents. The night smelled of dung and lavender. The mules—tied to poles and palms—neighed in a laughing staccato. In the distance, coyotes howled with fierce sexuality, calling to their mates.

By day, Marianne wore the dark shawl that covered her slender body, head and mouth. Only her eyes and nose saw and smelled the corruption around her. Grime, garlic, and goat sweat filled the market places. Sacrificial blood dried up on the steps of the temple. This was not Marianne's religion. It reeked of death and power, men of muscle, and the sword that murdered. Even the brightness of the sun couldn't sweep the streets clean of the destruction and hypocrisy. She hated the cities, visited only to gather the hidden ones, the women waiting to live and pray in the desert. Marianne knew the men; the royalty who still surrendered to the Goddess, the *Shekinah*, and sang the songs of prosperity, fertility, and immortality. They followed her into the desert as well.

Tonight in the heat, they all came together. And her rabbi was here, dressed in a single white robe, his eyes bent in passion, his tongue swaggering with guttural roars, his hands reaching out to the black heavens where the face of the goddess stole the night into her bosom.

There were twenty-four of them. Twelve men and twelve women. Marianne stepped forward, "Those of you in your moon cycle bury your blood into the sand with a lock of your hair. You others, prepare and beat the drum, shake the tambourine."

Three women fell to their knees and followed the ritual. They then moved outside the circle. Hypnotic music awakened the night. Men and women swayed with intertwined arms and legs, random yelps shot out from bellies and throats.

Marianne and the rabbi, hip to hip, eye to eye, rhythmically moved around each other. "Tonight, rabbi. This is the night. Union. Tantric union. It is the order of the cosmos. The creation that needs our seed. Our breath and hearts. Our bodies, our unity, sacredness of our union is the bounty of plenty. It is good. It is so." They kissed, hungry, and trembling. "Hold the energy. Let it rise to your third eye. Let it move the earth, stars, and galaxies."

One by one, as Marianne and the rabbi entered their tent, each couple vanished into theirs. The night swelled in orgasm.

Chapter 13: Fall, 1961 Crushed

Joel and Ruby moved on to sixth grade together. Joel grew his hair long and wore torn jeans and different colored tie-dyed T-shirts. She loved him and his dingy jeans. And always, they'd manipulate their way to sit next to each other so they could pass notes.

Every Friday after school, Ruby would watch television with Joel, eat Twinkies, and drink orange juice. Strange, warm, tingly feelings rose in her crotch every time she smelled the sweetness of Joel. He pulled her ponytail and stuck his head under her dress when she bent down to pick up a pencil. He made fun of her bent nose and he never stopped ringing her doorbell and running away. He laughed at her poetry and spilled juice on her drawings of the moon. She was thrilled around his energy; he was a wild mare.

November: winter blanketed over summer and fall and plucked the trees of their green, gold, reds, and blues. Navy-gray clouds darkened with bits of sunlight shadowed the edges of the sky. The heavens promised snow with their frozen glare hovering over the horizon. Ruby and Joel huffed into class one day and hung their coats in the closet. Alone between the soft strokes of woolen jackets and gloves and the smell of new snow, he touched her hand. Ruby felt a hot intensity.

"You love me," Joel whispered.

"No I don't." Ruby shushed him.

"What do you know?" Joel shoved her against the coats.

"You say, love, love, and then you ignore me after class."

"Guys don't hang out with girls." Joel leapt out from the closet.

Ruby followed him. Both sat in their seats. "Oh. You're afraid to let your creepy friends know?"

Joel shrugged his shoulders. "My friends have nothing to do with anything."

"Then why don't you talk to me when you're with them?"

"Because. That's why."

Ruby kicked his foot. "I have a secret."

"See. Girls are pests."

"You're just a jerk. Girls know that. That guys are jerks." She folded her arms in defiance. "I'm never going to tell you my secret."

Joel made himself busy with a math book. "Who cares? I know everything about you anyway."

"You do, huh?" She grinned, knowing she'd captured his interest because of the way he aimlessly thumbed through the pages, breathing hard. "If you say hello to me when you're with your friends, I'll tell you."

Joel held her stare and tapped on the book. "Maybe."

Ruby paused. Should she tell him? Her body shivered. She watched him watch her. "You've got to promise you'll notice me no matter who you're with."

"You always want so much from me, Ruby."

"I'm telling you something that no one knows. No one!"

"You bargain your big secret cheap."

Ruby bit her lip. Her eyes glared with a longing fury.

Joel's lids grew heavy with thought. "Damn. Okay. Okay."

Ruby released a tight breath. Wiped her face as if there was a spot on her cheek. She leaned forward. "I see angels."

"What do you mean? Where? Here?" Joel scanned the ceiling.

"No." Ruby frowned, pulled her turtleneck over her ears. "I'm afraid." She repeatedly slid her palms underneath her sweater.

"Of what?"

"Of other things."

"What things?"

"Of being Jewish."

"What?" Joel shuffled his feet.

"I can't talk about it."

Joel threw his hands in the air. "Tell me already."

"No." Ruby pushed against her desk.

"You little bitch. You're dead, Ruby fuzz face." He leaned back, crossed his heart. "I promise…if you tell me. I promise I'll never ignore you."

"Don't call me names!"

"Okay. Okay. Now tell me."

Ruby peeked over her shoulder, took a breath. "An angel called Marianne talks to me. Since I was very young. I wear her around my neck next to the Jewish star my grandmother gave me. See, look." She pulled it out from her sweater for him to see.

"Where'd you get that charm?"

"Rosetta."

"That lady who took care of your mother when she got out of the crazy bin?"

"Yeah. Her. She told me it's Mary Magdalena. And I think…" She looked over each shoulder. "Come closer," she whispered. "I think she's Mary, the Jesus's Mary. I don't know much about her. But I think she's talking to me."

Joel pulled Ruby near to get a better peek at the face on the pendant.

Ruby grabbed her necklace. "Do you think I'm crazy?"

"Because you talk to Mary Magdalena?" He smiled.

Ruby stared at him. "I feel stupid."

"What do you talk to Mary about?" Joel flopped back in his chair.

Ruby nibbled on her nail. "You believe me?"

"Yeah. Sure." He rounded his fingers around his eyes. Googling out as if he wore glasses. "I try and see things."

"Are you making fun of me?"

"Nope. Me and my friends, we experiment with…ya know." He put his finger to his mouth and puffed.

Ruby tugged on her sweater. "What! For real? How do you get it?"

"You know. Everyone does it."

"You'll die or something!"

"You can't die from smoking pot."

"Sooo?" She poked his arm. "You're a perv." Ruby wiped her hands on her skirt.

"You're nuts."

"Shut up! Why do I talk to you?" Ruby pushed out of her chair and stood up.

Joel laughed, "Because you can't live without me?"

"I can too." Ruby tightened her fists, didn't know where to go. Class was about to start. "Why doesn't the teacher come?"

"You can't live without me."

Ruby's face grew beet red, her fingers flipped about like octopus tentacles, and then she turned and gave him the finger. "I...I...I... *hic*, don't need you. Ev...*hic*..ev...ever." Ruby gritted her teeth. "Just because you put your finger up my...my...my... it didn't mean a thing." Ruby slapped her hand across her mouth, slowed her breath down, caught her fear.

"So you weren't asleep." Joel pointed a finger at her. "The TV was going and you pretended you were sleeping."

"Shut up. Just shut up."

"If you weren't asleep, then you let me. Yeah, yeah, you let me, touch you down there." Joel smirked.

"Yo...you...you're..hic...dis...dis...*hic*...dis gust.. ing." Ruby folded her arms, trying not to go into hysterics.

"You're a liar." Joel shot back.

Ruby's body shook. Why did she let him? What was wrong with her? Ruby ran. Hid inside the closet. Folded into the coats and scarves, blended into the dark. Kept counting over and over 1...2...3...4...5...6...7...8...9...10. Gone. Hiccups gone. She breathed. Pressed her lips together for strength. She wanted to wring his neck. Her heart pumped like she had run a hundred miles. Ruby placed her hand over her eyes. Tiny tears welled up in spite of her will. She let him touch her vagina. She told him about Marianne. Her head hurt. She pounded her forehead against the wall. *I'm crazy. I'm crazy.* Her body knotted up. Brightness seeped in through the cracks of the closet. A soft voice spoke to her. *"You did nothing wrong Ruby. You can stop being afraid. I love you. I'm here."* Ruby straightened her back. Shifted her jaw. Whispered with a loud strength, "I will not be afraid. I am Ruby and Joel is a big, stupid, ass!"

Suddenly a ray of light shot through her body and out of her eyes. The closet went dark.

A thin-skinned, crumple-eyed, balding man with a nice blue tie and brown jacket was standing by the closet door. "Get into your seat, Ruby. Class is starting."

Ruby blinked. "Fine, Mr. Pollard." And she marched toward her seat.

Out of the corner of her eye she saw Joel crunch a grin. She bowed her head away and stared out at a lone bluebird perched on a bare branch stroked by the dull sunlight.

She whispered, "I did nothing wrong."

"Yeah, sure," Joel smirked.

"Yeah, sure is right." Ruby opened her book and shut Joel out

Chapter 14: December 1961–January 1962, New Year's Eve Blues

Ruby stopped talking to Joel. Fine. Good. She didn't need him. Why give him her heart and secrets? It tore her up to see his sarcastic face and hear his oozing hurtful words. But Ruby had no control over fate.

That morning, it snowed. She ran outside to watch the slow ballet of flakes cascade from the sky. The icy cold snuck through her bones and she bundled up—in her scarf, mittens, and long faux-fur coat with large pockets, where she kept her favorite paperback *Catcher in the Rye*. Holden Caulfield was her hero. She didn't fit. Just like Holden. Maybe she'd run away to Manhattan? Maybe? If she got on a train and found the Edmont Hotel, maybe she'd find a way out of her life.

Suddenly a chill went up her spine, but not from the weather. She knew that feel, that hot/cold stare. She felt Joel. He was right there, on the other side of the short wall that separated their porches and brick houses, attached in rows all strung together by cement.

He pulled out a crinkled, skinny cigarette.

She couldn't control herself. He was too close. Who cared, really, what had happened between them? It didn't matter. Her unquenchable attraction for him vanquished her anger.

Ruby watched an orange dog pee against the oak tree in front of the house. *Poor guy. I hope he has a home. I hate seeing dogs that don't have a place to go.* She tightened the blue wool scarf around her neck. *Brr. Cold.* She looked over at Joel. He was wearing a thin grey pullover sweater and jeans, no shoes. "Aren't you cold?" she called out to him.

Joel sucked in a puff. "Yeah. Whatever. Pot makes it all better." He rolled his head back and twirled the smoke between his fingers.

Ruby didn't flinch; subdued her pounding heart with a breath. "Where'd you get it?"

He jumped over the wall, plopped down in a chaise, pondered the joint. "Doesn't matter. But, we're going to smoke it for your birthday. Tonight. At midnight, you turn twelve."

Ruby's eyes shuttered closed, trembling behind her lids. She straightened her back. "Who invited you to my birthday? Besides, I'm not talking to you."

He poked her and pulled her hair. "Really?"

"Really." Ruby slapped him on the arm.

"You done?" Joel stroked quote signs in the air. "With the *I'm not talking to you Joel because I let you touch my vagina* revenge?" He leapt back over the wall and grabbed the screen handle and blew her a kiss. "The argument is officially over for me, Ruby. Time to make up. It's your birthday. I'll be over tonight around eleven o'clock. We'll watch the ball drop, then." He took a toke, "Happy New Year's and happy birthday to you."

Ruby's stomach slid down into her crotch. A warm tingling made her close her thighs tight. She attempted to keep a straight face, not show any emotion. She turned her face away. She sucked on her lip, trying to gain composure. "I don't smoke. It's disgusting." Ruby's cringed. "I feel nauseous."

"I'll be there, Ruby. Time to own up."

Ruby fell silent, closed her eyes, bathed in the cool and calm of the day. "My parents…"

Joel interrupted. "Your parents are going out with mine tonight. It's New Year's Eve. And…and I know Leah and Pam are going to a sleepover."

"I forgot." Ruby's eyes circled in curiosity. "Why aren't you going to some party or whatever?"

"I planned to be with you tonight, Rub."

"You planned? Planned without thinking of what I want?"

"I was thinking of what you want, Ruby." He tapped on the screen. "I saw you sitting on the porch. Kismet."

Ruby shuffled her feet, hid a grin by chattering her teeth. "I've got to go in. It's too cold."

"See you later."

"The door will be unlocked." Ruby stood up.

Joel winked and pointed his finger to the sky. "Maybe Marianne made it all happen?"

What was she doing? She didn't know or care. "I'll see you later."

Later couldn't come fast enough for Ruby.

***

They lay on Ruby's bed, side by side on their stomachs, passing the joint, watching the frenzy of the crowd in Times Square on the 14-inch Zenith. The glitter, confetti, and cold night stars twinkled with anticipation of the new year approaching. 1962. Dick Clark counted down: *"Ten, nine, eight, seven, six, five, four, three, two, one. Happy New Year!"*

Joel flicked off the television. "Happy birthday, Ruby." He took a last drag and drowned the smoke in a glass of water sitting on the nightstand. "Not so disgusting." Joel pulled off his sweater, rolled off the bed and stood up.

His flat, washboard stomach, outie belly button, and smooth chest caught Ruby off guard and she stumbled onto the floor.

Joel put out his hand to hers, pulled at her toes. "Come on. We don't have to pretend anymore. Don't you wanna see?"

Joel turned off the small antique lamp. The room went dark, but the streetlamp light from outside her window slid in through the white shutters. Its smooth, sexy glow wrapped them in a shadowy light. Tips of dull, soft light framed their bodies, mystical and gentle. Ruby imagined herself as Brigitte Bardot.

"Come on." Joel hit his chest like Tarzan.

Ruby's hot, wiry lust for Joel took over her senses and mind. Slowly, one piece of clothing after another, they matched undies for undies, bra for sock, until they were both standing naked.

Joel edged a few inches closer to Ruby. She could feel his warm breath on her face, his sweet sweat and the tip of his hard penis against her vagina. Ruby pushed him back. "Not so close." They dry humped. His penis between her legs, rubbing, but no penetration. He held her ass and eased back and forth outside of her vagina. The light blanketed them in a thin translucent veil that revealed only the peaks and curves of each other's body. But nothing revealing was seen. It was a poetic moment and Ruby felt a torrid, boiling tingling—a rapture—overtake her being. She let out a small squeal, closed her eyes, and felt her body release in a way that she had never imagined. She opened her eyes and saw Joel's head roll back, breathing heavy as he yelped out. The two stared at each other, motionless, close to each other's skin, and then slowly drew a safe distance away. A gap they didn't trespass, and didn't touch one another again. She felt small, alone, and wet between her legs. Uncomfortable, sweaty, and humiliated, she melted into the rapture of the moment.

Joel put his mouth next to her ear. "I want you to tell me…" He stopped, disappeared in the folds of the room.

Ruby reached out, searched for him, blind and jittery. "Where are you?"

"I want you to show me how to get high without pot. I want to speak to Marianne." He was somewhere in the void of the room. She heard the clink of his belt buckle. He was getting dressed.

She stood frozen in the spot, "Joel. I don't know how it comes." She made a fist. "Is that why you came tonight?"

"You're selfish, Ruby. I'm gonna smoke with the guys. I'm leaving."

The door to her bedroom opened and slammed shut.

Ruby cried. Stuffed up tight into a ball. The worlds that inhabited her mind and body shook her senses loose, her emotions, her intellect a tornado of troubled anguish. The wispy darkness, its seductive embrace licked Ruby's bones. Exhaustion and emptiness drew her into sleep.

She slapped her body into the bed. Drifted off. Breathing hard, soaked in a cold sweat. Once she passed through into the dream world, Marianne spoke to her. A hazy outline of her the face, her red hair flowed into the void. *"Cry, Ruby, cry…hold yourself. There's so much more to who are you are. Cry for now. Go through the aches, doubt, fear…before you are ready to know me as yourself."*

Ruby reached in her dream, hot tears, dark circles, drowned in despair. "It's not fair. Any of it."

"Life is not about fair. It's life. You have to be a woman to live it." Marianne drifted away.

She woke up. The house was silent. "Mom, Dad?" A thin buzz of silence crept through the house. She rolled out of bed and turned on the black and white set. Natalie Wood and Warren Beatty kissed the screen: *Splendor in the Grass.*

Young love, angst, mental illness, cruel mother, absent father, psychiatric ward. Ruby was hooked.

Chapter 15: November, 1967 – Brooklyn College

Ruby sniffed the cool November air as she ran up the stone steps into the Psychology Building. The campus grass stank from marijuana—that's how much sucking and puffing went on between classes. It was a given, that at any 1967 college campus, students, and probably professors too, were high, tuned in, and tuned out to "Lucy in the Sky with Diamonds."

Wearing a thick black turtleneck, black tights, and a navy pea coat, Ruby breezed her way to class. She quivered as she shuffled through the crowd of lazy, long-haired boys and girls. Students piled in groups as Ruby pushed through the open metal doors. She wove through the crowd into the hallways of Brooklyn College. Books and papers tucked into her chest, she hurried toward her nine o'clock class.

To Morty and Claire, marriage to a rich, preppy Jewish boy was more important than a college degree. But, Ruby insisted on getting an education. Especially when, out of boredom, Leah had enrolled in college.

"Leah doesn't give a shit about college. I'm going if she's going."

Her parents didn't argue, and Ruby started her first year studies, while Leah met Howard Levine, a doctor-to-be, the man of her parent's dreams. Leah and Howard were pinned during freshman year. Ruby watched them cuddle, ogle, and hold hands. The perfect couple. Leah catered Howard's football parties, accompanied him on outings in the Catskill Mountains—actually hiking through woods. This was not the Leah she knew. Her sister hated the sound of a bird chirping in the morning or the roar of any kind of sports event. It was crazy bullshit

73

how civilly and tweedy-eyed Leah flashed her baby blues at Howard. What the hell was that about? The next minute she'd growl, sneer, and treat Ruby like an old dish rag; hassled her, calling her stupid, slapping her hand if Ruby reached for her blue shadows or pink lipstick, accusing her of wanting to grab the center of attention with her paintings and poems. Ruby knew that wasn't true. Her parents ignored her art. But they bought Leah a designer wardrobe to hook Howard.

Leah never made it through the second year in college. Once she captured and sealed Howard's affection, she became the "good" daughter. Morty and Claire, proud that Leah snatched a "rich one," gave her all the time in the world to shop, lie around, and wait for Howard to take her to a movie or Broadway show. Late at night, when Leah talked privately on the phone to Howard, Ruby overheard her sister say, "You got to get me outta this nut house, Howard. I hate Ruby. She makes my life miserable. And my mother's a bitch. You love me Howard? I love you. I can't wait to be married."

What a jerk. Ruby thought herself superior to her sister. She would be the first educated woman in her family.

Ruby decided to major in art history with minors in literature, education, and psychology. Learning about neurosis and pathology both frightened and excited her. Ruby worried that she was a full-blown schizophrenic. For sure, her mother was a borderline, defined as "an emotional hemophiliac" who bled emotions, was suicidal, and turned on everyone with rage at a moment's notice.

Watching *Splendor in the Grass* at age twelve had changed Ruby's life. Deanie, played by Natalie Wood, was a heroine for Ruby. She identified with Deanie's pain, her cruel mother who shamed and mentally tortured her for loving Bud Stamper, finally ending up in a mental institution. Deanie painted her angst, her lust, healed her own self-hatred. The finale was Ruby's favorite. Deanie returns to say goodbye to her old love and her mother. Wearing a white dress and hat, she is strong, proud, and alive, and leaves both behind to marry her psychiatrist. If Natalie could overcome, then so could Ruby.

Ruby found Dr. Rosenthal, a Jungian psychiatrist, when she turned sixteen. Saturday mornings and Wednesday nights Ruby typed resumes at an employment office to pay for her three-times-a-week therapy sessions. If it weren't for her art, Dr. Rosenthal, and prescriptions for Elavil, and Valium, she'd certainly be headed toward that ledge again, and not be running to class right now.

Around her, students were tripping out on LSD, cocaine, and other hard drugs. Ruby limited herself to hits of pot with Joel even though Dr. Rosenthal had warned her against it. Pot could set off her visions in a dangerous way, he said. It could increase her detachment and disassociate her from reality. But smoking pot deepened her paintings with a rich reality, bonded her and Joel in erotic and mystical ways. Ruby didn't take Rosenthal's warnings seriously. After all, it was only pot. And Joel—well, Joel was her soul mate.

Ruby pretended she was a typical teenager from a typical family. She straightened her curls, circled her eyes with liquid black liner, and highlighted her brows velvet brown. Her favorite attire was a tight sweater and bell-bottoms. Denial became an art. It froze her insides so she couldn't feel the shame and rage. She could turn her eyes and ears from the terror of her mother's yearly retreats to the Summit. Bury the fact that as normal family business, her mother went four times a week to a Fifth Avenue psychiatrist, Dr. Burns, and swallowed blue, pink, and white pills daily. She severed, fragmented, and deposited her heart and soul behind a steel shield, hoping one day she could leave all of it—all of the crap of her life—behind. Just like Deanie.

A student bumped her and smashed her shoulder against the wall.

"Schmuck!" Ruby screamed as he ran by.

She looked at the clock centered high on the pea-green wall. Damn, she had to get going. She entered the big lecture hall and found an empty seat. The professor, slouched over the podium, was god-awful with his puny voice, disheveled bushy brown hair, misshapen, bunched-up vest, and oversize trousers that swam around his thighs like a deflated tire. Ruby wondered how such a creepy man came to teach psychology. His wild, bugged-out eyes that never looked straight at you when he asked a question could terrify a rat.

"Today we're going to watch a documentary on touch deprivation." The chatter quieted. The squirmy professor shut off the lights.

The black-and-white 8mm was scratchy and had white slits running through the frames. Ruby twisted in her seat as she watched infant rhesus monkeys squirm and slam against cages. Monkey screams cut through her nerves and curdled her blood. Their eyes bulged with fear and their tongues hung from the sides of their mouths.

The narrator of the movie echoed through the room. *"This is what happens when infants are touch deprived. Psychosis and personality disorders occur even in these baby monkeys."*

Touch deprived. Yes, touch deprived. She heard right. Ruby trembled. She folded her knees to her chest and cuddled into herself to keep warm.

Ruby watched the little furry creatures rant and rave, pull their hair, squeak, chatter their teeth, bite their own arms and legs...starved for loving touch. She quietly sniffed back tears. Felt her legs shake. Wanted to vomit. She clutched her chest. Why did her heart ache like a fist had smashed into her chest? They were monkeys. Monkeys, for god's sake. She wanted to save them. Hold them.

Muted light pulsated against the walls. She scanned the lecture room. Students watched with serious intent. Was she the only one feeling sick? She held her breath and placed her hand across her stomach. Was anyone else alive? Red, blonde, brown hair, the backs of heads grew like balloons. Humming sounds punctured her ears.

The film grew foggy. Mother monkey sat in a separate cage... sitting, watching...biting her nails as if she were waiting for a bus.

Suddenly, the mommy monkey resembled her mother. Getting ready to play mahjong. Filing her nails, piling mascara onto her lashes as Ruby lay on the sticky bathroom tiles kicking and screaming. "Mommy, hold me. Mommy, touch me. Tell me you love me."

The monkey documentary became her story. Blonde mommy monkey looked down and belched, slapped her tush "I have to go now," she said. "Why are you so unhappy? Why are you on the floor? Get up. I have to go and show everyone that your father bought me a pink Cadillac." Small, little Ruby had no control over her mother's cruelty. Her mother's touch meant hard beatings and hangers. She hated the feel of her mother's hands and yet hungered for them to stroke her.

The lights flashed on. Whispers and shuffled sounds called her attention back to the room. Students were leaving. The last words from the professor's mouth were, "Test next week."

Ruby mumbled to herself. Test? Test on what? How many baby monkeys suffered because of fucked-up mothers? *A. 2. B. 300. C. A million?* What would her essay be about? How many baby monkeys will commit suicide before they get their mother's attention? Or which one would grow up and become a serial killer? Or hear voices of angels that make them insane or jump off of buildings? Or wind up in mental institutions or psychiatrist's couches?

As she gathered her books, Ruby leaned over and whispered to a tall, long-haired boy that hustled next to her.

"This is bullshit! What LSD trip are they dropping into our psyches? "

He forced a quirky smile and yawned. "We're just doing to the monkeys what we do to ourselves. Humans should be in cages, not the monkeys."

Her eyes widened. "Yeah." She shouted with assertion. "We do that to ourselves." Ruby blinked. In truth, she didn't know what he was talking about. She wasn't treating herself that way. Or was she? It wasn't her fault the way her mother treated her. Or was it? But for sure, she agreed humans belonged in the cages over the monkeys. "Yeah, yeah. Humans in cages." Her comment fell into an empty room. Everyone was gone. She slipped on her coat.

She wiggled through the row of chairs and thumped down the steps that led out to the corridor. Crowds of college kids bustled around. This way, that way, shooting darts aimed toward whatever bulls-eye they thought they were destined toward. For a moment, she was swept up in the kaleidoscope of ripped jeans. Red, blues, and blacks whooshed by and twirled her to a halt. She felt out of place in this ocean of academic fish. Flapping around, laughing, puffed up with their little fish fins, thinking they were going to conquer the world.

The hallway sped around her. Faster and faster. She couldn't breathe. She ran past the flesh, perspiration, and loud chatter. She almost tripped as she flew through the large metal doors. She leaned against the bricks and slid down onto the top step. Air, breathe, air. Huge oaks with perfect green leaves were stationed proudly along the walkway. Blueness and whiteness brushed across the sky. Nature's beauty at its best and all she felt was a claw ripping at her stomach. Hordes of people hopped and jumped around her and over her. Where were they going? What was the rush?

Suddenly a voice belted out a warning. "Better get off the steps."

When she glanced up, a raven-haired guy with lightening-blue eyes stood upright. She ignored him.

"Better get off the steps." This time she clipped him a dirty look. "Who the hell are you?" Before she could get the last vowel out of her mouth, he cuffed her arm and threw her onto the grass. Her books flew through the air and scattered all over as she landed on her ass, spread eagle. A bit woozy, her head fell over like a wet rag. To the left of her eye lay a dead bird.

A storm of protest marchers thrust through the doors of Boylan Hall and catapulted down the steps, shouting with raised fists, *"Ho, Ho, Ho Chi Minh. Ho, Ho, Ho Chi Minh."* Ruby belted out a cry as if Marines were attacking her.

She rolled over and picked up the little yellow and baby blue bird. *Dead. Oh my God. Did I do that? Did I kill the poor thing?* Her eyes filled with tears.

"No. No!" The blue-eyed guy bent down and cradled the small winged creature, placing it under a flowering red maple tree. "I saw it there. It was there before I pushed you down. I'm sorry. I just knew they were coming." He laid the bird under the tree as if it were his long lost friend. "I had this parakeet that flew out of its cage and smashed right into a wall. I watched it break its beak and slide down to the floor." He wiped his hands of the dirt. "Hate to admit it. I was ten and I cried. Thought I killed him. Kept getting birds and they kept flying into walls. I gave up on pet birds." He offered Ruby his hand to steady her to her feet.

For a moment Ruby softened. Averted her eyes away from the bird, slapped her hand into his grip and jumped up.

"Sorry about your birds," Ruby was distracted by screams and the rush of students. She shook her head. Hundreds of middle-class white kids called for their leader. Ho Chi Minh? Ruby shouted above the noise. "All misguided, cheering for a Vietnamese dictator who tortures his citizens." Ruby suddenly caught the young man's glance. "Oh, and thanks for stopping me from getting trampled." She cleared her throat and drew her eyes back to the commotion. "Lovely." She brushed dirt from her jeans. "Bunch of schmucks who don't even know what they're fighting about. Like to see them give up their Corvettes and allowances." She gathered her books.

The blue-eyed savior smiled and picked some leaves out of her hair.

She cocked her head away, wondered why he was grinning. "Don't you get that Ho Chi Minh starves his people? Johnson napalms little children so these, these so-called American protestors think Castro and Ho Chi are better than Johnson? The SDS—or whatever they call themselves—are morons. The world is run by a bunch of psychotics who probably didn't get enough breast milk from mama. Or maybe they were like the rhesus monkey babies. Now there is a midterm paper. Ho Chi Minh, President Johnson, and the rhesus monkey. What did they all have in common? *A. Mothers with no breast milk? B. Mothers who played too much mahjong and lost their minds and hearts to the seductive smoothness of oriental tiles? C. Mothers who didn't give a damn?"*

"You're funny."

"No I'm not." Ruby frowned, starting up the steps.

"Ok. You're not." He pecked his way up the long staircase.

She sliced a curious look at him. "That Psych One class, ever take it? Those ranting rhesus monkeys? Man, oh man."

The young man didn't budge from the step. "I'm more the jock type."

"I could tell."

"What do you mean?"

She pointed. "Jock haircut…"

"My name is Steve. Steve Berg." He held out his hand toward her.

"Ruby Goldsmith."

"Oh, you're Leah's sister?" He tucked his hand into his pocket.

She gripped her books to her chest. "How'd you know that?"

"I'm in the same fraternity as Howard. Phi Sig. He's a year older." He strolled close to her. "They're going together. Pinned. Right?"

"So what? Howard talks about me or something?" Ruby stiffened.

"Don't go paranoid. Howard doesn't confide in me. Everyone knows in the frat house that Howard and Leah are together and that Leah has a younger sister Ruby. Not too many Rubys around." His eyes washed over her and landed at her chest. "So you're Ruby. You some kind of hippy or feminist?"

"You looking at my breasts?"

He coughed, crossed one foot over the other. "No…well…Man, you're…"

"Here take a snapshot." She stuck out her chest and grinned. "You know, I think I know an idiot from your frat. Plopped himself down in the chair next to me at the library. He keeps asking me out."

A glint of recognition brightened his eyes. "Yeah, yeah. David. He's a good friend. Vaguely remember him telling me. Yeah, Ruby. Man, small world." He grinned. "You demanded he buy you a pack of Salems."

"I didn't demand it. I asked him." She laughed. "I don't even smoke cigarettes. I don't know why I asked him. Probably to get rid of him."

He kicked the step, "He said you were a cold bitch."

"Oh, yeah?" Ruby stared at the sky. "I just won't go out with him." She tapped her foot.

Steve leaned toward her, "Why?"

"My parents." Ruby tightened her grip around her books. "They got this I-gotta –marry-a-doctor fantasy thing."

Steve shuffled his foot. "What does that have to do with going out with David?"

"He said he's going to be a doctor."

"Most girls would jump at a guy like that." Steve winked.

"I'm not most girls." Ruby glared.

"Do I dare ask? What kind of girl are you?" He shifted from one foot to the other.

She turned in a huff about and walked away. "None of your business."

"Well, you know the guys talk about your sister."

Ruby halted. Turned. "Yeah? Like what?"

"That's she's got Howard by the balls."

"Really? That's nice to tell me." Ruby started to walk, then turned back. "So now the frat idiots say I'm a ball buster?"

"I don't know. Maybe. No. Kinda. The Goldsmith sisters. Ya know."

"The GUYS don't know shit about shit."

"I'm just shooting my mouth. I didn't mean…" Steve tried to grab her by the shoulder.

"Forget it. It doesn't matter." She almost tripped as she hurried away.

"Hey, wait. Come to the fraternity Saturday night."

She turned, blinked, kicked a pebble from under her foot. "Why?"

"Oh. You might like what you see." A cocky look perked up his face. "I'd like you to come."

She eyed him. "Isn't one Goldsmith bitch enough?"

"Maybe I like bitches." He tilted his head.

"I think you should see my shrink if that's the case." Ruby smacked her lips, stamped her foot. "Oh shit," she whispered. She had slipped.

"What? You go to a shrink?"

Ruby coughed. Why did she blurt that out? She had to cover up what she said, "I was just kidding." She raced forward. Took a few steps and looked back. He was watching her. She sighed. *Interesting.* This was the first time she felt a warm tingle for another boy besides Joel.

Ruby ran. Her feet crashed against the pavement. The trees huddled in, whispered, *rush, run, go.* She had to catch the bus to Rosenthal's office.

Chapter 16: Dr. Rosenthal's Office, The Truth Be Told

Five o'clock every Monday, Wednesday, and Friday, Ruby went to therapy. It had been kismet. Reading Jungian psychology journals at the school library, she stumbled upon Dr. Rosenthal's article, *Altered-states of reality and Schizophrenia*. It snapped her attention. At the bottom of the page was an asterisk, his name, and mention of his private practice in Brooklyn Heights.

That Monday, Ruby talked about the rhesus monkeys. "What a freakin' horror movie."

The doctor stroked his hand across his baldness as he listened.

"I wanted to vomit." She paused. "Didn't you once say I was touch deprived?"

"Yes, Ruby. You've been physically, emotionally, and mentally abused and touch deprived." He squinted his thin eyes. He waited. His cheekbones curved like mounds. "The film put a face to the words?"

"I'm one of those deprived monkeys." She folded her arms, tucked her legs under her buttocks, and curled into the corner of the couch.

"It's deep, the hurt. Very deep, Ruby."

Ruby tensed up. "Fuck them all! I hate them. Hate them!" The heartbreak, the schism in her brain, the cracks in her soul remained clogged up in her body. She wasn't ready to drink the oily mud of self-hatred that spawned from the abuse. Wasn't ready to transform all of that painful energy and use it to heal.

Dr. Rosenthal crossed his legs and pinched his glasses against his nose. "Sometimes all you can do is blame and hate until you're ready to see how it all truly affected you. So, get out all the hate, Ruby."

"I don't know. I don't know what I feel." She folded her arms. Ruby felt comforted by the doctor's familiar grey sweater, penny loafers, and the sweet smell of his pipe. He was a harbor she sailed into and dumped her anxiety. The smell of his sugary Old Spice cologne warmed the room, along with the cedar walls and cherry wood floor. His office felt like a woodsy cabin in the middle of the Catskill Mountains, enveloping her. Any minute, Ruby thought the chipper squirrel staring through the office window from his tree hole would offer her the meager crumb he nibbled on. "Since I was a kid I've had shit slapped all over me."

"Close your eyes. See the little girl in you. Feel her. Can you?"

She waved to the squirrel. "I don't know."

For an instant, the doctor appeared like cardboard. He sat quiet and distant. But, then Ruby noticed a flash of light in his eyes. A stare or knowing that violated her wall of defense.

"Why are you looking at me like that?" Ruby fumbled with her turtleneck.

"How am I looking at you?"

"I don't know."

"You keep saying 'I don't know'."

"Well, I don't know."

"You do know, Ruby. You're feeling it right now. I see it all over."

Ruby blinked and squeezed her eyes shut, not wanting to cry. She started to gag. "I…I feel like I'm choking."

"Breathe into the sensation. What's choking you?"

Ruby heaved, shifted around on the couch, tried to steady the palpitations squeezing her heart. "It's always the same. I feel like I'm dying."

"Stop holding. Breathe." Dr. Rosenthal kept delving.

She shook her head. "I just pretend." She turned. Stared out.

Dr. Rosenthal emptied his pipe, tapped it, and folded his hands. "You pretend so you don't have to feel. It's safe."

"My sister hated me the day I was born. I couldn't even turn to her."

"Did she tell you that?"

"Yes. She thinks I am turning my parents against her." Ruby fiddled with her sweater sleeves. "Everything is my fault. I should have never been born."

"That's a harsh thing to say that about yourself."

Ruby gazed at the ceiling. "Leah and I make fun of how dumb my mother is. How much we hate her. We call her the witch." Ruby paused, coughed. "Leah repeats our conversations to my parents, and tells them I hate her. My father confronted me on whether I hated my mother. I do hate her. But I told him it was a lie. That Leah hates her." She hit her thighs. "I keep doing that. I keep talking to Leah and she keeps snitching. Why do I keep trusting her? She always tells them everything. I'm so stupid!"

"Are you stupid to want your sister's love?"

"Since I was little, my father has told me to stop talking about stupid things." Ruby frowned closed her eyes. "I'll go far away and never see any of them again."

"Wherever you go, you take all your problems with you."

"My mother told me that if I say anything to my father that upsets him, he'll get a heart attack. He'll die. It'll be my fault. You know, because he has the heart condition. And if I get angry for any reason, he'll die. Or my mother will take a knife. And go crazy." She tightened the hold on herself. "I want to scream into their faces, smack them. My father could die if I really let it out."

Dr. Rosenthal leaned forward. "Ruby. If your father dies, it has nothing to do with you. You can't make him die."

"How do you know my father won't die if I get angry?"

"Does your mother have the power to know why or how your father will die? Does she have God's power to know when your father will die?"

"God? What does God have to do with this? What does God know anyway? If God knew something, then I'd have different parents. I wouldn't be sitting here."

"Do you feel abandoned by God? Are you afraid if you allow anyone to know how much you hurt, and how much love you need, that something horrible will happen? That if you love, God will take it away?"

"I don't believe in God."

Rosenthal quieted, rubbed the edges of his chair, "What do you believe?"

"I believe in nothing."

"Do you believe in Marianne?"

Ruby's eyes hardened, her lips pressed tight against her teeth. "How do I believe in a hallucination? It only makes me more crazy."

"Maybe she's your guide. We all have guides. I talked to you about how some children who are abused leave their bodies, split off to protect themselves, and see guides or angels. I believe that is what happened to you. We need to put all the pieces back together."

"You give me medication. Two different kinds. According to the abnormal psychology theories, I'm schizophrenic."

"The medications stabilize your moods. You had thoughts of driving your car into a tree when you first came here. Now you don't. Now you go to school. You keep coming to sessions because you want to live. I don't think you're schizophrenic, because you can tell the difference between the altered-state visions and the actual world you live in. There are forces that influence us. Beyond you and me. Inside of your subconscious. Marianne is a shadow life, a part of you, like a sub-personality. We all have different parts of ourselves that guide us. I think you have a gift."

Ruby's chin dropped to her chest. She sighed. "She doesn't feel like a part of me," Ruby swept quotes with her fingers. "A 'sub-personality.' I see and hear her like I see and hear you. How is that not schizophrenic? Or even having multi-personalities?"

"Look how you are talking to me about this. You know the difference. It doesn't matter how she comes to you. Can you trust what I'm telling you?"

Ruby sighed. "Painting helps me to create Marianne's worlds. Then I feel one with her. But otherwise, I feel nuts. How can Marianne make me believe in myself when she makes me feel abnormal and scared?" She threw her hands in the air. "I don't understand anything that's happening to me. All I know is, I'm fucked."

"I understand how painful this is for you."

"I tell Joel."

"Tell him what?"

"I tell him about my visions, my parents…I let him do anything to me. He makes me feel like I matter. Smoking pot, kissing, whatever I do is alright around Joel."

"You know that's not true. Joel hurts you. Joel is not your savior. Smoking pot isn't a good idea for you. It can set you off into psychotic break. I've told you that." The doctor tapped his fingers on the chair.

Ruby got up and grabbed her pea coat, stopped, and stood very still. Only the quiet hum of the radiator lodged in her ears. "The drugs you give me...I'm not sure what they do for me. The drugs I smoke with Joel make me feel alive. I'm fine." She put each arm through a sleeve.

"Ruby, you resist what you want...why?"

"Why? What do I feel? You keep asking, over and over. Okay. I feel rage. Dark, bloody rage. Like the color of Marianne's hair. I'm afraid of my rage. I'm afraid of Marianne. I'm afraid of being my mother. It's all choked up."

"Your mother is in you, but you aren't her. I'm on your side, Ruby. I'm truly interested and care about what happens to you." Rosenthal's energy was charged, He stood up. "Keep painting, writing. Let it scream, let it come out, Ruby."

"How do you hate and love someone at the same time, Dr. Rosenthal?" Ruby rubbed her hand against the doorknob, stared into the doctor's eyes. Around her neck, tucked underneath her sweater, down deep where no one could see, Ruby grabbed the medallion and Jewish star that lay on top of each other like two coins in a fountain. "I see Marianne now." Ruby squeezed the knob.

Dr. Rosenthal walked to the door, stood by her. "What do you see?"

"Her eyes, staring through me like a hot iron. Her hands reaching toward me. I feel sick inside."

"What does she want you to know?"

Ruby closed her eyes and asked, "Marianne, what do you want me to know?" A minute passed, Ruby opened her eyes. "She says the paintings will tell the story."

Rosenthal leaned against the wall, rubbed his hands. "Hate and love are bedfellows. You can't hate someone without loving that person as well. But the worst kind of hate is for yourself." He held the door open. "You're safe with me, Ruby. Can you feel that yet?"

She slammed the door as she left. "I never feel safe." She dove into the winter air. Its breath froze her cheeks and lips. Down the block, the trees were upright and naked, the cold sun shone on the cold metal of cars, everything around her was a tomb, a place to die. Life was killing her, closing down on her like a giant foot from the sky. She leaned against a Buick to catch her breath, shoved her hands into her pockets. Her teeth chattered, cars rattled by, her nose a red ice cube. She thought about Joel. A smutty shame ate at her genitals. It grew like moss up her spine. She screamed out. "Fuck! God help me!"

Chapter 17: Joel's Invitation

It was around midnight when Joel called. Groggy, Ruby picked up the phone.

Leah screamed, "Who's that calling now?" She turned over and melted into the mound of white covers.

Ruby's face glistened with a dreamy smile. "Yes, Yes." For a minute her heart beat wildly, then slowed to a regular pace. "Can I bring Susan?" She had met Susan Lenard in her archeology class. Both were obsessed with ancient Mesopotamia and Egypt. They hung out in Susan's strawberry-painted room on weekends, smoked pot, ate Twinkies, and drew Picasso-like pictures of sexual tantric positions. Susan's mother, who dressed like a burlesque queen and worked two jobs, was never home. Susan had free reign to come and go as she pleased. Something Ruby envied. Like Joel, Susan ignited Ruby's wild side. Claire disliked Susan and her mother, called them trash. All the more reason for Ruby to befriend her. Dr. Rosenthal's estimation of Joel stuck in her head. "He'll hurt you." Maybe bringing Susan would prevent her from jumping all over Joel.

"You met Susan at my house. She's got blonde hair down to her butt, really skinny. She was wearing jeans and a T-shirt with a skull and bones. She's got that one blue eye, the other brown?" Ruby could hear Joel thinking.

"Just get here by eight."

She snapped on the small lamp and immediately dialed Susan's number. "Wanna get high with me and Joel on Saturday night? You remember him. My next door neighbor."

Leah's muffled demand seeped from under sheets, "Go to sleep, Ruby."

Ruby covered the phone, "In a minute, Leah." She whispered into the receiver. "Well. Do you?"

"I already get high." Susan snorted like a pig.

"At Joel's house at eight."

"Yeah, I'm in."

"Good." Ruby hung up.

She flicked off the light, lay in bed, stared at the billowy shadows that crossed the ceiling. For a split second, she thought about Steve. Who cared about a bunch of straight-asses anointing some jock king for a day? Even though there was something about Steve, his calm demeanor, the way he looked at her with a glint of warmth, she wanted Joel more. Her thoughts were interrupted by Rosenthal's warning, *"You can have a psychotic break."* Ruby shook her head, tossed off the alert in her mind. Her hunger to be with Joel outweighed anything else. She'd smoked before and nothing like that ever happened. What did that mean anyway, psychotic break? A memory of her mother being carted off to an institution. *No! It's only pot. It's harmless. It only makes me feel good.*

The next day at eight o'clock, the two girls showed up dressed in black minis, tight sweaters, heavy black winter coats, and knee-high boots. They jabbered away as Ruby rang the basement doorbell. Joel answered wearing a white undershirt and blue jeans. The two girls looked at each other and giggled, held hands and stepped down into the den of sin.

The walls in the basement were wood-paneled and matched the cherry wood floors. The air was smoky with pot and incense. Sweaty-looking T-shirts hung from every chair and windowsill. Bologna and mustard reeked from every slot and crevice of the basement. Frayed jeans hung across a red upholstered chair.

"What a slob." Susan complained and held her nose.

Ruby didn't care. She smiled. "Who cares, Susan? You know?"

Susan shrugged her shoulders. "You've got this thing for him. Not me."

A slight ray of light slashed through the thick-shaded window close to the ceiling. Strokes of dusted light streaked the room. Every step closer into the heart of the room made Ruby shakier. Around her, soft grey hues played against the floor. Pounding footsteps from upstairs caught Ruby's attention. "Who's up there?"

Joel entered the room like a gazelle. His long neck rippled as he slowly strode across the room. "My parents."

Ruby threw her hands in the air. "Your parents?"

"Don't get your panties in an uproar. They never come down."

"Never?" She checked the stairs, stared at the closed door atop the steps that led down into the basement. What a break. Her parents banged on the bathroom door a hundred times if she was taking a crap. "You got the life. No one checks on you."

Strings of glittery stars hung like lanterns across the ceiling. They floated aimlessly. Hypnotized by their swing, Ruby fell backwards into the big-armed red chair.

Susan struggled into the chair with her. "Move your ass."

Ruby made more room for her to squeeze in.

"Well, well. Two peas in a pod." Joel laughed.

Ruby noticed that his big toes had lumps on either side. Ugly. She didn't like seeing that, went back to admiring his smooth porcelain face. His blonde hair bounced on his shoulders. A loose strand fell in his eye and he swept it away.

Susan elbowed Ruby and whispered incoherently in Ruby's ear.

"What is it?" Ruby growled.

"I got to go the bathroom." She skidded across the floor. "Now!"

Joel lit a stick of incense. "It's back there, remember." He pointed to the far end of the room.

"Yeah, I know." Susan darted across the floor and slammed the door.

"When was Susan in your basement?" Ruby's mouth curled.

"Oh. No. Yeah. I think one of my frat buddies brought her here one night." He stared off. "Crazy night. Crazy. Yeah. She was here."

"Why didn't you tell me you knew her?"

Joel winked. "I don't know. What's the difference?" Smoke curled around his body like a snake.

Joel plopped to the floor, sat by her feet cross-legged, and pulled a joint from his back pocket. He ironed it with his finger, took a match and lit up, took a long hard inhale, held the smoke until his face turned red, then released with a big sigh. A ripple of laughter escaped from his throat and he winked at Ruby. "Pay attention. This is good stuff."

He placed the crinkled, rolled cigarette onto the edge of an ashtray. From his back pocket he took a plastic bag filled with what looked like dead leaves, and pinched a small heap into a metal pipe. "Which one. Joint or pipe?"

Ruby stared at him. "I want to know why you didn't tell me you know Susan."

"I started this joint. Here, take it. Relax." His lids drooped and he put the pipe and bag to the side.

"I'm not done with this Susan thing." Ruby reached for the soggy roll of weed and her stomach grumbled. "I'm hungry already." She slipped the joint between her thumb and pointer finger, examined the white smoke and red sparks that popped from the tip of the joint. With caution, she reeled it up to her mouth and sucked in, once, then twice. The peyote gold rushed into her lungs. One more time she brought the weedy, crunchy smoke to her lips and drew in deep. A burning sensation ripped down her throat and up her head.

"Drag in deep." Joel facilitated her puff, his eyes all soft and sexy-like. "Dig in."

The hot orange edges flashed. Ruby coughed, almost choked. Then waited. Blinked several times. "What about Susan, Joel?

Joel ignored her question. "Ok, hot lips. Give it back." Joel snatched it from her mouth.

She didn't realize how long she had it dangling from her mouth.

Joel took several short snorts, closed his eyes and handed the reefer back to her.

Again, she took a few hits, handed it over to him. Ruby dug deeper into the chair. "And where is that damn Susan?" She eyed the bathroom door, wanted to yell out to her or get up, but somehow she felt like a sloppy Joe, messed up, and sinking into chunky meat.

"Never mind." He handed the weed back to her. He lumbered up from his seated position, twisted his body into a rock 'n' roller stance, fingered an invisible guitar as he slinked over to the record player. "Dangerous hot music." He pulled a record out of album and placed it on the turntable, flipped it on.

Ruby coughed. Lightness edged her skin against her bones as she released the next drag with a prolonged huff. She licked the saliva from inside her mouth. "Cotton mouth."

From the center of the record player a fiery red beam flashed.

It grew big and voluptuous, and insistent. The sultry rays whipped around the room and lassoed the corners and chomped at the walls.

Ruby whirled inside of 3D. She was the sound system.

"Jimi." Joel threw his head back and laughed.

Electrical music cruised up her spine and pricked buzzing up her hips and vagina. She involuntarily jerked forward.

"*EXEPeriennnnnnnnnnnnnnce!* Wow! Vibratory, hallucinogenic stuff Hendrix. Soul food." Joel strode back to her and grabbed the joint.

Joel's words glided through her. He appeared squared off, a Picasso painting walking across clouds. She gripped her thighs. Something was happening to her eyes and ears. They popped and sprouted music sounds, blinding her senses to one long wicked note.

"The red light is pregnant with the cells of the universe." Joel swayed back and forth.

Ruby growled, hungry. A smorgasbord of fruits and hot tamales swirled in front of her. She reached, and the succulent food disappeared. She wanted to eat…and suck on a tangerine. Dive between the musical cords and smooth rhythms that birthed from Jimi's throat. *HAVE YOU EVER BEEN EXPERIENCED…Do you want an experience?* Over and over *experience. Experience…*drummed her deeper into her wet pores. The room expanded.

"This weed is lined with LSD." Joel was lying on top of her. "Ruby. Remember, I already know you. Inside of you. Remember when we would watch TV in my bedroom. Your twelfth birthday. All that playing around, but never the real thing. You know? This is what you came here for. It's what you always want. And I do, too. This is it, Ruby. I'm here. Going in, digging, busting you in. You're a big girl now. No more pretending to be a good girl. Be a woman."

She heard her voice as a girlish squeak, "Shit! Fuck!" Joel head shape-shifted. She couldn't catch him. He was here, there. His body bold, heat, swayed, rocked around her and on her. A choked yell— *push him off,* but her body was a mash of confetti, shredded and flying through the air. Yes, they'd sixty-nined, finger-fucked, but she didn't want to do IT. "No!" All of her friends had lost their cherries by the time they were fifteen. She was scared to go all the way. Why was she saving herself for some twisted 50s paradigm of saving herself for marriage? This was 1967. This didn't feel right. Not this way.

"Come on, baby. Open your legs for daddy. Open sesame. Stop teasing me. Don't be a CT."

Joel words were mumbo jumbo. Soft whisper smells, strands of beads, music, and sirens blew her mind into pieces of lint and grey matter that encircled every part of the room. A woozy heady spin trapped her in a maze of music, shakes, and rolls. She wanted to scream. Instead she laid back, wrapped her legs around him. Her head bobbed in beat with the hypnotic jazz-rock. Her body wanted Joel's penis. Her head said no. Her body said yes. She let him enter her hard and fast. Just like he did at twelve when his fingers explored her vagina. This time it was the real deal. He was busting her cherry cream pie. *EXXXXXXXXXXperience* drummed in her head. The longer the sound, the harder Joel pumped inside of her.

Ruby opened her eyes. The walls and ceiling crumbled as she felt a stab of pain go up her genitals into her hips, then a hot warmth that made her moan and quiver.

"Give me more…another sweet taste." Joel's fat erection climbed deeper into her soft cervical walls.

His rotation and movement lit up her being, as big and as red as the burst of crimson light beaming from the record player. Each note jerked with Jimi's voice.

"I can't breathe." She groped her chest. Tore at her sweater. She heaved like a rabid animal, gasped and spit. Her eyes rolled. The room spun. She blacked out.

Chapter 18: Ancient Oasis

Mountains, the hot desert sun streaked Ruby's body. She thirsted for water. Above, the moon strayed behind dark clouds. A sudden burst and it transformed into a sunlit orange sky. A vibrant blue river blended into the horizon.

"Marianne is the river," a distant voice blew through the winds.

"Joel?" Ruby buried her toes in the clay-like soil. Cool and safe.

Ahead, an oasis. Women bustled around, washed and beat clothes against rocks. They had traveled far and needed to keep their clothes clean, free from the smell of sweat and worry.

A woman stood in the center, men surrounded her. Her wavy auburn hair cascaded down her back. She appeared fragile, weak, yet her voice loomed strong and confident.

The others put the wet clothes in baskets, their brown faces gritty from the sun. Camels and tents stood steady in the quiet sands. The other women joined the circle.

Ruby watched. The sun beat on her every nerve. Smells of heat and screeches of vultures pressed against her chest. Slow garbled voices strained through her ears. She could hear the women's thoughts. They were afraid, longing, searching for comfort and safety. Their attachment to Marianne, they'd protect her from the elements, the people—they honored her visions.

Marianne. Ruby felt her, saw her. The burden. So much for Marianne to take on her shoulders, this epiphany that set her apart from the rest. Marianne positioned her knapsack—filled with wheat and nuts for nourishment—around her shoulders. Her water pouch, thick and soaked, was strapped to her waist. She unhooked it to wet her throat, gulped several times then placed her palm over her eyes to block out the sun. The heat burnt her skin and her eyes swelled with sorrow. Her true love was dead, crucified. Could she make the sojourn into the unknown without him? The river led the way to the ocean, across into another land. That is the route, the path she had to follow in order to save her own life and the life of her unborn child.

Ruby inched toward her.

The woman looked up. "You're here." She adjusted, put up her hand. "Don't come any closer."

Ruby crumpled and fell to the ground.

At that moment, one of the men—his face buried beneath layers of red and green scarves—screamed, "Marianne! You lie. Why should we believe you?"

The group of women yelped, held their fists up in the air. "YAAAAA! YAYAYAYA!!"

"Your jealousy stinks. I tell you, he came to me in spirit. Now you throw the laws at me. The ones we all defied? The hole in my heart cries out to you. Why have you forgotten me? I'm left a grieving widow and you abandon me?"

Ruby held her throat. Sweat poured across her scalp. Scorched with fear, she called out. "Marianne."

Marianne threw a fierce stare at Ruby. "Stay away. Watch and listen, but don't participate."

Another man's voice scathed with rage. "Your womb rules your logic. Your emotions out of place. He healed your wild mind. Your grandiose visions…your melancholy. Now they're back with this betrayal that you are the prophet, God's messenger and savior. No! You lie."

"And I healed him from inner blindness. His lost memory. You want me to hide behind his shadow. No! I won't. You change my name, my lineage, and bury my female ancestors. My mothers and sisters." She held her belly. "But I won't pass that down to my daughter."

A rigid man with a graying beard came forward and pointed an accusatory finger at her. "Laws of Moses! You defy them."

She shooed them away. "I'm the *Shekinah*. Yes, I cried at his feet. I loved him. And they banished me from the tribe because of that. But I'm Marianne, Mary, whatever you want to call me. I am the prophetess. The face of the *Shekinah*. I am the divine woman who sees, hears, tastes and feels everything, just like Sarah, Leah, and Rebecca…just like the priestesses of my blood."

An aged man, strong in stature, waved his hand in the air. "The Law is good and great. The master taught the law, you make up your own. Blasphemous. You're still a pagan, one of the prostitutes in the temples. That's what you gave to the Master. Sexual favors."

Marianne threw the soggy cloth at his face. "I learned the ways of healing. I am his equal. You resist. Stuck in old ways. You think I am still lost and crazy? You want me to mold and rot as a woman. I will be sent to redeem woman in *Aserah*'s plan." She hid her face and sobbed. "Your rejection hurts and rattles the cells in my body. I need your love as I love you. I know the law, but you must breathe, eat, taste, and feel it, not just live it from your head. It is more than you think and pray upon. It is so much more."

"Go away, Marianne. Go to your hiding place. Just go." All the men started to scream together. "Go. Go."

The women rallied around her. Protected her from the men's stupidity and fear.

She lifted her hands to fight. "Receive the feminine face. My eyes, tongue, mouth!" She fell to her knees and shoved clumps of granules into her mouth, and spat at the men. She opened her arms, searched their faces for any sort of movement or compassion. The angry silence strangled her. She pulled her hair, pawed at her arms until blood trickled down her skin. "For all eternity, for all eternity my blood will wash over the earth." She lifted her arms to the heavens. She convulsed. "How will I be remembered? As his whore, his handmaiden, your keeper?"

Suddenly a crack of thunder jolted Marianne. Lightening encircled the sacred desert space. The light lifted her and she levitated. The men gasped as she dangled mid-air. She cracked a bird-like squawk, "I will return. I will."

Those were her last words. She disappeared.

Chapter 19: Back From Beyond

Ruby shot back into her body. The basement oozed into focus. Joel's body crushed her chest like a lump of sod. "You. Fuck you." Her anger and adrenaline pumped up her strength as she kicked him off. He dumped to the floor, sprawled out.

She fidgeted with her panties, leapt off the soft chair, blood and semen smudged between her thighs. Shaking and crying, she stumbled around. What happened to her? Her vagina ached. She pressed against the chair.

Joel was on the floor, passed out. Where had she gone? A dream? A hallucination? Dr. Rosenthal warned her of what could happen if she kept smoking. Was she psychotic now? That woman. That woman. Mary? Red hair, anguish, rage, her words burrowed into her heart. The *Shekinah*, the divine woman. A woman. She's just a dream. Her imagination. That's all it was. She shook her head. This time, Marianne felt real. Really real. Dr. Rosenthal had asked, did Marianne help her to believe in herself? Marianne, passionate to her vision. Strong. Ruby had Marianne's visions. Why her? She remembered seeing the rabbi's spirit when she was little. Now, Marianne's spirit and story. She held her head. *Shut up. Shut up. Go away. It was nothing. Nothing. I'm not crazy. NO!* She burrowed into her shame. Her body wilted and emptied into tremors and waves of guilt.

Joel lay on the floor. She held her hand to her vagina. The room spun. She gripped her chest. Susan. Susan. Where was she? *Have to find her.* She fell to her knees. The floor was hard, then spongy. Leaves rustled. They caught her attention. Lovely leaves.

In the distance, a figure emerged from the shadows. It was a man. He was lean with smoldering blue-grey eyes. He glided as if he were on wheels. He reached for her hand.

Ruby panted. "I'm sick."

He stroked her hair. "Such lovely red hair. I miss you."

"Go away. Don't touch me. I don't know you."

The vision vanished.

Joel grunted. Opened his eyes groggily. Then his head plopped back down.

Ruby kicked Joel in the shins. "It's because of you. You…damn. You did this to me." Ruby shoved him with her foot. "Get up. Get up." She jumped around, crying, shaking, and screaming

Joel mumbled incoherently. "I did nothing, Ruby. We're having fun."

Ruby swirled. Music pounded in her head, *"Foxxxxxxxy lady."* Boom, Boom, Boom. The floor vibrated. Joel stirred, his hand reached toward her.

"You bastard." Ruby kicked him again. "Susan? Where the fuck are you? I'm freakin' out!"

Ruby hobbled to the bathroom, opened the door and peeked in. No Susan. Damn. Through the corner of her eye she noticed the staircase. Ruby dragged her body toward the steps. She wrapped her hands around her thighs tried to move each foot forward. Shit. Shit. Ruby felt like a thousand weights were tied to her ankles.

Out of nowhere popped Susan. She stood at the bottom of the stairs. Wide-eyed and chomping on a Snickers bar. "I got hungry. Good smokes."

"Where the hell have you been? I didn't see you." Ruby clung to her arm, worn, frail. She fell on the steps. "I can't breathe, I'm going to faint."

"Been? You were in the midst of screwing your brains out." Susan chewed on the chocolate like a starved raccoon.

Ruby's voice lowered. "I'm…so afraid." She huddled over, tiny and tender, eyes roaming. Her breath was shallow.

"Afraid. Of what? Hot man. That's the way it goes. I'm not jealous, either. You can have Joel, too."

Ruby's face balled up and turned a beet red, hysterical, "You're a fucking bitch."A surge of rage gathered in her body. She stood up.

Susan shoved past her, snubbed her nose. "Miss high and mighty. Get over yourself." She turned around and snapped her fingers. "Miss General Electric refrigerator. Well, you're officially defrosted. You're just like all of us girls now." Her face hardened. "You'll see." She flicked a smile. She hopped down the stairs like a small child.

Ruby tightened her fists then collapsed into a ball. Susan plunked down the steps. Ruby plied herself off the step and slid out behind her friend.

"It's all grist for the mill." Susan sing-songed her way out the door. "All grist for the mill. You'll see. You'll want more and more Joel. Read Ram Dass. All *Grist for the Mill.*"

"We're friends. Why are you doing this?" Ruby hobbled after her. The door slammed with a deafening clap. Cold air slapped her senses in place.

"You want Joel, you can have him. We're not friends anymore."

Ruby froze in her step. She looked up. The sky was eternal and vast. She felt her heart pounding, her feet flattened to the pavement. "You're not making anything clear, Marianne. Why do you hurt me? I don't understand. You come and go and leave me when I need you." She placed her hands over her ears and screamed. "Fuck!"

Ruby ran home. Climbed into bed. Alone, terrified, she coped through the night, running to the bathroom, throwing up, then back under the covers. She made it through to morning, limp, and ragged. Got up drank three cups of Nescafe, took a hot bath and then slept until Monday morning.

Chapter 20: Winter, 1967 – Staying Alive

It was a barren and desperate winter. Ruby buried that night deep. Blocked it out. For two weeks, she upped her dosage of medication. But then she realized she'd run out and stopped. She knew she was playing with fire, but she couldn't, didn't want to tell Rosenthal.

Ruby discontinued her friendship with Susan. They passed in the hallways, cast daggered looks at one another.

But she was far from done with Joel. The spaces in her head were filled with thoughts of him.

Winter crashed down on Brooklyn like a nightmare. Her eighteenth birthday came and went like an abandoned shack. No one seemed to notice. Joel gave her the book, *Games People Play* by Eric Berne, dryly wrote inside "Happy Birthday. My one and only, Ruby." She threw the book in a shoebox. Hated the title and wouldn't read it. Games people play. She didn't play games. Joel did. And still, she met him in his basement, on the corner, in a candy store. She couldn't resist the sex. Susan was right about that. She wanted more. As much as she wanted to stop, she ached for Joel.

Spring rolled in with a demure coolness. Ruby had term papers, deadlines with art pieces, and physics to pass. Distracted by Joel, her grades suffered. She thinned out, became as skinny as a rail. She watched television for hours, ate bags of chocolate kisses, forget to eat full meals. Her parents screamed for her to come to dinner. She tuned them out with loud Beatles and Hendrix music. The more she listened to the Beatles or Janis Joplin and smoked her brains out, the more Marianne's presence intruded. She painted in her basement for hours on end. Her parents never looked, never asked.

On her regular visits to Dr. Rosenthal, she continued to lie about pot use. Never revealed what happened that night in Joel's basement. But, she showed him her paintings.

"These scenes seem surreal. More unstable."

"I feel alive in them."

"Alive or stoned?" Rosenthal studied the painting in front of him.

"They come to me from nowhere, where Marianne lives."

"You're hiding something. I don't think this painting came from nowhere." He puffed on his pipe.

Ruby stiffened.

"What happened? You look like you weigh as much as an ant. I'm deeply concerned."

Ruby twisted about. She wanted to run away. "It doesn't matter. I'm a free woman." She built a false sense of pride through denial. Ruby held to a picture of herself as the woman who danced in the starlight, sang bluesy rock and roll songs like *Shotgun*, and was fearless since she got herself through that horrific night. She walked on high-wedged shoes and bell-bottoms, swaggering her skinny body, thinking she was Miss America. Hiding her Jewish roots, born in a ghetto where the women wore wigs, long skirts, and covered their bodies and turned crazy from repression.

"Really? You feel free?"

"I can't lose you, Dr. Rosenthal."

"Why would you?"

"Because. I didn't listen. I need Joel and I don't listen."

"What happened?"

"I...I smoked with Joel... and I had a full-blown...Marianne...I saw her, I was there."

"And...?"

"And..." She looked around and touched her face. "I'm here. Somehow I'm here."

Ruby broke down, cried. "I don't know how I'm walking around. I don't know. I'm so afraid."

"I'm here. We'll work through this. You can do this."

"I can't stop yet. I don't know how I blocked it. Like a slingshot. I just boomeranged back. Dead. Numb. I doubled up on the medication."

Rosenthal's look sharpened.

"I stopped doing that. But, I can't let go of him, and I need you to accept me for that."

"I do. And I am responsible for you, Ruby. You can't take your therapy into your own hands."

Ruby nodded.

"I need your commitment, Ruby. I can't help you if you don't want to help yourself. I know how shameful you must feel. But I am not judging you, only deeply, deeply concerned for your well-being."

Ruby kept nodding.

Yes, Ruby needed Joel. Their hot, steamy time. Both indulged the other. His incessant search for some mysterious world beyond their relationship baffled and excited Ruby. He studied psychology and philosophy and became more engrossed in Martin Buber and Sai Baba. She frequented the Modern and Metropolitan museums, roamed the East Village streets studying artists who worked and lived in lofts and empty garages. She dreamt of living in Paris, walking through the Louvre eating french bread and foreign cheeses, drinking wine while Joel read and meditated to his heart's content. He wanted to find God. She wanted to forget there was a God.

They made a pact one night, watching a full moon from the steps.

Ruby started, "Pinky swear. Never succumb to suburbia, dull conversations, and babies. We'll live a gypsy life."

Joel laughed. "Sure." And he intertwined his pinky with hers.

As the snow melted and cherry trees blossomed with the onset of spring she knew it was a long road ahead to understand the pain that deepened her love for Joel. She needed to find a way to break free of her family's grip on her soul. Ruby was afraid to lose herself to Marianne, and afraid to lose herself to Joel. She was afraid of everything in her life. Her need to control and perfect a fantasy life caused Ruby to act out even more through her addictions.

She didn't realize she had already lost herself.

On one of her weekly visits to him, Rosenthal's voice heightened. "Ruby. Do you want to stop? The pot? Joel? You're traumatizing yourself. Over and over. Can you receive it when I say you deserve love, comfort, self-compassion?"

Ruby looked up. "I want to get well. I need to stop. But, I can't." She closed her eyes. "It was my fault. All of it. I always wanted sex with Joel. But...it's all confusing."

"You need to go into treatment, a program, Ruby. I can't help if you can't stop."

"No! No! I won't. Not like my mother. I'll stop. I promise. Please teach me."

Chapter 21: Summer, 1968 – Cabana Love

The seagull dove in for the kill. Underneath the surface of the shallow waves, a defenseless minnow was about to meet its doom. The sun radiated its heat like a soft whip against Ruby's back. She filled out the tiny red bikini with her curves. A cacophony of barking poodles and children's screeches filled the beach winds. Salt, fish, and the smell of tanning oil mixed to create the perfect, hot August day. Ruby had quit pot. Stabilized. Steady therapy and medications with Rosenthal. But she wasn't ready to let go of Joel. There was more here to understand. More to explore. More to delve into.

Far Rockaway Malibu Beach Club was for the rich. Blue-and-white striped cabanas encircled the blue pool area and huge yellow umbrellas lined the beach. Blonde- haired and brown curly-topped beach boys ran around serving the members cold drinks and crisp fries.

"Heat wave." Ruby flung her head back and soaked in the rays. Gobbled a salami sandwich. She knew how great her bod and face looked all fresh and tanned. She spied through the corner of her eye to see if Joel was gaping at her. Instead, he was intently reading. She poked at the cover of the book. *Games People Play,* by Eric Berne. "That book. Always."

"A game is an ongoing series of complementary ulterior transactions progressing to a well-defined, predictable outcome. Descriptively, it is a recurring set of transactions...with a concealed motivation...or gimmick. That is what it says here." Joel pointed to the passage. "I gave you this book. Remember? Of course, you never

read it."

Ruby ran her finger down and around his biceps. "Oh yeah."

He caught her hand. "Listen. You're doing it right now."

"What am I doing?"

"Seducing me, wanting my love so you don't feel worthless." Joel tossed the book next to him.

"You're not my shrink. Shut up." Her lips tightened around her gums.

He stroked her cheek. "You throw away your spirit. You throw away yourself. I don't get it. Don't you want to understand your visions? Understand God?"

Ruby swiped sand from her ankles, shouted, "GOD. HA!" Ruby eyed him.

"Why are you angry with God?" He stared off, followed the white gulls' flight, buried the slivers of sand in his toes. His fingers traced the soft curves of the beach blanket. "You of all people. You…you… see visions, hear voices, and you question if there is a God."

"Who says that's God talking to me? I'm no prophet. I take medication. Is that God-like?" She shoved her finger in his chest. "Even you made fun of me. My bullshit stuff. My psycho stuff. When did you become a believer? Gonna to wear a yarmulke and tizzies? Or whatever they're called?" She pulled up her bathing suit top, swiped the beads of sun juice from her cleavage. "You want the visions. Why?"

Joel stared down at the book while he sermonized to Ruby. "What prophet wouldn't be put into a straight jacket today, or on medication?"

"Why is that all so important to you?" Ruby swirled tanning lotion on her shoulders.

His eyes caved with anger. "I'm not a deli man. I'm not the Jewish kid. I don't believe in any of that. I want out of it." A cloud gently covered the blaze of the sun's grasp. "Don't you get it? You don't, do you?" He threw the book at her.

She tossed it back at him. "I don't want to read it." With a curve of her head she leaned her face back toward the sun, closed her eyes. "I'm reading Ram Dass stuff. Trying to figure it out. But I don't feel it. God is love, I'm God…I'm not into all of that. God is…is… I'm not sure. I don't know. I just want to be normal…oh, I can't get into this with you." Ruby stroked her neck, rubbed in the beads of sweat and lotion. "Susan turned me on to Ram Dass, bitch that she is." She pressed closer to him. *"You can fly around in the clouds, trying to know God, but you have a zip code,* Ram's words. I'm looking for my zip code, not my wings."

Joel kicked the blanket. "You're so needy."

"So? Doesn't God want us to need one another? I can't reach God. But I can reach you." Ruby rubbed her toes across his calf.

"I want it to be real." Joel picked up the tanning lotion and flung it in the air.

"I'm not real to you? This is not real?" She pinched his arm.

He slapped her hand away. "Cut it out. Is that what your shrink taught you?" He mimicked smoking a pipe and lowered his voice into a formality. "The only reality is the present, Ruby. So embrace your neediness and be real." He laughed.

"You're an idiot." She grabbed some chips from the wicker beach bag and crunched them down. "I'm the idiot."

"You're too much. Your whole family is too big for me to handle." He snuggled his toes in the sand.

"Are you copping out? Are you?" Ruby straightened her spine and turned her head with a jolt toward him.

"Backing out of what?"

"There's been no Susan, right?" Ruby folded her knees to her chest.

"I'm eighteen fucking years old, Ruby. You're eighteen. You and me…well, I'm not a hermit. What do I know? What do either of us know about anything?" He brushed his hair away from his face and pulled his fingers down his cheeks in frustration. "I want an adventure."

"Can't we just be together, Joel?"

"Ruby, I got a life ahead of me. So do you. This is the Age of Aquarius. Not the Dark Ages."

"I can't handle this conversation. I want to go…" Ruby started to roll up the blanket, threw in drinks and packs of chips, stamped her feet into her gold sandals.

"Wait. Calm down. Can't we have a conversation? Why is everything so black and white with you? You want to control everything." Joel grabbed her wrist.

"Control. Me? You're so conscious you blame it all on me!" Ruby plopped down and played with the bag of chips, smashed it with her fist.

Joel bent over and kissed her neck. Then her cheeks, her eyes, her fingers. She felt moist and wet and her heart beat fast. Her breath quickened. Soon his tongue was in her mouth. "Fuck me with your tongue. Now."

Before she knew it, they lip locked straight back into their private cabana. Away from the crowd, she couldn't get enough of him; his supple fingers, the rough edges of his nails across her back, the strong tug of his feet around hers. His sandy sweat smell. She wanted Joel to be so far inside of her that it would explode her consciousness into smithereens. Their bodies were greasy and sticky from the oils, the rough material from the lounge pricked at her skin. The smell of salami lingered in her mouth and on his skin. But she didn't care. It all was part of the delicious food for her soul.

"I want you in me forever." Ruby whispered while they lay tangled as if they were vines winding around a tree.

"I can't promise you that."

"I'm going to tell my father this week. This week, Joel."

Joel rolled on top of her, held her face. "Ruby, get out of fantasy land. I'm not living with you. You need to live on your own. Find out who you are." He rolled her off the beach bed and lifted her into his arms. "But we can dance like Fred and Ginger. Singing "Night and Day."

They laughed and circled around the humid room. The sound of the ocean engaged their naked bodies; alive and satisfied.

"You love me Joel, don't you?"

They swirled around and around.

"I don't know what love is. And neither do you."

Ruby dug her toes into the sand and swirled in his arms. "Isn't this love?"

"I don't know. Only time will tell."

Ruby grabbed her bikini, quickly dressed. "I need you to do this with me."

"Ruby, wake up."

"Joel...Joel...you have to...or I'll die." Ruby heard those words pour out like bitter herbs. Die. She would die without him? "At least share an apartment with me? Just see?"

Joel sat on the edge of the lounge, rubbed his forehead and neck. Pulled a joint from his bathing suit. Lit it. Puffed. "Maybe. I don't know. How can we make money to support ourselves? I wouldn't mind moving out. Maybe." He shook his head. His eyes burrowed inward, thinking, wandering around the idea. His face turned sullen, conflicted to say what was true for him. Then he blurted out, quick and short. "No. I can't, Ruby. It won't be possible." He handed the joint toward her.

"No!"

"Man. What's up with you and taking a toke? A long time. Huh?"

"Tell me you'll do it with me."

He was lost in the swirls of smoke. "Maybe. I don't know. No. I don't know."

Ruby heard maybe. Maybe was yes to Ruby. Maybe was everything. "Why can't you be more like Howard? He wants to marry my sister."

Joel's mouth dropped. "Howard? Your sister? Are you kidding?"

Ruby eyes drooped. Did she really say that? Was she trying to be like Leah with Joel? "Oh my god. Oh my god." She shouted and ran from the cabana.

Out in the wind and sun, she stared around her. Yes, she was trying to be just like Leah. She wanted to leave home through marriage. Be taken care of. By Joel. "By Joel." She screamed out.

Chapter 22: Last Week In August, 1968 – The Joel Fantasy

Ruby sat on the edge of her red and white ruffled bed. She planned her getaway. Type more resumes, start night school in January, find a cheap apartment. Joel always had spare hundreds. She didn't care if it was from selling pot or pumping gas. Ruby had her own ideas of things to come whether Joel agreed or not.

That night at dinner over half-baked, pinkish chicken and soggy mashed potatoes she said to her father, "Dad, I need to talk with you."

Leah eyed her curiously. Ruby ignored her need to know.

After a bowl of chocolate ice cream for dessert, a shower and change of clothes, Ruby and her father faced one another. She sat on her bed. He sat on Leah's bed. Ruby was dressed with a brown scarf tied around her head, a fake ruby dangling from her forehead, rings of gold and silver adorning her fingers, bell-bottoms flaring over her feet.

Ruby saw the doubt in her father's eyes, watched him study her. When she was little, she'd waited for his every glance and touch. For a moment she saw their vacation times in Miami. She was maybe seven or eight the day she and her father sat by the pool. The sun drifted lazily behind the ocean. The blue, pink, and purple dusk fell into the pre-twilight. The smell of chlorine wafted through the air from wet pavement around the pool's edge. The smooth ripples of the ocean sparkled like diamond flies and waited for the night to cover its illustrious blue translucent coat.

Ruby had fallen asleep beside her father. Everyone had gone to his or her rooms. All the towel boys were gone. Only Ruby and her father were left. It was her favorite time, the smell of sweet coconut oil, the soft salty breeze from the ocean beyond Miami.

Suddenly, Morty popped up with a snort. "Time for a swim." Ruby ached to flap in the pool water with him, but wasn't a good swimmer. He hopped off the lounge and dove in from the deep end of the pool. His usual breaststroke woke the sleepy waters, gave them their last jolt of play. Ruby loved to watch him swim back and forth, back and forth; a breath at the deep end, a breath at the shallow end, maybe fifteen laps. After his twentieth stroke and with a heavy breath, water dripping off his entire body, her father stepped out from the pool. His baggy green swimsuit hung like wet clay.

"Let's go. You gotta get dressed. It's almost dinner time."

Ruby followed behind as he wiped his arms and legs, then wrapped the towel around his waist. He slipped into his sneakers.

"I caught you sucking my cigarette butt this afternoon. I'm not going to ask why, but stop it. Eat chicken and vegetables tonight. That's healthy."

Ruby chewed her father's crushed butts, just to get the taste of what he loved. Just to wrap her lips around something close to his mouth. Her mother smacked her whenever she caught her. "Don't eat butts. Eat food."

Ruby wobbled to stay in stride with her father's large steps. She squeaked behind him in her rubber sandals like a little mouse all the way back to the hotel room.

A snap of her father's finger brought her back. "Well. What did you want to talk to me about?"

"I'm moving out." Ruby was stoic.

"Really?" Morty stared at her hands. "How many rings are you wearing?" Morty leaned forward and counted with his eyes.

Ruby covered her hands. "I work now. I type and make money. I want to be an artist. I'll take night classes. And maybe, uh maybe... Joel might...you know, be a roommate."

"Is that what that your psychiatrist told you to do? No meal ticket from me. Nothing. You're out and you don't come back." He placed his hands on his knees, his fingers fiddling.

A boiling wave of sweat swept across her face. "What do you mean, don't come back?"

"You can't make it in the world as an artist. Or with those flitty ideas of yours. And Joel? Joel? When did this happen? Joel is a wild kid. He has no responsibility. He won't take care of you. I do."

Ruby ground her teeth, clenched her fists. "I want this. And I can do this. You can't control me for the rest of my life."

"Your clothes, rings, that trampy red lipstick. Who pays for that? Joel? Typing resumes, you think that will give you the life you're accustomed to?" You'll live like a whore. You won't make it. You need a husband." He gripped his knees. "All boys want is one thing, Ruby. One thing. Joel's no different."

Ruby eyes darkened. "Maybe I want," she airbrushed in quotations, "'one thing' from Joel. Huh! Did you ever think of that?"

Her father slapped her across the face, leaving a red handprint. His force knocked Ruby off the bed and landed her on the red carpet.

Face hardened and screwed into a venomous stare of rebellion, she yelled, "I hate you more." She touched her cheek. "I won't cry for you." She started to throw bottles of perfume off of her dresser. She threw her French can-can doll at him, the one he bought for Leah when her parents traveled to Paris. "Here! French whore." She threw the doll across the room. "That's what I am. Yeah…yeah…I want to be a whore. Better than living in this freakin' horror show." She grabbed his hand. "Why can't you see who I am? Why? I need you so much, Dad, and you just hate me."

Her father's face turned a pale green. He swayed, cupped his head. "I don't hate you. Where do you get that from? You never listen to me, Ruby. I'm your father. I just want what's best for you. I didn't have a father or mother growing up. They died by the time I was fifteen. I had to make it on the streets. I had no one. I don't want that to happen to you."

"Calling your daughter a whore says 'I love you?'" Ruby slapped her father's arm. "I can't do this with you anymore, Dad. You can't keep telling me I'm stupid."

Her father held his chest, "Ruby, something…" A pain bent in his brow. His teeth clawed against his lip till it bled, then suddenly, he dropped; hit the floor like a cement block. The floor seemed to crack open.

"Oh my god. Oh my god," Her shaking fingers crawled along the floor as she bent down next to him. "Mom. Mom!"

Her mother stumbled into the room. Gazed in horror at Morty on the floor. "You did this. YOU. What do you want from him?" Claire ran from the room. Within minutes an ambulance took her father away. He was still alive when the paramedics arrived. They took him away down the dark road where oxygen tents, white jackets, and heart pumps waited for him at the hospital.

Her mother's green smock, black stockings and spiked high heels stumbled into the ambulance. "Stay here…stay," her mother ordered as the ambulance attendants whisked the door closed. "And don't call Grandma." The ambulance sped away, red lights spinning, cop cars following behind.

Ruby flew back into the house. She was alone with the plastic-covered blue couches and the shredding grass wallpaper. She dragged herself into the downstairs hall bathroom, splashed her face with cool water. There was a small brush with black knots tied and twisted in the bristles. Ruby picked it up and aimlessly brushed her hair, then wobbled back to the living room, brush in hand. A whooshing sigh escaped from the plastic as she sunk into the couch. What did she want from her father? Those words haunted her. Want from him! She lay down; folded her body against the plastic, fell asleep. She dreamt. A child running. It was Marianne. Ruby felt her like she felt her own breath stream through her lungs. She ran after Ruby. "Stay with me. Stay with me, Ruby. You rebel, but you never leave. Leave with me. Learn about love." Suddenly the dream transported her. Ruby stood in front of her father's deli. Her belly growled. Each time, the ashy smell of smoked meats filled her lungs. Sandwiches piled high, threaded with fat, grease, and garlic. The taste of corned beef and pastrami whirled in her mouth, thick with the juicy meat. The warm sumptuous morsels swept her to heaven. Behind the counter, her father winked. He saw her biting down into his prized sandwich. Ruby ate to make him happy. Rows of salami, turkey, and roast beef separated them. Then the song began. The counter men wearing their sticky, stinky white aprons sang in unison, "Ruby, Rambling Rose of the Wildwood." The serenade from her childhood. Her father blew her a kiss without even knowing she existed. Ruby's body jerked through the dream.

It was midnight when Leah crashed through the front door all smiley and uppity. Ruby woke soaked in perspiration. She rubbed her back.

Her sister strolled into the living room. "Why are you laying like that? Mom is going to kill you for being in here." She took a breath and swerved to the right then to the left. "Where is everyone?" she asked as she popped the last piece of a sugar cone into her mouth. She hovered over Ruby like a giraffe.

"At the hospital."

Leah cracked down into the plastic. "What! What happened?"

"I think Daddy had a heart attack. I had this fight with…"

Leah interrupted. Stuck her fingers into Ruby's biceps, came close to her face. She stunk of dry chocolate. She whispered into Ruby's ear, "If Daddy dies…if he dies…it's your fault." Leah's stare was stark and penetrating. Her eyes sank back into her head, like she had put a curse on Ruby.

Ruby hit Leah on the thigh with the brush. "Bitch."

Leah ran to the bathroom. Click, the door was locked.

Ruby ran after her sister, pounded on the bathroom door. "You think I care. You're not my sister. You're some monster, some bad witch. Even the boys at the fraternity say so."

Leah shouted, "Go to hell." Her curse seeped through the walls.

Ruby scooted up the stairs to the hall bathroom and heaved. She was in hell. Suddenly, the phone rang. It was two o'clock in the morning. Ruby raced to her parent's bedroom and grabbed the phone. She heard her mother and Leah's garbled words…all she could remember was her mother's order. "Uncle Seymour is picking you both up. Bring a radio." Then a dial tone.

As soon as she slid the phone into its cradle it rang again, but on her private line. Ruby picked up.

"Ruby?" It was Joel.

"What's up over there? I saw cop cars and ambulances. Did your mom try to jump out of a window or something again?"

Ruby slunk down onto the bed. "Why didn't you come over?"

Static wheezed through their conversation. "Look Ruby. I got to tell you something."

Ruby fell silent. "Tell me what?" She picked her eyebrows.

"I've decided to go to India." Static silence. "I know. I know. But this is a chance of a lifetime, Ruby."

In the background, Ruby heard a female voice. She recognized the familiar high- pitched laughter. "What's Susan doing there? Assholes.

Fuck you. Go to hell." Ruby slammed the phone down. Maybe her mother had the right idea. Just down a bottle of aspirin and slash her wrists. Then it's over.

A horn honked from outside. "Come down, Ruby. Uncle Seymour is here."

She peeled herself from the bed. Grabbed the banister and cruised down each step as if she were Loretta Young.

"Move it, Ruby." Leah shouted. "You're such a selfish…" Then she blurted it out. Right there in the rubble of the Goldsmith drama. "I wish you were never born."

Leah's words pierced her like an arrow through her heart. The wound was so clean and quick, Ruby didn't feel a thing. "Same to you."

"You're a real jerk." She hurried up the steps, grabbed Ruby by the arm and dragged her out of the house.

They left in a whirlwind. Lights left ablaze in every room of the house. Leah slammed the door behind, leaving it unlocked.

With a swift jolt into the backseat of the car, they were off. Ruby stared out the window.

"You girls alright?" Curly-topped Uncle Seymour was a kind man. He was her father's sister's husband. Odd, her mother hated him and her father's entire family. Ruby barely knew any of them, and yet Seymour came to save them.

She leaned her head against the car window. Watched the streetlights fly by. It was her fault if her father died. Hers and hers alone.

Chapter 23: Hospital - Morty's Heart Attack

The hospital echoed with sounds of quiet feet and smells of urine. Ruby, Leah, and short, stocky Uncle Seymour scurried down the corridor as if they were a family of mice afraid of the hidden traps. Seymour stopped by the ICU reception desk and conversed with a dark haired, pimple-faced nurse.

The sound of Leah's heavy breathing strummed in Ruby's ears. "Where's Mom?"

Leah jerked her head away from Ruby. Ignored her.

Seymour pivoted away from the nurse's desk and grabbed both girls' hands. "Your father's through those doors, Room 101. Only one of you can go in at a time."

"I'll go first." Ruby blurted. She took a deep breath and dragged herself toward the doors. Before she entered the ICU room, she leaned against the wall, closed her eyes. She clung to the door ledge, peeked in.

A plastic tent imprisoned her father. Tubes ran everywhere. Ruby stood by the doorway and stared. This was her fault. She did this to him. Claire sat in a metal chair. The back of her hair stood on edge, parted down the middle where it appeared she was bald.

Ruby stared at her father. He breathed heavy. Eyes closed, face white. Why couldn't she cry? Why couldn't she go over and touch him? Why?

Suddenly, Claire turned her head, coolly gazed at Ruby. "Did you bring the radio?"

Ruby shook her head no.

Her mother's eyes were stark and red. "You can't even remember a radio for him. No thanks to you, he's here."

Ruby kept hearing, *No thanks to you. No thanks to you.* She ran from the room, past the door, past her sister and Uncle Seymour. Down the exit steps and out to the front of the hospital. She sat down on a bench. Her eyes twitched and her heart raced.

No thanks to you. No more Joel. No more crazy ideas to move out. No more! She lifted her eyes. *Marianne. I want to understand.*

Suddenly there was a tap on her shoulder. Ruby turned. "Dad! What're you doing here? Why are you wearing that black jacket and hat?" Morty bowed and swayed. "I came to say goodbye, Ruby. I'm sorry I didn't take care of you. I love you. I'm sorry. I love you."

"No, Dad. It's me. I'm wrong. So wrong. I can't be what you want. It's me. Please, Daddy." Ruby fell to her knees, kissed his hand. "Look at me, Daddy. Look at me, Daddy. I don't want to admit it. I don't want to say it. Say that I NEED YOU! I don't want to NEED YOU. I DON'T WANT TO NEED YOU. If I need you, then I have to die. I have to sacrifice everything about myself in order to need you. I have to play by your rules. I have to do what you want me to do. I have to be your little geisha daughter. I have to massage your back. I have to make your salami sandwiches at midnight. I have listen to your complaints about Mom. I have to take care of you like a good little girl. You can't die! If you die, then I'm left being invisible. I'm sorry…I'm sorry…"

"Get up." It was her mother speaking. "Get up."

"Where's Dad? He was just here." Ruby's eyes searched in desperation.

"He's dead, Ruby. Dead." A shrill pain scorched through the air as her mother dropped to the ground, beating her chest. "He's dead." She screamed again.

Ruby sat next to her. Was it up to her to protect her mother now? She pulled her hair. No. No. No! "He can't be dead. Mom. He can't." She leapt up. Ran back and forth. She yelled. "Where are you, Dad?" Then she stopped. Knew. He was an apparition, a ghost. The same as when she saw the rabbi's soul. *Oh my god. Oh my god.* The summer night suffocated her. No moonlight to comfort the bleak hole in her chest. Not even a star.

Her father was gone.

Back on the sidewalk, her mother convulsed. Two nurses emerged from the hospital, tried to calm her mother.

Without warning, Leah stood before her. Blotched muddy tears ran down her face. Mouth curled with anger. "You fought with him. You!" She screamed and ran back through the hospital doors. Disappeared into a hazy fog through the hospital doors.

Ruby blended into the darkness. Shivered in frozen pain. Dry eyes, mouth, body. Numb. Nothing to shield her from her despair. Except her numb. She folded her arms around her body. Once again, her mother was carried off by hospital staff. Once again, Ruby was alone. A shiver rattled her. Once again, Marianne's voice, "I know your pain. I know."

"Stop. Stop. You're invisible, like me." Ruby ran back into the hospital. But the voice chased her. "I know. I know. I know." She ran into a bathroom, locked the door. Waited. The locust of images, the sounds, the sights buzzed and clanged, until she was there. Gone. Into another realm. Close and near, touching the hem of Marianne's time and place.

Chapter 24: Marianne and The Rabbi

Invisibility. A vapid, insidious predicament. Marianne's father had died of the plague. Her mother blamed her. Threw her out of the house. She was eighteen when she left home filled with grief and shame and wandered the countryside with the disheveled mystery man.

She took to the outer villages and balled up into the arms of the stranger who called himself rabbi. He gorged himself with wine, ate meat until bones shone from his saliva. At night, he'd sit lotus-style and ask Marianne to join him, his breath thick with certainty. Marianne felt his soul ache with sorrow as he called upon the ancestors to channel through his veins. He brought her to states of ecstasy through a simple touch or quick look that warmed the depression that ate at her without mercy. She cried blood cries, madwoman cries every night. She drank and ate and made loose-whore love with him. She soothed his brow and sang lullabies and they rocked each other to sleep. Who was she? Who was he? Soon she sat in long silences with him, as moons shifted from one phase to another. And one day he said, "Let's travel to India." The open fire blazed through the chilled air, the night sky solid with stars. The evening lit around their feet and heads as people tucked into their meager dwellings to sleep.

"Where's that?" Marianne threaded straw for a basket.

"It's a place where myths live and die." His eyes, soft and dreamy, wet from the smoky flames that lashed toward the sky.

"My grief lifted and left a yearning, but not to travel to this India."

"What then?"

"I'm a woman. Do I have to know what?"

He laughed and the wind chimed in. "Well, what do you know?"

She sniffed and wiped her nose. "I know how to weave this basket covered in my sweat, and devour everything inside of me, even my own madness."

He teased the flames with his fingers, never getting too close. "I want more."

"What is more?" She kissed his cheek. "You call yourself rabbi. What do you teach?"

"I teach the coyotes, snakes, and spiders to spin, howl, slither on their bellies, and drink the earth. I teach the flame to flicker when I smile. I taught you how to love and leave the past behind. I teach the people to treat others with an open heart and mind. I teach how to eat from a holy place. I teach to pray on the Sabbath. I teach that God is our savior. That man can move mountains if only they believed. Now, I need to be taught."

Marianne stood up, shoved her basket into a bundle. "I didn't leave the past behind. I live in the nightmares of my past. Eve, Sarah, Esther, Leah, Miriam. My sisters and mothers, they want to be heard and tasted, feel their burnt skin and naked sorrow. They've been forgotten, through years of idle myths and repressed rage and grief. I no longer regret where I come from. You helped me with that, rabbi. I can feel my body once again. And those feelings are charged with love and hate." She turned her head and gazed out to where the wild desert slept, "I hurt with the pain that my mother never searched for me. That she doesn't miss me."

He grabbed her by the arm. "Does this grief bring love?"

Marianne held her hand out to the sky. "I wasn't born from your rib. I was born from my mother, a woman's womb. The serpent winds around the Tree of Life, like the goddess wraps her legs around the gods." A soft crease burrowed her brow. "I'll return to the Temples of the Priestesses. I'll teach through my body. Inside is the messy truth. The chaos of feeling the woman inside is what guides my love. Harmony comes from madness."

He kicked her bundle. "They'll call you a sinner."

"And you? What do you call me?" She bowed and brushed the dirt from his feet with her hair, gazed up at him.

"I call you my instinct, my heart, and lover. Come here and bite my neck, Woman of the Night." He opened his arms.

She threw her scarf over her face, lifted the veil and stared at him. Hips swirling, she shouted, "My mother thought I was no longer a Hebrew. The blood in my veins is bonded to my foremothers. I am a Jewess. I want to come home, but they won't let me, since I've rebelled against the laws and took off with you." She tiptoed back. "I love you and I have to leave you."

"I'll follow you."

"Only if you're ready to die in order to live again."

"I'm ready."

A snap clicked in Ruby's body. A quick breath and shiver reframed reality. Dark night, whirling bands of color, drew Ruby down, around and back. Ruby was lying on the black and white tiles. How long had she'd been there? She staggered to her feet and groggily slumped over the sink, turned the knob and ran the water over her mouth and face. Where was she? She thought. Hospital. Hospital. Her father. Her father. *Oh my god!* Her father was dead. She ran from the bathroom, to words trailing in her head: *I'm ready. For what? For what? Marianne?*

Chapter 25: August, 1968 – Morty's Funeral

Morty didn't have a prepaid burial plot, so it was up to Sarah to make all the arrangements. Sarah chose a simple walnut coffin with a white cushioned interior. Her grandmother ran the show like a CEO of a company. Ruby was too numb to care. Leah clung to Howard like a clothespin.

Claire was unable to function with any coherency. She lay in bed mumbling, cursing, and downing Bayer aspirin, Valium, and other pills that blended into a rainbow of colors.

Every time Ruby neared her mother, she'd point an accusatory finger. "You did this to your father."

Ruby had to repeat and imprint what Dr. Rosenthal said. *"You can't kill your father."*

A late summer storm soaked the streets. Howard drove Sarah, Leah, and Ruby to the Stein funeral home. The place smelled of roses and sandalwood. Not of formaldehyde or dead corpses.

Hot and humid, the funeral proceeded. The room was stuffy and filled with dark suits and black armbands. Scattered throughout the funeral parlor were majestic floral arrangements of white lilies and red and yellow roses. Mitzi and Leo escorted Claire to the front row. Ruby's mother flopped forward, near fainting every minute, and kept reaching toward the casket. She whimpered and screamed, then quieted from the drugs cascading through her blood and brain. The parlor bulged with about two hundred people. Most wore sunglasses and black. The thick stench of death roamed each person's seat, tapped them on the shoulder reminded them that they might be next.

Sarah wailed like a wounded animal: an ancient cry to God. She beat her fists to her chest. "Why him? Why? I should go first."

Ruby never realized how attached Sarah was to her father. She stared at Sarah, no feeling. Just stared. Then she gazed at Leah. Head on Howard's shoulder, sobs. What did her sister really feel? There was no connection. No grief held between them. Strangers in mourning. Ruby still felt the cold venom of Leah's blame.

The day was blurred for Ruby. She stole a fistful of Valium from her mother's batch. Her eyes were glued to the coffin. She barely breathed. Inside laid her father, dead.

The elder of Rabbi Hersochwitz's sons officiated Morty's epitaph. "God gives and then he takes. We do not know the wisdom of His work. Morty remains with us, in our hearts and memories."

Blah, blah, blah. Bullshit. Shit fuck. Ruby thought to herself. She blocked out the rabbi's speech. She lived vicariously through Sarah's grief. Because she couldn't feel a thing. Even her toes were numb.

"All rise." The rabbi raised his hands. Everyone stood up and the funeral procession began.

Four men lifted the coffin. One of them was Leo. Another, Uncle Seymour. She didn't know the other two men. The family marched. Others followed.

Ruby looked over at her sister and mother. Nothing. Blank deadness emanated from their eyes. She gagged.

The crowd moved towards the tall oaks that edged the graveside. Ruby leaned against one, felt the roughness of its bark. The air was bright and yellow, smelled of bees' honey and wild daffodils. This wasn't really happening. It couldn't be. Soft sobs surrounded her. Ruby felt her toes sink into the roots of the tree. A slow creak alerted her to the inevitable. Her father was being lowered into the ground. Ashes to ashes. Dust to dust. A soft breeze whispered.

The Kaddish was recited. A long drone of Hebrew chants lifted her father's soul to God.

As the blend of song and music swept the mourners as one, Ruby searched for Joel. Behind the family seats were the Simons, their heads bowed, eyes saddened. Joel's hair flowed over his ears. She stared at him, sent vibrations for him to look over at her. But he didn't. Ruby fell back against the tree, sniffed the fragrance of the leaves that shaded her. Between the air, wind, and song, Ruby heard Marianne's voice. *"He's there and here, look up.* " Ruby tilted her head toward the sky and saw her father. He stood among the long road of clouds, wrapped in black silk. She remembered his loud Brooklyn gruffness, his sad eyes, the gentle way he taught her to ride a bike. Her mind raced. "Dad?"

She heard his voice in the silence of the prayer. "Ruby." His translucent body and sound faded into strands of mist and air.

Morty left the three of them wealthy. Sarah was bequeathed enough to live out the rest of her life. A vault stuffed with cash, stocks, and bonds added up to millions. Claire was livid with rage. "It's all mine." She didn't think her daughters should have any of it. Tried to convince them to give it to her, that it belonged to her. But Ruby and Leah held onto their inheritances. Ruby didn't know how to manage money on her own. Dr. Rosenthal's long-time friend and investment advisor helped her keep her inheritance away from her mother's greedy grasp.

Morty gave to them in death what he couldn't give to them in life: freedom. But money didn't buy freedom for Ruby. Her prison was self-made.

Chapter 26: Winter, 1968 – Crumpling

Summer bled into fall, fall set into winter. The year was scurrying, racing toward another birthday. Another month and she'd be nineteen. Her father's inheritance forced her to grow up to handle money matters, pay for school, mortgage, food, clothes, her mother's care. Leah avoided the whole situation; took the money and squandered it on material and menial things: a watch for Howard, a trip to the Catskills, expensive shoes. Even though her grandmother was made executor, Sarah didn't understand much about the legalities of her mother's mental illness or how to balance a bank statement. Sarah never learned to read English. She handed it all over to Ruby. She became executor and medical surrogate. Ruby grew up fast.

In late December, Ruby once more caught Claire leaning over the bathroom sink trying to swallow a bottle of Valium. Ruby grabbed it out of her grasp before she emptied it into her mouth. Claire was admitted for a stay of undetermined length at Summit House.

Trees turned into dead branches, homeless, stiff and monster-like. Ruby fell into drug stupors and painted without feeling or destination. Bright reds, blacks, and browns filled the canvases with images of fanged women, blood dripping from their mouths, hearts hanging from their chests. That was how she mourned. Inward, introverted, frozen in terror, her heart gripped in stone.

Piece by piece, Ruby watched her family crumble and crack without Morty. Leah waited a proper four months after her father's death before she left with Howard, who transferred to Boston University for the January semester. Both rich with family money, together they rented a luxury apartment. Leah packed her minis and faux furs, eyeliners, lipsticks and a toothbrush and was gone.

Claire was oblivious. Her mind had regressed to that of a two-year old. Sarah moaned the day Leah walked away, suitcases packed, into Howard's 1968 blue Plymouth GTX. "A child doesn't leave her mother."

Leah laughed at Ruby as she slammed the door. "You're stuck with them now."

Branded in Ruby's mind as her sister slid into the front seat of the sporty car was the way the cold sun hit hot against Leah's fur coat and black boots, and what her sister said. "I can only love Howard. I can't love anyone else. Stop trying, Ruby. I'm never coming back. I'm going to marry Howard and never come back." And that's exactly what she did.

Chapter 27: 1969 – Ruby's Birthday

New Year's Eve crawled into reality. Alone on her birthday. It was 3:00 AM. Ruby peered through the window of her bedroom and watched the ice tip against the bushes, streetlights, and cars. She smoked grass. She heard a door slam. It came from next door. Was it Joel? Hadn't he left yet? She wasn't sure. She flinched as she tingled, remembering his touch.

Tonight, she wanted him. Tonight, she wished she had run away to India with him. As her breath fogged up her window, a sudden sight jolted her attention. Two hazy figures ran across the street. They were familiar. It hit Ruby like a whip. The edge of the street's light caught them. Them! Susan and Joel, humping and grinding up against the lamppost. Both wrapped in heavy coats, scarves tied around each other's waist, as cold smoke escaped from their mouths. They laughed and kissed.

Ruby's knees weakened and she grabbed her chest. She opened the window and called out. "You shits, you. Why aren't you gone? Go to India. Get your dirty faces off the street." The air was quiet and the echo of her curse lay on their shoulders. A touch of cool air pinched her nose and chin through the screen. "Both of you cunting around like little monkeys and smoking grass…and tripping out."

"Go back to your safe little hole, Ruby." Susan shouted.

"Shut up, Susan." Joel pushed her away and stood beneath Ruby's window, like Romeo. "Ruby, oh Ruby, how art thou, Ruby?"

Susan ran out and slapped him. "How dare you." She screamed out, "Fuck you," and raced down the street across the gutter and disappeared.

Ruby screamed back. "Why aren't you kissing the feet of some Indian guru? You never came to the shiva. Or even called after my father died? You dirty crackhead."

His face contorted with anger. For a moment Ruby thought Joel was about to climb the oak, pull her out, and smack her. Instead, he threw up his hands and skidded down into his basement. "I'm sorry about your father. I am. I just…I just…I have my life to live, Ruby, my way. Not yours. I'm leaving soon, real soon." The screen door slapped against the edges of the doorway leaving a stiff clap of rage in the air. Then suddenly it cracked open again. Joel screamed up at Ruby. "I'm here only for tonight to pack last minute things. I am leaving in a few days."

Ruby wiped the window's mist. "Who cares!"

"So don't ask." Joel flew into his house.

Ruby closed her eyes. "Good night Joel. And goodbye." She flopped back onto her bed. Ruby fought the tears, the hurt of feeling so worthless. What had she done to elicit so much shit from Joel? What? She just wanted to love him. What did she do wrong? Ruby curled around like a snake. He was her love. Why didn't he want her? What was her next move? Her emotions drove her up and down like a wild horse. Fuck him. Good. Stupid fuckface. He was out of her life. For good.

She grabbed a book on archeology that lay on the table next to her bed. She thumbed through the pages. Lost civilizations buried in each chapter. A group picture of men and women in khaki shorts holding a vase, a spoon, a statue of a fertility goddess. Her thoughts wandered elsewhere. Was Marianne's home in the rubble of these ruins? She upped her pot smoking that night, and rummaged through the refrigerator, later consuming salami, potato salad, butter cookies, cream sodas. Food was her mutilator.

She played in her madness like a baby played in her feces.

Chapter 28: A Dream of Marianne

Feeling fat and full, Ruby slept. The wind whistled and haunted Ruby's dreams. "Go out. Go in." The voice beckoned. Ruby was transported into desert temples. People swarmed around, stood shoulder to shoulder, wet with anticipation, stinking with human sweat and greed. They waited for the great priestess to arrive. The white arches were adorned with red roses, and the scent of frankincense wafted through the hallways, open rooms, and marble floors. Snakes wiggled up the steps, biting their way through the crowd. The priestess arrived and shouted. "Come to me and find your religion." The crowd trampled the priestess until blood trickled down the steps.

Soldiers dragged her by her hair. People roared, fists in the air. "Traitor, sinner. Traitor, sinner."

Women cried, children ran, men froze. An angel descended and hovered above her. "Marianne. Wake up. You are free. There is no sin."

Ruby woke with a choked breath. Panic shook her. Red flowers on the wall. Clock ticking. Pillows puffed. She wiped her neck and forehead. She was dripping wet. "I'm here in Brooklyn." She glanced over at the clock on her dresser. It was only 5 AM. The phone shrilled. It was sharp and woke her. She lifted the received to her ear. Ruby cried out. Her hands trembled. "My mother slit her wrists."

Chapter 29: Same Night – Claire's Suicide Attempt

Ruby's mother lay in the rubble of her own hell. Somehow, Claire had stolen a knife and performed her dirty deed.

Ruby drove out to Long Island, dazed and morose. Sarah snorted and smoked most of the way. They arrived as Claire's life was being saved. The emergency room doctors stopped the bleeding, bandaged her wounds, and dripped new blood into her veins. Shades drawn, her mother's home away from home; a hospital room. Once again, Ruby watched her mother slither under sheets, an intravenous in her arm. Was it ever going to end? Why did she have to save her mother if her mother didn't want to save herself? Ruby stood over Claire like the Grim Reaper. *Oh, my mother dear, why do you break my heart so?* The walls in the hospital were a sterile blue and bore witness to her grief and loneliness.

Sarah was distant in the corner of the room as the hours ticked away. Lightening struck the night and frightened the stars. Its jagged edges lit the room like a neon flash. The wind howled and banged against the window, a death blow shook the room. Dull whiffs of alcohol made Ruby sneeze. Ghoulish silhouettes stalked above her mother's bed. Ruby wondered if dark souls were coming to take her away.

Not a chance. Her mother moaned, opened her eyes. "Mama?"

"Don't 'Mama' me." Sarah moved.

Her mother didn't notice Ruby. She only repeated. "Mama. Mama."

Day rolled into night. Claire became more awake. It wasn't long before her mother was throwing cups, pillows, and insults at the nurses who tried to feed her chocolate pudding and watery chicken soup.

Grandma Sarah was relentless in her disapproval. "Vhat's wrong with your head, Claire? You think God will put up with such a selfish girl? You aren't worth anything to your children."

"To her child." Ruby corrected her. "Leah is too busy to come home."

"Your sister is doing right. She is doing right." Sarah huffed.

"What are you talking about, grandma? Leah's a shit!" Ruby lashed out.

"Such language." Sarah sat down, folded her arms. "Look at your mother. Just look at her."

Ruby didn't want to look at her mother. Her face was a brow-less stucco mask, her wrists bandaged.

Her grandmother paced the floor. "Oy. Oy. No respect. How are you my daughter? I don't know how." Sarah admonished her daughter.

"This is your fault, Grandma."

"My fault? My fault? Oy. Vhat a thing to say to your grandma. Everything I do for you." She stormed out of the room, screaming. "Everything I do."

Claire jumped from the bed, pulling all the tubes and wires out and falling to the floor. The hospital gown flew open and her buttocks popped out. "Mama, Mama. Don't go."

Ruby picked Claire up by the elbow, pulled her mother back into the bed. "Don't do any more damage. I can't take it."

Two nurses and a doctor entered the room. "I'm Dr. Arber. Are you Mrs. Goldsmith's daughter?"

Stoic and calm, the three examined Claire. Took her pulse and heartbeat and checked her eyes and ears. One nurse inserted the intravenous back into her arm, injected medication into the plastic bag that flowed drugs into Claire's veins.

"Get away from me, you bastards. I want to die." Claire kicked up a ruckus. The medication began to work in her blood, her eyes fluttered, and soon she was asleep.

The doctor cleared his throat, buttoned the top button of his official white jacket. His salt and pepper hair cut neat and short matched the dull crack of his forced smile. "Sorry I didn't get to talk with you when I admitted your mother. Busy day. I'll need to keep her here for observation. I know she is a patient at Summit. We will transfer her back there when she's stable."

"Keep her here forever." Ruby's eyes clouded with grief.

"Do you need to talk to anyone professional?" The doctor placed his hand on Ruby's shoulder.

"I go to a psychiatrist."

"I'd appreciate it if you'd give me his name, please."

Ruby inched away. "What for?" At that moment Sarah returned, all huffy and red-faced.

The doctor shook her grandmother's hand. "I'm Dr. Arber."

"Can you help, doctor, can you help? My daughter does such things."

"Grandma. I want to get out of here. The doctor can take care of Mom now. I'm tired. I want to get out of here." Ruby tugged at Sarah.

Sarah moved toward the doctor, "You take care of her?"

He patted Sarah on the shoulder. "As best as I can."

"Come on, Grandma." Ruby couldn't look at her grandmother.

"You rush, run away. Vhat's your problem?"

Ruby stared up at the yellow stained ceiling. "I'm leaving."

Sarah wobbled after Ruby.

"Are you ever, ever going to tell the truth, Grandma? Ever?"

"Vhat truth?" Sarah huffed.

"Why are all of us crazy, Grandma?"

"No one's crazy except your mama." Sarah held her pocketbook to her chest.

"She's like that for a reason."

"No reason." Sarah drew into a cold space where no one could enter.

"Damn. All of you! All of you!" Ruby smashed the elevator button, several times over. A cacophony of barks and howls echoed down the hallway. "Did you hear that, Grandma?"

Sarah rolled her eyes. "Sha. There's nothing to hear."

Ruby heard animal cries, smelled the blood, the salt and felt the touch of fire run up her spine.

The elevator opened. Sarah stepped in and turned to Ruby. "You should be thankful. Your mother has no thanks. You're here. That's it."

"Grandma. Forget it!" Ruby entered the elevator and leaned

against the wall, scanned the ceiling. Damp and cold filled her eyes. Confused pain. Would she be lost forever? Fragmented shards of her life dangled in mid-air. What is the truth? Ruby pierced an angry gaze at Sarah. She was a rock. Tough. Ruby felt her blood harden.

Chapter 30: Marianne Vision Stories

The light fired the night. A cool horizon turned soft and warm, receding deep into the moon-sky landscape. The stars sparkled without sound or destination; solid, still, showing the way inward to Marianne's breath. Not even her tribal sisters could stop her from going off into solitude. She had to think. Sort it all out. The rabbis called her tramp, viper, sinner. Her monastery was the miracle of sight.

A messenger from Magdala carried the news. "Your mother is dead." He poured water over his sandy face, ate a piece of flat bread, and was gone. Head in hands, Marianne cried. She had not seen her in three years, since she beat her with a broom, calling her ungrateful and faithless. Her mother never believed in her. Only the laws were sacred, not a woman's experience of the laws. Why did she have to cover her head, feel shame to speak of her vagina, hadn't God made Eve naked? What was wrong with the body? Her body told her everything. Talked to her in her sleep. Made her see and feel things beyond human sight. She was the roots of the desert, the owls and snakes, the mountains and trees. The rhythms of her menstruation told her when the seasons blossomed and died, she felt the past in her cells, the future in her belly, the present in her heart. What else did she need? She needed the young rabbi, who understood. Who encouraged her, allowed her to feel the pleasure of orgasm that coupled them with God. He said he would follow. Where was he? Marianne prayed. But her body was silent. Only a tight ball twisted in her stomach. "When?"

"Six months ago." The messenger drank furiously from his water pouch. "I need to return." He ran back into the blackness.

Marianne watched the ragged man disappear. Folded into the night of her body, she sobbed for generations of dead mothers. Her limbs were heavy. She longed to feel the balance of the water jar on her head, be a part of the laughter of young girls being readied for marriage. But she was burdened with visions that drove her into the unknown.

Around her, wolves yelped and howled in frenzy, fierce in their determination to find their tribe. They wailed out their command to Marianne, "This is my desert. No humans allowed." Marianne returned their warning, "I am animal as well." She peed in the cactus bush, stripped naked, rolled in the rivers, ate ants and dead frogs. "I am the animal of *Shekinah*."

Marianne's kin thought she had gone mad. She was a witch, an outcast because she claimed to heal the sick, raise the dead. The sacred rituals "hieros gamos", spiritual sexual cleansing, the union to the divine. Mobs stoned the priestesses. Roaring with rage and disgust, "Prostitute. Unclean." Marianne barely escaped. Saved by a group of renegades, rallied to the edge of the desert shores and set free. It seemed like centuries since she was amongst the hungry crowd of witch hunters.

Marianne watched the moon turn into a half-breed of black and white. This was an omen. Flames from the campfire waved and convulsed. She stared into the hypnotic fire. From the center an apparition broke through the fire. A hand reached out to Marianne and grabbed her wrist. A voice spoke to her. "Tell your story. All the stories."

Pain shot fire through her veins. She grabbed her arms. A demanding order shot through her head. "Your dream is my dream. We dream together."

Marianne screamed. The temperature rose around her, winds screeched, and the voice of the vision devoured her.

"I'm here to give you the stories of generations. Our blood runs side by side. You died without telling. Your mother died and all mothers died, their stories buried. They died sick, rejected, and shamed."

Marianne wept. She fell to her knees "Heal me, *Shekinah*. The sacred stories will be written. I wake the host; through her pain the vision will wake. Ruby will surrender to the calling. A thousand centuries beat in her soul." Marianne dug her feet into the sand, and shouted, "I'm the forgotten one. I want to come home to my mothers."

Chapter 31: January, 1969 – Sleepless To Write

Fatigued and agitated, sorrow hidden between sighs and silence, they arrived home. Sarah rushed to sleep. Ruby dragged herself to bed as well.

Restless dreams stalked Ruby. Hazy remembrance of howls, pee, a woman, faded from her conscious mind and slipped away in her sleep mind. A sharp push, a burning sensation up her spine. A fire engulfed her hands. The pain was unbearable. Voices, rumbled. *Tell the stories.* Ruby woke with a gasp, wet and shaky. She tiptoed out of bed, rummaged through her pocketbook that she had thrown on the blue satin club chair. She found a crumpled joint; lit it. It couldn't hurt.

The blackness in the room blinded her. The room was warm from central heating, but a cool draft swept from between the walls. Ruby put on sweat socks and a pulled red sweater from her mother's closet. The fatty Jewish food smells of Sarah's cooking blended between the bleach that her grandmother used to wash the floors. She wandered over to the window. An urge hit her heart. She rubbed her hands together. Glared at the stars. Her paintings held the images of women's faces; their eyes told stories. Each stroke and image was a cry for the truth. Words beckoned to be written, translated from the souls of the women she painted. They whispered, echoed, and pleaded in her head. Marianne, the desert, her dreams, highs and lows, her bond to her fragmented, homeless lineage. Ruby extinguished the joint on top of the dresser, threw it back into her pocketbook.

She entered her grandmother's room, quiet and still, and stood by her bed. She leaned over and breathed in her grandmother's baby-oiled, wrinkled face. Sarah was the lock and key. What cruel memory did Sarah hide that she took out on her mother? Would Sarah tell her story so she could know more of her own?

She lay down next to her. So much was hurtling towards her. Six months down the road was the completion of her junior year. These last years were a bitch, trying to study, get passing grades. No Joel. No Susan. No friends. School, mother, grandmother, work, therapy. That was her life.

Oh god, her mother. A numbness tingled in her fingers. She twisted her hands in circles. She didn't want to feel anything. Next time, she hoped, her mother would bleed out. If that's what Claire wanted. Let her mother die.

Ruby sat up and edged to end of the bed. There she was. She and Sarah. Snoring, belching, kicking the covers. She was sinking. Sinking.

In her mind a story summoned her. *"Sarah left Mesopotamia, the only home she knew."*

Sarah snored. Yes. Sarah, her grandmother left the only home she knew. How did the trauma of her nomadic history play out in her blood?

Ruby ran down to the basement, dipped a thin brush into red paint, wrote across the canvas: *And the women gathered to listen.*

A cacophony of words fought their way onto the canvas. Images, graffiti, a foreign language to Ruby, a trance story.

Hours passed until her energy was soaked and depleted. She stood back, shocked. Scrambled letters sloshed over women's faces. Paint was matted on her face and hands. She squinted. What was all this? Fatigued, she dropped to the floor and fell asleep.

Chapter 32: March, 1970 – The Session

Blistering winds cut through Brooklyn and Ruby's bones. The hissing steam purred warmth into the Dr. Rosenthal's office. Ruby noticed how his books were perfectly lined across the shelves. Ruby hiccupped and looked at her wristwatch. She felt a quiet safety between the daisies on the wallpaper and the smell of pipe tobacco. The weekly therapy helped her to stay on track with her undergraduate degree as she worked to ground her own mind and feelings.

Ruby smoothed her black mini and played with the top button of her pink shirt. Her eyes were misplaced underneath the thick black false lashes.

"Can you look at me?" Dr. Rosenthal curved his fingers under his chin. His eyes were searchlights into her soul.

Ruby peeked up through the jungle of black furriness.

"Where are you?" He sucked on his pipe.

Ruby felt her chest relax. Beside the chair rested her black knapsack of a pocketbook. Bells, whistles, and toads lived in that pocketbook. Maybe her second-grade poem was in there. Ruby dragged it onto her lap. Fumbled through the maze of lipsticks, mirrors, papers, and whatever else. Found the Doublemint gum, unwrapped a piece, and popped it in her mouth

Ruby plopped the bag back to the floor. "I'm here."

They eye-locked. Both waited. She rustled in the chair.

"How's your mother doing?"

"Still crazy." Ruby chomped down on the gum.

"Will she be coming home anytime soon?"

"I hope not."

"How are you?"

"Still crazy." She smiled.

Silence rotated around them.

He crossed his legs. "Do you visit her…?"

"Not lately."

"What's going on, Ruby?"

A huge round bubble popped around Ruby's mouth. She laughed and scraped away the gum, spit it into the wastebasket next to her chair. "Ugh. That tasted like cardboard shit."

"I'd prefer you put that in a tissue or something."

Ruby rummaged around the garbage, pulled out the gum as if it were a toy from a cereal box, held it up, smiled, wrapped it in a piece of paper from the rubble, then flicked it back in the pail. "Ruby lips."

Smoke curved around Rosenthal's neck and head. "Do you expect me to pull a rabbit out of a hat?"

"What do you mean?"

Dr. Rosenthal leaned back into the cushioned seat. "What does 'Ruby lips' mean?"

Ruby frowned. "Nothing."

"I'd like to know."

Ruby shut her eyes. "My mother used to say that to me."

"How old were you when she said it?"

Ruby closed her eyes. "I don't know. Four, five or something…or fifteen. It was what she said to me."

"Ruby lips." Rosenthal tapped on his pipe. "What comes up?"

A book tipped half off the doctor's desk. It looked like it was about to fall, but it held its own. Ruby burrowed her brow, squinted, used her mind power, hoping to push the book off to the floor. After a minute she gave up. She pulled her arms around her chest and smacked her lips. "Crazy big lips, crazy little crazy mother. Crazy all the same."

Rosenthal leaned forward. "How does crazy feel and look?"

"Dictionary description. Just put my mother's picture and her name. Then the bloodline before Claire, way back to Poland. Then across the ocean, the seeds of crazy spread to America."

"Does crazy have a feeling?"

Ruby closed her eyes. Tucked her feet under her buttocks, "Tight in my chest, my belly. Tight. Pain. Shame. Fear. Nowhere to go. Alone.

Rejected. Torn to shreds by wolf fangs."

"Can you remember anything else when your mother said 'Ruby lips?'"

"That I wanted to be her close to her so bad, I'd take the tissue she'd pat her lipstick on and put it against my lips."

"Can you feel that?"

Ruby brushed her hair away from her face. "It hurts. My chest is filled with it. My heart yearns and I can't …I can't."

"You can't what?"

"I…." Ruby held her throat.

"Breathe into your throat. What are you holding back?"

"Fuck you. Fuck G-d. Fuck my mother, my sister. It's too big. It'll kill me."

"It will kill you if you stuff it all down in your body."

"No one cares. It doesn't matter. No one believes me. I've just got to get through school. Get out of school. Get away. Why can't I do it? Like Leah. She just left."

Dr. Rosenthal nodded. "Yes, she did. But do you think running away will make it go away?" He got up walked over to his desk and pulled out a pad and a carton of crayons from his drawer. Returned to his chair and handed it to Ruby. "Here, draw it."

Ruby placed the crayons and pad on her lap. Sighed. Pulled out red. She flowed through the spinning web of color and shape. Then blues, then greens, and purples. She remembered. "Miss Paula, my kindergarten teacher, was my first inspiration to paint." Ruby studied it. Held the drawing a short distance away. Her eyes traveled along the maze of images.

"What is it?"

Ruby twitched. She pointed to the center. "Rainbow edges, eggs with vines." Her fingers traced what she had created. She wrote on the pad. "Strangled. All the women strangled." She read it out loud.

"Is that how you feel? A strangled egg? Never cracked open or born?"

Ruby stared. "Never born?" She grabbed her stomach. "I feel nauseous." Ruby tightened her lips. "I want to scream."

"Go ahead, Ruby."

Ruby slinked out of the chair and slumped onto the brown plaid couch. Held the pad to her chest.

"The more you hold onto your rage, the more you'll act out or in on yourself."

A pillow flopped over her arm. She clung to it. Harder and harder she pulled at it. She started to gag and cough. "I can't…I won't."

"You're strangling the child in you."

"No." She struggled. "No!" Her scream cracked against the walls. She tore and pounded the pillow. "I hate you, hate you, hate you!" Tears peeled off her false lashes. Like spiders, they wriggled down her cheeks, down her neck. Her sobs rocked her. She kicked pillows. Her face was wet from spit and tears. "Mommmm!! My heart hurts. Oh. Oh." She held her chest.

"Breathe. Keep letting it out."

Ruby leapt off the couch, crying, screaming. "I hurt. So much. OHHHHHHH!" She sobbed and breathed, sobbed and gasped, choked, dry heaved. Tears of shame ran across her nose and mouth. She wiped the fear from her face. "I come from a bunch of crazy women. My grandmother hates my mother. My mother hates me. Leah hates me. I hate myself." She paced back and forth. "I see and hear things. Are they real? Am I nuts? My pain is bigger than the universe." She grabbed Rosenthal's arm. "I need to hold on."

"It's okay. It's okay."

Ruby breathed lighter, let go of Rosenthal. Sat back on the couch.

She wiped her eyes, spat into the pail, held her belly. "I feel it in my gut."

"Feel that. Hold it."

"I feel insane in this pain." Her crying smoothed into slow breaths. "I feel like I've been holding my breath since I was born."

"The pain, the trauma can ignite both the spiritual experiences as well as mental imbalance. You've got to move the energy of the pain, open your heart, your throat, and belly. You won't go insane if you do this, you can get to the other side. I know how hard it is. How much courage you need. But you can get the crazy out of you… and make it into a spiritual initiation into freedom and creativity. You enter into other realms and return with stories of vision."

Ruby turned. "Was my mother having a spiritual experience when she beat me? Or tried to kill herself?"

"You're mother couldn't do what you're doing."

Ruby's eyes wandered. "I remember. I was little. My mother

talked about angels. Then the doctors put her on medication and she never mentioned angels again."

"There are so many different reasons for what happened to your mother. Maybe she saw angels. She couldn't ground what she felt or saw. Medication works different on everyone. It made your mother forget. She didn't have the resources inside of her. Ruby, your visions can lead to something greater. I don't know what, but if you keep working the emotional energy, you can cross over into wholeness. All that strong female energy can help you. But if you get stuck in it like your mother, then you just might end up like her. You have to feel and accept all of you, Ruby." The doctor held his ground. "Change the generations of fear and grief. You're doing this. You."

"I don't understand how I can do that." Ruby grabbed a tissue.

"You don't have to understand everything. You have to trust."

"Trust? That's funny." She brushed her head to her shoulder, held it there for a minute then whispered, "What do you want from me? What? I need perspective, not perverted ideas about myself." She sniffed and wiped her nose with the palm of her hand. "I'm fucked no matter what I do." She shied from his gaze. "But the writing is coming. All over the paintings. I write. Fragmented stories. They make no sense." She got up and put on her coat.

Rosenthal walked her to the door, handed her what she drew. "Journal them. You can move through the terror and hear the voice as your own. It is not crazy to be different. It's crazy to try and be someone you're not." Rosenthal took a long breath. "Allow Marianne to be in you. Allow your mother's and grandmother's survival strength to be in you."

Ruby took the paper and folded it into her pocket. "Maybe my mother saw an angel that forced her to go mad. Is Marianne my life or death?" She turned, opened her mouth to speak, hesitated, then asked, "Do you think Marianne is Mary Magdalena?"

He held the door open. "I don't know."

She buttoned her navy pea coat on and whisked out the door. Bare cold limbs swaggered in the wind from the trees that lined the street. Fresh winter air filled her lungs. A faint smell of lilacs reached her nostrils. She tapped each car lightly as she strolled by. Her life. Where was she going? Her white Buick convertible was parked down the street. Slowly she approached the car. It was all part of the act. Black

Cher-like hair, mini skirt, and convertible. No one knew. No one. She didn't have a friend that she could confide in. Only crazy lunatics went to psychiatrists. She heard Dr. Rosenthal's voice in her head. *You're not crazy.* She leaned against the door and listened to the slow traffic beep lazy songs to each other. She fingered the sacred charms that lived beside her heart. *Show me the way,* Ruby pleaded. *Show me the way.*

She pulled the drawing from her pocket, read what she had written. "All the women strangled." The words vibrated through her.

***

Her grandmother fell asleep early that night. March winds persisted, howling and banging against the windows. She went to her basement. Paint was everywhere. Canvases scattered across the floor. *Paint, write, Ruby, paint.* At this point, that was Dr. Rosenthal's best advice.

Ruby fingered a joint and drew it in deeply. She knew it was wrong not to tell Rosenthal. But, whatever, she thought. She balanced the joint off the edge of a ceramic ashtray that she had sculpted in class. Sculpting was a new exploration. She liked the soft clay, the swish of the wheel, the smoothness turning hard. She won first prize for the goddess figurine at the college's Spring Art Fair at school. The statue was placed behind a glass case in the hallway.

A snap of a branch hit against the window. She sank into the lumpy, frayed blue couch. This was her sacred world. Her space. She lit the joint and sucked the smoke into her lungs.

She picked up a brush. Like an archeological dig, her art pieces were lost universes and faces. She painted it all devil eyes, fragile translucent breasts, and abdomens with roses growing from belly buttons. And always the woman: Marianne, her red hair sailed in dark seas amidst Lilith mermaids and moonlit waves. She'd never get her right. Smudge over smudge, stroke over stroke, feeling Marianne's power as she painted.

Beside her rested a book. One that she had read dozens of times since the first time Susan threw its title in her face: *Grist for the Mill,* by Ram Dass. She poked at it, drew it into her palm and flipped through the pages, randomly stopping to read: *"It is like the moment depicted on the ceiling of the Sistine Chapel where the hands of God and man are just about to touch, it's just at that moment that the despair is*

150

the greatest, when you reach up, that the grace descends and you experience the knowledge or the insight or the remembrance that it all isn't in fact the way you thought it was. If it happens too violently you decide you've gone insane."

"Yeah. Insane." She leafed through a few more pages then stopped: *"A desire to use this birth in order to become who in truth you are."* She took another drag of the smoke. And that is? One more time with a thrust so hard that the book nearly ripped apart: "Come on. Give me something I can use." The passage socked her in the eyes. *"If you get over the value judgments, you can listen to what it is you need to do without getting caught in all of the social pressures about marriage or no-marriage. The true marriage is with God. If you are marrying for economics, if you're marrying for passion, if you're marrying for convenience, if you're marrying for sexual gratification, it will pass and there is suffering. The only marriage contract that works is what the original contract was – to come to God. In fact, that is what everything you're doing is about."*

The ash from the joint ate away at the thin white rolling paper. A spark caught the tip of her finger. "Shit." She rubbed her finger against her jeans. She threw the book aside, clasped her head in her hands. She stamped out the joint into the tray. "No. No. No!" She slid off the couch and meandered over to her latest creation, picked up a brush, dipped it in the thick red oil piled on the palette, and wrote across the half painted canvas: *My cunt hurts.*

She slashed the oils, mixed them on the surface of her painting until it looked like mud. She dipped her fingertip into the red and meticulously placed a small perfectly round dot smack dap in the middle of the oily mess. "The end is the beginning and the beginning is the end, says the idiot to the moron." She fell to the floor and laugh-cried.

Ruby switched on a small lamp and scrambled to find something to write on. The only available writing material was a large drawing pad. Fumbling around, she found crayons and began to scribble thoughts. Thoughts that made no sense to her, but she wrote them anyway. She dated her entry.

March 15, 1970
My past haunts me like unrequited love. With passionate fury,

my memories awaken me from a deep slumber of denial and I find myself lost in the world in which I have chosen to live. I sleepwalk with ghosts that whisper in the night and I hold my ears, blocking their voices, aborting the emotions I once felt. I know if I ignore their lust they will bury me alive, never to recover to see the light of day.

My relationship with God has been dramatically dark and stormy with rays of joyful light at its best and infantile sucking at its worst. I believe if I suffer enough or if I am good enough God will grant me my dreams. When He doesn't anoint my every desire I hate Him like I hated my father for depriving me of fatherly love.

Most of the time I run around in circles pretending I am dancing so no one will know that I am terrified. I live on the edge of fulfillment. I touch the mouth, eyes, and lips of the unknown every time I blink or smell the fragrance of the sky.

My fantasies have built a prison around my heart. I can't feel anything but my wounds. I hurt like a broken wing and judge myself for being so small and ugly. This is my shadow. My shadow follows me like a stray cat, clawing my soul for milk juice. I can't seem to shake her no matter how fast I run, or how much pot I smoke, or how much I fuck. She is my incessant nightmare and before my head drops on my pillow at night she is the last voice I hear - and she says oh so sweetly: "You might die in your sleep tonight." Ah! HA! There I am...AH! HA! There I am. I walk the desert, crawl across the skies. I awaken your ancient knowing.

The writing was lightning through her fingers. Her arm ached and her back was spasming. She sat up, dropped the crayon. In the distance she saw a vague figure. A small girl with tight, matted auburn hair. She held a candle, lit match after match, a wind kept blowing out the flame. The dream child spoke to Ruby. Her voice echoed between the downpours of rain.

"I've come to save Mother Earth." She held out a ragged scroll to Ruby. "The story of generations. We worshipped the goddesses Asherah, Isis, Inanna, Ishtar, Ashtart, for twenty-five thousand years, from Babylon, Mesopotamia, to Palestine, Israel...until...until...they, the warriors destroyed the altars. Raped our healers, our prophets, sold them into slavery, burnt them at the stake. I've come to resurrect. You must resurrect."

Ruby's hand trembled toward her. But nothing was there, only her canvas with the image of a young girl dabbed in grays and dark blues. Ruby approached the canvas and stared into sad eyes of this girl, still wet from paint. Who was she? A deep sorrow washed over Ruby.

Chapter 33: That Weekend, March, 1970 – Fraternity Row

The night pavement glistened from the streetlamps. Wild howls trampled across the crisp air. Ruby didn't mind the cold. Wrapped in her faux fur and black leather knee-high boots and a skirt so short that it about kissed the rim of her underwear, Ruby scuttled down the street shaking, her lips frozen with excitement.

Fraternity row was only two bus stops from her house. It was a strange choice to go that night. But something drew her there. Check out what she had missed all these years in college. Three years since she turned down the invitation from that boy, Steve. Three years. Three years of hospitals, deaths, madness. It was about time to be a normal twenty year-old, feel young, not like an old cow. She needed to get away from her isolation and self-pity.

Ruby was an innocent to the crowds and noise. Locked away in her art room, oils and poetry, protecting her from the world, she didn't venture out much. Visitation to her mother was enough of an outing for her. In the past, she had thought Joel's basement was the only "Lucy in the Sky with Diamonds" that could give her the jitters. Getting high, eating bags of Wise potato chips and M & Ms, singing along to "Shotgun" and "I Wanna Hold Your Hand" was her idea of a great night. But that was all over now.

Long-haired guys and girls shuffled passed her, high on pot and laughter. She looked for the Phi Sig frat house. She remembered. Phi Sig. That was where Steve belonged. Finally, she found it. A two-story white Colonial. Ruby hopped up each step, past the beer drinkers and potheads and shoveled her way through the stuffed room. Loud music boomed and shook the floor. She couldn't even make out what the song was. It was all electric guitar and screeches. She shied back toward the door. What did she expect after all this time? Maybe that Steve guy wasn't even here. He probably forgot her. It was stupid of her.

What the fuck? She peeked around, searching for someone, anyone. She could barely move among the bodies dancing. Just a bunch of lunatics, tight jeans and smoke everywhere. Then, in the far corner of the room she saw him. He was the same. Handsome, blue eyes, tall. All smiles and bee-bopping like a jerky two-year-old. His baby blues were like a hot magnet. She was still drawn to him the same as she had been that day in front of Boylan Hall. She couldn't believe it. After all these years. It had to be kismet or something.

As Steve slinked through the crowd, the chaos slowed down to a ripple of a beat. The heat in the room rose from the dance of human frenzy. She watched Steve weave in, out, and around. Stopped to talk to everyone. He was moving toward her; clipped a wave and a smile. Ruby circled her fingers into the air, gesturing a reply then giggled. At first, she wanted to run. Then a hushed comfort grounded her feet to the spot. The closer he came, Ruby felt like the sun was approaching the night.

I only have eyes for you, spun through the room. Quiet rapture stole its way into the crowd.

There he stood, a breath away. Steve held out his hand to Ruby. A hushed one-two-three step brought them together. She placed her head on his shoulder.

Steve pulled her tight. "Hi. I'm Steve Berg. Relax. Take your coat off."

"I'll keep it on." He didn't remember her. Strange. He didn't remember her, but was drawn right to her. Ruby fell into his arms. She followed his every move and groove in his slinky hip movements and rhythmic sway. They were as unsuited as a Mickey Mantle and Marilyn Monroe, but there it was: the attraction of opposites. "I remember you. But you don't remember me." More warmth from beer, drug, and sex smells made her woozy.

He snuggled into her faux fur coat. "What do you mean?" He held his head back so he could take a good study of her face. "I know you?"

He kept staring. "Wait. Wait a minute. Leah's sister? Ruby? Right? Wow. Man. How is it we never bumped into each other? Wow. You're here. Man."

A quick change of a record and Ruby found herself doing the Twist.

Steve followed. "You want to get out of here?"

"Let's go." She grabbed his hand and eased through the crowd.

Steve caught her by the waist. "Where are we going?"

A can hit Steve in the back. "You idiots! Don't move. I'll get my coat." Off he went, pushing, and shoving.

Ruby watched his strong back and muscular arms nudge through the throngs of people. It was a jungle. She was happy to leave. It wasn't a place for Ruby, whose nerves were fragile. Being left alone in the middle of bedlam tangled her emotions into a knot. Everyone was on top of each other, touching, grabbing, suffocating each other's space, glued together, no room to breathe. In the corner, a guy with frizzed hair was vomiting; a girl with long red hair was taking her shirt and bra off, twirling them in the air. The rest were blurry shapes humping and hopping around like hyenas and kangaroos. She had to get out of there. Maybe she'd call Steve later. But she didn't know his number. Maybe she'd write him a letter. What was his address? She hadn't a clue. Just as she was about to make a dash, Steve's perky smile surfaced above the heads of the masses. She calmed down. At last he was next to her.

"The animals are on a rampage."

Ruby took his hand. Felt his gentle touch thread through her finger. Ruby didn't want to let go of him.

He held the door as they slipped out into the cold.

"Those people are lunatics."

Steve laughed. "Those lunatics are my friends."

The lamplights ran a halo around his face. It lit a map of his eyes, nose, and mouth. Mesmerized by his boyish strength, she lost control of her footing. A crack in the pavement caused her to trip. "Damn."

Before she hit the cement, Steve caught her. "Another save."

A frozen gust of wind slapped her face. She pulled her collar up. Leaned into him. "I don't do well with people."

"Well, you're doing okay with me. Come on, my car is parked around the corner. It's cold." Arm in arm, they raced down the block.

Parked between a black Corvette and a green Buick was his beat up black Rambler. He opened the door, ran to the driver's side and slid in next to her, started the engine. "Have to let it roll for a bit before I put the heat on."

Awkward moments fleeted by. The purr of the heater cozied up the car. Steve coughed and rubbed his palms together. Ruby pulled her skirt down. Long pauses between the rustling motor and Steve revving the accelerator passed. Neither spoke. Each adjusted to being together. Ruby started to hiccup. Her stomach growled. "I get the hiccups, sometimes, when I'm hungry or maybe nervous."

"Do you want to go to Chinatown?" At last he pulled out.

"Sure. I haven't eaten since this morning."

They came to the corner and the light turned red. Steve placed his arm around her and eased her near him. "This will help us warm up faster. Don't you think?"

Ruby played with the curls that flipped over the collar of his Brooklyn College Varsity Baseball jacket. "I don't know anything about you." She eyed his coat. "Except that you play baseball. And you're some kind of fraternity god."

"Ask me anything."

Ruby wasn't sure. The light changed to green. The night turned soft from the warmth inside of the car. People ran up and down the streets. Brick house after brick house, street after street, bare oaks stark in the shadows. A half-moon clung to the edges of the sky. Store after store, garages, candy stores, butchers, supermarkets dimly lit as they zoomed by, toward the bridge into lower Manhattan.

"What's your family like?"

"What?" Steve kept his eyes on the road.

"You said ask anything. So what is your family like?"

He kept his attention dead ahead on the road. "My parents. They're idiots." Bridge bumps and the soaring sound of wind slapped against the car as they crossed the bridge. It gave an eerie feel to the conversation. Steve grabbed the wheel.

"Really? Why?" Ruby eyes perked.

"I didn't think you'd ask me about my family."

"Why not?"

"Because, that's a lot to talk about right off. I guess, I just want to be with you and eat chow fun."

"Look. I understand."

"What do you understand? Just what?"

"You're not the only person who has family problems. Don't be such a jerk."

Before Ruby could blink, Steve rammed on the accelerator and sped across the bridge, tight, cold, and silent. They drove wordless, until they were in the middle of Chinatown. He drove around the blocks, searching for a spot. Ruby had never been there. Fascinated, she was lost in the shouts of fish peddlers, the Asian dolls hanging from awnings, little jewelry boxes covered in green and red silks. Bright lanterns cascaded across storefronts, steamy sidewalks fogged from the underground trains, and hordes of people covering the streets like a human blanket. Garlic, onion, soy, and tamari mingled with the car fumes. She remembered the old tale that she'd heard as child, that if you dug down deep enough into the earth, on the other end would be China. Well, there she was. Just on the other side of the bridge. China.

It took another fifteen minutes to find a spot. Steve turned off the ignition, stared out, hands still on the wheel.

Ruby backed up against the door. "Are we getting out?"

He tapped his fingers. "I don't know."

"What's wrong with you?"

Steve stared out. "My parents are getting divorced."

"Really? I'm sorry." She touched his shoulder.

"Are you?" Steve surrendered to her comfort.

Ruby leaned close. "My father died of a heart attack. My mother - who by the way, is in a mental ward - blamed me. My sister left with Howard four months after my father's death. I live with my grandmother…and…well…I see a psychiatrist." A gaunt shadow sucked in her cheeks and eyes. She was about to tell him of her father's ghostly visit the night he died. But, why should she? Why put herself out there that much? Then she'd be a jerk. "I wish my problem was that my parents were getting divorced." She shivered. "Look, I know it hurts you. I'm sorry. We've all got our shit in life to bear." She shivered. "It's freezing. Can you put the heat back on?"

He started the motor and turned the switch to heat. "You go to a shrink…and your mother…?" A car beeped. The driver, an irate smoker wearing a beret, motioned for them to pull out. Steve waved his fist in the air, waved him on. The wannabe Frenchman gave them the finger.

Ruby gave him the finger back.

"Maybe I better take you home."

Ruby crushed against the seat. "I truly am sorry about your parents. But can we eat at least?"

"I'm sorry about your parents. And…I'm not hungry. I gotta get home." He echoed.

They drove, hidden behind their thoughts and fears. Ruby didn't notice the wobble and jiggle of the old car's tires. She thought it was her anxiety taking over. Tall buildings blended against the darkness. Only a glimmer of light struck a window here and there, letting her know she was still a part of civilization. Somehow the ride back was longer than the ride going. Excitement had turned to emptiness. Ruby just wanted to return to the secluded ease of her paints, pads, and pencils. Listen to her grandmother's snorts and grunts as she slept. Go back into the mysterious terrain of Marianne's world. As unknown as her life was, Steve seemed to be a thicker place to break through at that moment. "Take a left here." Ruby pointed. "The second house over there." The porch light was on. Sarah wouldn't be up, probably didn't even know she was missing. "Thanks for driving me home." She opened the door.

"Wait." Steve touched her arm. "Can I call you?"

"Why?" One foot in and the other out, she turned.

"I like you."

"You do?"

"I'd like to try this again. Next Saturday?"

For a moment she felt nauseous, believed that it was a sign to say no to him. Then again…"Give me a call. RN 333-8281."

He tapped his head. "RN 333-8281. Got it."

Ruby hurried up the steps, fumbled with the key and opened the door. Threw her coat on the banister and dashed into the kitchen. She slapped together a lettuce, tomato, and mayo sandwich on white bread. She sat at the marble kitchen table. No plate, no napkin. She gobbled it like it was her last meal. Mayo covering her mouth, she glanced over at the basement door. Stomach full, proud of her ability to hold her own tonight, she got up. Step by creaking step she tiptoed down into the basement where her other life waited.

Chapter 34: Next Morning – Steve Calls, Sarah Falls

Nine o'clock in the morning and Ruby was painting. She drank a ton of coffee. Paced. Up most of the night, she slept in the basement. Woke every hour on the hour and continued with her vision. Marianne was thirsty. She painted her mystic eyes, her flaming hair and weathered skin. Ruby gave her a water bag strapped to her waist. The image of the woman crawling through the desert swept across the canvas. She resembled a snake slithering across the sand. What was she thirsty for? What did she need? Another story awaited in this picture. A man. A rabbi who wore white linen that wrapped around his slim body and touched his ankles. This man needed Marianne and Marianne needed him. She painted his body over Marianne's like a cloud of dust. Hot fire caused Ruby to perspire. She felt this urge of sexual love paint through her hands. The strokes of the brush embraced Marianne and the rabbi's genitals. She exposed their lust in the painting. Legs entwined, mouths open, hearts floating in air. Ruby painted with a fury.

She added strokes of red, purple, and blue to the sky. A slab here and there, harder, faster. What was in the eyes of her subjects? Then a mundane thought hit her. Would Steve call her? What was the difference? He ran around with the rats from college row. Maybe he was too straight for her.

She didn't have to wait long. The phone rang. Brush in hand, grungy and face and hands marked with different colors of oils, she grabbed the phone. "Hello? Steve? What's going on?" Ruby listened, sat down on the couch, "Okay. It's okay. You didn't do anything.

Please. Don't apologize. You're allowed to act out of it. I'm pretty out of it myself. Yeah, sure. I'll go out again. Yeah. It's okay. See you then." Ruby hung up the phone. Man, this guy really likes me. Ruby scratched her head.

A loud thump and glass shattering shook her attention. She looked up."Grandma?" She grabbed her stomach. Terror struck her in the gut. "Grandma?" The paintbrush dropped from her hands and she scrambled up the steps. Checked out the small den where her grandmother slept. No one there. Underneath the door of the bathroom, a thin light pushed through.

Ruby entered. Perfume bottles, moisturizers, shampoos, toiletries circled her grandmother. The shower curtain was wrapped around her legs. Her plump body, a dead weight on top of the throw rug while her left leg shook. "Grandma!" She knew the drill. Ran into her parent's bedroom, trembled as she picked up the phone. Call the operator. Call the hospital. Call the police. Which one first? Police. Dial. Ring. Ring. "Hello, hello? My grandmother, please…help. 1630 E. 51 Street. Hurry, please. No. I don't know what's wrong. Her leg is twitching. Yes, she's breathing. I think. Hurry!"

The bed skirt caught her foot. Ruby tripped, crawled back to the bathroom. Laid herself next to her grandmother. Spread her hand across her chest. She moved. Some breath wheezed from her. "Grandma. Please don't die. Please."

Chapter 35: June, 1970 – It Doesn't End

After having her stroke, Grandma Sarah could barely blink. Ruby had to hire a live-in nurse. Transitioning the den into a guest room was chaos. But the squat, strong, steely nurse Barbara was a godsend. Now her home was a hospital. It took three months for Sarah to move her fingers and feet. By May, she was sitting up and slurring words. She finally started rehabilitation in June. Ruby admitted her to the Grand Cypress nursing home near the Summit on Long Island so she could get the recovery care she needed.

It was freakin' hot and muggy the early part of the month. Ruby bought herself a new red Camaro. She was fatigued from traipsing back and forth between Sarah and her mother. A sporty new car gave her a feeling of speed and vitality. Steve stayed close, bought groceries, whisked Ruby away to a movie so she wouldn't sink into crying bouts. It shocked Ruby that Steve wanted to be a part of her life. She'd ask, "Why do want to get involved with my shit?"

"I care about you. Can you accept that?"

She tried. "It's new for me."

Sarah's broken hip from the fall put her in a wheelchair. The trauma affected her speech and the right side of her face. Her skin slumped into her mouth and her drool drained down to her chin when she tried to speak or eat. Although Sara began to take small steps alone, her eyes grew more distant, her speech more scrambled and her demeanor more distraught. Sarah was disappearing.

Again, again, and again. Hospitals. In and out. In and out. A revolving door of heartbreak and cold corridors smelling of despair and rubbing alcohol. A hodgepodge of mental and medical illness that Ruby couldn't control.

At the end of June, Ruby attempted to bring Claire home for a weekend visit. She thought she could handle her. Claire couldn't quite adjust. She left dishes in the sink. Her clothes on the floor. She couldn't walk to a movie or even go the hairdresser without falling into a full-fledged panic attack, throwing a rage, hitting herself with hangers and her own fists. Ruby had to rush her back to the hospital.

Dr. Arber organized another home visit the second weekend in July with a psychiatric nurse from Summit. Her mother didn't notice that Ruby had permanently removed the plastic from the couches. Claire kept saying how soft the cushions were and then asked when her father would be home. Ruby made her chicken soup the way she learned from Sarah. Carrots, onions, basil, salt, pepper, leeks, and spices that would make anyone's mouth water. Claire slurped it slow, with purpose and determination to avoid staining the rug, pleading, "Mama, don't hit me." Ruby couldn't handle her mother's infantile regression, her smallness, her need for Ruby to comb her hair and give her a bath. The mother she was terrified of was now fragile, benign, softened from anti-psychotic drugs.

Dr. Arber soon decided that home visits were futile for Claire. Ruby agreed and was relieved. She hung flowered curtains and placed soft yellow chairs for visitors by the side of Claire's bed. Ruby custom-made an automated Sealy mattress so Claire could adjust the comfort level and position of the bed. In addition to the care at Summit, Ruby hired a private nurse to make sure her mother's needs were attended to. That fresh flowers were placed by the window so the sun could wash their roots with light and fill the room with hope. To gaze upon the decay of her mother's physical beauty turned Ruby rustled and unkempt from anxiety. She'd try to boost her mother's daily application of red lipstick, a dab of mascara. She styled her hair into soft waves. Claire was unresponsive to Ruby's beauty regimen. Her mother was a feeble lump of skin and bones. Ruby soon lost satisfaction in fussing over her mother. Tired of her own false bravado, tired of trying to overcome her fate. Her damn fate. Ruby held her rage as she nursed her mother and grandmother. Went on automatic pilot.

In late July, Ruby called Leah. Her sister screamed, "I can't and won't come. I'm getting married and starting a clean life. I don't want any part of them. I don't know why you would." Ruby couldn't answer that question. At this point she didn't want to. That was the last time Ruby contacted her sister.

So there was Ruby, left to be the caretaker and daughter of the year. Her senior year was approaching, and with all her responsibilities, she struggled to keep up the pace and stamina. How she made it through her junior year was a miracle, with her ping-ponging routine: classes and study at night; visitation two times a week to Sarah, three times to Claire; painting, writing until sometimes four, five in the morning. Her exhaustion turned into a manic high. Dr. Rosenthal upped her anti-anxiety medication. It was survival therapy now. She needed him to just get her through each week. She rested at times on the weekend. Sometimes on Sunday she'd sleep the day away. Dreaming or hallucinating, not knowing the difference at this point. She was living off of pure will, youth, and denial.

Steve gave her a gold bracelet in August. She wore it proud and true. The heart charms jangled and clinked when she combed her hair or opened a door. She loved the sound. Their relationship formed mystically, as if they knew each other from past lives; they fit in ways that went beyond her understanding. He was a rock for her. An unexpected gift that she wasn't sure she deserved. He showed up, strong, loyal and protective. "I've got your back." He was a lifeline for Ruby. How could she be so lucky? Something had to go wrong. She'd do something to fuck it up.

It didn't seem to bother Steve that her family was the black plague. He saw Ruby as a Florence Nightingale. They'd go once a week for pizza, and once a week for egg rolls and chicken chow mein. He'd come on Saturdays and they'd play gin rummy or Scrabble and watch old movies. At times, he'd sleep over. She didn't smoke weed while he was around. The times she was alone, late at night, terror crept through her as the house creaked and groaned. She'd call Steve at midnight or even two in the morning. They'd talk until she fell asleep, the phone cradled in her ear.

One night, after Steve brought in Chinese food and merlot, Ruby opened up to Steve. She gulped down some wine. "I'm not a virgin."

Steve nodded. "Me either."

"I've had this crazy relationship with my next door neighbor.

Joel. Joel Simon. I took drugs with him…and I thought I was going to marry him…and he left me. Went to India with my supposed best friend. I hate him. But he was the one. I thought he was the one. I was obsessed with him."

Steve took her hand. "I have a past, Ruby. Her name was Julie. But now we're Ruby and Steve. We're the ones for each other."

With that, Ruby led Steve down into her basement. Without much explanation she allowed him to stroll through her art and her writings and see the other world Ruby lived in. Ruby tested Steve with this intimate view of her underbelly life, short of revealing her visions of Marianne. She wouldn't share the suffering battlefield of her fragmented soul. Afraid that psychotic pain would chase him away. She didn't want to lose him like she did Joel.

Steve wandered as if in an art gallery. Then turned to her with seriousness, "You're so much more, so much, Ruby. I don't…I can't…" He stopped, took a breath. "I want you to have everything. I want us to have everything." He picked up one of the paintings of Marianne. "Who is she? I feel fired and alive when I look into her eyes. She's so real. And…she also scares me."

"She's a tribal woman."

Steve placed the painting down. "She reminds me of you." He wandered, read the scattered poetry on the canvases.

"Are you afraid of me?"

"No. Never."

"We'll see."

Steve laughed. "Yeah, okay."

They made love for the first time that night. She took Steve by the hand and into her bedroom with its red flowers and the red scallop trim around the ceiling. Slowly, he undressed her, shirt, jeans, bra, undies. Then she undressed him, shirt, jeans, undies. They stared at each other's flesh. He touched her cheek, her neck, her mouth. She reached for his penis. "I'm hungry." She whispered.

It wasn't the passionate, sexual hunger that she experienced with Joel. But Ruby felt safe, alive and validated. Was this love? Soft, kind, and gentle? The deep warmth with Steve was easier for her body to handle then the dark intensity with Joel that left her empty and wanting. Ruby shoved Joel deep into her psyche. The medications Rosenthal prescribed quieted her, allowed some internal consistency. Or was it

Steve who grounded her? She wasn't sure. But the combination was her remedy for coping and living.

After their sexual initiation, Ruby left the bed. Steve rustled and tumbled in the sheets. She stroked his messed hair and went down into the basement. She felt a spark, some urge to paint, but it wasn't urgent. She pulled out a brush from underneath the stacks of art tools. Stared at an emerging painting that was incomplete. Marianne grew greyer and softly crept away in her ears and eyes. Ruby searched for messages, but only a wisp of faint images ran across her easels. Pastels, watercolors, and shades of yellows and golds bulged from the canvases. Women emerged from caves, walking across mountains and valleys, Egyptian garb and desert tents, eyes painted bold black and red moons. Ruby wrote a story of a priestess. She lost her home and was fated to be motherless, live among the coyotes and rattlesnakes. She searched for a lost tribe, stood before a tree of light, it cautioned her to see within…*take heed at the rivers and mountains that lead into cities… stay clear of the people.* Among the crowds she was to find her other half. The one who brought her the ecstasy of union. Ruby entered into a world of ancient ruins that broke hearts and lied to the soul-life. Ruby wrote. The writing and painting didn't seem to stop. Where was it taking her? Then there was quiet. A sudden reprieve. She felt detached. She looked around. A cave. A hidden memory. She wanted to be with Steve, not down here. She ran up the stairs and snuggled into his warm flesh.

She felt Marianne was gathering her strength inside of this new quiet. An incubation, a re-invention. Marianne nestled into her cells. Backed off for a short breath of time. Ruby ignored the forewarning in her body, that Marianne was letting go, in order to return with force.

Ruby rested. If only for a moment. She indulged in Steve.

Chapter 36: End of August, 1970 – Morning, Leah

Ruby sucked in the smell of the summer vines and wild flowers that surrounded the private grounds. Holding her hand to heart, she prayed that Sarah was stronger. She needed her grandmother, needed her tough hands, heart, and mind.

As she entered the facility, the cool air from the central AC hit her. Ruby shivered. She was smart to wear the blue sweater; adjusted the top button as she walked to the elevator. A few steps through the lobby and Ruby froze in her tracks. Leah was sitting, legs crossed, staring at her. All dolled up in a white dress, gold sandals, her blonde hair piled into a French twist. Who the hell did she think she was? Princess Grace?

"Hello, Ruby." She got up from the chair.

Ruby clenched her teeth as Leah slinked over, all puffed up like a peacock. Strange how fate turns and twists a life. Ruby pressed the elevator button, hid her shock, her angry surprise at Leah's appearance. "What do you want? Why are you here?"

Leah handed her a silky white envelope. "Here."

"What is this?"

The elevator door rang. Opened and shut. "A wedding invitation."

The light above them started to flicker. Once again the elevator dinged and opened. This time a group of nurses piled out, scattered in different directions. The doors hushed shut. Ruby turned to Leah. "You're kidding, right? You came all the way here to give me a wedding invitation. I didn't even know I'd be invited."

"You're my sister."

Ruby's face scrunched up with anger. "This is bullshit. Why'd you really come?"

"I wanted to see you." Leah reached out to her.

Ruby slapped her hand away. "I remember, Leah. I didn't forget what you told me. That you hated me. You left and didn't give a shit." Groups of visitors started to arrive. The lobby filled up with people. Ruby fidgeted with her sweater.

"I don't know how you're doing it, with Mom and Grandma. I can't, Ruby. I just can't. I don't want to."

"Can't? You won't. What do you want from me, Leah? What? You hate me, you hate Mom, fine. But Grandma? Why?"

"Grandma? Grandma beat Mommy. Grandma hated Mommy. The two of them beat each other. Then Mom beat us. How many times did Mom try to kill both us and herself? How many? And now Mom is where she belongs. I'm not going to save her. Let her rot where she is."

Ruby stumbled back. Grabbed Leah by the arm. "No. They screamed and fought, but…no…I didn't see Grandma beat Mom."

"You hid, Ruby. You thought Grandma was special because she taught you to make blintzes and chicken soup. You escaped into your little far off world with your paintings. Blocked it out. I didn't have that luxury. I saw and heard it all." Leah led Ruby into a quiet corner. "And even so. It wasn't enough what Mom did to us? We're screwed up. Maybe for the rest of our lives. Who knows if one day their sickness won't take us over? Howard is my only chance, Ruby. He accepts me. Even against his parents' wishes. They wanted him to marry some rich bitch from Boston, but he chose me. Me!"

Bewildered, Ruby searched Leah's eyes. Deep pools of remorse and sadness whirled inside her sister's pupils. "Why did Howard's parents reject you?"

"Because I want him for myself. I won't let them, especially his mother, control him with their money. Mold him into being the family ornament, something they place on their mantel. We don't need their money, as you well know."

Ruby laughed, threw her hands in the air. "Wow. You're good. So you control him? You get to be his controlling mother?" Ruby wanted to smack Leah. She twisted her fists to her side. "I held your hatred. I held it, Leah. What do you want me to do now? I can't just say, Okay.

Everything is all right? Now we can collude against Howard's family, like we did against Mom and Dad? Except you snitched on me to them. Made them turn on me. You're really nuts."

"Nothing is all right, Ruby. Nothing. I don't think anything. I came here to invite you to my wedding. I want a sister. I want family. Will you come?"

Distraught and confused, Ruby snatched the envelope and tore it up. "I hurt so deep…you come here. Now you want a sister. Do you have any idea what has been going on?" Her sobs caught between short breaths until she started to hyperventilate. "I can…can't breathe." At that moment her eyes rolled back. She bent over, held her head between her legs. Cried beyond control.

A doctor startled them. "Do you need help?"

Leah rushed Ruby by the arm out the back door. Once outside the two sat on the curb. The smell of eggs and bacon whisked passed them. Garbage cans surrounded them. Strange. Behind the hospital was a forest of tall oaks and pines. A dogwood swayed. A chipmunk scrambled across the gate. Ruby breathed, put her head down, held her hand to her chest. Wiped the sweat from her brow.

Leah took her pocketbook and placed it under her dress. Brushed off the dirt from her hem. "Shit." She stood up. "Why'd I wear this?"

"Because you're trying to be something you're not?"

"And what is that, Ruby. What am I?"

Two doctors meandered up the walk, drinking coffee. Stared them up and down then entered the building.

"I don't know, Leah. Who are you?"

Clouds gathered around the sun. Shadows blanketed the day and stretched out through the grays and blues of the sky. "I'll tell you a story, Ruby. One that I kept a secret. It's time you knew. Grandma was drunk and she blurted out something to me. I didn't want to believe her. But now it makes sense."

A chill of terror gripped Ruby. All at once, her perceptions were re-arranging and it threw her off balance, making her dizzy and nauseous. "I don't know if I want to know."

Leah tapped her foot, huffed, puffed. Pointed her finger, pulled it back, and brushed a hair from her eye. Her perfect hair-do was falling out and messing with her appearance. "Grandma was raped by Cossacks. Who knows who Mom's real father is…and…and…after,

Grandma couldn't have any more children."

The air stirred in the breeze. Like the quiet before the storm, Ruby twisted her head, fumbled around with her hair, and with a sudden burst, she leapt and slapped Leah's arm. "Liar! You lie to my face. Making shit up."

Leah pushed Ruby. "Damn, Ruby. You should be locked up like Mommy."

Ruby gripped Leah's arm then backed off. Plopped down to the stoop. Buried her head in her hands. "Maybe I do belong in a cage."

"I didn't deserve that. But I get it, Ruby. Your rage." Leah brushed off Ruby's rejection. "I don't care. I don't care if they die. Blood isn't always family."

"That's what you feel? That's it?" Her whole life Ruby wanted to know Sarah's secret. Her irrational cruelty toward her mother. Now she knew.

A young intern came strolling by. His eyes perked up when he spotted Ruby. "Hello." He held the door ajar. "Are you coming in?"

Ruby glanced over at Leah. The shadows shaded her face. It was hard to tell if she was near or far. "Are you coming?"

"No. You can go back to those crazy bitches. I'm going back to Boston."

The slender young man waited.

"I'm sorry, Leah. I didn't mean to hit you."

"Me too. I didn't mean to hate you." Before she left, she turned to Ruby, "I still want you at my wedding."

Ruby's eyes filled with years of torment and yearning, conflicted with fear. "I...I want to...I ... Just can't."

Leah stood for a moment. Stared. Swayed. Left. Her hair out of place, her dress wrinkled.

Ruby turned to the doctor still holding the door. "Thanks." As she followed him into the corridor, a whisper filled Ruby's head. "Dig deeper." Ruby's edges iced over. She had to survive. Ruby marched toward the two women who birthed her bleeding lineage. They survived war, poverty, and death. Her grandmother's grief and mother's pain stuck in her soul. Leah abandoned her. She couldn't, didn't know how to let her in, be her sister. Something neither had ever been to each other.

Ruby swayed down the corridor. Her hips caught the motion of ancients, the smell of heat. She started to perspire, wiped her neck and arms. She made it to her grandmother's room, collapsed into the chair next to the bed. Ruby closed her eyes. The women of the night lived in her cells. Suddenly, Steve came to her mind. Steve. Her hardness softened. Her ache vanished. From the distance, a muted image dripped through her thoughts. Marianne praying. Ruby saw the wailing walls. A brief window into Marianne's core called to Ruby. *Come to me. Come to me.* Marianne's voice had power. Ruby surrendered, didn't fight her call. *I'll survive in whatever way. Whatever way, Marianne.*

Ruby slipped into Marianne's being.

Chapter 37: Marianne and *Hashem*

From as far back as the age of six, Marianne remembered the sacred temples where the priestesses initiated young men and women into the rites of passage, the sexual rituals, the union of prophecy, through their body and soul. Monotheism outlawed the fertility rites of passages. Made the priestesses and priests ugly sinners. Prostitutes, they were now called.

Brave and filled with pride, she snapped at the snakes and spiders, ran from the campfires, the tents, the manna left over from meals, and found her way into the heart of the city. She hid behind pillars of what were now considered pagan temples. She watched the men and women enter trance, float in sacred pools, touching, laughing, whispering and praying. Naked, drenched in sweat and the moon's heat. They all seemed mad with passion for *Yahweh* as they ravished their bodies in the curls and humps of strange cries that seemed to heighten the night's electricity. Wrapped around each other like vines, they howled with joy and ecstasy, free and wild, groping toward each other as if they were gods and goddesses to be worshipped.

Marianne watched and felt the heat rise from between her legs, up her spine, through her arms, her chest, till her head was filled with hot light and she saw the stars, earth and universe. She sped into the hands of angels and heard the voice of the Divine Mother vibrate inside every organ and cell. Her eyes shot open and she felt a hundred feet tall. Bigger than any mountain and stronger than any barbarian. The bursting flow of life was never-ending. She was in the center of that violent eruption. It turned her inside out and outside in. It evolved her mortality into immorality.

The family's pilgrimages to Jerusalem excited her. But now, bands of tribes swarmed across the desert to worship the One God, *Yahweh*. She was angry at *Hashem* who forbade the young girls from entering the sacred fertility rooms. Shamed the people away from worshipping the Goddess. There wasn't even a Hebrew name for Goddess. The *Shekinah*, the feminine face of G-d, was the only one mentioned on the Sabbath. When Friday dusk swirled in, the feminine smoke from the candles swept through every Hebrew mother and daughter's fingers. But, they had forgotten Her true face. Her true body and soul. Sarah, Rebecca, Leah, and all the Hebrew matriarchs walked behind, in the shadows, afraid of their calling, their sacred sexual calling to cleanse the earth with their intuitive bodies and spirits. Women's bodies and the Earth's body were one. And if the female body and her power were annihilated, then the Earth would rage and the body would die.

Marianne, now a woman, was a renegade, an outcast. Her tribe huddled, sleeping under the moonlight, and echoes of howls comforted her loneliness. Each person lay inches apart, flopped over like sleeping fish. She wanted the priestess life. Nothing mattered to her, not even the scorn of her family. She would have that life. Even if it made her insane. Even if they called her a prostitute. She did not care. She had to train herself to shut down her need and pain for her family.

She had a different road to walk. A way of being a woman that even she didn't grasp or understand. She was at the mercy and surrender of her soul, laying herself at the *Shekinah*'s feet.

Chapter 38: At Sarah's Feet

Ruby lay at her grandmother's feet and wrote the Hebrew word, *Shekinah* on the blank page. Sarah snored, tossed, and threw the crinkled sheet off her body. Her stomach protruded from underneath the cotton hospital gown. Up and down, up and down, her loud breathing expanded her belly like a balloon. What if what Leah said was true? No, Leah was a liar. She'd do anything to get attention. She shoved the journal into her bag.

Ruby nuzzled her head into the sheets. In the quiet, she heard the soulless soles of the nurse's shoes squeak down the hallways. What was she going to do? She looked up. She imagined her mother walking the corridors of the psychiatric wing. Did her mother know? Ruby shook her head like a dog wrestling water off its fur. No. No. Her grandmother's screaming criticism toward her mother, Sarah's scathing words to Claire, 'stupid, shamed, no good." If Leah were right, her grandmother's resentment toward her mother would make sense. Her grandmother hated her mother. She blamed her mother. It was all a mess in Ruby's brain. Did her dead grandfather know? Did Sarah lie to him? But she must have been pregnant. Damn. So many questions.

The faucet dripped and pinged against the metal sink. Outside, a buzz of quiet hummed across the floors. Spots of sun hit between grey holes in the room. Ruby scratched her skin. What lurked in her cells? Cossacks? Russian Cossacks? A quiver ran through her like a mini-earthquake. She leapt off the bed and grabbed her bag. She stood over her grandmother, her hands frozen in rage. But then she'd be like all the women in her family. Using harsh words and steel hands to murder the life out of each other. After all, she already hit Leah. What next?

Ruby sulked out into the hallway. A nurse passed by. "Nurse." She waved a hand at her to get her attention.

The nurse halted. "Yes?"

"Is there a Jewish chapel or something here ?"

"Down to the left. It's a uni-religion chapel."

"A what?"

"It's for everyone. I call it that." The nurse glanced at her watch as she sped off.

The stench of bleach made Ruby's eyes tear up. Around her, attendants pushed carts with meals for the sick. Trays of applesauce and pudding neatly packed and ready to go. It made Ruby gag.

She walked toward the hallway, turned left through two doors. The hallway was dimly lit. A champagne color washed the walls. Tiles sparkled with tints of blue and gold. It was serene, like a prayer. At the far end Ruby saw a big red arrow pointing right. Big letters painted in purple read CHAPEL. To either side of her, random doors were painted in various colors like a crayon box. Each door labeled; staff, counseling, research, family remembrance. What was this place? Curiosity tilted her head. Straight ahead was her destination. The Chapel. She moved toward the arrow. Amazing that this beat-up hospital had a wing for those who wanted to meditate, center themselves away from the dread and doom of their troubles. A swoosh of energy up her spine pushed her toward the chapel.

She opened the door. Inside were three long pews to both the right and left. Light forced its way through the thick mosaic glass windows. A painting swirled in bright reds, greens, and yellows. Flames of the burning bush; Moses on his knees receiving the Commandments.

Ruby slid onto a bench. The hard wood struck her buttocks like a rod against her spine. Ruby studied the sacred mosaic of Hebraic content. Swells of longing, fear, and curiosity illuminated Moses. She turned her head, and to the far left, a face of a woman shone from a bolt of clouds. A cloth covered her head, she held an infant in her arms. Her eyes glowed like the moon. Ruby knew that this was the Virgin birth. The silence in the room deepened and drew her inward. She'd never seen Moses and the Virgin in the same scene. Together, they conjured a mysterious spell. She shuffled her feet and crossed her hands on her lap. Mythologies mixed together. Other religions were not present. The Judeo-Christian culture was the main story.

Yellow and orange flames shot from the center of the glass etching. Red tones clawed their way to the top of the fire and carved each commandment, each law into the stone. Ruby screamed. "No!"

From the edges of the window another image emerged. Stones arranged into steps and climbed into the foothills, snakes skirted among the rocks and pebbles. A young woman with red hair waved. Her face innocent, her eyes familiar. Ruby squinted. Marianne. This was Marianne. A lost child. A lost woman. A voice, *"Come with me. Come, Ruby."*

"How, Marianne?" Everything was wrong. She was just like Marianne. Lost, rejected, wandering the desert. What if it was true about her grandmother? "Do you know, Marianne?"

A tap on the shoulder. "Ruby? Your grandmother is awake." Ruby jumped and turned. It was Steve.

She grabbed Steve's hand. "What are you doing here?" She stood up and hugged him.

"I know your schedule." He looked around, curious. "Are you all right?"

"There are things I haven't told you. There are things…"

Steve tugged at her hand. "It's okay. We have time. What's immediate is your grandmother. Let's go." He circled his arm around her waist.

Ruby pulled, kissed his hand. "You just don't know. What you see is not what you get, Steve. There's more to it than the paintings, the therapy…more…I don't know how you want this…this life with me."

He swept his hands through her hair. "What I see is what I want. I see your heart, Ruby. The rest doesn't matter."

Ruby's heart beat hard in her throat. "It will. It will matter." Ruby straightened and tapped her foot in a steady meter. "I have to pee." Peeing was good, Ruby thought. It gave her a time to feel what was next. Rest for a moment. Peeing was good. Peeing was human.

As she sat on the toilet, she saw desert and orange clouds.

Chapter 39: Grandma Sarah's Message

Steve accompanied Ruby back to her grandmother's room. He kissed her on the cheek. "I'll wait." He meandered into a small waiting area where a young red-haired man sulked by the window, and a tiny, dark woman read a book. Steve turned and waved. "Come get me if you need me."

Ruby forced a nod and walked down the corridor. She edged into the room. It smelled of steel and old shoes. "Grandma?" Ruby hovered over Sarah.

Her grandmother grumbled and spat into a cup. She threw the cup on the floor. Her aged fingers wiped across her mouth. Her eyes glazed over. She was propped up against the pillows. The side of her mouth drooped into a sling that curved to her chin. *"Ma...ma...la."*

Tubes hung from every edge of her sheet. Sarah's head jerked back, her eyes rolled, and she was still. She didn't appear human. Sarah's wrinkled skin sagged like an old mask, plastic, unreal; her cheeks sank into her bones, her face a grayish hue. Each squeaky breath her grandmother struggled to inhale stabbed at Ruby's heart and tears bubbled in her eyes.

"Turn around. *Shayna madalah.* Turn around."

Where was the voice coming from? It sounded like her grandmother. But Sarah was unconscious.

"Here, *bubbalah*, here."

Ruby made a fast one hundred and eighty degree turn. Sarah flapped like an eagle in the air, her crinkled hospital gown draped loosely around her waist. Her grandmother's breasts hung in full view.

"Grandma?" Ruby yelled. Her grandma floated in the corner of the room. Stunned, Ruby tripped over her own feet, picked herself up, touched her grandmother, who lay under the covers. She was solid and warm. She gurgled phlegm in her throat.

"I'm still up here. I talk better when I'm out here. That body can't give anything no more. Look up, Ruby. I know you see."

Ruby felt her feet melt into putty, goose bumps waved up her arm. Again the visions. A surge of anger tore at her gut. "NO. I can't bear this. No. No. I don't want to carry this weight." She bent over, grabbed her stomach. "You hurt me. Why did you lie?"

"Listen. Listen, *rubalah,* I'm dying. And you must live. I did what I thought was right."

"Why did you tell Leah?"

Her grandmother was translucent, peeping in and out of the molecules of light and the sound of the whirring air conditioner. "I was drunk. Stupid. I didn't vant for anyone to know. I grew tough and I wanted to forget. Forget that they wanted to burn me because I read the tea leaves, the palms. I saw the future, but not my own. The soldiers raped me. Killed my family. Because I saw things. The ghetto vitch. I came to America with death on my back. I wanted to be quiet and live the old ways, be quiet and cook the blintzes, light the candles, stop all the crazy *meshuganah* things in my head. I thought I'd beat it out of your mother. Beat it down, beat the Cossack blood out of her. Didn't want your mama to see things in her brain. When I light the candles…I make blessing that turned to a curse. But you got it. You got it. But you…you…you…must have a blessing. No matter what. You Jew. You always Jew. A blessing and a curse." Sarah started to fade. "Leah makes curses, too. It's a choice, *bubbalah.*" Her grandmother evaporated and left a gash in Ruby's mind.

Ruby whisked over to her grandmother. She was lying in disarray, mumbling, ravaging through a scrambled world between life and death. "You give me a choice? You? You gave me the pain in my heart, you robbed me of a mother, a…a…crazy screw loose that hangs out of the side of my brains…a homeless home. I'm a fucking nutcase." Ruby cried. "I'm so alone with all this loss."

She shook her grandmother. "I'm so angry. We could have loved one another. You taught us to hate." Ruby shook Sarah until the tubes rattled around and the heart monitor did a jig with beeps and lines. "You can't make this right in death. Leave me to figure this out my fucking self." Ruby dragged herself to the window. Looked out at the blue, the still trees, the sun that spoke in the language of light. This was where she was, on this Earth. Here in this room, in this body, at this time. *I'm too young. And feel too old,* she whispered to herself as if in a trance. She crept alongside her grandmother's bed and entwined her fingers through her grandmother's crooked hand. She squeezed and kissed Sarah's fingertips and rubbed them against her face. "You damn old tough fart."

A soft rap on the door alerted Ruby. She averted her gaze over to the nurse who stood in the entrance. "Your grandmother needs sleep."

Ruby nodded. A shudder came over her. Her mother. She needed to see her mother.

She ran down the hallways. Rushed toward Steve. "I'm going to see my mother. It won't be long. Do you mind? Can you wait here? It will be about an hour."

"Don't worry. Do what you have to do. I'll keep an eye out for your grandmother while you go." Steve's tender hands thumbed through a sports magazine. His eyes held Ruby's with ease and acceptance. "Go. I'll be here."

Chapter 40: Claire Claws

Claire scooted to the end of the bed and tipped the saggy mattress off the frame. "Oh, your hair is so nice." Ruby flinched and jerked as her mother touched her soft curls. Now she thought her hair was nice. For years she had combed it like it was a rat's ass. It was a sad scene to witness her mother's will crippled under heavy drug prescriptions. At the same time, it turned her into some sort of sweet lady who knitted sweaters.

Her mother smelled like Ivory soap, the scent that Claire claimed was soft and pure. But the little girl in Ruby knew better. Even now, she wanted to sneak into her lap, wrap her arms around her mother's waist, beg her mother: *love me, pick me up and cradle me.* But there was no mother to be found. A memory twisted Ruby's neck from side to side. Claire running down the street, naked, screaming, tearing her hair from her head. She had only been three when that psychotic episode ripped through Claire. Her mother chased after Ruby like an alligator. She opened her mother jaw. Claire locked onto Ruby's arms and legs and pulled her down under into the tub water. Ruby struggled, "I can't breathe, Mommy, help." She almost drowned in the snot and goo of her mother's dark mental illness. Her mother wanted to murder her children like Medea. If her father hadn't been off from work that night, Ruby would have been dead.

Ruby neared her mother.

Claire was scrawny, wilted. She sat like a toddler, feet hanging over the bed, playing with her cotton hospital gown, smiling, "Come here." Her mother rubbed her hand in a circular motion on the blanket.

"Where's Daddy?"

Ruby sat a foot from her mother's hand. "Daddy's dead, Mom."

Her mother's eyes ticked. Her hands groped under the gown, anxious, ready to pop like a stun gun.

Ruby stood up, inched snail-like toward the wall, leaned against it, folded her arms in a shield of protection. Her mother's hands frightened her when they were restless. A bowl of oatmeal sat on a tray in front of her. It had turned to a glob of mud. The spoon stuck to it like glue.

"Are you hungry, Mom?"

Claire shook her head no like a shy child.

Ruby wedged away from the wall and sat next to her mother. "Mom." She extended her hand close to her mother's shoulder then stopped, changed direction, and patted her hand. "Mom. I want to understand." Ruby could felt her mother's coldness.

Her mother stared down, lost in a sea of green linoleum that shone under the iridescent lights. She tucked her gown under her bottom. "Where's Mama? I want Mama," Claire cried.

Overshadowed by her mother's whimpering, Ruby nuzzled her head onto her mother's shoulder. "I want that too, Mom. I want a mama, too."

Claire hunched away from Ruby to break free of her daughter's dependency, her eyes fluid with fear. "I won't share Mama. I won't."

A heavy-set nurse entered, pushing a cart filled with cartons of milk and Jell-O. She interrupted the mother and daughter communion. "She won't eat. It's a problem. And she hits. Even with the medication, she throws tantrums. Can you make her eat?"

"If you get her some fresh oatmeal. This is rancid."

The nurse picked up the dish and threw it on top of dirty plates. "I'll be back."

Claire scrambled under the covers and spooned a pillow into her chest.

"I don't want to eat."

A sudden urge to lay hands on her mother boiled through Ruby's blood. Images flooded her; a circle of women, praying, mixing herbs, intuitively she knew the healing of the ancients arjuna for the heart, bacopa for mental illness, and bitter melon for diabetes; placing crystals; apophillite for mental disorders, fluorite for Alzheimer's;

apace; tears for grief, malachite for emotional trauma and healing. Ruby saw a ritual of healers. They chanted and danced with Marianne.

Ruby was alive, fired up; pulled the sheets from her mother and stood over her like the sun. She opened her hands and strange incantations sang through her. Ruby was afloat in a mystery of things beyond her comprehension. An energy guided her hand toward her mother's head and heart. She couldn't fight it. She couldn't think, or move by her own choice. In a trance-like movement she reached toward her mother.

"No. Go away." Her mother bit down hard on Ruby's finger. "I'm putting a curse on you."

The pain of her mother's teeth dug into her skin, broke flesh, blood trickled down her finger. "Ouch. Man. Shit. Fuck. Damn." She ran into the bathroom, turned on the faucet, cold water slammed against the wound. Ruby squeezed down on it with a towel.

Ruby flipped down the toilet seat and sat. She repeated *I don't care, I don't care. Leah's right. She got it right. Go away. Far away. Why do I care? I've got to get out of here.* She got up and looked in the mirror. She grazed her hand across the mirror. It squeaked against her palm. What if she broke the glass? What if she took it and just ended it all for her and her mother? Her body started to shake. Sweat beaded around her head and under her breasts. She felt that urge. That urge to die. She was about to crash the glass with the shampoo bottle when she noticed a man by the door.

"Hello?" It was Dr. Arber.

Ruby froze. Put the bottle down. Her hand was wrapped with the bloody towel.

He edged toward her to help, guided the tangled towel away from her hand. "Come with me." He rushed her to emergency and examined the wound. "Nothing serious." The onset of wrinkles etched the corners of his eyes. His breath was stale and heavy.

"What happened?" He swathed medicinal alcohol and a soothing ointment on the injury and swirled a gauze bandage around her finger. "Would you like to talk in my office?"

"What are you doing here?" She followed him down the hall and into a small cubicle. His desk was mass chaos. Files, books, empty, stained coffee cups and cigarettes crushed in ashtrays.

"I'm affiliated with the Summit. I make rounds here on Long

Island. At the Grand Cypress as well." He pointed for her to sit on a leather couch. He filled out the big leather chair like the Buddha.

"I think it's important that you understand what is happening to your mother. She is a borderline-schizophrenic. Difficult. Very difficult. All we can do is give her psychotropic drugs. But she refuses to take medication and won't eat. We might have to put her on a feeding tube."

Ruby wrestled with her legs, fumbled around. "That doesn't help me understand. I need more."

"In simple language, your mother hears and sees things that aren't there. She feels in a way that she can't connect or attach to people. Possibly can't love. Her emotions are like knives and she hates herself and others. She's paranoid, thinks everyone is against her, thinks people are out to get her. Her emotions bleed out, like an open vein. She's delusional. She can switch her mood in an instant. Her depression leads to suicide attempts. Extreme anxiety and panic cause her to experience deep feelings of worthlessness. She is self-destructive, impulsive, self mutilating." Arber took a deep breath, stopped, waited.

"I've watched her self-destruct. And try to kill me and my sister." Ruby felt her heart palpitate in her throat. She swallowed, but it stuck there like undigested food, She sped up, talked fast through the panic. She didn't trust Arber enough to freak out in front of him. She breathed, tried to calm herself. "It's so hopeless. So dark."

"There's no solid answer. It can be genetic, set off by abuse. Brain chemistry. We're never sure."

"I've struggled with all of this, Dr. Arber, in my own therapy. Can I have this sickness? Is it random? Is it inescapable?"

He pulled his chair close to her. "Do you ever think of suicide? Not able to release painful feelings, paranoid, difficult to be in relationships?"

"Sometimes my feelings are so painful I want to die. But it passes. My therapist encourages me to write, paint, work through the feelings."

"So you see or hear things?" Arber's eyes closed in on her. Sucked her in as if she were one of the case studies he was writing up.

"It doesn't matter." Ruby felt her insides clench. She didn't want to talk to him. Didn't want to tell him about Marianne. She didn't know him. And he couldn't even help her mother. Why should she trust him? "I only talk to Dr. Rosenthal. Thank you."

"What medications does he have you taking?" He stood up. Frustration curled his lips.

Ruby got up. "That's none of your business."

"I'd recommend a psychotropic medication."

Ruby's eyes simmered with anger. "I'll sign the permission to put my mother on a feeding tube. I'll sign whatever it takes to keep my mother alive."

Arber, paused, then got up. "If you go to the nurses' office, they'll go over the paperwork with you. If you have any questions just call me."

Ruby leaned against the door. Her face drained of any color. "Is that it?"

"No. You're going to have to put her in a nursing home. Summit can't handle it. I think you could get her into Grand Cypress. I'll help with the admission and details. They have a psychiatric wing."

"Fine." Ruby ran down the corridor. Her heart throbbed. Her eyes foamed up with tears. Nothing was going to save Sarah or her mother. How could she save herself? This coming year was her last year of college. September was a month away. Then classes started. She had to get through it. Living another year in the house might kill her. The ghost of her childhood rested in each room. In the mornings, she smelled her father's Old Spice, her mother's Chanel No. 5; in the bathroom, drawers of makeup waited for her mother to come play. Purple, blue, and brown eye shadow became dusty and faded. The loneliness shredded each vein, knotted every muscle in her body.

She pushed through the doors. The administrative office was ahead. She'd sign for her mother's feeding tube. Sign her into anywhere, anyplace.

Chapter 41: Monday, August 1970 – The Session

Rosenthal's office was cool and comfortable.

Ruby pounded his desk. "Why are you giving me all this bullshit?" She kicked her sandals across the room. Jumped out of the chair and paced. Her eye caught the tilt of his duck painting. It was off center. Damn ducks.

"What are you talking about?" Sweet pipe smoke whirled into clouds around Rosenthal.

"I am a borderline schizophrenic like my mother."

"Who told you that?"

"I told me that."

Rosenthal shot a clipped, controlled look. "Take a breath. Sit."

"I talked to my mother's doctor, Arber, yesterday. He gave me the whole spiel about her mental illness…and…I must have it…I have it. I have it! He recommended anti-psychotic medication. You're letting me walk around believing I'm special or something. But I'm as crazy as my mother. It's in my genes." Ruby held her head. "Oh my god! He said I'm not on the right medications. You got to give me something that will stop it…stop all of it…I don't want it. I don't want to wind up with a feeding tube up my nose or ass."

"Ruby, you're not mentally ill. I'm giving you medications that won't impede your process. Auditory and visual experiences have been portrayed in biblical stories for centuries. Indigenous and varied cultures and religions see this as a natural rite of passage. Carl Jung, Martin Luther King, and Winston Churchill all heard voices. It can be a spiritual awakening. It can be set off by trauma, illness, or life-threatening situations. Drawing, painting, music, journaling, and dreams are all ways to channel this experience. Can you hear me at all?"

"What're you doing to me?" Ruby heard chimes and dings resounding in her brain. She hit her head against a pillow.

Rosenthal raised his voice. "You're making yourself ill by thinking you are ill. There was no one to help your grandmother and mother. Now they are trapped. You've got to listen, Ruby. You've got to hear me."

"Hear what? Tell me to pretend to be a woman. Find myself? I feel so scattered, like a ball of splinters and shards." Ruby heard a shofar blast. She covered her ears. "No! What's the right medication?"

The room tightened like a hand around her throat. Ruby stroked her neck, moved toward the doctor, then stopped. "I can't breathe."

"I know. I know. I know, Ruby, you've got to calm down. You're having a panic attack. Calm down."

Ruby growled. "I can't stand it. I can't stand being this way." She tore a button off her shirt.

His fingers fumbled around in his pocket, emptied a bottle of small white pills. White dots tumbled everywhere. "Here." He threw one into her mouth. "Chew. Breathe."

Her rough breathing turned down a notch. She felt the warmth of the pill fill her nerves and muscles. "That's what I need. That's what I need. The crazy pill. The crazy pills."

Rosenthal felt her pulse, shook his head, sat up and hunched over. "Stop. This is unacceptable! You are in the process, Ruby. Don't stop it now. You'll suffer more if you do. You're under a lot of pressure. The anxiety and stress will exacerbate things. You need to trust."

"I don't want to be your little experiment. Just make the delusions stop. Make them stop."

"You want it all gone, Ruby?" Dr. Rosenthal sat back in his chair.

"Yes. That's what I want." Ruby pushed her feet against him. "Please."

He moved to the end of the couch. "You're stronger than your mother. You won't wind up in an institution. I know what Arber wants. They'll turn you into a zombie, Ruby. You'll be empty. And the medications don't always make it all go away."

"I don't care."

"It will come back to haunt you, bite you in your butt."

"You don't know everything." Ruby shouted

"Neither do you." Dr. Rosenthal stood up. "Nor Dr. Arber."

"I'm not asking, I'm telling you."

"You speak with little trust in me, Ruby."

"Trust! I hate that word."

"I'm human. You're right, I don't know everything. But I do know, if you can let go, work through the terror and the trauma, you will find a great light in you."

"I'll get your license taken away. I will!" She stood up.

Dr. Rosenthal went to his desk, pulled out a prescription pad. "Valium and Elavil. That's it. I won't give you anything stronger."

She grabbed the prescription. "I'm through with therapy."

"If you want medication renewal, you'll have to see me once a month. We'll need to keep adjusting dosage. If you get pregnant one day, we have to discuss options. Side effects could be devastating for the fetus. Or for you if you go off without supervision."

"I'm not getting pregnant anytime soon, or maybe ever!" She folded the script. "I'll find some doctor who'll give me something stronger. Something, damn, something…someone who doesn't see my mind as a spiritual journey, but as crazed and out of control."

"You say that, but you won't."

"You're deranged, Dr. Rosenthal."

"If you are so crazy, why aren't you locked up like your mother? Numb, sick, and lost. You won't stop painting, writing, seeing, hearing what you see and hear. Do you really want to stop now and give in, collapse, not reach your potential?"

Ruby wiped her mouth, studied Rosenthal, picked at her curls. A battle raged in her. A tug of war. Who would she be without her art, the voices, the chaos? She didn't know. Didn't know the answer. Her heart hurt down her arm into her belly. An ache that grabbed her soul. She rubbed her chest. She didn't know. "I don't want to think about any of this anymore." She walked out and slammed the door.

Dr. Rosenthal called out, "I will see you in a month, Ruby. Don't go and find some doctor that would be happy to make you the walking dead. I know you can hear me."

Ruby breathed. Ran down the hot pavement. Was this the beginning or the end? A new moon, a different sun, and a different life. She'd never tell Steve about Marianne. It was her private psychosis. Depression was one thing. She knew Steve handled her mood swings. But not the hallucinations. He'd never marry her if he knew she was one big LSD trip. This story was her swirling current, her wave to ride. But how? How? How could she live? Medications? No medications? Paint the stories. Write the stories? Would this make her sane? Ruby stopped. Her head pounded. She rubbed her temples; fierceness and fatigue drew her listless. She dug her fingers into her scalp then scrambled around in her pocket. Whisked out a joint and brought it to her lips. Instead, she cracked it in half, threw it down and crushed it under her knee-high boot. She shook from her toes up and screamed until the air molecules trembled. "No more."

Chapter 42: January, 1971 – Steve's Heart

The new year rolled around and Ruby turned twenty-one. Marianne's face bled in and out like soaked watercolors. Shades of black and gray took the place of the Hebrew woman's stark tiger eyes. Random poetry, love/death, God, love, Joel, Steve, short spurts of angry words, sorrowful prayer, and unconscious narratives rolled across journals. She now had a box filled with the writings, none of which made sense to her. None that eased the pain, but instead brought obsessive yearning and a restlessness with no name.

Only the smell of burnt brain matter was left; a still pond of buzzing sounds, like baby bees flipping around flowers. Ruby called it 'the fading.' Rosenthal's medications discharged some of Marianne's rapture at times. There were phases of intense creativity then phases of intense moodiness and darkness. She fought and resisted so much, everything blended into mud. Either way, she did heed Rosenthal's warnings. It frightened her to be a slab of putty like her mother, and it frightened her to flow in and out of mania. So she stayed on his prescriptions, visited him once a month. She shared little beyond, "I'm fine." Or, "I'm depressed." No analysis, only adjustments of dosage. Somehow she had a sense of when she was a plain Brooklyn girl or when she was in some sort of cosmic insane asylum. She found a way to surrender, be in limbo with her own journey.

Steve encouraged Ruby to keep painting. He brought new warmth and calm to her life. A flurry of paintings rose out of the fading. Bold colors draped and smudged with palette knives, oils splattered with sponges, toothpicks, collages of faces, wrinkled women, young children, and fashion models all arranged in rows like the evolution of womankind. Her mind quieted, but her creative juices flowed with vibrant paintings of impressionistic value and tone. She didn't need pot anymore.

Ruby was to ready commit to the next stage of her life. The winter unraveled with a gentle fury, long days of dark cold, heavy rains came and went.

On her twenty-first birthday, Ruby asked Steve to move in and help her sell the house. She wanted a new life. He immediately said yes. They clinked champagne and ate caviar at an exclusive restaurant in Manhattan. Steve gave her half-carat diamond earrings and whispered in her ear, "forever."

"Do you mean it? Really?"

"I see your heart. Through it all. I see your heart. Can't you see mine?"

Ruby placed the earrings in her lobes. Waited. Stared at Steve. Placed her hand on his heart. "I see. I want to feel."

"Let me in." Steve grabbed her hand.

"Help me sell the house. We'll make our own life."

The obstacle to listing the house was Leah. She owned half of it. Steve handled all the legalities, found out who Leah's attorney was. Ruby relied on Steve; he was her only chance. They grew closer, more intimate, a couple tightening their grip together, saving each other from the harshness life brought. They mingled like vines, attached to each other, dedicated and rooted.

Steve graduated and secured an entry-level position in a real estate investment firm, Goldman and Rubin. He worked long hours while Ruby painted into the night. Their two o'clock in the morning rituals of tomato and cheese omelets, grilled cheeses with pounds of butter, and dark coffee and chocolate chip cookies created a world of their own. The proper professionals were caring for her mother and grandmother, and for a moment in time, Ruby felt free. She felt a certain symmetry between the family that was dying and the one that was being born.

Ruby designed her future. She wanted to be a wife. Wear a ring on her finger that told the world she belonged to someone. That she wasn't a neglected soul without anyone to love her or for her to love. Love became a romantic prelude into a new imaginary, delusional world. Love and marriage were her new destination. A full bounty of ordinary with her feet planted firmly to the ground. She'd control her destiny, not psychiatrists or invisible ancestors who stole her sanity. She would be straight and steady, straight and steady. Yes, Ruby would repeat her mantra *straight and steady, Ruby, steady and straight, girl,* every night to herself in the mirror. Yes. Yes. Yes, as she gulped down her medications. Nothing to the left, to the right, behind, up or down. Just straight ahead. Her mind a wild mare now tamed. And that was her life. She switched one fairytale for another, one compulsion for another.

But floodgates are meant to be flooded. Steve was the mint and aloe vera soothing the rash of paranoia that lay beneath the surface of Ruby's skin. Steve. Steve. Steve. Soon he'd be initiated, taken through the pagan ritual called Ruby Goldsmith.

Chapter 43: Diamond in The Rough

Valentine's Day. It was a brisk afternoon and the hot chocolate Ruby sipped was yummy. The creamy warmth brought a smile to her face. She cuddled close to Steve's side as they strolled down Broadway. The two matched in their mod clothes; Ruby wearing a black mini and navy pea coat, Steve in black bell-bottoms and short leather jacket. Steve's hair swept across his ears and down below, almost touched the edge of his jaw line. Ruby's hair was pulled into a side ponytail with bangs straight across, framing her dark-lined eyes. Together, they were the perfect 'now generation' couple.

They walked arm in arm down Times Square. They had just seen the movie *Love Story,* the newest tearjerker.

"Why'd she have to die?" Ruby frowned.

"Love is never having to say you're sorry. That would go over big with you." He pulled her closer.

She cupped the warm drink and smiled. "Well, it was corny, but thanks for taking me. It was sweet of you. I know it wasn't what you wanted to see."

Sunday in New York. Broadway bright, lively signs of musicals adorned the buildings, *Tommy, Hair, Jesus Christ Superstar.* Ruby felt her stomach jump with excitement. She grabbed Steve's hand. "Let's go see *Jesus Christ Superstar.*"

"When?"

"Now. Tonight."

"Now?" Steve sat down on a bench and pulled Ruby next to him. "I had other plans for us."

"I just have to see that play. We can grab a bite. Maybe go to the Modern Museum then cop some tickets for the seven o'clock show."

"*Hair* is a smash. Let's go see that."

"Steve. Come on. Please." She gulped down the drink. "This is cold." She jumped up and threw the cup into a large waste can, sat back down and snuggled into Steve. "Do you like the watch I gave you?"

Steve rubbed the gold Piaget Polo watch. He examined the piece with pride.

"No one ever gave me anything like this." He stared at the gold piece, twisted his arm around, grinning like a little boy who just ate the last cookie in the jar. He turned to Ruby with a serious gaze. "Ruby, we're good together? Aren't we?" He tapped the bench and squeezed her hand. "But…but…well, I've been offered a position to develop land in Florida. It's an amazing opportunity. And…"

"You're leaving? What do you mean?" Ruby's eyes moistened, her face laced in fear.

Steve's eyes swelled with anticipation. He crossed his legs, hunched over, then sat up straight, placed his arm on the edge of the bench, unzipped his jacket and pushed his hand inside.

"What's going on?" Ruby poked at him, trying to pull his hand out of his jacket.

"Stop." Steve pushed her hand away.

The cool air captured the sunrays. Ruby shivered. "What is wrong with you? I demand to know! Are you leaving me?"

Steve's mouth dropped. "Ruby. No. No." He leaned over and touched her face.

Ruby avoided his embrace. "I can't take one more person leaving. It's too much for me."

"Ruby. Babe. Ruby. No. No." Finally, he lifted a small velvet box out of his jacket. "Open this."

She tilted her head and took the box from his hand. As she flipped open the lid, the sun's light jumped off the surface of a two-carat square shaped ring. Edging it on either side were two baguettes and strung along the band were several smaller diamonds. "Oh my god."

Steve got down on his knee and asked, "Ruby, will you marry me?"

Ruby grinned. She had caught her man, reeled in the lone fish that would make her life decent. He slid the ring from its case and held it. "Well?"

A sun halo bulged from his head and body. His glow warmed her belly and filled every empty space of her cells. He was Gabriel, blowing the ram's horn, Sir Lancelot charging on a white unicorn to save her soul. Jimmy Dean, stirring passion in her genitals…but, but…her mind scrambled into a hospital room where her mother and grandmother lay dying. Her hand dropped to her side, her eyes thickened in a cauldron of worry. "Do you want me to move to Florida with you? Leave my mother and grandmother? How can I do that, Steve?"

He stroked her hand. "We can visit every month."

"What if they die and I'm not there? And I want to finish school. Graduate in June."

The trees rustled against the air. An overcast cloud suddenly blew across the clips of sky jammed between the skyscrapers and apartment buildings. Steve tightened his grip. "We'll figure it out. I promise."

Ruby looked away. "I can't leave as long as they're alive."

"Do you want to be with me?"

"Yes. I do. And…I'm afraid."

"I know you are. And I will protect you."

"Protect or control?" She plopped down on the bench. "You can't understand."

"I understand that I want to marry you and take care of you. Isn't that what we've been headed toward this last year?"

Ruby extended her hand toward Steve. "Put it on."

"You sure?"

"It's complex, me, my family. But…I don't want you to leave without me."

"You can fly down to Florida on weekends to visit them after graduation. You have four months to be with them." Steve grabbed her chin, "Look at me." His fingerprints indented her cheeks. "Look, Ruby, I've a month to take this position. I'll fly back and forth. We'll get through this. We can wait to marry until after you graduate. We can do this together. Us."

Ruby unglued his fingers from her face. "Why?"

"Why what?" Steve's eyes filled with confusion.

"I don't get it. Why would you do all of this for me?"

Steve placed his hands in a prayer over his heart. "I don't know. Maybe it's because love is never having to say you're sorry?"

A warm belly laugh rumbled through her defense and defiance. "Yes! I want to marry you."

Steve slid the ring on Ruby's finger. They hugged, kissing with longing and hope.

The two jumped up, crisscrossed through the streets, dodging through the crowds.

Chapter 44: June, 1971 – To Sarah's Grave

Summer splat with heat and mug. It rained all that week after graduation. Then Sarah fell into a coma. Dr. Arber phoned Ruby at five in the morning. His painful words froze in her mind. "Your grandmother isn't going to make it." The phone stayed cold in her hand after she heard the news. Tears backed up into her stomach. She threw up. She wasn't prepared for this day.

Lucky that Steve was there for her graduation. He held her close as he took the phone from her hand, put it in the cradle and held her. "I'll cancel my meeting."

"No. Go."

"No. I'm going with you."

The oaks and sycamores were soaked; their musky sweet fragrances filled the summer air with an aromatic afterglow. The pavement was soft and slushy as Ruby and Steve ran toward the nursing home, her umbrella pulled inside out by the wind. Steve struggled to close his. They entered the lobby, threw their umbrellas aside in the waiting room. Steve clasped Ruby's hand.

Ruby twisted her engagement ring around and around her finger. Depression sat in the pit of her stomach as she breathed in the aroma of brewed coffee that escaped from the cafeteria. The rich heaviness of her mood ran through her body. She squeezed Steve's hand. "Stay close."

Exhausted and disheveled, her hair an explosion of frizz tied into a tight knot, she wore a strapless flowered dress, light pink sweater, and flip-flops; no make-up to cover up the fear that trembled on her lips.

She had to go, had to be the one who helped guide her grandmother's soul into heaven.

With dread and caution she stepped toward the elevator. Steve, strong by her side, pushed the button and the elevator sped up. A short ride to death's door. The doors opened. Ruby eyed Steve as they stepped out. The corridor seemed shorter, smaller. Snores of patients roared in her head. Her heart pounded hard. The smell of decay led her toward her grandmother's room.

Two nurses and Dr. Arber were beside her grandmother. All the tubes and machines were off. A translucent silence, an otherworldly energy permeated the air. Ruby felt the presence of something beyond, but she saw nothing except her grandmother's stiff, white body.

"She's gone, Ruby. I'm sorry." Dr. Arber stood back, gave Ruby room to say goodbye. He truly emanated a deep sorrow. "We did everything."

Steve whispered, "What do you need?"

Ruby touched his cheek. "Just for you to be here. Don't leave me."

"I'm right here." Steve inched away, leaned against the wall.

Ruby kissed Sarah's hand. She sniffed her neck. Hoped to smell something alive; the Palmolive oil on her skin or the smell of a blintz. But Sarah was gone. Her face was placid, quiet, cloudless, and still. *Sarah, Sarah.* Ruby heard her grandmother's name echo through her blood. Sarah was dead, leaving Ruby alone with murky memories of ancestors who died back in Poland. She'd miss her snores, her tomato-y meatballs, and tender boiled chicken. The smell of cigarette smoke and vodka that lingered on her breath and in her hair. Grandma Sarah. Grandma Sarah, her wrinkled eyes and knowing glance. This woman, her grandmother, lay in the arms of God now. And Ruby inherited her pain and determination, leaving her with a thousand questions.

Ruby yelled, "Grandma, damn…what do I do now?" Ruby pounded her chest where her heart lay beneath the skin of her past. She turned to Dr. Arber. "What do I do?"

"You grieve."

Ruby stared out the window. "I grieve doctor, every day. No tears come anymore. What do I do next?"

"That's up to you."

Chapter 45: June, 1971 – Till Death Do I Part

The sun hit hard and steady against the morning sky. The cemetery stood amongst weeping willows and blazing red maples. Their presence reminded the mourners that in their sorrow, God's majesty was omnipresent. Together the trees were fire and air. It was alchemical nature at its best. The wind guided the spirits that lay under the shade of trees up toward the heavens. Kaddish prayers for the dead swept up into the sky. Most of Sarah's friends had passed. No family. Ruby gripped Steve's hand. His fingers, an anchor of patience and tenderness, kept her grounded. Ruby's eyes followed Hebrew words as Steve recited the song to God.

At that moment she had only Steve to give her an identity, a place in life. Her own body and face gave her nothing. It was no longer a mirror to her self-knowledge, just an empty cup. Steve was her destiny for now.

***

A week later, they married in Rabbi Gutman's study under a humble golden *chupah* draped in velvet. The simple, wise old rabbi who had *bar mitvah*'d Steve officiated their wedding. There was no smorgasbord, no big band or *havanagilah,* no best man or maid of honor. The two agreed, no fanfare. Maybe later on, when things were clearer in Ruby's life, they'd have a reception. But the truth was, they didn't have anyone they wanted to invite. Their lives had been so wrapped up in each other that they'd lost touch with any friends. Before they married, Ruby questioned him over and over, "You're sure? You know what you're marrying when you marry me?" Steve's

205

answer was always their inside joke. "Love is never having to say you're sorry." Ruby learned to trust his words. Take them as the rock of commitment between them. Yet at times, over a cup of coffee or while painting, she'd shake as if stricken with the flu, delirious from fever, waiting, wondering if Steve would leave.

His divorced parents were the only guests. Ruby barely knew them. She watched them with severe caution, saw Steve's body weaken, his shoulders roll over, his confidence wane around them. Once, they'd trekked to Manhattan for Passover to his mother's lavish, antique French-decorated apartment encased in beige and light blue walls between Lexington and Park. Steve's upper crust mother Dorothy—a bank president's daughter—was polite and smooth. She welcomed Ruby with a slight coolness in her warmth. The only time Ruby had met Steve's father had been the previous year on Thanksgiving. He lived on Bedford Avenue—where the rich Jews lived—in a five-thousand-square-foot, five-bedroom, three-bath, stone-and-brick home. Steve had grown up in the house. When they arrived for the family holiday, Steve was pissed that George, his father, had redecorated the mansion in modern décor with straight blacks, reds, and whites. The art nouveau furnishings mismatched his father's unkempt, swirling, loud personality. Big George, who had an empire of car dealerships, hugged Ruby too many times, with too much sensuous gusto, and she nudged Steve to leave early. But George insisted they stay for blueberry pie and vanilla ice cream. Ruby complained of a migraine. They left as the ice cream melted on the crisp crust.

Ruby didn't really want them at the wedding, but Steve, who rarely saw them, felt obliged. Ruby stood distant, took note of his parents' every move. His father showed up for the wedding plump for the picking, suited up in a navy Armani, black-dotted tie and some god-awful cologne that stunk of cedar and wild horses. His mother— sophisticated and swank in a simple black dress and pearls—came with her new boyfriend Henry, who was balding but had a warm curly smile. Steve's younger brother Mark was off somewhere in Africa with the Peace Corps and couldn't get permission to leave. So there they were, the five of them in Rabbi Gutman's little sanctuary of biblical texts, surrounded with a spiritual ease that comforted Ruby in a way that made everything minimal and lusterless. Ruby was content with this scene of marriage. Perfect with it, in fact, as the rabbi pronounced them man and wife. In a strange way, the rabbi's blue eyes felt like home to Ruby. There was a calling in them, a way back to something that Ruby remembered as a child. At that moment, she missed her odd and sensational visions of Marianne. Longed for them. Were they gone? No, she felt, no, they waited for her.

But as Steve placed the ring on her finger, she forgot her past, smiled with assurance as he broke the glass and they kissed.

Their agreement: Ruby would move to Florida and they'd fly up two weekends a month to visit her mother. She knew they had to start a life that was theirs. Leah agreed to sell the house, and the transaction was done through their attorneys.

As Ruby and Steve packed up the last residuals of the Goldsmith home, the phone rang. Reluctant, Ruby answered. A voice whispered, gentle with compassion. A glaze of fog washed over her eyes as the doctor on the other end spoke, "Your mother just died."

Ruby hung up, too paralyzed to talk. Without looking up, without a ripple of movement, without texture or tone, she relayed the message to Steve. "It's over. My mother's gone."

A tiger of a cloud clawed its way across the bright sky and hid the sun. Ruby looked up. She remembered as a child, particularly on beach days, how she'd find odd faces of queens and kings, animals, castles and mountains shaped in the fluff of the clouds.

***

Impatient to leave and build a new home with Steve, she went to Dr. Rosenthal.

"I'm moving to Florida."

"There is a good psychiatrist down there. Dr. Zerkomentora. I'll send him your records." He sucked on his pipe, cool and unattached. "Ruby. Whatever you think or feel about me, I have always been on your side."

"Fine."

That was that. The road of new horizons lay before her.

Chapter 46: October, 1971 – A New Life

The steamy breeze from the bay waltzed across Ruby's face. October in Florida was uncomfortable and muggy.

A three-bedroom townhouse along Biscayne Bay disguised the fact that she was living in the South, where they still hated Jews. Ruby read the newspaper as she ate a bowl of oatmeal on her wraparound patio, feet perched up against the rail. She slapped her wrist as what seemed like the hundredth mosquito that morning sucked her blood. The headlines of a school strike caught her eye and stopped her mid-scratch. Teaching could be a way back to herself.

Since the move three months before, Ruby had felt listless, unmotivated. Her mind was a razor's edge of doubt and grief. She needed to stop her head from roaming into darkness. She had to push, force, and shove herself from past images of her mother and grandmother lying in their coffins. "They lay in peace," the rabbi repeated at the eulogy. Peace. Fragmented pieces, but no peace.

Ruby accepted Dr. Rosenthal's referral to Dr. Zerkomentora. The forty-something doctor had pimply cheeks and bad breath and was more than happy to charge $200 a session to keep her on medication. She visited his small, smoky office in North Miami for half an hour once a month. Her medications were a ritual. Like brushing her teeth.

She stuck to her decision: no more psychoanalysis, venting, screaming, or talking about her feelings. Her medication kept her mind and emotions as steady as possible. But still, a mild kind of walking depression crept in every morning. Her morning mood waited for her like a glass of vinegar, sour and drab.

She modeled the extra bedroom into an art studio where she mindlessly slashed canvases with oils and acrylics, wrote senseless yearnings full of grief and regret through the night. She painted ghosts, coffins, eyes. Ruby had become alarmingly, twiggy thin due to the fact that her diet consisted mostly of juicing fruits and vegetables, tofu, black beans, and brown rice.

Her dark moods intensified living among the good ol' boy mentality and southern sluggishness. Collins Avenue, hotel row, the hustle and bustle, coconut milk, sunscreen, Wolfies, and the smell of sauerkraut and knishes were remnants of her Florida childhood memories.

Florida's flat land was paved with eerily empty streets, a random bus here and there, no trains to hop on to visit a museum or go to the theatre. Orange juice sun-land, grapefruit trees, tall palms, and forever blue oceans pressed against beige-white sand lined with pink shells, egrets, and flamingos with their skinny legs. These were Florida's cultural sights. No Bloomingdales, Macy's, or Waldbaum's supermarkets. Only Publix. It didn't carry *yartzheit* candles. Chinese restaurants with checkered tablecloths that served milk with lo mein and eggrolls. Why had she moved, again? Start a new life with Steve? Even the gargantuan palmetto bugs in this tropical climate were alien, and creepier than any Brooklyn roach. The lethal depravity coiled Ruby's nerves into a volatile combination of tyrannical anger and collapsed sadness.

Her bliss was long strolls along the quiet beach at sunset. She'd slap her toes in the white crested waves, her eyes blinded by the hot sun, perspiration moistening her tanned skin. But Ruby couldn't go another month without work. She licked the bowl and sighed. Teaching was better than nothing.

Barefoot and clad in the white shirt Steve had worn for work the day before, she opened the French doors that led to the sleek marbled kitchen. The feel of the cool wood fanned by the central air conditioning coated the soles of feet with pop and vigor. She stuffed the dish into the washer and hurried off into the shower. Quickly blew out her mass of curls and piled them on top of her head. She masked her lashes with mascara, dabbed red lipstick on her lips. She threw on a bright blue ankle-length skirt, styled her white shirt with a brightly colored bead necklace and large red hoop earrings. One last glance at her fake persona of a happy woman ready for fun in the sun, she grabbed her portfolio and bag filled with art supplies and dashed out the door. She glanced at her gold Rolex. Ten o'clock. As good a time as any.

Chapter 47: Afternoon, October, 1971 – On Strike

Ruby pushed through the angry crowd. White shirts, bandanas, and Lee jeans swarmed around her. Posters swung in the air, bullhorns heightened screams in voluminous cacophony, "Pay raise. Pay raise." Swarms of discontented employees circled like wolves every which way. The smell of stale pizza, crushed cigarette butts, and cold coffee reminded of Ruby of her college days.

"Scab. We're on strike." A filmy spit splat at Ruby's feet. She tightened her grip on her portfolio and art case filled with pastels, colored pencils, and drawing pads.

"Asshole." Ruby marched through the mob.

As she walked toward the school she noticed that there were few windows, no bricks, no steps. Just a neat, square, indefinable drab yellow building. Nothing that shouted, "Use your imaginations, kids."

Once inside, the noise was higher pitched. The old familiar school skunk-smell hit her face. Students ran through hallways, slammed doors. An authoritative female voice blasted from a loud speaker. "All children in classrooms now! If any child is found running, roaming or racing through the halls you *will* be expelled."

Like bees darting to honey, the students buzzed and flew through the corridors.

Ruby approached a rusty blue door that read *Mrs. Rheinholdt, Principal,* and knocked.

A muffled voice replied, "Come in. Please, come in."

Ruby snuck into the office, stood still. A white-haired, small-framed woman, hands held over her ears, sat behind a chipped oak desk. As soon as Ruby entered, the frenzied woman straightened up and stroked the sides of her temples. She cleared her throat. "And you are?" The elderly principal rustled papers around and clicked a stapler mindlessly as she spoke.

"I'm Ruby Berg. I'm here to teach art. If you can use me today, that is." She rubbed her nose.

"Really? You seem unruffled by the goings on. You know you're crossing a picket line, don't you?"

"This strike gives me a chance to get a foot in the door. I'm passionate about teaching art to children."

Miss Reinholdt raised a brow. "You are, are you?"

"Yes. I am." Ruby shifted from one foot to another and gripped her art belongings. "I have samples to show you…and…"

"That won't be necessary. I need you today."

A blast of sirens whirled from outside. Mrs. Rheinholdt whizzed her chair around to face the window. She rolled up the blinds. "Someone's fainted. Good. That will keep them quieted down." She swirled back. "Now. I'm giving you the fourth and fifth graders. There'll be three shifts of children, half-hour time slots. The younger ones are going to watch a film. I've ordered security to pile them into the lunchroom, which doubles as an auditorium." She stopped and scratched her white flat hair, "Many students aren't attending class because of the strike."

The principal glanced at her watch. "It's ten-thirty. I'm closing school at noon. So do what you can." Her fingers were bony and laced with age spots. "Thank you, my dear. Maybe if this works out, we can have you on as a regular." She held onto Ruby's hand with an unusual strength. "The only thing…no dangling earrings and bright flowery skirts. I like to keep it toned down. You understand? Besides that, thank you again."

Ruby fondled her earrings. "Okay. I'll do what I can with the students." She took a breath and glanced down at her outfit. "Just point me in a direction and I'm there."

"Down the hall, first door on the left." Mrs. Rheinholdt swiveled her chair to watch the commotion outside. "Thank you, dear. God bless."

"Well…God bless you too, ma'am." She giggled and ran out of the office, trotted to the classroom.

Three security guards blew whistles and waved children around like they swatting flies. What was she doing here? She didn't know how to teach. A degree in fine arts didn't mean she knew anything about the minds of children. What if one of her whacked out mood swings invaded her in the middle of the classroom? What if…what if…she fucked them up because she'd say something weird, did something that was too arty, too freaky. Too…? *Stop!* Ruby stood still. Her mind was compulsively musing. *Shit.* The medication didn't stop her insecurities and doubts, only the visions. She calmed down, took a breath.

Before long, she entered the classroom. Ruby counted thirty heads seated at moveable desks. Kids were talking, reading, or sleeping. It was a mix of cultures.

Shoulders back, she marched into the room and placed her bags onto the lopsided desk and clapped her hands. "Wake up. We're going on an exploration today."

None of the children paid attention. They continued to engage in the nothing they were doing.

Ruby sat on top of the desk, lotus style. "We can sit here for the next half hour and ignore one another or we can do something that will jiggle your sorry asses."

That did it. The children slowly rose out of their comas and scoffed their deadpan eyes at her.

"Look. School bored me, too. I didn't care if one and one made three. I'm not that kind of teacher. I'm an art teacher. I have a trippy day planned for you guys. I may not be back after today. So I don't want to waste this moment." Ruby looked around. "You. With the black T-shirt and smart aleck grin. What's your name?"

"Leon." A tall, thin boy with braided hair and a face speckled with newborn pimples perked up.

"Ok, Leon. Come up to the board and write any word you want to write. I don't care what it is. Anything. Then tell us why you wrote it."

At first the willful Leon studied her as if she were a piece of white chalk.

"Come on, I dare you." Ruby egged him on.

The rest of the students muffled gossip and giggles until they started to pester him. One girl with a thick side ponytail, blue headband tugging down her wild hair and Jesus-on-a-cross earrings, poked her head up. "Yeah, Mr. Big Shot. Go ahead. What's the matter with ya?"

Another boy with an out-of-control head of frizz leapt from his chair and rapped Leon on his shoulder. "Mr. Leon, teach us, man."

215

The lanky eleven-year old stood up. All puffed up and swinging his arm like a gorilla, his mouth dropped. "Yeah. Any word?" He turned and challenged Ruby. "What's your name, teacher lady?"

"Call me Ruby." Excited to get something going, Ruby straightened her attention toward this offbeat young man.

Leon strayed up toward the blackboard, picked up a piece of chalk and wrote in bold letters. MOTHERFUCKER.

The children hooted and howled. "That a boy!" a short, skinny girl with a pile of twisted braids and colored clips shouted out.

Ruby took a deep breath. "You think you scare me? Think I never saw or heard that word? Or even said it myself? What's your point?"

Leon spun into a Jackson 5 twirl. "I don't care Ms. Ruby, what you got. Like you said, you'll never come back. So why should I care?"

Ruby pushed off the desk. "I said I don't know if I'll be back, but I didn't say I didn't care."

Leon folded his arms. "I feel not'n. Not'n at all."

"Good. Great. Feel nothing." Ruby pulled out the colored pencils, oil pastels and pads handed them to each student. "You! Leon. Write, draw, do anything you want around the word. Anything."

Leon eyed her. He grabbed the chalk. The students waited in anticipation.

Leon moved smooth and slow and drew. Images, shapes, dark, light, dragons, stabbings, jails, a heart with a knife through it. Frenzied and lost in his creation, he moved like a water snake, gliding through the ripples. Filling up the board, he reached the edge and came to a screeching halt, threw the chalk to the floor.

"Stand back and see what you've created." Ruby encouraged him. "Now the rest of you do it. Just do anything on your pads."

Her instincts served her. She had chosen the one student that led the pack. A hushed marriage of crayons against paper, busy hands in motion, writing, drawing, deep in their bodies, the students freed themselves from the jails they built around their hearts in order to survive. Ruby sucked them in. It was a good meal. Juicy and alive. She identified with them, their pain. They might see her as a fleeting handful of salt, but she knew their insides, their souls, and she could feel a holocaust a mile away.

These discarded kids became her terrain, her home, her garden to grow.

Chapter 48: Fall, 1972 – Somewhere to Go

Mrs. Rheinholdt held to her word. Ruby was hired as a full-time art instructor for the following year. Rumor had it that Ms. Ruby allowed students to paint and write stories, even if they used four-letter words.

Then something shifted inside of Ruby. The more attached she was to the students, the more she accessed the artist/teacher in her, the less her marriage worked. Once her savior, Steve was now the wall that stood between her and her artist's life. The higher he climbed the money tree—making partnerships, attending cocktail parties, engaging in idle talk about trips to Europe and five-bedroom homes, golf weekends in Key Biscayne, and dinners in exclusive restaurants—the more Ruby felt like a clown, a fake impression of herself.

She went back to her easels and began to slap paint around canvases. Attempted to conjure up images. All she could muster were shaky lines and curvy charcoal faces. Her desire was misty, her longing lacked luster. But in that murkiness, the writing became more dominant. One sleepless night, she asked Marianne: *How do I fill this empty void with love?*

I cry and cry and cry. This question rocks my soul, as the earth shakes beneath a quake. This empty place, this place where light struggles to enter is the place where the great spirit of the feminine lives.

You are human and yet you are searching for love in a way that takes you away from that void. The void is the answer. It is the mystery. And how this void affects you as a woman, loving in different ways as the sun loves us in different ways.

We have made rules of love. Marriage is a rule, and yet it fits if you have truly found your other. But there are others who might come on your path that give you pieces of yourself. I know you ache to know what is right or wrong. But there is no right or wrong. Maybe you are not ready to know. Maybe you need to journey into yourself and experience the fragmented pieces and find the true answer within.

Does this sound confusing? Life is confusing. How did I know the rabbi was my other? I didn't. There were others for me. You only know of him, because he was my last. But there were many until I knew him. I was his equal. He gave me the final piece and then there was only me to know.

Every entry seeped into the cracks in her heart. Was she talking to herself or was this Marianne? Something tugging and tearing, something ancient and erotic. She wanted more of this inquiry. More of this burning unknown. The writing grounded her, transported her into herself. It was different than the paintings. With her paintings she floated out of her third eye into a buried civilization.

Ruby thought about renting a studio on the beach. Giving herself alone time to write and paint. But she was afraid. Afraid of losing Steve. Afraid of conjuring up feelings dead and gone. Afraid of finding a stranger within that seduced her away from her safety. She clung to conformity and bordered on a breakdown. She gossiped with teachers about the latest nonsense; massages, facials, acrylic nails, juicing vegetables to cleanse and stay thin. Who was the best yoga teacher, what meditation brought inner peace? She wanted respectability. She hung off of Steve's arm at company dinners and cocktail parties like one of his cuff links. Ruby played the game, stuffed her emotions down, her hunger down, her past down.

Ruby didn't want to ignore the forgotten life bursting at the seams. And yet, she mastered the art of denial, while living in delusions that seemed real.

Ruby pushed hard against the student's creations. Forced them to go deeper and deeper. Let all hell break loose. She introduced guided imagery to stimulate the student's imaginations. Imagistic music played as she stimulated their senses beyond the stars, suns, and universe.

Then one afternoon, a tiny voice called her name. "Ms. Ruby."

Ruby looked up from the drawing she was examining. A frail, sad-faced, disheveled little student named Carlita stood by her desk. She always sat in the back. Never made much noise. Ruby thought her etchings mystical and curious. But the little munchkin would never speak to Ruby, and Ruby thought her too fragile to confront. She placed her hand on Ruby's shoulder.

Ruby patted her hand. "Are you all right?"

"Do you see Mary?" The student's big brown eyes sparkled with curiosity.

"Mary who?" Ruby blinked.

"Mary Magdalena. She told me to ask you." She held up a drawing with Marianne's face.

Ruby blinked. She began to perspire. Her hand shook. Ruby swallowed, held the child's hand. "What makes you ask that?"

The girl played with Ruby's fingers. "Mary helps me. I pray with her." Carlita's breath was shaky. "My daddy shot my mama. She's in heaven. My daddy's in jail. I live with my grandma and she hits me so I'll go to sleep at night. She says a good smack makes you tired, better than anything else." She teetered forward, about to fall down.

Ruby caught her, horrified at the child's confession. "Oh, my god!" Ruby's voice rose.

Students stared.

Ruby stroked her hair. "I understand, Carlita. I understand. I'll help you. I promise. As soon as class ends, we will go the principal."

Carlita's eyes welled up in tears. "You must be an angel. You'll save me from hell?"

"Carlita, you're the angel. You're never going to hell."

"Mary talks to everyone who hurts bad."

Ruby stroked Carlita's tears away. "It's going to be okay."

Carlita rubbed her eyes and wandered back into her seat. Went back to drawing. Before class ended, Carlita placed a drawing of vines wrapped around a body on Ruby's desk, and disappeared without saying goodbye. Shocked at the child's drawing, similar to the one she once drew in Rosenthal's office, Ruby mindlessly tore it up. Held her twittering panicked breath. Smiled to cover up the rising anxiety and disjointed memory.

At the end of the day, Ruby rushed to Mrs. Rheinholdt. "Carlita's grandmother is beating her."

"Call social services, Ruby. That's your job." Rheinholdt shuffled papers around her desk like spinning tops.

"Will you back me up?"

Rheinholdt's gaze locked onto a piece of paper like it was a biblical text, held it close to her face. "She told you, not me."

"What's the number?" Rigid, squeezing all her anger into her belly, Ruby's chest heaved.

The principal slammed drawers open, tossed aside notepads until she found the list of emergency numbers. She slapped through the pages. "Here, here it is. Take a pencil."

Ruby took the pencil. "Okay. Go."

"788-4000. Extension 202." Rheinholdt closed the book and returned to her clerical duties.

"Why don't you care? What is wrong with you?" Ruby threw the pencil back on the desk.

"Listen. I've been there. All idealistic. Thinking you can save a child. They're all the same. These children. All the same. She's probably making it all up anyway. I've met Carlita's grandmother. She's a hard working, good woman. Goes to my church." She handed her Carlita's file. "Here."

Ruby scratched her neck. It was red and irritated. She snatched the phone and dialed. "Hello? Yes. My name is Ruby Berg. I'm a teacher at North Frontier Elementary. I want to report a case of abuse." Ruby read from the file, "Carlita Ramona Munez. 131 SW 3rd Street. Okay. Okay. What do you mean? She told me. Her grandmother beats her. She told me. Gees! Okay. Thank you." She hung up. "The case worker will be sent out tomorrow."

Ruby slammed the door as she left Rheinholdt's office.

****

The next day, Carlita wasn't in class. Ruby called and called, but the recording kept repeating. "This number has been disconnected." Mrs. Rheinholdt wasn't surprised, nor remotely concerned. Dryly reacted, "An old story that I have no control over."

Ruby's distress mounted. Two weeks passed. Carlita stuck in Ruby's head. Her energy changed. Hyperactivity and anxiety increased her compulsion to drive the children to paint. She brought in crystals, gongs, and music to stimulate the children's souls. Lectured on creating their own reality, meditating with them, forming ancient circles of prayer. She felt a pressure in her head and gut that caused her to throw up at night.

Ruby needed connection. Needed to know she wasn't crazy. Steve. She had to tell Steve.

Chapter 49: Dinner With An Intimate Stranger

That night as Steve ate a bloody steak and downed a Coors beer, Ruby nibbled on grilled tofu, brown rice, and veggies. Ruby rambled on about Carlita.

Steve listened with light intent. Scarfed down his meal, shook his head, gave an *uh, huh,* here and there. "These kids, Ruby…you can only do what you can do. Don't get so involved."

"Don't get involved?" She sipped a glass of water. "Don't you see? These kids, they remind me of me…"

"Come on, Rub. Your father never murdered anyone."

"But my mother…Steve. My mother, my sister…it's in my body, my genes." Ruby wiped her mouth and cried out. "You don't get it. I need you to get it."

"You're getting yourself sick."

"I care about these kids." She threw her fork down. "Why am I doing this with you? What makes me so needy for your understanding?"

"Ruby. I hate seeing you like this."

Ruby shook her head. "Seeing me like what? Stop talking to me like I'm a two- year-old who needs a lollipop to shut her up. This is it. Me. What do you want me to be?"

Steve slid his chair near her, pulled her onto his lap. Ruby resisted. "I don't want to do this. I'm not your baby doll." She ran into the bedroom, slammed the door and counted the popcorn dots on the ceiling. She fell asleep rolled up in the blankets, her clothes damp and used. Soon, she felt Steve's nakedness slide along her back. His strong arms wrapped around her, his legs tangled with hers. He whispered, "I don't want a baby doll. I want you."

"You don't even know who I am. I want you to come to therapy with me."

Steve's arms stiffened. "What do you mean?" He pulled away, sat up on his elbow. "You don't even go anymore."

"I know. But the medication is not the answer for what is happening in our relationship. I can't do this. I need to be heard. I feel like I'm trying to be something I'm not. I don't want to stay together because it's safe. I want deeper conversations."

"Do you love me?" Steve cupped her face, looked into her eyes.

"Oh please, Steve. Do I love you? Love takes work."

Steve drew her closer. "Work?"

Ruby pulled away. "So, you're all normal and I'm the crazy one that you take care of so you get to feel superior?"

Steve inched away from her. "You think you're the only one who needs taking care of? I need to be heard!"

Ruby touched the edge of his fingertips. "That's why I want us to go to therapy. Find our way through this together."

"I'm so tired, Ruby."

"Me, too. I'm exhausted." Ruby started to drift into sleep. Her dreams transported her into a cave, where blackness engulfed her. Deeper into her dream, she heard the scream of desperation. A familiar voice, Marianne's message. *"Dig deeper. Find yourself. If you don't tend to what is hidden within, what is within will destroy you."*

Ruby jolted up in the bed. Opened the drawer and pulled out a journal. *"We deceive our partner when we make him or her into an object, and we deceive ourselves when we call this love."*

Chapter 50: Next Day – Witch

Rheinholdt stormed into Ruby's morning class. An ear-splitting scream broke the busy buzz of the student's imaginations. "I want to talk to you, now!" She marched out.

Ruby turned to the children, "Keep drawing." She followed the principal into the hallway. She tapped her foot. "Yes. What is it?"

"You're fired. You're a devil. This is a Christian community." Rheinholdt paced.

Ruby tightened her fist. "What are you talking about?"

"Get out. Get out now. I thought you were someone I could trust. You're crazy."

Ruby's face reddened. She felt her body tremble. The walls spun, slinked back and forth in her vision. "But you know what I've done for these students."

"You've poisoned their minds. With your crystals, and weird music that sounds like you're hypnotizing the kids. Taking them into Jew stuff, making them turn against The Lord Jesus. Believing there's more than Jesus. That they can do and think whatever they want. Making them think they can be God."

"Where is this coming from?"

"These students aren't God. Parents are stunned and fuming. You've gone too far, Ruby."

"You're a Jew-hater. That's what this is about." Ruby shouted.

"This is my school. And…and you're out. You don't belong here."

"Anti-Semitic. The whole system." Ruby leaned close to her.

"You're right. I'm a witch-devil and I put a curse on you."

She ran. Stumbled outside into her green Toyota and sped home. Ocean light, palm trees, clouds floating past the hot sun calmed her down. She attempted to turn on the air-conditioner. It was broken. Of course, why not? Let everything go wrong. Light beads of sweat layered her neck. Her underarms soaked the edges of her dress. Her Shalimar now smelled like dirty socks. She opened the window and let the Florida air swirl around her face. The warm flow only irritated her. She slammed the dashboard. She wanted a hot dog, to play red light, green light, feel her grandmother's hands, smell the garlic and parsley. Leah flashed through her mind. An ache grabbed her chest. She rubbed it. She felt so far away from anything familiar. She made a sharp turn. The wheels screeched. She thought of Joel and India. What was he doing right now? She kept breathing to prevent herself from passing out. Keep breathing. Keep breathing. She had to make it home. She blasted the radio. "Lean on Me" wafted through the speakers. Who could she lean on?

She arrived home, stumbled out of the car and trampled through the front door. To her surprise, Steve was sitting at the kitchen table drinking a Schlitz.

Ruby staggered to a wicker chair and swiveled around like a two-year-old. "What are you doing home?"

"It doesn't matter." He scraped the label off the bottle.

"What's going on, Steve?" Ruby kicked the opposite leg of the table. "Look at me. What's going on?"

"One of the partners had a heart attack." Steve slumped over. "His wife left him…and then the next thing, boom, heart attack. He's not doing good. They don't know if he'll pull through."

"Which partner? Wow."

"George. He's thirty-nine."

"I'm sorry. That's rough. His wife left him?"

"Yeah." He looked away.

Ruby touched his cheek. "Look at me."

"I can't."

"Why?"

"I don't know what's going on between us." He flinched at her touch.

Ruby slid her head into his hands. "What are you feeling?"

"I feel out of control of my life." Steve stroked her hair.

"George didn't have a heart attack because his wife left. You know that?" She perked up. "This is about your parents. You're afraid we're headed for a divorce?"

Steve rubbed his temples. "Going to therapy means we're headed for a divorce. I know it. If you don't love me, just say it. You're off in your worlds that I can't enter into. I'm working all the time. I thought we could make our lives normal. I don't know what I'm doing. Life goes just like that." He snapped his fingers.

"What are you saying?"

"I don't know. Maybe it's all hitting me. I've been so strong. Trying to be the man. Trying to make you safe. I don't feel safe."

"So. Don't be strong. Be whatever is true for you."

"My father had heart attack when he was forty. I could be headed there."

"You never told me that about your father."

"I've been so angry and pushing him out of my mind."

"I understand. You know I do. Don't you?" She slid the chair closer to him. "Think about how we got married. Think, Steve. Both of us running away from our past. Therapy was survival for me so I wouldn't go down with the ship. But therapy for us would be an anchor. You know what I mean?"

Steve got up, slumped over the refrigerator and grabbed another beer, flipped off the cap and drank. His Adam's apple chucked in unison with each slurp. "Let's have a child. That will settle both of us down."

"Are you kidding? Are you listening?"

"I'm ready." Steve leaned back into the chair.

Ruby shook her head. "No. Fuck no. And No! I'm not ready on any level. I just got fired today. I'm not ready. Can't you see? How can I bring up a child? I can't even grow up myself. I'm so fucked up, I'd fuck up a child. We're both not ready."

"Fired? Why were you fired?" Steve's eyes drifted into deep pools of fear.

"Because I'm a Jew-witch."

"What the hell does that mean?" He put down the beer.

"It doesn't matter. All I was doing was trying to teach the kids to love themselves. Let them express through art. Not be afraid of who they are. But maybe I was just trying to make myself feel better and escape from my own problems. Live through them. Maybe I was just manipulating these kids? I don't know anymore."

Steve's eyes softened, he put up his hand. "Stop. Let's stop for a minute. We need a minute. Let's go for a light dinner. Walk along the beach. We need to just do that. Let's just do that."

Ruby sighed. "Okay. Yeah. Let's just try to be together. I need to relax. My brain feels like it is going to explode."

They both took long breaths. A vacant space grew between them. They grasped each other's hands.

Chapter 51: That Night – A Choice

Ruby tossed and turned that night. Cried out from her dreams. Steve tried to comfort her, stroke her back, but she pulled away. Felt anxious and uneasy to be touched. She was far gone in a world he couldn't enter.

Around her were the voices. Strange, hard and soft aromas strung through vibrations of lavender, then mud and arid dung. She climbed the stones, her footsteps into the mountains, away from the villages, the people's sweat and gore, scabs, and leprosy of the soul. She was the one. She was one chosen. She heard beyond in her heart's ears, in her gut, her eyes. Everywhere, the others stood in their untouchable, iridescent bodies. Her dreams kidnapped her mind. The drugs couldn't stop the onslaught of her subconscious.

Many beings came to call upon her that night, nipping at her ear, pulling at her skin, licking her toes. Ruby dreamt that she walked to the kitchen. Hungry for Oreos. She opened the refrigerator. Tiny creatures ate them. The ethereal beings snuck into her cells, her DNA. She tried to pull them out like splinters. Around her generations spoke to her from the leaves, the rosebushes in her front yard, from everywhere. They were behind floating molecules, her mother's stormy eyes, Sarah's tough skin. The ancient women danced in circles with Claire and Sarah.

They came in small pieces, small dots of light, then grew into arms, legs, mouths, faces, eyes, dark eyes, fierce eyes, determined eyes. Determined to speak. *We are here. Your female ancestors.* They say, *listen, you're building the temple. You're building your temple.*

You're the maverick queen, pitchfork in hand. You must stand and tell the others. We don't fly, we walk the earth among you. Bumping into you in your dreams, waking you from sleep where you are falling, down, down into the abyss, to awaken out of the nightmare.

One voice repeated, over and over. *I won't stay away, Ruby. I'm Marianne. I'm the warrior of the heart.* Ruby saw her bloodthirsty eyes. *I am the soul. The feminine.*

Ruby struggled to awaken. *Wake up!* She was paralyzed. *I'm in your bubbling blood. Bubbling mind and bubbling voice that stutters the words of truth.*

With a gasp, Ruby shot awake. Soaked, shaking, cotton-dry mouth, she licked her lips. She turned her head left, then right. Nothing. Steve. Steve. Where was he? "Steve." Ruby called out. No answer. Over on the end table, the clock read 4 AM. *Oh my god.* Where had she been? She wiped her neck from the night sweats. Subtle sounds ran through her. Faint whispers tugged her back. She slapped her cheek. *Wake up,* she shouted at herself. *Get your ass out of this bed. Now, Ruby.* She clawed at the covers. This is real. This room. The fan. The shutters. The whirring of the air conditioner. The smell of burnt coffee. *This is real, Ruby.* She slipped out of the bed. Still wearing her clothes from the day before. She wiggled out of them, stood naked. What was she going to do with her life? *Just what, Ms. Ruby?* She stroked her breasts and thighs. Nausea swept through her stomach and throat. She ran. Head over the toilet, she heaved. Flushed. Watched the water circle down and around. Down and around. Down and around into the earth.

"Are you alright?" Steve shouted.

"Where were you?"

"I needed some water. Do you need me?" Steve shouted again.

"No."

"I'll go." Steve's words lingered.

"Where?"

"To therapy with you."

Ruby placed her head against the cool bathroom tile and cradled her body.

"Thank god. Thank you, Steve. I'll arrange it."

Chapter 52: Two Weeks Later – Couples Therapy

On a clear Florida day, Steve and Ruby sat on a paisley couch in the waiting room of Frank Luria, MSW, a marriage counselor recommended by her psychiatrist, Dr. Z. He was supposedly the "best" in the field.

Steve left work early that day for the session. He was still in his suit. He ripped his tie off and balled it up into his pocket. Ruby, comfortable in a white granny skirt, white T-shirt, and gold sandals, studied the room. Back issues of *Time*, *Newsweek*, and *The Miami Herald* were piled up on a rectangular glass table. Nothing frilly to read in this office. Steve picked up a magazine and thumbed through it.

"You nervous?" Ruby touched his hand.

Steve fumbled with the magazines, sniffed the air. "Does it smell like bad breath in here?"

"Yeah. You're nervous." Ruby took a nail file from her pocketbook. "I need a manicure."

Ruby glanced over at Steve intermittently as she spruced up her nails. She eyed his tight jaw and tousled hair. What would come out of him? Minutes seemed like hours and Steve soon removed his jacket. Ruby crossed and uncrossed her legs. She was about to bolt when the door leading to the private office opened.

"Steve and Ruby Berg?" A slim man with a minor belly bulge stood in the doorway. From the looks of it, he was in his early forties, and wearing a green polo shirt, jeans, and brown shoes. His bright brown eyes and stubbly beard reminded Ruby of a magician about to grab a rabbit out of his pants.

He smiled and a chip on one front tooth caught Ruby's attention in such a way that she could see the football that broke it as a teenager. Ruby didn't know if she was just having another delusion or was actually getting a psychic hit. And why didn't he get that cracked tooth fixed anyway? His laid-back demeanor surprised Ruby, who was used to formal, intellectual, bigger-than-life shrinks. His pastel blue socks and unkempt hippy hair filled her with a sense of relief.

"I'm Frank." He stuck out his paw of a hand.

Steve caught the therapist's hand and stood up.

Frank then turned toward Ruby and held out his hand. "Hello."

Ruby gripped his hand, wanting to show an air of confidence in her handshake. Instead, she stumbled as she reached out and almost knocked him over. He caught her fall. Ruby grinned, pushed herself upright. "Sorry." She looked down at her feet.

"No problem." Frank waved them into his office like the Pied Piper. "Come in."

Light streamed through the room from the large window that overlooked the riverfront waters. A blue couch and leather armchair were positioned opposite each other. A picture of Frank holding a bass in his hand and photos of friends and family decorated the walls. Among them were group photos of vacations to Italy, France, and mountainous regions that Ruby couldn't identify. Placed randomly around the office were African masks, goddess sculptures that, remembering them from art history class, Ruby believed were of Isis and Astarte. Placed on hand carved tables were sculpted lamps made from tree bark and stone. "A sanctuary," Ruby mumbled and snuggled into the soft cushions. "Is that the Goddess Astarte?"

Steve accidentally elbowed her as he slid onto the couch.

Ruby snapped a cold look at him, "What? I can't ask?"

"What are you talking about?" Steve edged toward the other side of the couch.

Frank sat. "Not a problem. Ask away."

Ruby kicked off her shoes and tucked her feet under her skirt. "No. It's a stupid question. Forget it."

"No question is stupid in here." Frank's eyebrows rose.

"Not according to my husband's elbow." Ruby glared at Steve.

"I don't think your husband influences anything you say or do."

Frank's eyes widened with a dark curiosity.

Steve smiled. "Oh you got it, Frank. Nailed it."

"What did I get?" Frank asked.

"Yeah, what did he get?" Ruby squinted at Steve.

"It was an accident that my elbow hit your arm. Right away you blame me for whatever."

Ruby blinked. A clock ticked. A bird chirped. Steve's words muffled into a strange buzz that crept into her ears. The smell of lavender captured her attention. She sniffed, searching for its origin, but there wasn't any incense, candles or flowers in sight. A snap pulled her back into the conversation. "What do I blame you for?"

Steve fumbled with the buttons on his shirt.

Ruby tightened her jaw. Tears of hurt filled her eyes. "Why are you acting in this puffed up way?"

Steve crumbled into a tight silence.

Frank made a time out sign with his hands. "Okay. Can we start at the beginning? Why are you here, Ruby? And why are you here, Steve? Who wants to talk first?"

"Didn't Dr. Z tell you anything?"

"I want to hear it from you."

Ruby glanced over at Steve. She watched him watch her. Why couldn't she feel anything? He was the same Steve. The boyish grin, the earthy groundedness, the warmth of his firm body, and constant, committed, solid eyes. What had changed?

"I feel lost. Alone. I want to feel closer to Steve," Ruby began.

"Tell me more."

"Can I talk? I would like to talk." Steve placed his hands on his knees as if he were getting ready to leap into a relay race. "I...I... damn...I don't know what I want to say." He sighed and leaned back. "It all gets jumbled up in my head."

Frank nodded. "Breathe, Steve. Calm down. Take a minute and see if you can locate a feeling."

Steve closed his eyes, barely allowed his breath to flow. Struggled to let his shoulders relax, control his hands from gripping his knees. He started to shake. First his lips trembled, then his eyelids, then his entire body. "I'm so angry."

Ruby reacted. "You're angry?"

"You have all your feelings, but I've kept mine quiet. Down and squelched."

"That's my fault?"

"Okay. Ruby, what bothers you about Steve's anger?" Frank smoothed his hands across the fabric of the cushions.

Ruby slouched over, put her head in her hands. For a few moments she was unable to look either man in the eye. Ruby clung to the couch.

"What do you want, Ruby?" Frank asked.

"I want Steve to listen to me. Really listen."

Steve turned to her bewildered, soft pain whitened his face. "That hurts. You think I don't listen?"

Ruby's eyes teared red, hot with emotions that surfaced like a slow boil. "I don't want to hurt you. I know you think you know me. But, goddamn! Do you really understand?" She faced him. "I feel you in my heart, but there is a wall I can't climb over. It's not you. I judge myself for so much. I'm afraid to open up. I want to. I just can't."

Steve grabbed her hand. "What is it that you think I can't hear?"

Ruby shook her head. "I can't. It's something that I can't…I don't know…it's so hard for me. I'm afraid."

"I'm as afraid as you are. And I'm angry. You wanted me to be honest. Isn't that why you wanted me to do this?"

"Yeah. But it makes me more afraid." Ruby folded into the couch.

Frank jumped in. "Fear. A good place to start."

Ruby stared off. "I started a long time ago." She saw the little girl who wanted to fly off the roof. "I was very young. And so ashamed."

Chapter 53: Marianne Calls To Ruby

Coyotes howled. Marianne was dressed in linen. Sweat flowed down her neck as her knees slipped into the velvet sand. A crack of thunder rattled the earth. It electrified the wind. Marianne fell into the arms of the turbulence.

She looked up. Above was the mountain to climb. There lived the *Shekinah*, the fire of the Divine Mother. Her name forgotten among the tribesmen.

Marianne now wandered the desert, searching for salvation, damning the warriors who had raped her spiritual sister's vaginal blood, destroyed the altars, and burned the feminine sacraments and scribes. She was pregnant with a fatherless child. The rabbi dead. She would birth this infant into a world that no longer sang the song of women. She'd teach her newborn the poetic words of creation through the seduction of the siren's call, the trance of dreams and prophecy, tolerating the unknown pain of not belonging. Her tribe of women, the temples, the rituals were gone. How would she live? 'Goddess' banned from Hebrew words. The *Shekinah* living in the ashes. Marianne knew she had to continue the lineage of women prophets. The God of herself must tell the story. She had get through to the other side. To the end of time.

She cried out. "Listen. Hear me, oh Isroyeal, *Adonai*…Holy of Holies, *Shekinah*, take me home. Sarah, Rebecca, Leah, I have not forsaken you. Don't forsake me."

She traced the Star of David in the sand, kissed it. Her mouth filled with grit and she held her belly. "Show me the way."

She started to climb the mountain. Its edges tore at the soles of her thin sandals. Stones, dust, and ragged peaks; she had to meet with her god and goddess. One could not live without the other or evil would permeate the world. She carried the torch of her soul. The Shabbot, the seven layers of the feminine, the cleansing. The fire lit the sky from atop the mountain. It raged in volcanic splendor. Her baby kicked inside.

She held tight to the vines and rocks as she ascended into divinity.

"I must carry and wake a new generation." She searched out to the sky, "Ruby. Ruby. Ruby."

Chapter 54: Winter, 1972 – Mirrors

As the season changed with dry, cool insistence, Ruby and Steve hunkered down into the therapy. Ruby found herself feeling more alone, distant; yet yearning more and more for what, she was not sure of. A black hole, an empty space: Ruby watched it grow from within. She battled with oils, acrylics, and molding clay. She threw canvases away. Wrote, obsessed with words and images that carried her into a time that had no meaning to her life with Steve. All these lives she was living. How did she make sense of them to Steve. Who and what was happening to her?

The more Frank pushed them to face the reasons they got married, the more Ruby felt abandoned and alone. She had always seen herself as the abused child, the wounded one, the insane one. The motherless and fatherless infant. Now she had to receive Steve's emotional deprivation.

At first, Ruby pouted, tightened, fought the onslaught of conversations that pried her open like a rusty jar. She hated hearing Steve's needs, feeling his touch, his desire to be heard. In Rosenthal's therapy, it was all about her. His incessant assertion to hone in on her spiritual and artistic channeling as a doorway into her wholeness. Ruby rejected that therapy. Now she again longed for the attention to be focused only on her, use her insanity as a reason to deny the world.

Steve became a mirror of all the parts of herself that were cold, distant, clinging, numb, manipulative, and collapsed. Her family's deaths and their abuse couldn't be the reason for her pain and emptiness in her marriage; it could only be the revelation for her mortality and choice to live. Steve was no longer someone she could dump her life on.

The session that day irritated Ruby. "Why do you wear shorts to every session?"

"My shorts aren't the issue."

Without a flinch, she blurted out to Steve. "I want you to save me and then I feel disgusted and repelled when you do."

"I don't want to save you anymore, Ruby." Steve rubbed his chest. "I feel this sharp pain across my heart. I'm afraid I'll get a heart attack, like my father."

Frank nodded. "Both of you close your eyes. Put your hands on your own hearts. Breathe."

They followed Frank's guidance. Moments passed. Silence and soft breathing charged the experience.

Steve burst free. "I feel hurt. Attacked and used. I see the little boy running and running." Steve shouted.

Ruby rubbed her hands together, held them to her eyes. "You think I attack you, Steve, use you?"

"I'm performing. I think I need to prove something to you. I feel inferior to all your art and your family. It's so big." He opened his arms wide. "Your problems win over mine."

Ruby stared at Steve. "So how do I know what is real with you? How do I trust you?" She paused. "I don't need that shit on me."

"I took on your shit. Didn't I?"

The two glanced at each other, then away.

Frank handed a pillow to Ruby, then to Steve. "Here."

Each one grabbed a pillow.

"Now, breathe, deep. Feel whatever sensations, feelings, anything that comes up. Breathe and let out a sound. But when you do, look into each others eyes."

Both did as Frank guided. Ruby's eyes remained wide, attached to Steve's every movement. She watched him huff, grunt. She gripped the pillow, tears started to wade across her eyes.

Both grappled, wriggled in discomfort, holding, staring, then pounding. Steve hit hard against the pillow, cried out. "I'm so alone. Alone. Alone." He fell into, down on his knees, sobbing.

Ruby was stiff, holding, until the sound caught in her throat exploded. Her mouth twisted from the pain. A roar, a stark growl, rolled from her belly. She was on all fours, screaming, crying, then dropped into a thin thread of exhaustion and weariness.

Then silence. Both apart, yet drawn to each other's pain. Each collapsed without a word, still eye-to-eye, intent and intense.

"You both have a long way to go. I'll want to see both of you individually and as a couple. Ruby, I want you to start sessions with my wife, Regina. That is the only way I'll continue. I want you both to be responsible for the depth of where you need to dig. It's a painful revelation to come into intimacy and selfhood." Frank leaned in. "So. Are you both in or out?"

Both nodded yes and in unison said, "In."

Chapter 55: June, 1982 – A Perfect Denial

Ruby felt ten years pass like lightening. Looking out at the clear blue sky as she lay out by her pool, she tried to remember when she became so apathetic and hazy. Thumbing through *The Sun-Sentinel* she saw an opening for an art show. She closed her eyes. Wondered if she could ever show her work. *No. No.* She shook her head. What for? Her art was for her healing - Marianne's healing - and she didn't feel brave about any of it. Still she was the girl, odd, broken, and lost.

Summer. Whew. Florida at its worst. School was over and she didn't have a routine. Taught art two days a week in a private school. Kept it conservative with charcoals, water colors, palm trees, beach scenes, vases and fruit. Nothing to ruffle any feathers. She frequented a bookstore called Heaven's Door. She loved to sit on the cushy chairs in the back and smell the fragrances, mists, the musk and fabric of mystery that lived in the air and on the shelves. She loved this home away from home.

The sun was strong. She wiped the sweat from her brow. As hard as she tried, she couldn't completely wean off the medications. Dr. Z. played with the dosage. Sometimes he decreased, sometimes increased them. Once, without telling anyone, she tried to go cold turkey three days straight. She threw up and shook incessantly with random visions. That was a disaster. Told Steve she had the flu. Didn't do that again.

A rumbling edged along Ruby's nerves, spurts of anger and depression came and went. She shrugged now. Restlessness made her jumpy. It was normal to mask her unhappiness. Writing and painting was medicine, kept the dark, chaotic visions and voices at bay. A double life. Inside outside. Ruby the channeler, Ruby the wife, teacher and suburbanite. Another wave of tremors shook her hand. She held tight to the newspaper, read without reading. She tightened, froze her emotions. She glanced at her watch. Had a therapy appointment later. Life as she knew it. A photo album on the table. Ruby grabbed it, thought for a moment before gazing through it.

Regina and Frank had become the Holy Grail, like walking, showering, flossing her teeth, drinking a cup of dark, steaming espresso. Regina was a Cuban beauty with blue eyes, steamy black hair and the hint of an accent from her homeland. She played guitar and sang Latin melodies that she'd written. Frank wrote poetry that boiled the soul and titillated erotic connection.

The sacred couple taught intimacy as a sacred journey. Ruby and Steve escaped into daylong meditation retreats with them. They learned to grope into each other's eyes, touch and stroke each other's bodies, repeat mantras that enlightened their weaknesses as strengths and brought them closer to each other's core being. They learned that fighting was an art, a practice of feeling, expressing and listening, that a good argument was passionate and life transforming. Together they learned to scream, laugh, and cry. Ruby opened the album. Leafed through. Pictures, scenes, memories.

They traveled to Greece, visited the goddess shrines with Frank and Regina. They meditated under the moon, sailed, salt in their mouths, feta cheese and phyllo pastry in their gullets. Travel helped them forget that they didn't have extended family to gorge turkey with on Thanksgiving or Passover. Mostly, it diverted them from thoughts of parenthood. The ten years compressed their relationship into the present and they grew up.

In August, Frank and Regina took a group of six to a small village built on the tip of France, where it rested against the sea. It was a steamy day. Ruby and Steve dressed cool and casual, sunglasses, sunblock, and sneakers. The splash of salt sprayed on Ruby's face. Steve stood behind her.

The group scattered around as Frank spoke and Regina took notes. "History claims that the two Marys moved to Aix-en-Provence. Mary Magdalena lived on a hill now named La Sainte-Baume, and when she died she was buried in the church at St. Maximin. In 745, because of fears of invasion and ransacking, her relics were moved to Vézelay. In 1279, King Charles II found the Vézelay shrine with its inscription explaining why the relics had been moved. He built La Sainte-Baume convent on the hill. In 1600, Clement VIII had the relics put into two stone coffins: one for her body and one for her head. During the French Revolution, many of the sacred locations were destroyed, and in 1814, La Sainte-Baume convent was restored. In the Catholic tradition, the tomb of St. Mary Magdalene is in the crypt under the basilica of the town of St. Maximin. Jesus healed her of the seven sins. But the number seven means wholeness, completeness and the feminine. Regina and I believe that Mary held the spirit of the *Shekinah*. The feminine face of God."

At that moment, as the sun dug its heat through Ruby's skin, she saw. The boat, the two Marys. From afar, Mary waved. A whisper cradled Ruby's ear. Ruby screamed. "Mary. Get out of my life!"

Everyone turned, startled by Ruby's outburst.

Steve grabbed her by the waist. "What are you talking about? Why are you so upset?"

Ruby had pulled away and ran. The visions were back.

Ruby threw the photo album to the floor. Tore the towel from her waist, buried her head in it. Things were out of hand. But, she could get it back into control. She swallowed hard, sat up. Therapy. Always the therapy.

A month after the trip, Ruby and Steve were in session with Regina and Frank. The four sat in a circle on the floor. It was a Saturday. Steve was in his running outfit, Ruby a granny dress. Frank and Regina served chamomile tea and butter cookies. The two were dressed as if about to go sailing.

Regina asked first. "What happened in France?"

"It doesn't matter." Ruby tossed a cookie into her mouth. "I'm better now."

Regina took Ruby's elbow. "Come, let's talk alone."

They walked into Regina's adjoining office. Whites and yellows, brightness painted light everywhere. Easels and canvases were against the wall.

Ruby sat on a huge orange beanbag. "You redecorated?"

"Yes. A renewal since the trip. Now, tell me."

Ruby rubbed her shoulders. "If I do, I don't want Frank or Steve to know."

"I remind you. This," she brushed a finger between her and Ruby, "is confidential." Regina, closed her eyes, took a breath. "You see or hear Mary Magdalena?"

"How do you know that?" Ruby leaned up against the cushy bag.

"We were in France talking about her and you screamed out 'Mary, get out of my life.' Remember? I can put two and two together."

Ruby lips trembled. "It's too hard to talk out loud about."

"Do you think hiding this will help you?"

Ruby shook her head. "When you hide something for so long it becomes natural."

"Not a peep for ten years, Ruby. What else are you hiding?"

Ruby's face reddened. "Other things."

Regina eyes deepened into a sea of confusion. "I thought we were helping. Are we? Am I? What have you been doing?"

"You and Frank helped me to have a life with Steve. My own life, that's a different story. I'm used to taking care of myself."

"Well...that's not going to work anymore, Ruby. Whatever you're hiding will bite you on the ass one day."

Tears waved through Ruby's eyes. "I'm sorry. I need to leave." She opened the door, peeked into the room where the two men were talking. "I'm leaving, Steve. See you at home."

For the next few weeks, Ruby watched sunsets. Drank coconut milk.

Now, she drew the ocean and intracoastal waves in Van Gogh swirls from her patio. Where did she belong? If she opened up to Regina, it could be a tremendous outlet. She didn't have friends to trust. Most often, she spent time alone strolling along the beach, the sun strong and comforting, her feet sliding into dampened sand, her childhood a lost memory between her toes. She found places to go. Coconut Grove, window-shopping, buying a funky top, or getting her hair straightened in some small avant-garde hair salon. She sat on sandy mounds and mused with the ocean waves. Her silence drew her inward, down deep into a place where she stopped hungering for the outside world. She visited Viscaya. The mansion stole her heart, gave her solace. She sketched and wrote, went home to paint for hours. Maybe she could trust Regina. Maybe. But, bringing Marianne to the surface...a trail of terror tingled along her skin like knives. Ruby coasted over the events leading to where she was now. Sitting, not knowing what to do.

It wasn't long before Steve changed the tide at a session. "I want a child."

Ruby just shook her head. "No."

Frank pushed the subject. "What do you want, Ruby?"

Ruby stiffened. "I like our lives. I don't want to fuck it up. Or possibly fuck up a child."

Steve's foot shook. His sandal fell off. "Why is my biological clock ticking and yours isn't?"

"Didn't you hear me?"

"Talk, Ruby." Frank insisted.

Ruby, tightened, her jaw hard and cold, she thought, rolled her eyes, "I need more time."

Steve shook his head. "For what?"

"Ruby?" Frank held out his hand, holding Steve's question.

Ruby stared at Frank's receding hairline. His ruffled shirt and creased shorts. Part of her felt a chill of wonder at the possibility. The other side of her feared for her life. Sucker punched. About to faint. She breathed. "Frank, how do I learn to be a mother? I never had a model of one that showed me. It's not natural for me."

"How you treat yourself, how you listen, self-care, express, is the same way you mother, Ruby. You can't plan how. You live how. You learn as you go. Just like you've been doing."

"That's it. Learn as I go. Wow, that's a way to have a child. What if I become my mother?"

"Do you believe that will happen?" Frank waited.

"Yes." She turned and saw Steve's stillness and anxiety. "And what about being on medication? I can't be on it if I want to get pregnant. Can I?"

Steve shook his head. "Is it safe for her?"

"There are risks. But they are low. Worse to be off of them than to suffer with mental and emotional reactions."

Ruby kissed Steve on the mouth. A sweet whisper of warmth swam through her heart. Steve deserved a child. At the same time she knew that wasn't enough of a reason for her to get pregnant. The urge was there, but the fear was greater.

A choked scream tightened in her throat. She gulped. Forced a strained smile. She fiddled with her skirt. A child. A road map with no directions. "Why is it so important to have a child?"

"To continue our faith. Our lineage. Our love. Our family." Steve insisted.

She glanced over at Steve. His eyes open, tanned, his body alert, smiling. Somehow, he resembled a golden retriever. All sloppy and slurpy, ready to run for any ball she threw. This was the next step. She stared at the river through the window. Slow waves rippled from the boats. Serene. Then suddenly, a speedboat tossed the water into whirlpool of turmoil. Slapped the other boats, rocking and tipping.

Ruby lingered. Spoke with focus that disguised the scream in her throat. "A baby? A baby." She held her belly. "You're sure?"

"As sure as I can be." He reached for her hand and squeezed.

"I need to talk with Regina. I'm processing a lot right now."

Steve slipped back into couch. Pouted like a wounded puppy. "Damn. Ten freakin' years, Ruby."

"I'm not saying no. It's a big decision and a lot for me to handle. Do you understand Steve? Can you ever understand whom you married? Do you want to stay married to ME?"

"And you to me?" Steve spat back.

The three sat, disengaged. Ruby opened her mouth about to say more. But a slow tide of fear washed through her. Her words trickled into pieces of air and drifted away. A child. Selfless love? At that moment she knew. The ten years of therapy anchored her marriage, but she never truly surrendered.

An egret squawked. Ruby jumped. Where was she? Oh, yes. Here on her patio. So much too soon.

Chapter 56: The Session – Faith?

Dressed in a black, ankle-length dress and gold sandals, Ruby told all to Regina. Marianne's messages, paintings, stories waiting inside. She fumbled, cried, trembled. "How could I have a baby not knowing what will happen to me next?"

"It's a leap of faith." Regina slipped next to Ruby on the couch. "You're not the first person who has had visions and messages and believed they were crazy. But, Ruby, look, look at you. Look at where you've come from. You're not like your mother. Can you trust that something different, something amazing is happening to you?"

"I don't have faith right now, Regina. Or trust."

"What will it take?"

"I don't understand anything and it terrifies me. I barely hang on."

"Your faith, and Marianne's faith will save you. We can take it step by step. One piece at a time."

Ruby laughed. "I can't fucking do that. I don't have that kind of discipline."

"It's up to you whether you can or can't. And, you might have more discipline than you think. You've accomplished a lot in spite of all the tragedy and trauma."

"Medication. Or I'd behind bars."

"I doubt it, Ruby. Medications do just so much." Regina leaned forward. "I'd like to see the paintings and read your journals."

Ruby pulled out a beige-orange journal. Opened to a page. Handed it to Regina. "Here, read this."

Regina took the book. *Mama. Stop.*

I wanted to tell you as you died, as you sat drugged on anti-psychotic medication, barely breathing, feeding tube up your nose and down your throat, because you refused to eat. I wanted to tell you as you threw me down the stairs, pulled my hair, slapped me across the face, hit me with hangers, tried to drown me in a tub of sudsy water when I was six. Mama, I wanted to tell you, as you held a knife to my throat, stood on the ledge of our window in your bra and underpants, rain pouring down and you wanted to jump and kill yourself. Mama, I wanted to tell you, no scream at you, no, grab you by the hair, squeeze your breasts and grasp your cold hands and say STOP. FUCKING STOP YOU CRAZY BITCH."

Ruby smiled, "And then there are the Marianne journals."

"You don't scare me Ruby. But it seems you want to scare yourself."

"Why would I want to do that?"

"I don't know. To stop yourself and hold yourself back? Afraid of your own power? Used to being small and hating yourself? Take your pick."

"I can't get into this, the fear…I don't want to. I'm going to go. I'm really tired."

Ruby left Regina's office. She drove to the beach. Parked and stared. The waves slapped and hushed against the sand. The day was overcast, dark clouds in the distance. Hurricane season was in full swing. Drops began to fall on her head and arms. She ran back to the car.

Steve was watching the weather station when she walked through the door. She heard the report. *Winds to the north, a front coming in from the South, tornadoes in the west.*

"I have to see if I can do it."

Steve perked up. "Do what?"

"Keep trying to get off the medication. I don't know the outcome. I just want to try."

Steve's eyes turned pure and bright. "Are you sure?"

"I don't know. Steve, there are some things I have been dealing with…it's hard."

"What? This is the time to tell all."

"Tell all. It's a real job to tell all." Ruby couldn't look at Steve in the eyes. She had an idea of what detox was like. "I have no clue what I'm doing. Having a baby, being on medication…it's overwhelming." She sat next to him on the couch. "I just don't know."

Steve grabbed her hand. "All we can do is try and see."

***

New Year's Eve rolled in. Steve had joined an exclusive golf and tennis club. There they were, in the crystal, gold, and turquoise dining room to celebrate Ruby's thirty-third birthday. Ruby studied each woman's shape and swag. The large diamond jewelry, the red lipstick, the whispers and laughs, all the women huddled ready to show and tell their boobs and asses. The men, whiskey, beer, open shirts with dark jackets, bored or impressed with themselves. Ruby shook her head. "What are we doing here?"

That's when Jim the plastic surgeon, and his wife Joan, the recipient of her husband's profession, glided into their lives. It was a serendipitous meeting. The two marched straight toward Ruby and Steve from among the wolf pack.

"We played doubles." Jim held out his hand.

"Jim Brennan." Steve stood, shook Jim's hand and sat.

Joan's smile broadened. "I watch you draw. I'm amazed that you have that talent. I love that. And you don't play tennis or talk to anyone. I like that, too."

For whatever reason, Ruby fell in love with Joan. Her verbose laugh, curvy hips, and natural blonde hair, the smooth way she slid her hand across a glass. The way she balanced Jim's heady, puffed-up doctor veneer fascinated Ruby. Joan cursed shamelessly and stood a foot taller than Jim. Joan was fleshy, warm, and had intense liquid eyes. She reminded Ruby of Brooklyn, stoop ball and hide n' seek.

Jim's jagged jaw outlined with a goatee, made his receding hairline seem attractive and mature. He wore clear-cut square glasses that enlarged his brown eyes. It was huge change for Ruby and Steve to befriend a couple.

Joan crept under Ruby's skin that night. She admitted that she hated her father. Hated playing the doctor's wife and that she was in AA. She drank ginger ale and ate a big steak. Ruby and Joan had a lot to talk about. To Ruby's surprise, Steve shared about therapy, talked about having children, and his fear of failure. Jim shook his head, saying, "Yeah, man. Yeah." It was like a truth serum had been poured into their water. For the first time, Ruby felt excited to get to know someone. Before the couple left, Joan said, "I like you. We'll talk more. Lots more." Kissed Ruby on the cheek and hugged Steve.

Jim gave them both a thumbs up. "You guys are a breath of fresh air. No bullshit. We'll get out of your hair now. But not for long."

After they left, Steve slid a new diamond wedding band on Ruby's finger. They finished their dinner, drank champagne, ate penne pasta with basil cream sauce. Jim and Joan brought new hope for something different to happen in her life. Friends. Something she never truly had.

A friend instead of a therapist to talk to. Another woman who wasn't afraid to tell the truth.

Chapter 57: 1983 – Too Damaged

From her bedroom, Ruby watched the summer wind slap the palms. She wrote: *"She wrestled, out of her own dark slime, images that capture her primal essence of the animal-like nature she tried to escape. Going into the uterus of the Great Mother, she reconnected with the seeds of her own creativity."*

Anxiety mounted. She stopped writing, pulled her fingers through her mangled, frizzy curls. It brought back her mother's frustration at trying to brush the tangles. Her younger insecurities started to resurface.

Dr. Z was against weaning her off the medication. Regina supported it. At the end, it was Ruby's choice. She got to a lower dosage, but the detox was challenging. She had sleepless nights and cold sweats. A series of dark dreams set off panic attacks. She started to feel undone, unmade like her bed. The eleven years of therapy wilted in her veins as she tried and tried to get off completely.

She guzzled a steady flow of merlot and chardonnay. Sometimes a bottle each day. At the moment she was holding her third glass.

Maybe she was too damaged to love, have a baby? What did she know about mothering? She placed the glass of wine on her dresser, pulled out a pair of wedged shoes and bell-bottoms, dressed, pretending that she was carefree. Ha! That was a laugh. She knew she was a Jew. Jews are never carefree. Their hobby was to worry to death. How would this child, if born, escape that? Were Steve's genes strong enough to overcome the terror of mental illness? And what about Steve? His parents were divorced. His family was cold, distant, numb. What kind of a child would they make together? Maybe she'd never get pregnant because her ovaries were paralyzed in fear.

She opened the patio door, held a sketchpad, charcoals spread across the glass table. She stared out at the blues of Florida sky and water. Along the horizon she saw her ancestors hand in hand. Sarah never dreamt of living in a five-thousand-square-foot house with wood floors, couches styled in Southwest décor, lots of mauve and beige on the walls, safely tucked into a gated community. Sarah wanted freedom from Cossacks and Nazis, a hot glass of dark tea, a piece of mondel bread, and a cigarette. That was Sarah's escape.

She sat on the patio chair, drew. Why can't I just find peace with my chronic sadness? I can't make it go away. A rapid series of drawings emerged that filled the rest of the journal. Ah! Marianne's face. *There you are.* Ruby brushed away the charcoal and stared into the eyes of her nemesis.

How many years? How many would pass until Marianne's presence made sense?

Chapter 58: June, 1983 – Friendship Secret

Ruby sipped on pekoe iced tea and sprawled across the lounge chair. Oiled in SPF 30 sun block, she couldn't prevent the sun from browning her like an Israeli Sabra.

Joan slithered her buttocks across the tile toward the pool and wiggled her toes in the cool blue waters. A splash and Joan leapt in, swam across with dolphin grace. All the tennis mommies ran around the pool. Children tucked away in pre-schools, daycare, or with their nannies, they lived the good life.

Joan rose from the chlorine waters like a mermaid from an old Scottish myth. Her blonde hair matted on her shoulders and back, her soft rose skin tanned pink, her full- moon lips and high cheekbones edged to the ridge of her grey-blue eyes that held a hidden sadness. Most times, Ruby studied Joan's face like she was Vermeer's *Girl with the Pearl Earring*, her facial mystique the opposite of Ruby's dark desert looks.

"Come in for a dip." Joan dried herself with a soft blue towel, wrapped it around her waist.

"Stop it." Ruby stirred the ice in her tea.

"It's hotter than hell." Joan slapped her with the towel. "If any day is going to be the day, this is it."

"I'll shower later." Ruby gave her an annoyed stare, pulled the towel from Joan's grip and threw it on the soaked ground. "Why do you have to do that?"

"What?" Joan raised her brow. "I'm just saying."

Ruby shifted in her seat. "You know how it is for me and water."

"I'll go in with you. You won't drown." Joan covered herself with a short black pullover.

"It's not about that." Ruby furiously swirled her straw in the dark tea."Let's drop it. Okay?" She took her straw and blew some tea at Joan.

"Stop it! You can be such a child." Joan wiped the tea beads from her cheeks, leaned her head back to catch the sun's rays. "I just think you have to face your fears. Be more positive."

Ruby bit away at her nail bed like a squirrel. "Positive thinking? That crap makes me numb. Like, the other day when I said I felt sad, you said, write a gratitude journal. I needed your warmth, not a homework assignment."

"Okay, I'm not brilliant. Maybe I try to fix things. I know I want it all to be right. I want to see you smile. I need your smile."

"I know you have good intentions. But I'm happy just to be out today. That's more than enough positive for me."

"Yeah. Enough with the hermit, tortured artist thing. I guess you're right. You're out among the living."

"I don't necessarily think I'm among the living at the tennis club, Joan. I'm not even sure if there are humans among this crowd. There's enough plastic surgery around that I wonder if there's a reptilian race hiding out here."

Joan smirked. "Don't you have any social graces?"

"I don't speak the same language."

"You know, dear friend. I might be one of those reptilians." Joan lay down on the lounge chair next to Ruby.

"I converted you. My charisma stripped the scales off your body. And, oh my god, we found a human heart underneath." Ruby smiled.

"Or maybe you're the one converted. You live here. Eat here. Shop here. So what's your excuse, reptilian queen?"

Ruby squinted, her fingers twisted around the moist glass. She stared off as her jaw clenched. Placed the glass down on the small table next to her. Ruby thought she saw a spider crawl across Joan's neck and went to smack it away.

"Hey." She swiped at Ruby.

"Thought I saw a spider."

"Ugh." Joan brushed herself off with a shudder.

Ruby shaded her eyes with the palm of her hand. "Do you have to wear that gigunda ring even at the pool? It gives me cataracts."

Joan admired her six-carat, pear-shaped diamond. "I like the shine."

"Why do I hang out with you?"

"I make you laugh, oh dark lady of the night. And I put up with your moods."

"Why?" Ruby turned on her side toward Joan.

"You know why."

Ruby kicked her thigh. "Come on."

"Okay. You need reassurance. Okay. Well, because, uh…because you're brilliant, and funny and honest, and you don't judge me for anything. You're the friend I have outside of my AA and sexual recovery group that understands the horror of abuse." Joan eyes saddened. "And I am attached to you."

Ruby reached for her hand. "Thank you. Thank you." Ruby looked around. Rubbed her nose. "Joan, I need to tell you something."

Joan leaned in. "What?"

The sun steamed up. A calm of the pool's freshly splashed chlorine waved against the tiles.

"I've been trying to wean off my medications. Steve wants to get pregnant. I'm terrified." Ruby paused. " I…I see and hear…voices, faces…of…of who I think is…is…Mary Magdalene. Steve doesn't know." Ruby froze, waiting for Joan's response.

Joan sat up. "Why didn't you tell me this sooner?" She stroked Ruby's arm.

Ruby picked on her cuticle. "It's been going on since I was maybe six. I just know…or believe I have my mother's mental illness. Somehow, my childhood abuse set it off. I hate all this medication. But it's just too hard to get off. I'm terrified." She twisted in the lounge chair. "My paintings are more than my imagination. I hear and see things that are not from me. They show me stories." Ruby looked up at the sky. "What am I going to do?"

"You've got to tell him." Joan stroked her cheek.

"I don't know how. He'll leave me. I know it."

"He might be angry you lied…but I don't think he'll leave you."

"How do you know?"

"Steve won't leave you."

Ruby laid back and punched the lounge cushion. "I can't wipe out everything that goes on in my freakin' Alice in Wonderland brain trip. I'm drinking." She drowned her thoughts in the floating clouds. "What the fuck!"

"What happens when you have these hallucinations?"

"They hurt my body. Like a flu. My organs twist. She…Marianne wants me to listen and write the story. Her story. I don't get it…I paint and she's there. I dream and she's there. She is pounding at my door, wanting me. I can't stand it."

"You're amazing. I don't judge. You're amazing." She fingered Ruby's necklace. "Is this her? Mary?"

"It was a gift." She squeezed it. "Yeah. Amazing. I have a past. A wicked one. An unfinished one. A Joel Simon past. The man who fucked me into insanity."

"Joel Simon. Dr. Joel Simon?" Joan shook her head, waved her hands.

"How do you know him?"

"I read his book. *Mind over Matter*."

"Fuck that shit. I gotta go. I'll talk to you later, Joan."

"Please, Ruby. I've told you about my father and what he did to me. The midnight visits when I was nine. You've seen me at my worst. My guts hanging out."

Ruby stopped, her head slumped to her chest. She turned like a schoolgirl caught with her hand in the cookie jar. Ruby slid her arm through Joan's. "I'll do my best, Joan." Ruby drew a cross over her heart with her finger, held up her hand, "I swear. But I got to go. I have a therapy appointment." Ruby got up.

Joan reflected Ruby's devotion. "I swear, too."

They parted to opposite ends of the crowded car lot. The tar was thick and lumpy; the sky thick with red clouds, threaded through a grey sky. Torrents of rain exploded and chased them to the Mercedes they both owned, Joan's white, Ruby's red with a beige convertible roof.

Ruby slammed the car door and waited. The rain beat against the windshield. Rain. Rain, Ruby thought, the universal milk of the divine. Rain, it carried rivers across oceans and beyond. Rain, the symphony of pit, pat, patter against the pavement. The rain converged and united her soul with human flesh, drop by drop with every human, dead or alive, her ancestors' names written on the pellets of rain.

Ruby started the motor. The sky was loaded with rain, loaded with pain. Far away in the mist, she saw the little girl about to fly. Once again she heard a voice scream. But this time instead of *"Stop,"* the command was, *"Go. Fly."*

She revved the accelerator and flew.

Chapter 59: Same Day – Regina's Question

Regina's hair was tight in a bun and drew her cheekbones into soft mounds. "Come sit, Ruby." She patted her hand on the carpet.

Ruby plopped down. "I've just come from the club with Joan. I told her. I needed to tell a friend. She told me I had to tell Steve." She sprawled out. "I can't keep up with anything. Everything is moving so fast. The scenery passes me by and I don't remember the faces or frames of things."

"Ruby. Do you love Steve?"

The room dulled behind the shades and shadows. Musk incense deepened Ruby's breath into her groin. "I feel angry that you ask me that question."

"Good, feel angry."

Ruby rolled on her side. "Joan wanted me to swim today. And I felt that dead stop inside, my breath just stopped. I went numb and blank to my toes. It's all still there. All of it. And it's coming out."

"Ruby, we've been going in circles. When are you going to touch inside and allow yourself to feel and see?"

"Why can't it be simple?"

"Breathe, Ruby. Close your eyes for a moment. Just breathe."

Ruby surrendered. Minutes passed. The ticking of her life beat away. She wanted to cry, but couldn't. "Nothing makes sense."

"Does it have to?"

"My heart hurts. I can't sleep. I'm sad. I feel trapped and lost. A flash of knowing turned to rubble and regret. I want to break free of myself. What is the answer? I can't hear it yet."

"Listen, Ruby." Regina's voice softened.

Ruby drifted inward. The room fell into a trance. "I cling to life in a way that strangles the life out of it. I want to suck in life, but it sucks me dry. I'm going to die. I know it."

"Stay with that." Regina placed a pillow in her hands. "Why will you die?"

"I don't know. I deserve to die." Ruby punched the pillow, tore at its threads. She strangled the pillow screaming. "Do I love Steve? How the fuck do I know? I can't live with him and I can't live without him. I sound so pathetic, don't I? So I take out all my anger on him, because I'm stuck between worlds that don't match." Ruby threw the pillow. "I don't want to do this. Not again. I can't go into the vortex again. That demonic LSD trip."

"Maybe you did die. Or maybe the part of you that hates yourself will die. A familiar protection. You want to kill off your soul?"

Ruby held her stomach. Sobbed without relief.

Regina held her ground. "Let it burst."

Ruby was motionless. She froze ."It's too deep. Too painful. I'm afraid of myself. What I'll do."

"I know. And there is so much life that you have to live."

"What if I don't have long to live?"

"You're being called to do what you are meant to do. What is your purpose in life? You're being called."

"It's easy to give some spiritual sound bite. What do you really know? It's all just a big experiment."

Ruby got up, grabbed her bag and slammed the door. She opened her bag and shoved two pills into her mouth. Waited with erratic breath.

Chapter 60: Same Day – Warrior

By the time Ruby arrived home, her stomach was a spasm mess. She pressed the garage door opener clipped on the sun visor and ran like a frightened raccoon straight to the bathroom and threw up.

She left a trail of clothes and sandals behind like her entourage. She slid naked into the green quilt and pillows. The wicker fan stroked the air and whirled coolness in the bedroom and her body. It churned her legs and thighs. AHHHHHHHH, cool air. She leapt up and pulled all the shades down, lit three candles, and slid back under the smooth sheets and mile-high pillows. In the middle of the bed lay her journal. She opened to a page. Ruby read an excerpt from her journal out loud.

Warrior ~
Is someone who has been brought to their knees
Only to stand again
Take me down, I'll already be there waiting
I've been baking cookies and finger painting,
Dusting tables, folding the laundry
Meanwhile I've unlocked the back door,
Found my way into the sacred garden,
Camouflaged by the light...
Waiting like a hawk, like a hunter, like a tourniquet,
Squeezing pulse rays dripping grandmother poison
Which is always far worse than the ones
I alone ingest I take care to care, take no more
Pitchfork in hand I stand against it, blades of light
Checkmate this state of ignorance

Go ahead, permission to peel back the banana for your seduction
Against the wall I push splitting me taking what is not yours
Divide and conquer as you wish
Medicine women dance around me
Chanting and singing, cursing
And spitting into the fire
Medieval women who burn cookies, shit on dust rags
Fuck with their fingers and still dive for pearls
Come for me they come in to me
They fight for me
I fight for the messages they have passed down
Brought to my knees
Every morning by prayer
You cannot stab me any deeper
I am already there
Take me down
Whatever you're going to throw
Make sure you throw it hard with everything you've got
I'll take it I'll feed it to my pack of wolf mothers
The harder you push me down in the dirt
In the judgment...I will still be...I will still stand...again
In the garden you fill us unwanted with anger
Buckets of coal and lava
Volcanic diamonds sequester
Bones, breasts, vaginal fossils still rest
In ungraceful positions
This is my home, my temple to worship in
Left in the midst of discarded images
In this garden of pagan trash I ask for more please...
Bring me again to my knees I've been waiting
I'll be waiting knuckles bare, palms bare

She felt voices stomp through her veins. Ruby found a home in pages of books that inspired her painting and writing: *Gospel of Mary, When God was a Woman, The Pregnant Virgin, Hildegard of Bingen, Chalice and the Blade*. The authors wrote about a world where women were mystics.

She flipped through her journal, searching for a quote she had written from *The Pregnant Virgin* by Marion Woodman. She found it. Consumed the words. *"No amount of therapy or analysis can heal a heart that does not trust. Women need to know that to face their darkness as strength, not a weakness. This movement toward wholeness speaks to women in a new language that is heard at first with no words. Her emerging voice defies all she has been taught: to be good, to be spiritual, to be of value to the world. A woman's entry into her void from lack of recognition and dissatisfaction with society. She seeks the void to her know her divine nature."*

Ruby placed the book on her chest and snuggled into a womb-like position. Her divine nature. Regina's words, *being called*. She needed a reprieve. Rest.

She sank into the bed sheets, picked up the remote and began to surf the television. The Spanish-speaking station caught her attention. It was some cheesy soap opera. The dark haired, dark eyed woman on the show waved her hands, cried, and tore at the shirtsleeve of a dark, handsome young man. Her tears flowed endlessly, yet her mascara never ran. Ruby raised the volume. She didn't understand Spanish, but she loved the sound of it, the poetry and rhythm, the smooth sound of quick lips. She liked to feel the words instead of figuring them out, analyzing them, wondering what they meant. The passion in not knowing. Feeling their pain and hunger for love captivated her. Ruby felt the actress's angst. Crumbled when her lover wouldn't kiss her. And as lovers do, they turned away, then back, and ran toward each other. They pleaded. Love me, love me, love me. "Amore. Amore."

Soon she tired of the Spanish novella. Nobody loves like that. Only neurotic women who believed men on white horses searched for the golden chalice. She clicked to the next station. Re-runs of *I Love Lucy*; next station; *Animal House*, food fight, next station; some cooking show, flipping white fish and some slimy white liquid, yuck; next station; rich and famous people, who cares?; next station, she clicked off the television and stared into space. The shadows that ran across the ceiling calmed her. She wanted to live in the dance of the grays and blacks, sway and feel the mystery of their shapes; their non-human forms that changed into nothingness as they danced.

The phone rang while she picked up an invitation from the local JCC that lay unopened on the dresser next to her bed.

She tore the envelope apart and the phone rang again. She knew it was Steve. She stared at the phone. She picked up, said nothing. Just held it to her ear.

"Hello?" Steve was agitated.

She fingered the JCC card.

"I hear you breathing. What are you doing?"

"Nothing."

"Nothing?"

"Where are you?"

"Bed." She chewed at the edge of the card.

Silence.

"Ok. I'll be home same time."

"I don't know what same time means."

Ruby clicked the phone off. She knew she was a bitch. She picked up the phone dialed him back. "Can I speak to Mr. Berg?" She waited.

"Hello?" His voice was low with a hint of anger.

"It's me."

"I'm dictating."

"I'm sorry."

Heavy breathing. "I'm working." Steve was curt.

"Steve. I'm sorry."

"I got to get back to work."

"I'm sorry, Steve."

"It's not enough anymore." He hung up.

Ruby slid the phone gently into the receiver. She had created a monster, bringing Steve into therapy. He needed more. More. She shook. She didn't want to be with anyone else but Steve. Was that fear or love? She rubbed her stomach. It growled. She felt a twinge of hunger but she didn't want to eat. She flipped the remote and clicked the TV back on. A commercial for toothpaste. Suddenly, she realized she was holding the envelope. She pulled out the card:

JCC of Broward County
AUTHOR of *Mind over Matter* AND SPIRITUAL TEACHER
Dr. Joel Simon, Jungian Psychologist, Hypnotherapist, Past
Life Regressionist and Reiki Master. Student of the lineage of the
Kabblistic traditions and teachings
Lebowitz Wing, Jewish Community Center in Davie, FL
Date: 7:30 PM, July 14th
Fee: $50.00

Ruby dropped the card, watched it weave in slow motion through atoms of air. Joel was here? His lecture was a month away.

An ocean swept across the television screen; white waves, sun streaked crystal beads. Ruby breathed deeply. Something ominous was about to happen. She felt it in her bones. A man on a beach wore a blue shirt with red flowers. His long hair blew in the wind.

The man on the television narrated. Eyes serious. "Hawaii, where the mysterious goddess Pali lives. Lava flows from her vagina." Ruby leaned forward. She rubbed her ears. What had he said?

Ruby felt wetness between her thighs. She peeked down; blood. She tumbled out of bed. She dug her feet into the cherry wood floors and ran to the bathroom. She fumbled through the drawers to find a tampon. A voice called her name, *Ruby…it's time to come home… Ruby.* A low whooshing vibrated in her ears. She ran back to bed took a pad and wrote in bold print, *HOME, HOME, HOME…*

Chapter 61: A Dream

Ruby slept hard that afternoon. She fought the dream. A bald woman pointed the way. The woman sewed a map of the galaxies like she was an alien Madame DeFarge. "What is that?"

"Touch it." The woman slid Ruby's hand across the bulbous planets, edges of stars and meteorites. "What does it tell you?"

Ruby opened her palms and gathered the fabric of the universe in her hands. "It feels alive."

The woman's startling blue eyes slanted into shapeless mounds. Only her pupils remained visible. "Alive in you." Ruby looked into the woman's eyes. Brown and familiar, light streaming. Closer and closer. Ruby felt her eyes strike her heart. Marianne. It was Marianne.

"Come home, Ruby. I need you." Marianne touched her head and disappeared.

A sudden shift in perception came from a light in the dream. Leah leaned into the brightness. Her face ashen against the beam of white. Ruby called out, "Here, Leah. This blanket is for you."

Leah turned and faded away. A shudder of breath awakened her to the urgency of contacting her sister. She woke with Leah's name on her lips.

"Hello." Steve stood over her. His tie unraveled, his suit ruffled, white shirt undone at the top.

"Wake up, Ruby." Steve hovered over her. "You're going?" Holding the JCC invitation.

Ruby rubbed her eyes, cleared the filmy sleep from her sight. "What?" She threw off the covers.

Steve crushed into the mattress near her. "So you're going to see him."

"See who?"

"Miss Independent. Ha!"

Ruby pushed up against the pillows. "What does that mean?"

"You think you're entitled to do or say anything."

"This is the twentieth century. Women can vote now."

"And cheat?" Steve eyes darkened.

"What are you talking about?"

Steve dangled the JCC invite in his hand. "Bullshit."

"Why would you think that?"

"Dr. Simon? From the time we first met, Joel was there in the background. You'll never get him out of your mind."

"He's a childhood nightmare that I thought was a friend. But he holds a key. Maybe he can help me understand what happened to me. Wouldn't you want that for me?"

Silence. Steve glared at her. His eyes thickened with power, "I thought you hated him."

Ruby slipped out from the covers. She threw a white silk housecoat over her naked body. "You don't believe in me, Steve. I need you to believe in me."

He grabbed her. Fingered her necklace, the Mary pendant and the Star of David. "You've worn that forever. I know that nurse gave you the pendant and your grandmother the star. But I still don't understand a Star of David and Mary Magdalene together."

Ruby held her hand over his. "It's a reminder of what I still need to know."

Steve unfolded his hand from hers. "What is that? Ruby. Huh?" He threw his suit jacket down on the bed. Left the room. Ruby followed him. He sat by the black granite counter, twisted back and forth in the stool.

Ruby poured herself an orange juice and Steve jumped up and prepared a protein drink. The noise from the blender shattered the air.

"What do you want?" She sat down by the counter, leaned her head against her glass. Licked the top. "I apologized."

"I'm not sure for what." He poured the drink into a big green plastic cup.

"For everything."

"Good. Feel that apology down to your toes."

"My apology is not guilt. It's real." Ruby said.

"We're not getting anywhere."

"Where to you want to get?" Ruby asked.

"I'm sorry. But, Joel? Why would you consider seeing him after all these years?"

"It's a lecture."

"It's not just a lecture"

"What do you know? He's a professional now. An author." Ruby's face turned red.

"Your face is red, Ruby." Steve pointed. "What are you hiding?"

"Nothing! Why don't you trust me?"

"Just don't go, Ruby. I'm serious. We've got our problems, but Joel isn't the solution." He took a gulp of his drink. "Go talk to Regina. Don't go to this lecture."

"You think she'll get me pregnant faster? Getting off meds takes time. And then…"

"Please, Ruby. I can't do this with you, Ruby. You're not getting off of anything. If I knew you didn't want children…"

"I never said that. I'm trying to get off the medications. I'm so mixed up."

"I think it would help if you thought about someone other than yourself in this situation."

"Fuck you, Steve! All I did was think about other people. My mother, grandmother, Leah. Now you! How dare you say that to me? I'm desperate to heal. Desperate. You want to make me feel selfish about that?"

Steve ran his hands across *The Sun-Sentinel*. "Let's go to a movie. Get out." Steve plucked through the paper. "We need fun. Some fun."

Ruby placed her hand on his shoulder. "Don't ignore me."

"I just need a time out."

Ruby repeatedly wiped down the counter. Then strayed over to the windows and pulled down all the shades in the family room and sliding glass doors. Dark, she wanted darkness.

Steve got up and pulled the shades up one by one. "I need sunlight."

Ruby turned to Steve. "I miss an overcast New York, grey clouds, and tiny rain taps against window. Sensual, filmy, sweaty. Maybe we need a trip back. See your parents?"

"Are you for real? I don't even know what part of the world they're in."

"I'm desperate. I don't know what I'm saying."

"You're not the only one who feels lonely." He picked at his cuticle. "But all I got in me is to go to a movie." Steve slugged down his high-energy drink. Started to wash out the cup. "That's why, Ruby, that's why we got each other. For better or worse." He pushed against the sink. "Don't go to this lecture. I don't know what I'll do."

"Are you threatening me?"

"Do you realize what's at stake here? I need your commitment."

"You got it when I married you." She went back to the counter, grabbed the newspaper. "You're right, we need a break." She studied the movie selections. "*The Gods Must Be Crazy, Bachelor Party, The Natural.* What do you think?"

Steve plopped down onto the stool, held his head. "I don't want to lose you. And then there are times I wished you'd just leave. Go. Or I should go."

Ruby leaned against Steve. "I know how hard this is for you, too. I can't be or do what I'm not. Nor can you. I have a past, Steve. Not a pretty one. You know that. I ran away from it. It's haunting the shit out of me. I'm scared of losing myself forever. I've got to understand. Joel was there. He knew my family. Do you understand?"

"A damn lot he cared, leaving you to go to India."

"We were stupid kids, Steve. It's not about you. Why do you keep forgetting? I came to you in this fucked-up package. I can't just make it go away like a headache." She gripped the newspaper. "Let's see *The Gods Must Be Crazy.*"

"Ain't that the truth." Steve swung out of the chair. "I'll change. How long will it take for you to get dressed?" As he strolled away, he turned, "I can't stop you. But I still don't know how it will go down for me." He rolled his eyes. "And, I don't think exotic degrees and fame necessarily changes anyone, Ruby. He's still a bastard in my book."

Ruby ripped the edges of the newspaper. "Maybe. But pharmaceuticals didn't mend me." She got up and pulled down the shades. "And for that matter. Neither did Rosenthal or Frank and Regina." She wobbled into the bathroom, took off her robe, slid into the shower, turned on the water. She wiggled her fingers and teased the drops until it was comfortably warm. She leaned against the slick glass. Her insides twisted; she cried. Dare she go and see Joel? She turned the shower off, grounded her feet as to not slip. She wrapped a towel around her body and covered herself with the silk nighty that hung on the doorknob, scrambled to her green vanity chair, twirled around and stared at herself in the magnified mirror. Bulgy bags around her eyes. "Yuck." She applied her make-up, skillfully patted away the darkness. "Steve, where are you?" Her dark wavy hair began to dry into a maze of ringlets pushing against each without purpose or direction. She called again. "Steve."

At that moment Steve strolled in.

"Where've you been? I've been calling out." Like the artist she was, she laid out all the colors of shadows in front of her, dabbed from one to the other. Wanted the most dramatic effect on her eyes. Swiped one smooth application of foundation fully across her face.

"I was outside, having a beer with the full moon." Steve leaned against the marble counter.

Ruby stopped. "You had a drink with the moon?"

"What's so surprising?"

Ruby raised her brows. Wondered. Why didn't she pay more attention to Steve's poetic nature? "Sorry. I just…" Ruby went back to her face palette.

"You thought I was watching some basketball game. Right?" He jerked a half smile.

Why did one minute she want to jump and kiss him and the next vomit from the smell of his natural body oils? Why? She placed her attention back on her smooth cheekbones. "Don't bother me. I need to get dressed." She crimped her hair with her palm.

"I can stop bothering you forever, Ruby." Steve left the room.

Maybe she was going too far? She might destroy the one thing, the one person who was there for her? "Oh God. I'm the idiot." She blew her hair straight, bangs hung like a hinge over her brows, highlighting her big brown eyes. Got up and dressed.

"Where are you, Ruby? I'm waiting." Steve shouted.

Ruby leaned against the sink. The faucet dripped. She tightened the handle, strangled it until the drip stopped. "I'm coming."

Chapter 62: A Week Later – Do or Die

Frank and Regina sat opposite Ruby. It was mid-morning. Ruby eyed both of them, fiddled with her fingers, a muddled mess. A mosquito bit Frank's arm. He slapped it dead. Regina crossed her leg. The couple drank the usual exotic tea, dressed in matching linen and silk.

The hum in the room raced with Ruby's heartbeat. Shaky, she could barely breathe as she shared her story. "Here it is. Joel was my first lover. The man who knows my every crazy thought, crazy mother, crazy family. He saw. He was my first. He knows my secrets. I had my first full-blown hallucination with him. He…is in town. I need to see him. Need to find out what happened. What I left behind. How he saw me. What he remembers."

Regina put up her hand. "Slow down."

Ruby took a breath. "Just tell me. Should I go and see him? Steve is kind of threatening me if I do."

Frank flicked his cup. "We're not going to tell you what to do."

"Oh come on, Frank. You have an opinion. You have lots of them. And you, too, Regina."

Regina's eyes narrowed with curiosity. "Why do you think it is so important to see him?"

"I was obsessed with him. He evokes that primal side of me. The side I repressed after he left me. Our relationship was left in a middle of a sentence."

Frank and Regina moved about, but didn't say anything.

"I need a yes or no."

"It seems urgent and unfinished for you." Frank shook his head.

"I closed the door tight on him, on my life. I shoved that part of me, Joel in me, into a fog, into a box of shit...I hated myself. Hated him. And then he left for India. My father died. It's all unwinding. Everything stopped. Even the writing and painting. I'm in the obsession. My blood is bleeding. My nerves shocked back. Time has caught up. The past is in the present. Now. Synchronicity for something to be known?"

Frank spoke. "What is the synchronicity you see?

"To put Humpty Dumpty back together. To find all the pieces I kicked under the bed. Blamed everyone for. Joel is a loose nerve, a split in me."

Regina chimed in. "I suspect he is part of the abuse. What seems normal. The abandonment and neglect. Pleasure and pain."

Ruby squeezed her hands against her chest. Her eyes fluttered. She started to perspire. Her short jeans skirt and T-shirt started to stick to her skin. "If I say it out loud again...then...It's not just Joel. It's somehow Joel...and...that night in his basement...."

"Say what out loud?" Regina leaned over and grabbed her hand.

Ruby felt the room spin in slow motion. A merry-go-round dancing around and around. "I...I...Mary, Marianne Magdalena... Yes. You're right. I see and hear her. Or I believe it is her. It's all raveled up with Joel, my mother, grandmother. I don't know." Ruby started to hyperventilate. "I can't breathe...I..."

Regina and Frank rushed to her side. Frank rubbed her back. "Take deep breaths. Long and in the belly. You're safe."

Regina poured a glass of water. "Here, sip this slowly."

Ruby pushed it away. "I'm...okay...I'm okay." She grabbed onto to the both of them, calming herself, pacing herself until she felt grounded. "Thank you."

"If you panic just telling us, what will happen if you go and see Joel?" Regina asked.

"I don't know. But, if I don't see him, this will stay bottled up, ready to explode any minute. Like you said, Regina, whatever I don't go to will break me."

Frank leaned against the pillow. "If it's unclean sweep it up. This is your life, Ruby. You have to heal it in the way you need to heal it. You and Steve have been through more than most couples. "

Ruby closed her eyes. A kaleidoscope of colors popped around like water lilies. She drifted in the river of diamond shapes. She shook her head to clear it.

"I feel selfish, afraid, hurt, ungrateful, greedy and stupid. But, I need to go."

Frank handed her a tissue. "What's his name again?"

"Joel Simon."

Frank eyes widened with shock. "Dr. Joel Simon. The author of *Mind over Matter*?"

"Yes." Ruby wiped her eyes and neck.

Regina stroked her hair. "I think the universe is at work here."

Ruby laughed, threw the tissue in the trash. "I hate that expression."

Chapter 63: July, 1983 – Joel's Return

Crowds of people swarmed into the Lebowitz auditorium. It unnerved Ruby and she bit down hard into a Baby Ruth. She sat in the back row between a grey-haired woman with chopsticks in her hair bun and a buxom blonde in jeans wearing a T-shirt with *Peace* scribbled across her chest.

Ruby tapped her foot against the seat in front. The woman turned with an agitated look. "Please. Stop kicking the seat."

From a distance Ruby thought she heard her named called. Once, twice, three times: a big scream. "Ruby, over here." Ruby's eyes wandered from head to head until she saw Joan's hand wave. The shine of her diamond flitted through the air.

"Shit." Ruby slapped her hand to her knee. Joan was a bloodhound.

Next thing she knew, Joan dragged Ruby out of the back row, straight down the aisles, right toward the front row, smack dab in the middle. She held up two tickets. "I read the paper. I knew you'd be here, hiding." She led Ruby into the seat, "You think I'd miss this?" Her *budinsky* friend examined Ruby close up. "You look like you're ready for him. Perfect, casual black dress. Sexy sandals. All Jackie Kennedy like."

"I should have never told you about Joel." Ruby snatched the program out of her hand.

"You tell me everything." Joan swiped her bangs to the side.

"I'm not going to cheat." Ruby crumpled the flyer.

"Look. You don't have lie to me."

"This all is just a juicy soap opera to you."

Joan turned her head slowly in Ruby's direction. Targeted a long gaze at her. "Ruby. I might act like frozen Japsicle, but I do have a heart buried under the iceberg. I love you."

A loud, ear-piercing screech shot out of the microphone. A tall, boyish-looking woman with a short bob tapped the mike and repeated. "Testing, Testing, Testing." She seemed satisfied after deafening most of the people in the audience and left the stage. The lights lowered and a lone spotlight tightened in the center of the stage. A hush of anticipation came over the audience.

Ruby squeezed Joan's hand. "Hold me."

Out walked Joel. Tall, blonde, and handsomely matured. Toughened skin that looked like it had seen some darker days, an intensity in his eyes that sparkled with a light touch of the comical.

Ruby gulped.

"I got it, honey. He is hard-core stuff to drop. Even for me, whose vagina is somewhere in Antarctica."

He leaned into the mike, "Hello, I'm Dr. Joel Simon. I thank you all for coming here tonight. I hope I can ignite your deepest urges and awaken the possibilities that live within each one of you." Joel picked up the mike and moved closer to the edge of the stage. "You know, all of us, you and me, are part of a universe that wants us to be fully alive, and fully human. Present to receive the flow of our true current, our stream of life. If for a moment, or just in this short time that we have together, you can let go of who you think you are and just feel who you are without judgments, shoulds, or have-to's, you just might know what your true passion is in life and give up whatever doesn't serve you. Then you can enlighten the world with just being here now, without any pretense or defenses. You will experience the joy of saving just one person, and that would be you." Joel's eyes wandered the room. "But you have to be willing to face your demons, hear the voices that tear you away from what is familiar. As Joseph Campbell said, "In order to live the life you want, you have to give up the life you're living." His presence was like a lightning bolt.

Ruby knew his startling eyes were coming for her. Every person in the room panted, waited for his next word. But his eyes stung to a halt when they met Ruby's. The audience's attention hung in mid-air. As he recognized Ruby, a glacier of surprise mounted; a hundred memories, the past came to dance with them. Silently he mouthed her name, each letter curled around his lips and melted like ice cream down his throat. R..U..B..Y.

"Oh babe…you're in trouble." Joan whispered in her ear.

Ruby soundlessly spoke the word, "B..U..L..L..S..H..I..T."

A burst of laughter exploded from Joel. At first, a low rumble of curiosity vibrated through the room, then some giggles, and then the audience was in an uproar, laughing with Joel.

"Idiots. They all just think he's the laughing Buddha. Morons." With that, Ruby stood up and marched towards the door.

Joan stalked after her. "Wait up."

"Joan. Please. I need time." Ruby weaved through the crowd holding her stomach, about to vomit. Confused and rattled, she turned. Joel's eyes followed her.

The audience settled down into a jolly hush. Then applause. Joan was behind, far away, blending into the maze of heads and claps. Even through the entrance from where Ruby froze, both Joel and Joan's eyes chilled her. She threw up her hands, yelled out, "I'm sorry. I'm sorry."

Helpless, Joan crossed her heart with her finger, held up her hand.

Chapter 64: Afternoon – Psychic Knowing

Red and green lights glared in Ruby's eyes. Stop and go traffic drove her crazy. Someone honked behind her. Cars were lined up, waiting for her to move. She flinched and looked up. Green light. "Okay. Okay!" She waved her arms and accelerated, turned down Powerline Road and drove until she saw the sign Quiet Waters Park. That's it. Quiet Waters. She'd go there. Dozens of cars were ahead, wanting to get into the park. What was the story? She banged the wheel and poked her head out. "What's holding everything up?"

Finally she came to the entrance booth. A pudgy, bouncy-breasted woman with Pippi Longstocking braids stuck her head out of the guardhouse. She yawned. "Renaissance Festival."

"What?" Ruby fumbled through her purse looking for singles.

"The park is only open for the festival. Ten dollars."

"Shit. Yeah, okay." Shuffling through the bills, she found a ten. "Here." Handed the money to the bored woman.

Ruby drove around the curved entrance. Twisted bark and cranky branches lined with bushy arms waved along the path. She loved the smell of the forest road, loved the old, witchy trees that whipped the hood and sides of her car. After twenty minutes of cursing and rotating around the lot, she caught a sword fighter and damsel in distress walking towards their car. Thank god. Ruby steered and followed them. It took forever for them to leave, between their kissing and hugging and whatever else. She swerved in quickly and threw her keys into her purse.

Signs guided the way toward the main grounds. The dirt road led her into the sixteenth century. An enchanted village; merchants selling Merlin hats and wands, crystal balls, artisan's booths, food and drink, wooden toys, unique pottery, clothing fit for kings, jesters, queens, and minstrels. Magicians strolled about pulling coins and balls from people's ears and shirts. Women dressed as wenches laughed and jostled with the crowd. Ruby roamed about fascinated; the land of King Arthur and Maiden Gwendolyn, when rocks spoke and clouds and stars wrote the histories of grand societies.

Intrigued by an archery contest, Ruby watched. A tap on her shoulder dismantled her attention from the two competing knights. Ruby jumped and barked, "What is it?"

A brunette stood there, hair swinging around her shoulders, intense green eyes, wearing a high-necked emerald velvet gown. Ruby burst into tears. "I'm sorry, please, I didn't mean it. I'm just edgy."

The woman held up her hand. "My name is Marion. I am meant to read you."

Ruby raised a brow, "You're *MEANT* to read me. I don't want to seem rude, but I don't think so."

"I'm meant to read you," she repeated. "Fifteen minutes for twenty-five dollars." She pulled a pendant out from underneath her dress. It was a ruby. "Ruby? Yes?"

The hair on Ruby's arm sizzled. "Really? That's a coincidence."

"Come to my booth." She brushed her skirt in a circle and led the way. She pulled out a chair.

Ruby shrugged. "What the hell? I've got nothing else going." She plopped into the chair.

Marion rolled up her sleeves to reveal an elaborate tattoo of dragons and forests. "Place your hands in mine."

Ruby gently laid her hands into her palms. A tingle stung throughout her body.

The fortuneteller took out a tarot deck. "Shuffle and pull three cards."

Ruby pulled from the top, middle, and bottom. She laid the cards face up.

Marion's gaze deepened. "Three major arcane cards. The Fool, The Lovers, The Magician. You're in for many changes and challenges."

"I could have told you that." Ruby folded her arms.

"Well, my dear." She put a tape into a recorder and pressed a button. "You were born with sight. This is the Magician. But you see it as a curse. You're stuck being a victim to your past. The Fool. You're tortured and needy. You push your life away and can't receive what is right in front of you. You try to get love through head games and manipulation when your body leads you to your heart and soul. There is a past love and a present love and a future love." She pointed. "The Lovers. None of them will ever give you self-love. You are lost in a maze of self-hatred. Your hate will turn to love. That's your path. Rage is the opposite side of the coin of love and passion. Sacrifice and inner work. Give up the medications and you will know everything, including whether or not the voice you hear and the face you paint is Mary."

Ruby perspired. Her face clenched, her dress stuck to her thighs.

Marion continued. Rambled on in a trance state. Her eyes flitted. "Human love disappoints you. The only source of love is God. God cannot force you to receive your life. You fight life! You fought it when you were born. Nothing is perfect...not even God. SHE is still growing and becoming along with us. This man. I see this man. His name...J...J...Joey? You think he can save you? You think so? You have to save you. You have to listen. See. Feel. Live your life, not someone else's."

Marion's words were fire and cold ice.

Ruby shivered. She gripped the edge of the table.

Marion got up and placed one arm around her waist and one behind her head.

Ruby breathed slow and steady. "His name is Joel."

Marion let go of Ruby, sat down and stroked each card. "Yes, Joel. At the end you will have two daughters. One will come from your womb, the other won't." She pushed the cards back into the deck. "I'm through." Popped open the recorder and handed Ruby the tape.

Ruby face tightened as if struck by a stun gun. "I'm never having children." She opened her bag and pulled out twenty-five dollars.

"I know. You don't want children. You're terrified. But in the end, you'll be a mother and mother many. You have to go find your woman." Marion's mouth curled. "Don't make this life about you, Ruby. You're bigger than that."

Marion hugged Ruby with great generosity. "Oh, one more thing. You'll be going away. It will be a choice to leave."

"I'm not going anywhere."

"We'll see." Marion waved in a young woman in blue shorts and a tank top. She sat down. "And that necklace you're wearing. Don't ever lose it."

Ruby grabbed the chain that had grown longer as she grew and cradled it with a fierce strength. Making her way out, she noticed a small statue of a naked woman wrapped in snakes sitting on a shelf. She picked it up and stroked it. "Who is she?"

Marion stopped, peeked over her shoulder. "Excuse me for a moment." She smiled at the young woman who impatiently bounced her foot. She walked up to Ruby and admired the statue. "The *Shekinah*, the feminine face of God. *Asherah* in ancient Israel. Take it. It's yours. It's your lineage. Your grandma lost her way, but she's helping you now. She's here."

"Grandma?" Ruby hugged the statue looked around. "Grandma!"

Marion closed Ruby's hands around the statue. "Now GO." The psychic returned to her customer.

"This is so crazy. But thank you."

"I'm not crazy just as you are not."

Ruby wandered through the boisterous crowds. Dazed and shaky she felt as if she had just stumbled down the rabbit hole. She returned to her car and laid the statue on the seat. Turned the ignition on. She inched the rear view mirror a bit to the left and studied her swollen eyes and cheeks. She stared intently at her lost and lonely face and whispered, "I see you." She pulled her car out of the parking space. "I need a drink." Not the best choice. She didn't care how it mixed with her prescriptions. She remembered her grandmother's handbag and the schnapps, the vodka she slugged. Now she wanted to carry on the tradition. She wanted to drown everything out the way her grandmother did - with booze.

Chapter 65: Same Day – The Bar Woman

The corner booth next to the panoramic window was a quiet spot. It gave her a majestic view of the long dark highway; the only friend she allowed to get close to her that night as Ruby squeezed up against the leather-cushioned seat. Cars swooshed by as beams of light reflected the faces of all her broken promises back into her mind's eye. Each painful memory crossed over like snapshots in a frayed photo album. Tears welled in the corners of her eyes. Between the meds and the alcohol, her eyelids were light and fluttery. She touched her lips. They felt spongy and wet.

"Want anything else?"

Startled by the waitress' presence, Ruby jerked and wiped her eyes. "No." As the waitress meandered away, Ruby whispered, "Just my life."

A woman slid in next to her. Her twisted white hair, dark green eyes, and nose whiskers that dangled from the edge of her nostrils made her resemble a Scottish terrier. She smelled of cigarettes and onions.

"Want a drink?"

"Drink. Drink. I drink." Ruby held up her glass. "A drink with a little ol' Brooklyn girl, me?"

"I have a story to tell you."

"Mary had a little teeny lamb?" Ruby laughed.

"You need to listen." She grabbed Ruby's elbow.

"If you keep touching me, I'll scream. I promise." Ruby tried to cross her fingers over her heart, but they slid away as if rubbed in baby oil. "My fingers are Jell-O."

"You're so self-absorbed." The woman inched away from Ruby.

"Mwahh? Me?" Ruby waved to the waitress who leaned against the wall smoking.

The server flicked the reed to the floor, crushed it with the heel of her flat shoe. She wove over to the table. "Yeah."

"Two whiskeys. Yeah." Ruby giggled.

"Thanks for the generosity." The old woman bowed her head.

The waitress wiped her nose and walked away.

The woman tapped her finger against the glass, gazed out of the window. "The view tells the story."

"You keep talkin' about some story? I've got a story. Yeah! I do." Ruby rested her head on the table.

"The story." The old woman winked. "You need to worship the bones of stars and moons."

Ruby wrapped her finger around the sticky glass saltshaker and squeezed. The waitress placed the drinks down and whisked away. She watched the moist droplets slide down the shot glass. "What the fuck does that mean?"

The lady slugged down the whiskey and coughed. "You need to come home, Ruby."

"How does everyone know my name? Marion, Marianne, you. What the fuck is up with that? How do you people know my name?"

"We're all the same woman. We're all Marianne. Healing doesn't change the past, it brings you peace in the present. Acceptance of what is. If you don't receive your life, Ruby, you'll never heal or tell the story."

Ruby leapt to her feet and was about to leave. "Shut up with the story already!"

The vagabond grabbed her hand. "You need repetition. You're thick."

"Stop. You're driving me nuts."

In the background, Ruby heard a voice whisper, "The storm is coming."

Ruby shuddered in a whisper, "A storm is coming." She searched the night skies. The moon was full. Stars playfully glittered. She turned to the old woman, "I want out of here."

Ruby dashed out to the parking lot, jumped in her car, and drove home in a frenzy. Blurred vision, shaky hands. This was dangerous. She accelerated, needed to get home. She needed Steve. Always relied on Steve to soothe her. But would he be there for her? How much strain could the marriage take? *I'm a mad woman who lives in a shoe.*

Headlights and frantic turns of the wheel. She slapped her face. Picked up a bottle of water lying on the seat next to her, drank until she felt her mind clear a bit. She saw the statute lying on the seat rolling back and forth as she drove. She had to get home. Not get killed on the road. No! Finally, she made it to her driveway, grabbed the statue, rushed in and stumbled to the couch, hugging the Asherah.

A sound made Ruby jump. Her eyes darted open. Steve peered down at her. His tie loose, hair all messed up, suit worn from the day. She rubbed her eyes, took a breath and blinked. "Did you say a storm is coming?"

"No."

"No?" Ruby blinked.

"No. Where have you been?" Steve bent over, smelled her breath. "Pew. What the…where have you been? And what's that statue?"

"Nowhere. Nothing."

"You reek, Ruby." He grabbed her arm. "You drank on your meds? What's wrong with you?"

"I don't care. I can't stop. Something is going to happen. Something scary. I don't feel natural inside. My insides don't match."

"What's happening?"

"I hate him. But seeing him…it's opened a can of worms. I feel them wiggling in my organs."

"You saw Joel." Steve stormed away.

"I'm not finished talking. I'm…I'm going to vomit." She jumped up and ran to the bathroom. Asherah slid out of her hands and fell to the floor.

Chapter 66: Early August, 1983 – Tragedy Strikes

Ruby wore tennis shorts and a tank top on a stifling hot day. It had been two weeks since Joel's lecture. Zucchini, squash, and broccoli at Wholesome Foods refreshed her mind. Then her cell phone rang, the latest and greatest on the technology market.

Ruby tightened her grip on the cart, ignored it. This was the first time in a week Ruby had left the house. She relished walking through the neat aisles of salad dressing, chocolates, peanut butter, roasted chicken, rib steaks, unique sauces, gourmet cakes, tofu, swiss and pepper jack cheeses - all the scrumptious foods that ignited her senses but gave her stomach a hard time.

Her phone rang again. Ruby thought it was probably Joan. Her friend was relentless to connect with her. But Ruby wasn't ready to talk. Joan had stuffed an article from the arts and leisure section of *The Sun-Sentinel* regarding Dr. Simon's visionary approach to mental health and healing in her mailbox. He came to Florida to market his new residential healing center, The Westfall Wellness Center and Institute out in California. An alternative and spiritual training facility for those suffering from trauma, abuse, and addiction. Ruby shoved the article into her drawer.

She plunged the metal scooper into a heap of walnuts. The phone rang again. This time she answered. "Hello." She squeezed a melon. "What's up, Steve?"

Ruby shuffled from one foot to another, smelled the sweet fruit, placed the cantaloupe in its correct place in the pile. "I'm shopping for dinner. What's so urgent?"

She nuzzled a sweet potato in her hand. She dropped the potato. The news that Steve told her made her tumble to the ground. A knotted scream turned into a heavy sob. She fumbled, trying to catch herself against the cart, which jerked and rolled into the lettuce table and sent tomatoes flying and slipping over each other to the floor in a pile of mush.

A young woman dressed for yoga, strolling with her bouncy blonde pigtailed child, grabbed Ruby as she was about to topple over. "Are you all right?"

Ruby squeezed the woman's hand. "My sister."

Chapter 67: Same Day – Accelerating Home

Strapped into her red Mercedes, strips of blue and white clouds chased after her. She time-warped every light, swerved around every elderly driver, and was a ghost to the cops that hid in bushes. She passed the guardhouse through the resident's entrance, wove and streamed along the tree-lined streets, each home emerging like pillars and castles from behind elaborate landscaped entrances. As she turned into her cul-de-sac, she noticed a white Camry parked by the edge of the driveway. Who was that? Didn't matter. She curved her car around the circular driveway, slammed on the brakes and ran toward the front door. From behind, a hand grabbed her arm. Alarmed, she screamed and kicked, "Steve, help, Steve!"

"No, Ruby. No. It's me. Me. Joel." Ruby face squirreled up into a twitter, her chest heaving anxiously. "Joel? What the fuck? What are you doing here?"

Joel wiped his forehead, beads of sweat dotted along his thick hairline. "Your friend Joan got me past the gate. Calm down. I'll tell you all. Let's just talk, please, Ruby. I had to stay. Figure it out. I had to find a way to figure it out."

"Joan? Damn that girl. Go away." She pushed at his chest, raced toward the door. "You don't get to figure anything out. Not with me. You didn't give me that chance."

Joel leapt after her. "I can help you. I can. All these years. I know what's happened to you. You've got to let me help."

"I don't 'got to' let you do anything. You shit. You come back and you tell me that, Mr. Big Shot, egocentric, molester-disguised-as-a-guru, back from the spiritual clouds of all knowing. Are you kidding me?"

"No. I know. I know you'd think that about me. But…damn Ruby, we're not kids anymore, and I was a schmuck, but I never stopped thinking of you. It's because of you I slept on dirt mats and sacrificed and tried to find the truth."

"What bullshit are you selling me? I know you. You think you can make some big plan in your mind and I'm just going to go along with it? Just like in high school. Same old, same old Joel, thinking only Joel exists." Ruby slapped his face. "Why don't you just stay gone?"

Joel didn't flinch. Face and eyes clear, a spot of softness threaded through his stance. "Okay. That was years in the coming. And your reaction to me says you haven't gotten over me." He handed her a card. "Call me. We have to face our karma. I run a residential healing center called Westfall. You can heal there. It's not just about me. It's you and both our lives. Everyone's lives."

Her eyes tightened, her mouth twisted. "Karma! You made a choice. That's your karma. I need to go, my sister…I need to go." She threw the card into her bag. "Go back and sleep on the dirt and mud and whatever spiritual shithole you chose, but don't make it about us. You left me. Now I get to leave you."

At that moment the door swung open, Steve jumped, pounced at Joel. "Get away from my wife!" He slam-dunked him to the ground. They tumbled over, squawking, belching out monkey screams, fighting each other.

"Steve, stop. Stop it!" Ruby bounced from one foot to another. "Stop! It's Joel. Stop!"

The action crumbled. Steve grabbed Joel by his shoulders. He kept a firm grip, then let go, stood up. He edged back, wiped the dirt from his white pullover. "Joel. Asshole Joel. Why are you bothering Ruby? Get out of here."

"Man, Ruby. You let it all fester into a bitter blob of blame." Joel climbed to his feet. His khaki shorts were ripped by the pockets and buttons had popped off of his short-sleeved shirt.

Steve carved a knife-like stare at him, twisted his fists, kicked some pebbles, and stormed towards the house. His anger rumbled out like a cannon ball. "Your sister is on her deathbed and you waste your time with this creep? You take care of this." He grunted and mumbled, punching his fists all the way back inside.

Astonished, Joel reached toward her.

Ruby pushed him away, rushed toward the open doorway. A twig bit her thigh and a trickle of blood spotted her skin. She grimaced and hit the branch that attacked her as she marched toward the house. "Get out of here, Joel. I didn't invite you back into my life." She slammed the door.

Joel screamed after her. "Yeah, you did. You showed up at my lecture."

Once behind closed doors she peeked through the etched side windows, watched Joel slug down the walkway.

"It's him you stare at? Him? Then I don't give a shit."

Ruby grabbed Steve's hand before he could move, reeled him in. "Just tell me. What's going on? Forget Joel."

"It's not all about you." He took a breath.

"Just tell me, Steve! Now you're making it all about you."

He wiggled away from her touch. "I got a call in my office from your sister's attorney. There was a car accident. Head on. Howard died immediately. Your sister's holding on."

Ruby clutched her chest, "My sister. My sister!" Ruby stormed into the living room, threw her bag on the chair, laid across the shag throw rug. "Leah's been dead inside of me forever. Now she's more alive then I can bear."

"She has a daughter."

"Oh, my god!" She pulled her knees to chest.

"Her name is Hannah. She's, I think eleven, twelve or something, and she's been left to us."

Ruby's mouth dropped from shock. "Stop. This is crazy. Leah can't die. A daughter? What? No. She wouldn't give her daughter to me."

Steve edged down next to her. "Ruby, we either get on a plane tonight or you might never see her again."

Ruby's body tugged, battled whether to go, not to go. No. No. *A daughter, Hannah*, circled in her head. Sobs dangled and her body trembled. "Her daughter?"

Steve paused, a sigh of sorrow escaped.

Ruby kneaded at her stomach. "Why would Howard and Leah…

this is not real."

Steve nodded. "It's a nightmare."

His words jumbled in Ruby's head. She tossed about on the floor. Something touched her hand. She lifted her palm. It was Joel's card. It had fallen out. She stuffed it back in her bag.

Ruby noticed Steve watching her. Their eyes shot past each other's glare.

Steve whispered. "I'll make flight reservations." He placed his hand over hers, held it there for a second. "I don't know what we're facing. But it's you and I facing it."

Ruby gazed past the reds and gold of her living room, the blues and greens of her bedroom, the perfectly lined deck furniture, beyond the baby blue pool water to the breezy palms, the mangos and oranges that dripped from the branches of the tropic growth. Where in the beauty of the day did this horror belong? Her mind sped, raced to a thousand lifetimes ago with Leah, Morty, Claire, and Sarah. Then there was Ruby. A family. Gone. Her head spun, echoes clashed against each other's shadows, they repeated *You're next. You're next. You could die next.*

Ruby pinched her arms mindlessly. Leah has a daughter? Hannah? The psychic's prediction, a child out of the womb. She looked up at Steve. "Howard's parents? Why wouldn't they take Hannah in? Why us?"

"Howard was estranged from his parents. I don't know much else."

Ruby lifted herself from the floor. "You don't have to come with me."

"That's fucked up, Ruby."

"I know." At that moment she broke, fell into Steve's chest. "I'm all fucked up. I can't feel anything. I'm...we've got to go."

Chapter 68: That Night August, 1983 – Leah's Death

Ruby's hair was a bomb of a mess. The sweaty red shirt and jeans she had traveled in were wrinkled and ragged. The smudged mascara that caked down her face showed her exhaustion. Carry-ons only, they rushed out of the airport. Steve, a ball of stress, flagged down a cab. They arrived at the hospital around eight o'clock. They found Room 202A and approached the doorway.

A middle-aged man dressed in hospital blues was standing over the bed. Ruby peeked around him, wanting to catch Leah's eye. Steve stood by Ruby. Fear furrowed his brows, his eyes flicking from Ruby to Leah.

Ruby walked in. "Are you the doctor?"

He turned. His eyes, tinged with seriousness, rested on Ruby. "Yes. You are?"

"Her sister."

"Yes. Come in."

Ruby moved towards the bed and looked down at her sister. Yellow eyes, swollen face, broken breath, arms and legs twisted, splintered in casts. She screamed. "Leah!"

The doctor spoke in a quiet manner. "The cancer spread into her brain, her blood, her organs. It metastasized."

The soles of Ruby's feet folded into the floor. She was about to faint. She gripped Steve. "But, it was a car accident. She...what? I don't understand."

The doctor placed his arm on her shoulder. "Do you need water?"

Ruby grabbed his arm. "Please explain. Please."

"She's dying from cancer, not the car accident."

"But, but...but..." Ruby was bewildered.

The doctor grimaced, wiped his upper lip. "She allowed the cancer to go undiagnosed. She never came in for treatment. She hid it. The daughter was in the car with them. A miracle she wasn't hurt. A double-edged suicide. Cancer, car accident." He took a breath and moved to Leah and took her pulse.

"How did she hide this? No one could ignore this. This is insane." Ruby waved her hand. She paced. What had Leah done? What? Why? Ruby's mind raced, she flung herself at her sister's feet. The air in the room floated in circles, grabbed her tongue, her throat. Suffocating. She was suffocating. She rummaged through her pocketbook, found the stash of Valium she kept. She slid two under her tongue. She didn't want to feel.

Ruby buried her face in the sheets.

The doctor tapped the intravenous tube. "Maybe another transfusion will wake her a bit to talk for you. I'll get the nurse." He left the room.

In a few moments, a harried nurse replaced a bag of fluids. She sat on a chair in the corner of the room.

Leah's eyes flickered. Their translucent haze invited Ruby into her sister's death. Leah flopped her head to the side, whispered. "Ruby."

Ruby fondled her sister's hand. It was cold, foreign to her touch. She'd never held her hand. Heart-stricken, Ruby wanted to save her.

Leah squeezed Ruby's hand. "Did I do anything wrong?"

Ruby blinked, breathed deep, trying to stay strong. "No. You didn't do anything wrong."

Leah closed her eyes. For years, Ruby had bolted her heart shut, rotted from the estrangement between Leah and Ruby. And for what? Pride? Hate? Love? Ruby didn't know.

Time broke and crumpled in Ruby's hands. At that moment, a tingle ran up her spine. A small hand on her back, gentle like the flutter of a wing, tapped her. Ruby turned. It was a young girl, maybe twelve, thirteen, with lost blue eyes and stormy red hair. A torn jean jacket, layered black skirt, scrunchy for her ponytail, with lacy socks and black sneakers, a typical Madonna look-alike. Across her forehead was a thick bandage, her right finger in a cast. Their eyes touched, glanced, barely able to hold the other's grief. Each examined the other, two ships lost in a foggy sea. Ruby shivered. Her nose was Ruby's nose. At once it hit Ruby. *Oh my god, this is Leah's child.*

Hannah's face froze in knotted tension. The young girl slipped her hand away from Ruby. She edged back an inch, not wanting to connect too long or too close. "You're Ruby." She peered over her shoulder. "And Steve?"

Steve nodded.

Hannah glared at Ruby, "I look like you. I hate that." A hard sob escaped. She straightened up to stifle it. Hannah's eyes held a dead stare. Her hands raked and dug into her mother's bruised arm, swollen by toxins from the breast cancer. Her voice trembled; she pushed to her mother's side. "Mom!"

Ruby wanted to scoop Hannah in her arms. She was moving toward her when a scratching cry screeched from Leah's throat. Her hollow pain poured out from her darkness. Death contorted her as she turned and bowed on all fours like a dog about to pee. She collapsed on her stomach.

The nurse untwisted and adjusted the wires attached to Leah. Scooped her back into a comfortable position in the bed. Beeps and mechanical yelps shook the machines, red lights lit up. "Please step away. Move back. Please."

The three backed up against the wall.

The doctor returned. He examined Leah. "She's close. Do you want me to get a rabbi?"

Not one of them answered. The three huddled together, as if to protect themselves from an approaching thunderstorm. Ruby came forward, stood over her sister. Looked down at her, a need to wake her from her tomb, raise her up like Lazarus. Sister. Her only sister. The heartbreak and pain of the empty closure. Years of estrangement, bitterness, blame. Nothing left. No goodbyes. No touch. No explanation.

Ruby knew it by memory, not by rote, but through osmosis she learned the Kaddish prayer. So many times, each yarzheit when she lit the candle for her mother, grandmother, and father, the prayer for the dead. For their souls to lift to heaven. To be with God. She had to help Leah cross over. Inside, she battled the no, no, no, she didn't want to be the one. No! She heard Regina's words, "What is your purpose?" It appeared this was her purpose. To pray for the dead over and over, and survive. The vigilant warrior. The one who eats her prey for spiritual food. Her prey was prayer.

A choking breath lingered in Leah's body and then released. She was gone.

Ruby screamed. "This is my last memory."

Hannah slumped to the floor.

Steve gently lifted Hannah, held her by the arm. He placed his arm around Ruby's waist. Together they recited, "*Yisgadal v'yiskadash sh'me rabbo, b'olmo deevro chiruseh v'yamlich malchus…*"

Hannah stroked Leah's head. The young niece clung to every word, every syllable of the prayer.

Ruby and Steve continued, "*b'chayechon ovyomerchon uv'cheyey d'chol beys yisroel, baagolo, uvixman koreev, v'rimru omen.*" Four more verses and all three hummed the final amen.

Like a baby wolf, Hannah howled, "I want my Grandma Ellie and Grandpa George. Where are they? I want them!" Hannah ran, fell, picked herself up. "Grandpa, Grandma?"

Steve chased after her and almost slid in the shiny corridor. "Stop, Hannah. They're not here." He caught up to her and grabbed her by the arm.

Hannah fought like a pitbull, tried to kick, even bite him. "No. No. Get away from me. Get away from me." She pushed at him. "Why do they hate me?"

Steve held onto her for dear life so she wouldn't fall. He was the caretaker of her torn heart. He stroked her hair, kept cradling her, shushing her, leaning into her pain. "It's okay. I'm not going to hurt you. Please trust me."

Hannah dropped to the scuffed, chilly floor. "Why'd my grandparents leave me here with you, and, and…her?" Red mournful eyes filled with tears.

"I'm sorry, Hannah." Steve plunked down next to her.

Hannah stomped her feet, pulled her hair from the ponytail, threw her scrunchy, wailed as if her skin had been torn from her body. "How can they blame me?"

"It's not your fault, Hannah. Please."

At that moment, Ruby stood above like an avenging angel. "Hannah, you're coming home with us."

Hannah eyes widened with a deepening horror, she lifted her arm, and swatted the air. She yelped like a wild animal. "NOOOOOOOO, fuck you. No!"

"She even talks like you." Steve blurted out.

Through the corner of her eye, Ruby caught the orderlies entering Leah's room. She heard the word *wait* shout through her body, and the urge to stop them from taking Leah away. The silence of her scream skipped like a pebble across her skin. But then the ripples spread out, thinner and thinner until the *wait* turned into a stillness and inaction. In the distance, the wind, trees, and rain hurdled a roar and stirred the unlived part that sat in her chest.

"Hannah?" Ruby erased the image of her sister being carted away. She stood in Hannah's line of vision so she wouldn't see the spectacle.

There was nothing left. No reason to stay amongst the sick and dying. Where were her tears? She wanted them now. But they were gone. "We need to go, now." Ruby bent over and buttoned Hannah's jean jacket.

Hannah was spent, her eyes swollen. Steve pulled her up. Guided Hannah toward the elevators.

Ruby followed behind. Her peripheral vision caught a slim figure with red hair run down the hallway. Ruby turned. Nothing. No one. She studied Hannah. Her face. Her eyes. Familiar. Hannah looked… she resembled, oh yes, she looked like. *Oh my god.* Marianne and Ruby combined. No. Couldn't be. No. Was it true? Or was she in a delusion? Stress brought on these imaginings. A mountain of stress was hard to climb.

"Hannah?" Ruby touched her shoulder.

The young girl pulled away. "I know I'm supposed to go with you. But I can keep living at my friend Amy's. My grandparents don't want me. They say they can't look at me. They hated my mother. They say it's my mother's fault their son turned on them and is dead now. That I have the evil blood in me. Why do I have to go where I'm not wanted?"

Ruby shook her head. "Your grandparents are wrong. And Steve and I want you."

"Yeah? So why are you only here when my parents are dead? Where were you all these years?"

"You're right, Hannah, that we haven't been in your life. But I want you now to come home with us."

The elevator opened. Steve and Ruby entered.

Hannah hesitated. Looked like a frightened raccoon. She walked into the elevator and huddled in the corner.

The door closed.

Chapter 69: May, 1984 – Hannah

Demons pushed against Ruby's mind as she woke that morning. She rubbed her temples as a dull headache approached. Tiny dots of blue and green swamped against her closed lids. It had been nine months since Hannah became part of their household. She gazed out the window as she lay in bed, clouds silent, wind tipping the waves, and thought about Hannah and the difficult relationship that had spawned.

Steve and Ruby met with the guidance counselor after Hannah's third month in school. Ruby knew that the chubby woman who held her bangs off her face with a bobby pin didn't have a clue how to talk to Hannah. But she wasn't having much headway, so she was desperate for any information.

The floppy, pear-shaped women reported Hannah's progress. "She doesn't talk much. Her grades are average. She's isolated. Her classmates are afraid of her. She angers quickly."

Ruby scoffed at her lack of insight. "She lost her mother and father tragically. What do you want her to do? Dance on the desks?"

Hannah had the cursed blood. Ruby could see that. But she tried the conventional suggestions; communicate over a cup of tea, take her to movies, out shopping, to lunches hoping to build trust. But nothing opened Hannah. Nothing.

Ruby took her to a grief counselor. For weeks, Hannah resisted. "I don't want to go. She doesn't know what she's doing. Don't be nice to me. Just leave me alone." Hannah seethed over dinner one night while Steve was working late.

Ruby poured a glass of lemonade. "How do you want me to treat you?"

"Don't treat me like anything. I don't want to talk. Can't you leave me alone?" Hannah was a dark closet, closed to the public.

Soon, Ruby lost interest in being the good aunt, or trying to be some kind of mother that she wasn't cut out to be. She let Hannah stew in her own juices. Allowed space for her to come forward when it was right.

The more Ruby left Hannah alone, the more her troubled niece stalked Ruby. In her studio at night, Hannah became a fly, buzzing around Ruby's creations. At first, Ruby felt controlled by Hannah's presence, suffocated and uptight. But she soon forgot her niece's shadow huddled in the corner of the room. That is when her paintings started to deepen in their color and images. Faces of women seared through the paints with alchemical fire in their eyes and barks of wolves gurgling in their throats. The more Ruby painted the more the voices directed her. At first in whispers, then a low chatter. She began to write random ideas, thoughts, and stories again with the paintings. The faces on the canvas were variations of Marianne. At times she saw Hannah's face in Marianne's. Ruby wondered. Where did Hannah get such red hair from? Her mother had reddish-blonde hair as a child. Howard's family? A skipped gene? Who knew? It was odd and exciting, all the thick redness. Entries into journals: Blood red forests, Sarah, smoke, fire, desert, *Shekinah*. Puzzle pieces.

Other days, Ruby sketched women squatting, their vaginas exposed, their mouths open in anguish. Hannah's curiosity grew and she drew closer to the easels lined against the wall. Then one day, Hannah picked up a brush and painted. Hannah's closeness alarmed Ruby. Her body quivered. Her hands shook. Soon she adapted to Hannah's presence. Once in awhile, Ruby showed Hannah how to use a palette knife, or blend colors so they wouldn't muddy out. Hannah blossomed into an artist. Hannah's passion to paint excited Ruby. On the other hand, she prayed that Hannah didn't have the gift. It was enough that Hannah had Ruby's looks, but now her niece's soul followed in Ruby's footsteps.

One night while they painted, Hannah said, "You're painting me."

Ruby kept painting, poker faced. "No. It's not you."

Hannah flipped her brush on a palette. "It's someone who looks like me. And a little like you."

Ruby wiped paint off her brush. "You can't control what comes out of your mind when you paint. It just comes."

"Yeah. That's what I like about it, and it scares me too."

"What scares you?" Ruby smashed red paint across her canvas.

"My thoughts and feelings. You know what I mean? Sometimes I'm so sad it hurts my whole body. My brain feels tight and terrible thoughts happen."

Ruby turned to Hannah, white and blue paint splattered on her hands and face, "What terrible thoughts?"

"I don't want to talk about it."

Ruby understood the fear in Hannah's silence. Left the conversation alone.

Art bonded them. Tornadoes of energy whirled as they painted. When their creative juices died down, the two retreated as strangers. Even after a full night of writing and painting, sometimes Ruby would cry over a cup of tea. In the soft distance, Ruby would hear Hannah sob as well. Steve slept through it all.

Ruby continued to drop Hannah off at school, pick her up at day's end. At breakfast and dinner they talked about the latest movie or the awful teachers at school. Hannah never mentioned Leah or Howard. Never talked about painting. Never talked about anything of significance.

Each morning at eight o'clock on the dot, Steve would stumble into the kitchen, drink a quick cup of pre-brewed coffee and hurry to work. He'd come home between six- thirty and seven exhausted, and drink his Schlitz before he took off his suit. Some evenings the three sat outside, watched the white sun turn orange, listened to the crickets, and bathed in the warm breezes. Soon the nothingness tired one of them and they'd march off to bed. On the outside, it was business as usual; on the inside an unsettling tremor rocked each of them.

Meds continued to ground Ruby, but nothing blocked out the emotional pain. Her dreams were epic, trekking through deserts, mountains and caves, Leah lying in her coffin, running in space. Many times she woke exhausted, overcome with sadness. She struggled against her crying bouts.

Dr. Z, Regina, and Frank conferred and felt it best that she stay with the dosages and medications prescribed, particularly since the tragedy. Her sessions with Regina went from once every other week to twice a week. She stopped teaching, stopped cooking, just stopped. Talks of pregnancy ceased and keeping Ruby stabilized was the goal. Staying the course with her paintings kept her contained, engaged and focused. She didn't care any longer if the stories of the paintings were real or not. If her rambling writings were sane or insane. They gave her meaning and substance, a solidity to cling to.

Chapter 70: Break and Down

Ruby woke this day with a different movement inside of her. She needed to create an atmosphere of calm and nurturance. She wanted to talk with Steve and Hannah. Really talk. Get to the core of the emotional estrangement.

Ruby climbed out of bed, dragged herself into the almond and blue bathroom. She splashed water on her face, brushed her teeth with Colgate, rinsed, untangled her hair and threw on the white empire dress that hung on a hook behind the door. She covered her cheeks with apricot blush, painted her lips with shiny pink gloss to disguise her mood, hoped it would transform her into Betty Crocker. Ruby stared at her tired eyes in the mirror. She swung open the vanity and reached for the Tylenol, downed two and placed the bottle back. At the same time she downed two 10mg tablets of Valium and a 20mg of Elavil.

One last time, she gazed in the mirror and messed with her hair. She sighed, flicked a curly strand behind her ear and walked out of the bathroom. She strayed over to her dresser, peeked over her shoulder, and opened the top drawer where her bras and panties were tossed around. She slipped her hand under a black lace thing and glanced at the card Joel had given her. Yes, she'd kept it. Something inside of her heart demanded that she keep it. *Maybe, someday* was always in the back of her head. She never let Steve know, but at times before they'd close their eyes at night, he'd ask, "Do you ever think of him?" Ruby never answered that question.

In the back of her mind, Ruby thought of Westfall. It was a

possibility beyond the revolving medication door. Hannah was that glaring smudge for Ruby, and the reason she knew she needed to go further in her healing. Her teenage niece lived in a world that Ruby understood. Hannah's dress grew dark, her eyes sunken, her young years blemished with emotional scars. She was so much like Ruby. Hannah strolled around the house wrapped in layers of scarves or ponchos, wearing moon earrings or big crosses, dark red lipstick emphasizing her pouty lips. She'd slink in like a snake, sit in the corner, knees to chest, and stare out like a zombie.

However, this Sunday, in spite of Ruby's ritualistic morning moodiness, she decided to cook up a brunch. Wanted to apply the eons of therapy. Enough is enough rang in her ears. Enough was enough. Time for change. Things had to change.

Her shiny steel pots hung above the stove; waiting for her to scramble up omelets, fry up cinnamon french toast, all crisp and chewy, put out raspberry jam and marmalade. She brewed coffee and tiptoed across the cherry wood floor toward the toaster. A comfy brunch, just the three of them. She laid the whole wheat buns flat, perfectly matched side by side, and pushed the bake time to level six. She set the table with apple-green linen napkins, arranged the floral china in the center of the bamboo placemats. Bottles of chilled Dom Perignon and bubbly apple cider sat on the black slate counter, tipped to the side in the ice bucket, their smooth backs up against the steel container. Ruby took two crystal glasses, poured half-orange juice and half- champagne into them, filled up a third glass with cider, and positioned them next to the silverware. She stood back, hands on hips, shook her head as if admiring her subjects. The illusion of safety and perfection.

Steve entered the kitchen huffing and sweating, ruffled up in his running shorts and Aspen T-shirt. He plopped down into the cushioned wicker chair, closed his eyes, and sniffed the aromas that greeted him. Sunday brunch was a ritual for Steve and Ruby. It was once a time where they hooked up and grabbed each other's thighs to spark passion into their marriage. Ruby slipped into the chair next to Steve. She played with the butter knife. Steve responded by flipping a napkin into his lap. All cozy and picturesque by the bay window, hummingbirds swilled around the cage singing their seductive song. All was deadly serene as they sipped their mimosas.

"I'm happy you're trying, Ruby."

Ruby fiddled with the corner of the napkin. "I'm feeling cold." She picked up the knife again and slid it along her arm.

Steve flipped the newspaper on the table and read.

Ruby turned her attention to the loveliness outside the window. The architecture of the day built a sunny face with pink clouds on its cheeks. At that moment, as the wind chimes blew a sweet clang, Ruby flipped the butter knife. She slid it up and down her arm. She wondered. What would it feel like to just dig into her skin? It was so smooth, the steel. *No. Put it down, Ruby.* Thoughts wandered through her mind. The knife. Put it down. She started to obsess about the knife. Then unconsciously, her fingers guided the dull blade against her wrist. She dug its edge into her skin until an indent etched into her vein. She kept digging a tad deeper.

Steve leapt forward and slapped her hand, "What the fuck!" His chair crashed against the wall as he grabbed Ruby's hands. The knife tumbled and clanged across the floor.

Ruby weaseled away from his strong hold, "What? What's wrong with you?"

"You're crazy." Steve shook her.

A vacant gaze chiseled her eyes. She stared at the knife lying on the floor. "It was unconscious. I didn't know what I was doing. I didn't."

Steve shook her. Her hair fell across her face into a mess of curls.

A flicker flushed through Ruby's dead eyes. She clung to Steve's arms. Her eyes adrift, her mouth dry with confusion she pleaded, "I'm here. I won't do that again. I promise. I'm here."

Hannah stumbled into the kitchen. Her hair tousled, eyes folded with sleep, her cotton shorts and short T-shirt exposing her young tight stomach, she yawned. "What's going on?"

Ruby ran to Hannah, touched her cheeks, smoothed her hair, wrapped her arms around her waist like a vine twisting around a fence.

"Aunt Ruby, what's the matter? You're scaring me." Hannah held Ruby. "What's happening, Uncle Steve?"

"You never called me Aunt before. Or hugged me back." Ruby calmed down.

Hannah edged out of Ruby's grip. "I'm sorry." She sat at the table and drank the glass of apple cider.

"Why are you sorry?" Ruby asked.

Hannah shrugged her shoulders. Looked away.

All three sat, waiting for a miracle to drop into their laps.

Ruby's voice dropped. "What happened in the car, Hannah? Tell me."

"Goddammit." Steve slapped Ruby's hand. "Why are you asking that now?"

Hannah's mouth twisted.

Ruby walked over to Hannah. "I need to know." She reached toward Hannah.

Hannah flinched back. "I can't. Just can't."

Ruby shook her head. "I have to leave. I can't go on this way."

Steve flopped into a chair. "I don't know what to do anymore. Why isn't Regina helping?"

"Why do you have to leave? Why?" Hannah asked.

Steve grabbed her hand. "You always have a home with me. Don't ever worry, Hannah."

Hannah breathed deep. Returned Steve's grasp.

Ruby hunched over and cried. "I don't know what will happen, but I need to get well. I can't keep taking medication, being terrified, feeling so alone. I need to leave. Nothing is helping me here."

Hannah marched out of the room, slammed the door to her bedroom. Steve bowed his head. It hung like a tired old dog. "Where are you going to go? Where? Huh? What are you thinking, Ruby?" He glared at her. "Hannah needs you."

"Don't do that, Steve. Don't. I need your support and help. I've got to go. What else can I do? Can't you see that?" Ruby eyes sought his approval. "You can give her some stability. And warmth. Where else can she get that from? I want to, but…"

A sudden flicker of insight dawned in Steve's eyes. "You're not. Oh no. Oh no, Ruby. I won't have it."

Ruby wobbled out of her chair and stood. Brushed the creases from the hem of her dress, leaned over and kissed Steve's open mouth, wanting to pass on the fever of her need. "It's what I need to do. How else can I ever know anything, if I don't understand myself? I've tried everything, everywhere. Joel offers something else…and he knows, he was there with me…it's not about me and him."

"And how long would this romp in the woods be, Ruby? This

skip down memory lane?"

"Please, Steve. Please understand. I want to get well."

He shook his head. "I can't stop you. I'm fed-up, and angry."

"I need Hannah and you. I just need myself more." She kissed him one more time, his lips, his hair, his musky taste, his comfortable arms. "Okay." She let go of him, marched into the bathroom, slid open the mirrored cabinet, counted, one bottle, two bottles, three bottles. She fondled them. "You've all got to go."

Steve's voice traveled from the kitchen into the bathroom. "I don't like this, Ruby. Do you hear me? Do you?"

She held the bottle of Valium in her hand. She studied the bottle, rattled it like a maraca, her eyes drew in deep, brown, drifting like wood down a river. She slumped over, "You can't make it safe anymore."

The door crashed against the wall. Steve edged in like volcano. "Since I was young, it was either or, either or, either, choose, your mother, your father, chicken, or pot roast, this shirt, this college. My family fucked with my head. You fuck with my head." He held the bottle of champagne, wavered in the doorway. "I can't stop you. And I can't know what is true for you. I can only decide for myself where I belong."

"I've got nothing, Steve. Nothing. I've believed for so long that I deserve to die. I'm afraid that if I'm happy, I'm betraying someone. I don't know how to be me. You have to see that. I'm a ticking grenade."

The burnt orange walls, the crystal fixture, the smell of suds, the toilet humming, wiggling water, wooziness from inebriation collapsed on them. Ruby conjured up some energy, "How do we come together when we need to grow apart first?"

Resignation set in. On the cold stone floor, they sat, Indian style. They passed the champagne to one another in silence.

"I've seen so much death I can't see life. Not even my own. I've been running away and running after. No more running." Tears swept down her face. "I don't want to be safe anymore. I want to feel alive." Ruby licked the last drop off the bottle. "Time to take that leap of faith."

Chapter 71: That Night – The Note

Ruby packed. She made the call to Joel. Told him everything. He set up all the essentials for her stay at Westfall. Strictly business. Ruby wanted it that way. "I feel sick seeing you. And I'm sick not seeing you."

She reserved a seat on Continental Airlines to California on the red eye. Before she left, she knocked on Hannah's door. 'Born in the USA" by Bruce Springsteen vibrated.

"Come in."

"Can you turn that down?" Ruby screamed over the music.

Hannah complied. Quiet.

"Do you hate me, Hannah?"

"Not anymore."

Ruby stooped next to the bed, rubbed her temples, pawed the edged of the mattress. "I have an illness, Hannah. I'm afraid. I need to get better." She looked straight at Hannah. "I want to heal, deep inside. I want to get better for you. For our home together. I'm not going on a joyride. I'm going out to California to heal. To be someone that can give you safety. I'm not running away from you. I'm running to you, to myself. I don't know what else to say."

"You're sick like my mother." She pointed to her head, "In here. Inside here. Like my mother!"

"You're mother gave up. I'm fighting for my life. For our lives."

"I can't stop seeing my mother…the way the cancer ate her. I saw…I wanted to kill myself too. Like her. I hated her. My grandparents. I tried to talk to them. They were mean, treated me bad. I knew my

Mom had some sort of awful illness. She looked so thin and gray. Every time I tried to call a doctor, she'd scream at me. Threatened to jump out of a window. I was so scared. I didn't know what to do. My dad was so busy fucking his new girlfriend. That Italian whore. My mother was dying and my father didn't even notice. She could barely walk. Can you imagine? My father didn't even notice. Finally, I took the keys. I ran downstairs. I said, "Dad, you have to drive Mom to the hospital. She's sick." He said, "Call 911." I ran back up. He hated Mom. She raged and raged all the time. Slept in a separate bedroom. Sometimes didn't come out for days. Finally, my mom let me take her down the steps. My father was reading the newspaper. He grabbed the keys. Stared at my mother then at me. He picked my mother up and carried her to the car. He said to me, "Get in the back." He got my mother in. Put on her seat belt. Started the engine. Started to drive. He drove fast. My mom. She had this strength. From some freakin' place. As he drove, she leaned over and rammed her foot on the accelerator, turned the wheel and we crashed head-on into a tree." Hannah sobbed. Beat her thighs. "I wasn't hurt. I was in the back and nothing got me. But, my father, my mother. Oh fuck. Oh God. I had a few scratches. What the hell? How did I live? Why did I live?"

Ruby grabbed and held her. "It's not your fault."

Hannah fought Ruby's embrace. She didn't want to be comforted by her. Ruby was stronger and wouldn't let go. Hannah fell into her arms and cried. "You did nothing wrong. Nothing. You couldn't have stopped your mother." She rocked her, wiped Hannah's tears away.

The sun sliced through the window. Hannah pushed Ruby away, slid off the bed. She pushed the armoire six inches from the wall. Behind it, where the floral wallpaper was slightly torn, an envelope was taped to the wall.

"Here."

Ruby hesitated then walked over to Hannah, "What is this?"

"When I cleaned out my mother's drawers I found this. It says "To My Sister Ruby" on the envelope.

Ruby hesitated and reached for the envelope. "I don't understand." She fingered the paper.

"I don't know." She licked her lips. "I was scared to give it to you."

Ruby slid her finger along the seal and broke open the envelope.

Unfolded the white paper. She began to read:

You were always stronger than me. And now I'm giving you my Hannah. I cherished her, hurt her, and abandoned her. Just like Mom did to us and I did to you. You're the only one I can give her to. No one else can understand her or what she would need. You have to take care of her. I'm sorry. I'm sorry. I'm sorry. Leah.

Ruby sank down to the floor, clutched the letter. "Hannah, I...oh, Hannah. I blame myself. I've been a coward." Ruby cried. She looked up. Hannah was gone. Ruby shook, frantic. "Hannah!"

In mere seconds, Hannah returned. She gripped a painting.

Ruby arched, eyes alert. The painting; colorful women shaded in blues, purples, reds, greens. Quiet waters, reflections of sky and moon. It took Ruby's breath away.

"I try to paint what you paint."

"It's remarkable." Ruby touched the edges of the canvas. "I'm coming back. I promise. You're so important to me, Hannah."

Hannah grabbed the painting and leaned it against the wall, "I can't lose you, Aunt Ruby."

"You won't. I promise."

Hannah frowned. "How do I trust you?"

Ruby gripped Hannah's hand, "We have the same strong blood." She held her face by the chin, stared at her dead straight in the eyes. "Do you hear me?"

Hannah slumped, "How long will you be gone?"

"I don't know. I don't know."

Chapter 72: July 7, 1986 – Ruby at Westfall

Ruby plopped her rear onto the mattress. Dull blue washed the walls with solemn comfort. Floral pictures of nondescript flowers hung about the walls. Lace curtains, a smell of lilac. Probably some sort of deodorizer. Ruby sniffed. Had to put some oomph into this room. Too bland. A short breeze clipped her face. The French doors were open to the acres of forest protecting the estate.

She glanced over at the calendar on the desk. Two years, two arduous years, but she was clean from drugs. Ruby never thought she'd be there so long. The healing was far reaching. A year of unyielding pain, grief, and terror. The second year, stabilization and integration.

Now only herbal remedies, Bach Remedies, color-puncture, acupuncture, vegan diet, juicing, guided imagery, and meditation kept her steady and centered. Then there was the deeper work. The cellular work. Still, her thoughts pinged, ponged, past, present, altered and other worldly. Ruby was blanking out. Sometimes forgetting dates, people's names, and where she was. But it was getting clearer, more stable.

A yellow bird chirped. Ruby caught it's tail end as it flew away. Outside the road curved. She remembered curling around the mountain as the taxi skirted the edges of the railed cliff. It seemed like yesterday. Below, ocean and a dozen or so seagulls danced across the horizon. She remembered the round stout driver who held the wheel with one-handed confidence, familiar with the unpredictability of each turn. Ahead, a random car here and there passed by in the opposite lane. The cabbie sang along with a Frank Sinatra tune, "Stranger in the Night."

She hummed a verse, thinking, remembering.

As they rounded further up the mountain, a river emerged from the middle of the sky. The river she now walked around every day. It swerved its gleaming body across acres of a lush green forest. Set back against the clouds, three stone mansions were seated among trees. Stone and brick gated the community.

The road poured into the driveway that welcomed visitors. The buildings deepened into the ground. A buried city known only to those who sought Utopia: pristine, untouched, as if civilization didn't exist. The wheels of the taxi cracked and crunched against the pebbles. Cherry blossoms, willows, and sweet-colored tulips played with the birds and bees. Westfall Estates, its grandeur, its majesty reigned beyond the world. The "rest home" awaited her.

When she arrived, she pledged to herself to stop everything. Stop brushing her teeth, combing her hair, picking out a new outfit to wear. Stop having to behave like she was happy that the sun rose or was grateful for all the money she inherited from her dead and insane family. Stop acting. Stop. Just stop.

Something popped in her head. Ruby walked to the table by the window. She was just thinking about the cab ride. She wanted to recall full days, full memories. She picked up a book. *Quantum Physics and Consciousness*. She tossed it. A sandalwood candle would make a difference. She'd have to call and request one. To the left, to the right, end tables and mundane beige lamps. No phone. She leaned on the chair and looked down. Chains bolted them to the floor. She walked over and touched the lamps. Also nailed to the table.

She blinked. She was high in the mountains. Joel popped into her head. He interacted with Ruby for the first two days. Set up her room, got her papers in order and created a program. It was surreal, sitting opposite Joel. Him being the teacher, the coordinator. He was professional with no shenanigans. "Ruby. I'm going to sporadically check in with you. Kimi will be working with you. When the time is right, and you are ready, we'll do the work we need to do together. I think Kimi is the best healer to help you through this. Not me. She's more of an expert in this area than I am. She'll let me know when it is right." Over the next two years, she saw Joel maybe ten times. To update on her progress. Once during that time, the third visit, Joel was silent. Stared endlessly into Ruby's eyes, the way he did when they were young. It made Ruby quiver, feel the old heat and passion they shared. She shook her head. *No*.

He felt it too. "I was so stupid, Ruby. I feel…what I feel doesn't matter. I have to stay committed to my path and you to yours. I promised my teacher. I promised. I have to go."

"There's the Joel I remember. Always having to leave. Find something he's never going to find. Funny, you're bringing me in home to myself, and you're still wandering the world."

He left the next day for an excursion in Peru. He came and went, went and came. Checking in on her. Making sure she had whatever she needed.

Kimi took care of her. She had to trust. Not Joel, but her gut. Things were happening. She was more stabilized, more able to manage the visions, the intense energy, moods, her dark energy receiving more light.

Steve and Hannah. Always, in and out of her mind-body. Weekends, holidays, Manichevitz wine, matzo, scented candles, Chanel perfume, they brought little things, new paint brushes, tiny charms for love, peace, and infinity to remember them by. She couldn't forget either of them. She made a promise. Every time they left, it took a toll. Ruby sat in silence for days. Was she wrong? That is what her sister asked before she died, "*Did I do anything wrong?*"

A knock. She didn't answer. "Go away. I'm not ready"

Sole-less feet scurried away. But no. Another knock. "Can I come in?" The voice was smooth, sleek, careful.

Ruby realized that she was naked. Touched her stomach as if stroking a baby's rear. "I have to get dressed. Wait a minute." She rushed over to the drawers, pulled out shorts and a T-shirt. She clumsily dressed. A brush on top of the dresser. *Okay*. Brush. Brush. Her hair still knotted like an old spool of wool. "Come in." Ruby's eyes widened.

The door opened. Kimi. Okay. She got a hold of it. "Hi, Kimi." Something was different about her. Something. What? Her hair. She was wearing it loose, down her back. It was the color of owl's feathers and shone like the fur on a chocolate brown Burmese cat. Ruby giggled. Her eyes were as tiny as she was small. Maybe she was a rat. A human rat with blue jeans.

Kimi leaned against the dresser. "It's time."

Ruby stared. Kimi's eyes spread across her face as she smiled. They were blue. Did rats have blue eyes? Her teeth were large and hung over her lip like chipmunk. Ruby laughed.

"What's so funny?"

Another glance and Kimi's face was full, brown, her cheekbones highlighted in a deep reddish shine. Behind her, Ruby witnessed an old woman with braided white hair beating a drum. "Is that your grandmother beating the drum?" She pointed. "I see her behind you."

Kimi nodded. "I suppose." She picked up Ruby's flip-flops and dangled them back and forth.

"What do you want from me today?"

"Your attention." Kimi waited. Still as the sky before a storm.

"I want red curtains and red paint." Ruby searched, her eyes roamed about as if uncertain in her decision. "And I want scissors."

Kimi licked her lips. Her eyes wandered. They paced around Ruby's face.

Ruby ground her foot into the floor, "I want to put another coat of red paint on the wall. I want red curtains to match. I want to cut my hair."

Kimi stood up. "I'll cut your hair. And you can paint and put up the curtains. I'll help. It'll be our project."

"You won't know how to cut my hair."

Kimi slipped toward to the door. "I'll cut it the way you want." She left like a ray of dust light.

Ruby perched herself into a chair. Waited and waited. Next stop. Next moment. Next. Hurry up, Kimi. Ruby's foot shook. It was a race against time. Ruby never knew when she'd transport into another realm. This was when her anxiety mounted into terror. But she learned to keep her trembling under control through deep breathing and little yelps, praying, asking for help. Kimi advised, "When you are most faint, afraid of the life channeling through you, keep breathing and surrender. Keep breathing and allow. Nothing can hurt you. Just be still and know you are safe." For Ruby, life and death hinged on those words. She repeated Kimi's medicine words, validating, allowing the space, the latitude and longitude to calm herself. Meet Marianne face to face. Not through random encounters. But walk right up to her square in the face and say, "Hey Marianne. What's up, girl? I'm right here. Come and get me." It was just a matter of time.

The doorknob jiggled. Ruby's foot stopped its dance. She held her breath. "It's open." But no one entered.

Chapter 73: The Calling

Ruby wove her fingers together. She held her breath, her face flushed, shook her hands, released. Her nerves fired up each time she watched.

Kimi flicked on the video.

"I need a glass of water." Ruby stroked her neck. "Make the sound loud."

Kimi handed her a glass of water. "Here is a pad and pencil. Write down anything that comes to you. Try to remember to allow the writing to just come. Do it as we have practiced. Place the pencil on the pad and your hand will move. You have to empty. Surrender. You're doing a great job."

Ruby gurgled some water, placed it on the desk. Squeezed the pencil and placed the pad on her lap. She perched at the edge of the couch.

Kimi clicked on the VCR.

Ruby's speech was throaty, sultrier, with a slight Middle Eastern accent blended with a Brooklyn twang. Ruby glued her eyes and ears to the footage. Jumbled words, at first incoherent, at times bits and pieces, then more fluid, poured out.

Marianne spoke through Ruby. It began with a request. "*I want to come home. I ran away, afraid...didn't want to be crucified. Like great-great grandmother Sarah left Mesopotamia and Grandma Sarah left Russia/Poland. What is in my heart? All women deep in their cells, the memory of being obliterated, annihilated, their voices and stories twisted into dust and ghosts. Grandma Sarah was raped.*

She hated herself. Left Poland, bitter, delusional, and psychotic. Grandma Sarah of Mesopotamia, priestess, so lonely, alone in her vision. Marianne sobbed.

My love was dead. I left pregnant with child. I was lost. After my love died…so much longing. Where is love? My body is sexual love and sacred love. I had to find the Shekinah through blind faith. Fear, desperation, the courage, the strength to be vulnerable. I feel the rage of my ancestors, Sarah, Leah, Rebecca. The Jewess in my blood. The feminine carries the blood, the heritage. When the ancestors were slaughtered, future generations of women went insane. Lost the direction of the knowledge. Forgot who they were, that they are the Earth. Hearts broken and torn. Sobbing deeply, Marianne pounded her chest, reached out with her hand. My heart breaks open to all the hurt and sorrow. We walked for forty days and nights, grieving, angry, not knowing. The land of milk and honey. Generations of women forgotten. They became psychotic, the fallen angels rebellious against creation, fallen women, shamed. We're empty for love. The void full of injustices, inequality, cruelty. Humanity paid the price when the feminine was obliterated. We were tortured, millions slaughtered as witches. We are healers, saints, and medicine women. The Church burned us alive. Marianne fisted in rage, growled, We are Mother Earth. We want to love this earth, the human body. I gave up everything. You, Ruby, you, out there. Bring me home. Open your hearts. I am Jewess, Prophet. Madwoman. Savior.

Marianne shifted Ruby in the chair, cleared her throat.

He came to take me out of the ritual temples. I was a holy prostitute. He came to me! I didn't want to give myself to any one man but he held me captive in his chemistry, in his allure…something that I couldn't control. Together, we followed something beyond. We followed each other and rebelled against tyranny. My depression lifted from his kiss. Alive in splendor. But then something happened. I started to dance and swirl and see everything between the lines, feelings that made no sense…irrational…urgent to find the woman in me. The woman in him. What did I love? It would seem I only loved him, not even myself. I drank from the rivers, I ran with the moon, I baked the challah for Shabbot. I prayed the morning prayer. Saw in my belly eye, my gut knowing, that the way of the feminine would die. And mankind would suffer. I drew the eye of the storm in the sand.

Traveled into the underworld and faced demons. What did I do? What did I learn? I fought the dark angel. No one listened. They laughed at me. Scorned me. When the rabbi - my love - died, they saw, men wrote my history, my autobiography, not me. But, you learn from me. Marianne curled, eyes cast downward, a shadow falling across her face. You must have a child from your womb. Hannah is your child. She is the daughter. Find her in your DNA. Give her the day and night. Give her the body of sensuality. Give her your heart. Give her everything because she is the future. The daughters are the future.

I am a Jew. I hunger for the feminine...the old ways, the trances and prayers that created prophecy and peace. I need to become whole. To heal the women, bring together the gatherings and circles to heal. Teach the mysteries. The body is the guide. Wisdom comes from within in the cells, the skin, the bones. I am a Jew; help me find my way back into the tribe, the female clans, who worshipped the blood of the vagina. To change the world, you must change yourself. Undo what has been done. Clear out the past first, then peace can come. Not before.

Marianne placed her hands in prayer to her heart, rocked. *Holy. Holy. Holy. I give you the stories of generations, the myths, the legends. You are the scribe. Write stories. Paint stories. Awaken the sleeping body and mind. Transcribe them to books. This will not be easy. But, I beg you. Don't run away. Please.*

Black and white static vibrated behind the glass. Kimi clicked off the tape. "That's all on this tape."

"Don't, don't shut it off. I want to look. Really look at me - her, whoever."

Kimi pressed the button, froze the frame.

Ruby came close to the screen, slid her hand across its smooth surface. "That's me. That's me all crumpled up? Am I sleeping? Am I her? I feel Marianne's longing. Her ache. Longing. To be whole and one. To be at peace." Once again she touched the cold screen.

Kimi touched Ruby's shoulder. "She's calling to us all."

"I don't know how I can do this. So much to interpret. There are at least two-dozen journals. I am still healing. How can I give this to others? You're the Algonquin. You're wiser than me. Why not you to take this task?" Ruby hunched down into the sofa, laid her head back and sobbed. "I'm so scared. Who'll believe me?"

"You answered the call, Ruby. Better for you to accept that truth."

Ruby sipped out of Kimi's teacup. "Marianne wants to come home. But I don't know what that means." Ruby got up and walked toward the door. "The fragments are coming together, the puzzle pieces. Marianne wanting to come home to her Hebrew sisters. How can I be the one to know that?"

Kimi sat by Ruby's feet, rubbed her calves, "Just by allowing. Trusting being you. No one ever knows the entire truth. You have pieces of the story. It'll become whole as you continue to become whole."

"How can I hold all of this and live a normal life? I'm a Jewish girl from Brooklyn. Who am I?"

Kimi smiled, "It's a paradox. It doesn't make sense. But does it matter? Go for the ride. Fighting it just makes you sick." She went to her desk drawer and pulled out a large black book. "Already you are starting to organize your thoughts from Marianne's thoughts. In here. These are your interpretations. You're writing all of this in a conscious state. I've been reading it. I'm lost in it. And it ignites and jolts me."

"Give me that."

Kimi surrendered the leather journal to her.

Ruby held the book to her cheek, hugged it for a moment then thumbed through the pages. "I remember. There are six videos. Right?"

"You see. Progress." Kimi emptied her teacup and placed the steeped bag on a tray. "Close your eyes, Ruby, breathe."

Ruby adjusted her dress, pulled her feet underneath and did as the doctor ordered. "I still don't understand. Anything."

Kimi's eyes watered up. An outburst of tears threw her body to the ground.

"Why are you crying, Kimi? What's wrong?" Ruby rushed to her side.

Kimi rubbed her eyes. "No. This is not about me."

"I want to know."

Kimi got up and walked over to the cabinet and reached for the chamomile tea leaves, boiled the water and let the leaves sit, waiting for it to strengthen its brew into something hearty to drink. "This tea saved me one night." She stirred then licked the spoon. "I was in one of my drunken stupors, vomiting bile, couldn't stop. And this tea came to my rescue. I poured it onto a heating pad, wet and hot, and bathed my body in its warmth, and drank the remains of it until I slept a deep sleep with no regret. She sat back down and looked at the sky. "I've hidden my past. I've guided you, but you're journey has jolted me to feel things I have squashed. I am moved to share my story. I've been judging myself. How can I be a healer, when I am still healing?"

"Aren't we all still healing? Look at me? I'm not walking on water. I don't know what the fuck is happening. Don't you tell me to trust?"

Kimi wavered in a pensive stare.

"It's only fair." Ruby threw the book on the chair.

Kimi sipped the tea and straightened, her face tightening. "I'm a recovering alcoholic."

"Tell me. Remember, as Marianne says. It is every woman's story." Ruby crawled to the couch, spooned against the pillows.

Kimi stared off and put her hands over her face. "I lost my son. Leukemia. My husband left. I set off to travel the world to find a way to heal my pain." She melted into her story, tears glowed in her eyes. "Joel helped me. Gave me a reason to be."

"Oh god. I...I'm so sorry."

"My father was a drunk, his father, and his father. It's in my blood. My mother and grandmother turned the other cheek. Took their abuse. Like so many of the grandmothers and mothers. I got pregnant never knowing who the father was. It took my son's death to smack the living daylights out of me. It took a breakdown, it took the world coming to an end, a long damn end of everything...and now I'm here."

"I'm so very sad. How old was your son?"

"Three."

"Three?" Ruby, twisted her hands, shook her head."I'm afraid to have children. And you lost your child. I'm so selfish."

Kimi sat up. "You have Hannah. And, you have done the best you can do. As I have. And as Joel has." Light and dark outlined the lines around her eyes.

Ruby rubbed her chest, her eyes beaten with sorrow. "My heart, wow. My heart aches. We are taught to be tough and hard in order to survive. Our feelings shamed. It's a web of deceit." She stared out, eyes questioning and distant. "I don't know if I still love Joel. If I love Steve. Or what love is. I know it starts with myself, but there are so many layers. So much we don't know and think we know. And we know shit."

Kimi's eyes softened and she tapped her cup, "Many, many, many layers. And all we can do is let go."

Ruby picked up the remote and switched the tape back on. Again the words of Marianne slurred from Ruby's mouth. *"Holy, Holy, Holy."* She freeze-framed her image.

"I'm the most unholy person there is." She clicked the tape on and off. "I was really drugged up and hallucinating. Joel laced the marijuana. I transported into Marianne's world. She said I had to work on my life before I touched her. I've hated her for making me crazy. Hated my mother for being my worst nightmare. My grandmother hated my mother because she had been raped by Cossacks and blamed my mother with her own self-hatred. The hatred handed down to all the women in my family. And who knows how many mothers back in my lineage have self-hatred. Where was the love? I can't think, I can't, my head…my…" Ruby screeched.

"Ruby. Listen to yourself. You're making contact. You're connecting the story. We cannot hate unless we love deeply."

Ruby dropped the remote. Entranced. Gone. *"Schma Isroyel… Schma Isroyal…bring me home. I'm dying…dying….what's left of me is dying."* Ruby's eyes widened, her spine curved and she perked up straight and confident.

Kimi tilted her head…"Marianne?"

Ruby's eyes broke open with desire. "Yes?"

Chapter 74: Marianne in Ruby's Flesh

An ancient temptress scalded the heat of Ruby's lips. Marianne spoke.

Kimi stood back. Didn't dare interrupt the transformation. She flipped the switch on the video camera. A whizzing sound rounded about inside the heart of the camera, snapping Ruby's every movement.

"I'm deeply disturbed. The *Shabbat* candles aren't lit." Ruby rummaged about, snatched a cotton blanket from the couch, laid it upon her head and let it cascade around her body. "Rabbi, you must get me the candles. But before, you must kiss me so I can know we are one in prayer." She snapped her fingers. "Go. And then let in the others."

Kimi fumbled around trying to find candles, but to no avail. "Sorry, Marianne. We need to go to the temple to light the candles. Will you follow me?"

Ruby twirled. "The energy ignites right here."

Kimi tried to lead. "Let's go to the temple."

Ruby dragged the blanket over her face and her body and slinked to the floor. "No, I'll stay here." She grabbed Kimi's face. "My heart breaks, Rabbi. They all reject me. I can't be who they want me to be. I can't stay quiet. They say woman cannot, do not see such things. Does not study, does not lead. You died and then I had to hide. Afraid all the time that I'd be the next to be crucified. I moved across the ocean. Alone. With our baby. I must pray tonight. For your soul and our baby's soul. The little angel. The little soul. Died in my arms. Her soft body. So soft. Too frail to make the journey. I couldn't live without you, without her." She straightened the cloth over her head. "If we are to be Holy, we must light the candles. Grieve and love. Love and walk the edge."

Kimi held out her hand to Ruby. "My baby died too. I know. Come. Let's create the circle."

Ruby hesitated, then followed her through the waiting room, hand clutching Kimi's shirt. "Who are these people?" Her body erect, alert, her eyes studied each person.

The group huddled in a swarm of whispers, buzzing like night flies around her.

"Tell them to go away. I didn't do anything wrong." Ruby blanketed her face.

Kimi comforted her with a gentle tug, "They are not judging you, Marianne. If you look closely, you know all of them." She pointed. "Over there is George, and then Ruth, and David and Sonia."

Ruby laughed. There was a Twiggy-like woman; her blonde hair stark straight to her chin, her blue eyes outlined black like a raccoon. She wore a purple shirt with yellow and blue polka dot shorts, her toenails, painted an iridescent pink, protruded from her flip-flops. George raised his hand. A floral scarf twisted around his forehead. His long ponytail, ragged and unwashed, stuck to his neck like an old neckpiece. He ooh'd and ahh'd, twittering about like a five-year-old. His need to be seen drenched all over and consumed the others like a hungry toddler. "Marianne, please Marianne." He wiggled around in his spot to be recognized.

Then there was David, all wolverine and ready for action with his Davy Crocket hat and overalls. His eyes were warm and loopy. Last but not least was heavy-set Sonia, draped in a white linen ankle-length dress, bald, a red moon and dove tattooed on her arm.

"Oh, I see them. Yes, I see them." Ruby weaved through the small gathering as she spoke. "Why do you follow me? I can see you all have your own visions."

Ruby stopped, turned. She pulled the blanket off, tore her dress off and tossed it in the air. "I want to run naked. I want to go away. Far away." She was vulnerable and raw, reaching upward, her body soaked and quivering in naked sweat. "Every day I grind my toes like a gypsy, dancing to the music of the tambourine. Like Miriam who pranced across the Red Sea, banging her tambourine. Ruby sang.

"Hey Mrs. Tambourine Girl sing a song for me. I am wasted and there is nowhere that I'm going to." She laughed.

Kimi attempted to cover Ruby with the blanket. Ruby kept throwing it off.

Soon everyone was tearing off his or her clothes. They were wailing, contorting into a knotted mass of skin and bones. An orgy of flesh melted into a mass of bodies.

Ruby jumped, clapped, and raised her hands to the heavens. Her knees wobbled and folded and she fell. "I've lost my words to tell my story. Her story. All the mothers and sisters have lost their words. They're all dead. I can't hold this any longer. How many letters, words, sentences? How many? They're caught in my throat, in my vagina. I'm between lives. No more words. Ohh…damn it all. I'm damned. Why don't you leave me alone?"

Mounds of crusted, dark, light, black, white hands begged in prayer. It was a holy snake pit that blossomed into a lotus of people petals, crying to be set free from their agony. They believed that Ruby led the way, or more likely, that Marianne led the way. Ruby ran and ran. Left them behind to wallow in their own stupor.

Kimi pulled out a walkie-talkie, "It's Ruby. She's on the loose."

Chapter 75: Sacred Wild Side

The rain hit the roof with gentle patters. Ruby snuggled into the blanket and spoke from a transcendent reality. "I'm in the desert. The sun streams down. Surrounding me are mountains, the steam of arid light brushes against my body. I open my heart and I feel the day. Feel today. Just feel. Hear my breath. In and out. In and out. Feel my body. The physicality of it, how it holds emotions, its sensations. Right here, now." She lit candles and waved her hands over her face, placed her palms to her eye.

Kimi sat next to Ruby, touched her arm and stroked it. "Don't worry. When you go into terror, you lose it. It's okay. You're safe. We have to keep working through the terror."

Ruby leaned against Kimi's shoulder. "Why don't you just chain me up like the chairs and lamps? That would be better."

"Bullshit." Kimi's face was intent, sharp, her mouth trembled, her fierce and alive. "I don't have compassion. At this point you truly know better. And you know it. You know it!" Kimi grabbed Ruby's wrist. "You're in the fire, the ride. Scream from the highs and lows, but keep digging, finding your ground. Don't go back into that, I'm not good enough, woe is me!" Kimi's voice was ironclad with conviction.

Outside, the crickets sang, the wet air was filled with pine and fresh cut grass. Ruby sniffed. "The smells of this place, the sounds, comfort me." She shook her head. "The urge inside is so strong. I will listen and write. I will." Ruby fluttered her fingertips like butterfly wings over the flame. "I gather up the energy and find myself, ground to my feet and hips…allow the vision, emotions and voices to come in…like a painter, a writer, I am telling the story without my words, without my language, just the feelings that guide. I feel Marianne. The thump of her heart, the dryness of her breath, the feel of her sundrenched skin. I drink her. Like water. I screw the top on and plug up any leaks, and the water flows inside the container. The truth is…I feel so alive when it happens. I feel every sensation, emotion, memory. It's so big, bigger than I've been able to hold. I don't think I have the right, or the worthiness. I react, become young. I become a child and scream a tantrum, because I don't want to be responsible. I don't want the job. I am trying to grow up, respond to the calling, not react into a mental breakdown." She held her stomach. "It's all in my emotions. The feelings…when I tame the feelings and follow them, it just happens. When I let the feelings guide me, the crazy thoughts calm down. But I have to feel deep, into the depth of my soul, my vagina, my body. Strong feelings, like a lightning bolt. I heat up. Energy. You've helped me, Kimi. You brought me to this place." Ruby's face folded into generations. Sarah, Claire, Leah contorted her features, alchemical changes to her appearance. "I'm all of them, my family, the women…except…for whatever reason, Hannah is the one. She is the one that will inherit the truth." Ruby caught herself, stopped talking. "I don't really know what I'm saying."

Kimi blew out the flames, pulled the candles out of the holder, placed them on the table. Picked up a red crayon and began to draw circles on the wall. "What you have to offer the world is a miracle. Hold onto your faith. This is your time."

"I don't want to save the world. I want to live in it."

Kimi laughed and threw the crayon down. "No one can save the world. Moses led the people, but he didn't enter Israel. Esther tried to save the Jewish people, but she didn't save the world. Marianne. She had vision beyond. You can give others a new perspective, a new understanding that she was human and of a great spiritual heritage. Marianne has given you that privilege. And Hannah has been given to you to pass it on."

Ruby slid on the bed next to Kimi, picked up the crayon and began to draw a large-bellied woman with snakes coming out of her head. "That is what Marianne feels." Ruby lit up with surprise and continued to draw. "I feel that from her. She's very insistent on getting that through to me." Her drawing became stronger, more exaggerated, the woman's hands and legs extended across the wall, her breasts hung. Ruby jumped up on the bed, tiptoed to reach the ceiling with her drawing, fill up the wall with this Amazon woman.

"Miriam was cursed with leprosy when she wanted to head one of the tribes. But she led the Israelites across the sea, frenzied in her glory. All the women were crazed with passion for God. They longed for this great love."

Kimi whispered. "The great love. The longing. The feminine."

Ruby kept drawing, "Home. Home is in my body. Home is in my womb where the *Shekinah* lives."

Kimi perked up. "Who's saying that? Ruby? Marianne?"

Ruby dropped the crayon. Smiled. "I believe both of us."

Chapter 76: Three Months Later, January, 1987 – Grounded

The day dripped of just the right amount of January coolness. A hint of mint and pine mixed in the air. Coyote and wild geese serenaded her. Ruby watched a caterpillar wiggle its curly body along the rim of the banister. It slid slowly, stopped, remained silent and still, then slid again; there was no rush or destination, no time or intent to its movements. The little green being was in the hands of destiny, just as she was.

Ruby sighed, pulled her red wool shawl snuggly around her, and pulled her blue granny dress under her naked feet. She had been reading the journals. Perusing the first six. So much to understand and integrate.

Nature was good medicine for her today. She sank into its solid embrace, secure in what the moment offered her; a retreat, a reprieve from the deep work. It had been years since she felt any relief. But now she drank in the full, rich beauty that surrounded her, savoring it like a gourmet meal. Suddenly, something quivered Ruby into sweats, trembling, stopping her flow. Something was coming. She felt it. She felt Joel was near. She shook off the feeling and continued to read.

Ruby closed her eyes. Around her were the voices. Strange, hard and soft aromas of lavender, then mud and arid dung clung to her nostrils, strung through the vibrations. Ruby saw Marianne climb the stones, her footsteps forging a path into the mountains, away from the villages, the people's sweat and gore, scabs, and leprosy of the soul. Marianne was the chosen one. She saw beyond the fear. The other mothers stood in their iridescent bodies, Sarah, Rebecca, Leah, Miriam, Esther. Their stories half told. Half truths. Still to be told. They spoke to her from the leaves, the rosebushes in the gardens. Ruby read, "*Woman as the body of life. We are the heavens that walk the earth. But there is more to know. To live. It is endless. Stories of love, hate, sorrow and miracle. Tell them all.*"

Ruby felt a hand squeeze her shoulder. She shuddered. The journal hit the floor with a thump. Unprepared for any human contact, she stumbled to her feet, her eyes burrowed with uncertainty. "Oh my god! Joan!"

Slender, tired, a big smile across face. Her body melted into a black halter, simple and clean. "Ruby!"

"Joan. Joan!" Ruby squinted.

Joan's eyes paled, lids quivered about to cry. "I've missed you so much. It's seems like a million years."

Ruby edged around the rocker, came a foot closer, stared into Joan's eyes. She locked into Joan's every twitch, facial tick, pores of her skin. "Joan? Joan! You're half the size of yourself. Why are you here? Why are you here?"

They hugged with ferocity.

Joan eyes wandered to Ruby's neck. "You still wear the necklace."

Ruby clutched the dangling charms. "Why are you here?"

From behind Joan, inside the crack of the door, a man's figure stood in the shadows. He leaned against the French doors. Then he slowly moved forward.

The closer he came, the more familiar his face. Blonde hair, square jaw, strong frame. It was Joel. Ruby glared at her friend, a collapsed confusion sunk in her chest.

"Hi, Ruby." Joel stood beside Joan. Dressed in bell-bottom jeans and white shirt. His spicy fragrance radiated and dusted the wind that crept across the porch.

Ruby covered her head with her shawl.

Joel spoke first. "Kimi says you're near. That you're managing and guiding the messages more easily. That your recovery and integration is coming along."

Ruby studied the two, a detective, sniffing their presence, feeling her way into the energy that seemed to bond them. "You're here together?"

Joan shot a look at Joel. Joel caught Joan's concern and clipped a quick nod. "Yes."

Ruby felt a betrayal flick through her body, her eyes stern, cold, alert.

Joan spoke. "We've all been supporting you. Steve, Hannah, Joel, Kimi. We only want your well-being."

Ruby blurted out, "Joel and Steve! And you? Hannah? Really? When did this happen?"

Joan stepped toward her.

Ruby flipped her hand up to stop her from getting closer.

Joan fixed a grip on her hip. "Ruby. We all want your health. We all have your back."

Ruby tightened the shawl. "This is strange. Too strange. Stranger than Marianne talking through me. Stranger than my mother's face without makeup. Stranger than my grandmother's, oh, stranger, damn, than…stranger…"

Joan threw up her hands, "Stop. I get it. Listen, Ruby when you left, soon after, Jim left me."

Ruby's tilted her head. "I don't understand."

Joel jumped into the conversation. "We met after the lecture when she helped me find you. We've become friends. And…"

"Oh, like we were friends, Joel?" Ruby flipped her hand at him.

Joan interrupted, "Joel brought me through a terrible depression." She crossed her heart, held up her hand. "See my hand, Ruby, see, I'm swearing the truth. Nothing torrid or erotic." Frustrated, Joan drew a long sigh, tapped her foot. "I'm here to get a rest from my own life as well. It's been a long, dirty divorce." She placed her hand over her heart. "I love you Ruby. I'd never hurt you."

Ruby rubbed her neck. She threw the shawl back onto her shoulders. "You always pushed, Joan. I pulled and you pushed." She wiggled her fingers at Joan, an infant needing to clutch. Joan slipped her hand into Ruby's. "I trust you. I do." She squeezed her hand. "I'm sorry about Jim. I don't think I'd be wrong guessing that Jim ran off with some bikini-waxed princess, ass-suctioned, big-boobed younger plastic surgery addict?"

Joan's sad laugh softened her eyes. "Yeah. I saw it coming, but looked the other way for a long time."

Joel motioned to Joan for permission to speak. He held his palm up mid-air. "Girls. You can catch up later. Ruby, we have work to do today."

"We do?"

"Brooklyn. Basement. That was a core moment for you. Whatever there is left to be remembered and released, I'm part of that with you."

Ruby lost herself in the buzz of the crickets and bees. "Yeah. I know, Joel. From the time I stood on the ledge at six. Then, that night in your basement. It was the first bi-location." She whispered." You drugged me. Took my virginity. Made promises. Then left. I can feel all of that still. It holds in me. Tears at my heart."

"I was a arrogant coward. I'm grateful you can forgive me." His eyes shifted with hope.

"I don't know if I've forgiven you Joel. I just know I have to face my demons."

Joel put out his hand to lead her. He nodded to Joan. "We'll come and get you."

Joan touched Ruby's cheek. "Go."

Ruby hugged Joan. "Did you see Hannah and Steve before you came?"

"They're doing good, Ruby. But, they miss you."

At that moment, a strong urge to feel Steve's arms around her. Sit on the edge of Hannah's bed and talk. Westfall wasn't her home anymore.

Ruby eyes roamed over to Joel. She walked past him turned with a swift clip, "I'm ready to die or live. Maybe both. Are you, Joel?

Chapter 77: Reliving Love, Pain, and Prophecy

Ruby's life now came to this moment.

Kimi was moving the couch and chairs against the wall when they entered the therapy room. Curtains closed, a dim lamplight shone against the walls. The room transformed into a mystical porthole, a time warp into Ruby's unconscious. In the center of the room was a big red armchair, frayed, faded, food stains and smelling of years gone by. Ruby flinched, her mind flipped to Joel's basement. "You kept it? How? That's freakin' off the wall!"

"I knew somehow I had to keep it. It's a remnant. It holds the energy. I sat in that chair often, remembering, regretting. I could never let it go. I've kept it in storage. Took it out. Put it away. Now it can complete its purpose."

Ruby slid her hand along the old velvet fabric. "A time machine?" She walked around the big old chair, sniffed, patted and laughed. Her mood soon turned into solemn waves, sporadic trembles, simple cries. Her face changed form, wolf-like, about to snap. "It's alive, this chair."

"I'm sweating." Joel wiped his hands together.

Ruby crawled into the chair. "Afraid you'll lose your mind, Joel? Or your heart?"

"I'm afraid I won't ever lose my mind or find my heart." Joel grinned.

Ruby wondered who is this man? He didn't have the rough edge, the big-shot, I'm-a-god attitude. She searched for the seducer, the misogynist, the vampire who wanted her soul-blood. Wanted to steal her secrets, the mystery and intensity of her womanhood. Now he was only a man, with skin and bones that stood in front of her, vulnerable in his fear. He no longer held power. He emanated nothing but humaneness. Joel's earthiness made her heart race. She breathed deep. Now, even more she was drawn to him. A deeper remembrance of her young love for him pounded in her chest---a time when she wanted only to hide in his arms, run away with him.

Ruby thought about life back in Florida and New York. Steve popped into her mind. The man who never left, but their marriage narrowed her choices of who she was. Safety did that. It made her one-dimensional. Material and afraid. Once, she slid credit cards through slim slots to satisfy the hunger in her belly like she forced her body through the tiny hole of lies she told herself, every time she spent too much, or gave too much, or overstayed a situation too long. She needed to take that karmic credit card and rip it up, so she'd have her debt clean. No longer the suburbanite, the city girl, or daughter, sister, wife or mother. The pain of her childhood, memories, life/ death. Despair. So much pain. Her heart needed to close to the past, not forget, but simply close the curtain, just like her wallet, because what she was buying back was her life.

Ruby curled into the chair. She was diving into her psyche ocean. Now she could participate through her own free will. Ruby closed her eyes. Her hands gripped the edges of the soft fabric. The chair massaged her memory. Held the story and cells of a past life. She breathed. She wanted to go there. Back. To the room filled with dull light, a flickering of candles, the beat of electric guitar… *experrrrrrrrrrrrience*. The color of her soul, the bones of her body, the colors of yellow, green, and red swirled inside and lifted her in. She learned how to transport in moments. Let time collapse into a surrender.

Joel came close, his breath minty, wet, he touched her third eye. "Breathe," his voice a whisper from the past. He tapped different points around her face and upper body. "Breathe. I'm here now. Breathe. I'm here now. Allow peace to flow." The collusion of their energy caused Ruby to open. Dry heat, the cries of coyotes, the wandering of her blood boiled; Joel's presence reeked of sex and abuse.

She screamed. "Get off of me, Joel. Motherfucker. I hate you." Tears choked in her throat. "No. No. I don't hate you. I love you."

She slammed the arms of the chair. Then fell to the floor kicking, screaming. "Hate you. Hate you. I hate you, mom. Blood everywhere. Love me, Joel. Love me!"

A deep heave of her breath and she was quiet. Desert and sun. Lizards, spiders and camel dung. Hot, sweat arid juice of life.

Marianne screamed at her. "Don't touch me."

"I'm ready, Marianne. I'm ready to touch your hem."

She had given herself over to Marianne.

Ruby eyes flickered, slept in the dream. It led her back, back to that time, the entrance into Marianne's world, through the hallucinations, the rape, the scorching of her mind, her heart, the battering of her soul, the sacrifice of her voice, allowing others, the men, the disciples who stood around, they robbed her of her life, defined who she was. The altars destroyed. The stars, moons, the herbs, the allowing, the full bodied women, their dark skin, their spiritual sacred sexuality, their ovaries filled with the intensity of stark, raw emotions. The women of the night, the temples, the men who raped, the spoils of war, women and children. Marianne was there and the rabbi was by her side. "Rabbi." Ruby cried, clutched her heart. "Joel. Rabbi. Are you here?"

"Ruby, I'm here." Joel whispered from behind.

Ruby screamed, trembled. "So much hate. I'm broken, broken apart. I hurt and hurt." Ruby roared. Her face turned savage. She tumbled on all fours, heaved and let out wildness, sounds of the jungle, it ripped from her belly belting the air with unending torment.

"AHHHHHHHHHHHHHHHHHHHHHHHHHHHHHHHH." Blotches of tears, sweat, blood tears, and violation. Her body jerked. Her eyes rolled, violent screams rattled her throat. Blood trickled from Ruby's wrists. "I loved you. You died. You left me. You all left me. I'm so alone."

Kimi leapt and wrapped a blanket around her. "We need to get her to a hospital. We need to get her to a hospital. What's happening? We got to get her to a hospital. Now!"

Joel fell to his knees, "Hold her feet. Hold her feet, Kimi. I'm going to hold her head. Do it. Do it now. Don't lose it now. Pray. Do your prayer."

Kimi slapped her hands around her ankles, she repeated over and over, chanting, bowing, crying, delivering the message to Ruby,

"*Mother ease my pain, mend my broken bones, teach me to mourn, bring me wholeness. Mother heal my shattered, torn heart, so I can use the gifts of my wounds, and allow you to use me in service.*"

Joel hands circled Ruby's head, he called out, ran his fingers across her spine, "*Hashem, Hashem. Hashem.* Show me the way. Show Ruby the way. Heal, Marianne. Heal Ruby. *Shekinah, Adonai.* I am grateful for all you offer us today." He held her wrists.

Ruby's eyes flipped open. The bleeding stopped. The red stains disappeared. Ruby's body jittered, her hands shook. She shot up. Joel and Kimi cradled her to a sitting position.

Ruby's eyes, a lighthouse of brilliance, hurriedly scanned the room, stared first at Joel, then at Kimi. A dam breaking, a flood of generations, of words, a story, a catharsis, all that Ruby held as foreign. She was the voice; the carrier, the one who had to have her say. Her voice, the braille written across her tongue and gut, the carvings of scribes in her heart. Finally, the garden of pain spilled forward. Ruby held her neck, squealed and coughed.

"It needs to come. Let it come, Ruby." Joel held his hand an inch above Ruby's head.

"I'm, I'm…it's all around me. Inside of me. The faces that are torn from my bones. I need to undo the lies of my father's ignorance, the violence of my mother's sorrow, the coldness of my grandmother's isolated and bitter life. Leah's death. I ache for them. They shake my body. Shake it with fear." Ruby threw the blanket from her body. She stroked Kimi's cheek. "Don't let go of me."

Kimi jerked a bit, her breath erratic, sharp. "I won't. I promise."

"I need to speak. I need to say…Marianne needs to say. We both need to say."

Joel pointed to Kimi to make sure the tape was rolling. Kimi ran over, clicked on the camera and ran back. "Go ahead Ruby or Marianne. Say whatever you want to say."

Ruby cleared her throat. She began, "I can speak. I can hear. I can feel. Truth doesn't please anyone but herself. No numbing, no escape. No stuffing Twinkies or pot, or pretenses down her throat. I see you, Kimi, Joel. I am holding on. I'm staying in. I'm coming home." She straightened, bowed her eyes away, a student to herself then held her head high.

"Who are you, Ruby or Marianne?" Joel asked.

"I am here. I talk for Ruby and myself. It is all our story." She stroked her arms. "My skin is smooth, wet and burdened with the caked blood, crusted and sticky. I am thick, pulsating, red, bulging beats. Deep down the mother scar, the crack of the bone, the tear of skin, the blood that bleeds from the heart. Love me, says the little girl, love me, pick me up and cradle me. But there is no mother to be found. No mother except the one sitting on the edge of the toilet slitting her wrist. She runs through the streets, naked, screaming, tearing her hair from her head, she runs after me like a alligator opening her big jaw, her sharp teeth pull me under the tub water, I can't breathe. Help! Help me. I am drowning in the snot and goo of the darkness of the mental illness my mother carries. She wants to destroy her own children. She is Medea, murdering her children."

"Why did the mothers die?" Joel questioned.

"I carry a hump of pain on my back. This is the burden that carries self-hatred, resentments and jealousies, of loneliness and despair. My sister's death. Leah. I placed the flower on my mother's dead body. The last time my father grabbed me, before he died and said, "I love you." A declaration he never expressed while alive. I carry the black hole of hungry, unfilled love. The black hole that needs the *Shekinah* to fill me up so I can be human, aware and remembering. They are in my cells. They wake me and, terrify me…and gave me life. I miss them so."

"Where do you come from?" Kimi asked.

Ruby panted, took deep breaths, grounded her arms around her chest. "I come from the writing on the cave wall. I come from the hunt, the dust, air, water and wind. I come from hunger and desire to express, create and be free. I come from an ancient knowing that eludes me in the shadows of my unconscious. The belly of the divine feminine, the matriarchs that lived and loved for twenty-five thousand years. The woman who spoke to the Earth, the mother within. I am that woman from the Hebrew lineage, the one who prayed to Asherah. The *Shekinah* outside the temples. I am the resurrection. I saw the spirit and soul; I taught that there is no sin, except the ones we create. I never left the matriarchs, the Israelites, the women of the dust, earth, and moon. I walked the waves in the dust for forty days and nights. And then they took our voice, our knowing, put headdresses over our faces and knowing. The woman became original sin, born from a man's rib. How long do we accept that as the image of truth? When do we birth ourselves from the female ovaries, womb, uterus. How long?"

Joel asked, "What is next, Ruby?"

Ruby wagged her head. Her eyes scorched like the desert. Her voice changed to a Middle Eastern accent. "We chose each other. Sarah, Ruby's grandmother, and my ancient grandmothers. They traveled through Poland, Russia, Canaan, Mesopotamia, Israel, cracked apart in the Diaspora when the temples fell and the Israelites scattered to the four corners of the earth. I come from the struggle of addiction, chaos, and holocausts. From Passover dinners and blaring songs of the shofar calling out to the heavens, sun, moons, and stars to forgive my transgressions. I come from millions of women slaughtered during the Crusades, who were psychics, healers, shamans, medicine women, spiritual teachers. I come from the *Shekinah*, the burning bush, thousands of years of wandering the desert to find the home of milk and honey. I come from a long line of warriors who walked into ovens and were burnt alive. I come from smells of frankincense and lavender, mixed in with fat, grease and oil. I come from the American assimilation, the pickle barrel that my grandmother Sarah hid in to escape from the pogroms. Cossacks who threw rocks and stabbed Jews with thick blades and knives and hung them from their porches. I come from a God who wanted us to know the twist of the planets, the body of the universe, the Tree of Life. We are universal women living very personal lives. Ruby and I come from the same loin, the same stars and moon. She knows me, I know her. Now, she is hearing me talk for all the great-grandmothers who lost their voice and souls. They long for love in every crack of their soul and heart."

"What is the Jewess?" Kimi asked.

"A Jewess gazes at herself in the mirror with dust on her hands through desert eyes and sweeps the generations in the name of *Hashem*. My soul came to America and lived the American dream of abundance and opulence, the smell of money and fear on my breath. I come from the mysteries and a strange unwelcome grief that asked 'Do I exist on this Earth?' I am from another galaxy that channels knowledge through my body. I keep digging to the other end of nowhere to find the ground to stand on. I am seeking, dying, living to know where I come from. My body is restless, moving, wanting to know the faces of my lineage…the ancients, the old souls, the battles of truth and the child who crawls toward the Star of David, where heaven meets earth. I feed my soul with God, never truly knowing Her name."

"What does Marianne want me to know?" Ruby cried out between her channeled words.

"I need to be loved for who I am. I need to feel my deep sadness and deep love. Without love and recognition I am devoured with gluttony, lusting after life, an addict ravenous, fierce to drink life like a chocolate shake with a hint of vodka in it. I feel this tearing of my stomach, it rips and sheds, like a mutilation of my inner self. It is never- ending, this search to be held by maternal arms. My soul is anorexic. I eat and starve, eat and binge, and purge, binge and purge. I want life, but then I throw it up. Afraid for the intimacy of life, afraid I will be tortured for needing love. I don't know where to anchor. Marianne is you and I, Ruby. She is hungry to work through you. Know herself today as a woman wanting to know herself. Her story was lost between the lines, between empires and religious sects that made her hate her body and give herself away. She didn't know how to love without a man, and now I am learning to remember how to be a woman and love with purity. It's painful to remember that you've been forgotten."

"Why do we forget?" Kimi questioned.

"We don't forget. I learned from the edge of the rails, the ocean's roar, the slaps of cutting waves, sailed across from Poland. A cold place, a hard place where Sarah escaped from the camps. There her mother died, her sisters and brothers, disappeared into the dark forests of blood, where bodies lay topside, no graves, no burial rites. Raped like all young Jewish women, slaughtered so they could not birth another generation. But, I'm back. We're back." Ruby smiled. "I see. I see. Gabriel blowing his horn, Miriam playing her tambourine. I am here to watch the thousands walk across the continent. At first one in spirit, then split apart like the atom that exploded into separate tribes, separate nations, separate countries. I am here to receive the call of the wild, the women waving from afar, waving, coming home… coming back."

My grandmother crossed the ocean in a pickle barrel. She left behind everything, every picture, fork, spoon, tear, touch and connection to her roots. My mother swam in her grief, the women of my family fought to stay alive, fought to find love, fought to forget there was a past to their beginnings. But they couldn't wipe it all out, couldn't forget; they tried, with fancy cars and large diamonds plucked from the sky, gambling junkets and big brick houses with mezuzahs attached to the doors, where they kissed God's lips every time they entered the house. This is their remembrance; the witness of a people who survived, but didn't know what it meant to be happy or alive, or satisfied. An undying lust for life that never quite got quenched. I learned so much from these women, these people, this world. I have no way of knowing anything except I stand on the earth, sun shining, oaks swaying, moon behind the rim of the stars; and down below is me, you and others, watching, waiting, delivering the past from womb to womb to reinvent the secrets that are encoded in our cells." Ruby cleared her throat, "This is my prayer. Stories upon stories. Generations upon generations. Real stories. Personal stories that create a new myth of woman."

The air stirred. Joel watched Ruby's every move, alert, vigilant, his eyes and body like a hawk, ready to catch her. Kimi, a steady force of compassion and commitment.

Ruby blinked. She stared at Joel. "And you. Our story is unfinished. And it has only begun the stories. This is the beginning." A tremor shook her, a gentle tear beamed from the corner of her eye. "And thank you."

Joel closed his eyes, rubbed his chest. "I know."

A shiver trickled across her face, her eyes wide-open, filled with a twilight beauty. She threw the blanket off of her body, studied the dots and imprints of dried blood on lower arms, rubbed her wrists. "Shit. I'm alive! Oh my god I'm alive." She sniffed under her arms. "Man, I need a shower. I need a big juicy, cheesy burger and I need to sleep for about a year."

Kimi touched her head. "Are you all right?"

"I am for now. I am for now." Ruby drifted off, sleep devoured her.

Chapter 78: Homeward Bound

Dawn crept across the tips of trees. A glow of sleepy light spread like butter. Ruby hadn't slept. Her knees folded into her chest, washed and clean as a baby after her morning bath. She counted the rows of yellow, pink, purple, and blue flowers that bunched together as far as her eye could see.

Ruby held a piece of paper. On top it read Joel Simon, PhD. She sniffed it. The smell of his sweet spice drifted up from the edges. It read, "There's more for me. I don't know what. But you have a home, I still don't. I will always love you, Ruby Goldsmith. Some day… some day. It will be ours." Joel left for Burma a week later, just as Ruby prepared to return to Florida. Both had their own path to follow, and yet she knew that they were meant meet again. Buried deep she knew he was her rabbi. He awakened the sleeping tigress---but not now. Not now. She folded the letter into a neat square and placed it in the suitcase between the meager clothes she'd worn during her stay at the institute.

Ruby crossed over to the window. Someone was running on the bike path. Puffing hard, hands and legs in unison, her hair scrambling in the wind, her dark shorts and red T-shirt clung to her curvy body. Her thick, bronzed thighs, the sweat that glistened from her neck, in union with the pavement, her body grounded, free to run. Ruby felt this movement. She was ready to return to Steve and Hannah. Leah, her mother and grandmother's faces, passed through. She touched her lips. "Ruby lips." She whispered. "Life isn't fair, Grandma. But what else do we have? What else? It's not for us to know, only to keep living." She placed her hand on her heart.

A knock interrupted her thoughts. "Open," Ruby shouted.

Kimi and Joan strolled in. Kimi wore a simple blue shift that grazed over her body, folded between her breasts, the cloth waved across her belly and hips like sand dunes. She smelled like the beach. Her hair a wild jungle, yet perfect in the way each hair twisted and curled into braids that fell down to her collar bone. Joan, hair tucked into a ponytail, face soapy clean, no make-up, was wiped clear of her sadness. She wore a black strapless cotton dress that downplayed her sophistication, but emphasized her natural beauty. Joan placed a suitcase by the bed.

Joan sat on the edge of the bed. Kimi leaned against the wall, her silhouette touching the body of the great goddess Ruby had drawn.

Joan leaned forward and kissed Ruby's cheek.

"So. What's all this about?" Ruby got up and paced.

Kimi put a finger to her mouth, "Just one minute." She ran out. In less than time could beat, she returned. She carried a box with twenty-four black journals and ten tapes inside. "Here. Yours. I just dated everything. It's all your words. Marianne's words. Create the amazing with them."

Joan barely kept her composure, clapped her hands like a schoolgirl. "No more shot's around."

Ruby bundled the treasures into her chest. She stared at it for several minutes, as if holding a baby for the first time. "*The Book of Generations*. My work is cut out for me. I don't know what it all means. I don't even know why or what or how. I own my path, my destiny. I don't question 'why me' anymore. That is a waste of time. But, I'm still so uncertain what this… this story, what all these stories mean to me. To others?" She stared at the two. "I still don't know who I am. What I truly want. Or where I am going."

"I feel a burning in my stomach." Joan piped up. "Something is going to happen, Ruby. Something more…. I don't know. Something else."

"I feel it, too. And emptiness, a whirlwind. Things are not in place. Nothing is in order." Ruby packed each book and tape into the suitcase Joan had brought. "I'm not sure of anything." A quick light shot through her eyes. "I am only first finding my footing. We'll see. Or I'll see. Or whatever." She laughed. "At least I don't think I'm crazy anymore. Just nuts." Ruby smiled, and then started to cry. She grabbed the two women held them in a circle hug. They fell into each other's arms, their feet touching, kissing each other's cheeks.

"You're my tribe of misfits." Ruby pulled the three down to the floor. They hung together like a chain link. "The story continues."

She knew in order to free the stories, find the truth in them, that she had to free her life. Live them in some way that was not clear. The stories were transcendental teachings, of what she was not sure. At the same time, they were intimate and personal. They transformed her into a magician, a sage, and still she remained Ruby, only human.

Chapter 79: Full Circle

Ruby stood by her doorway. She was home, surrounded by birds of paradise, palms and wild bushes that blossomed red curvy flowers and dark green leaves. The smell of Florida summer was thick with mugginess, orange and grapefruit that sweetened the air. It was close to three years since she had been home. She released her bags to the ground. They plopped on the cement with a loud thud. For a moment her breath shook, the color in her cheeks turned red, the heat rose up from her belly, and she felt adrift. She caught herself before her anxiety dropped any further than her chest, and took a deep breath.

It was strange being here. Weird as the day she was born and heard the angels tingle in her ears. Did she belong here? She stroked the carved columns around the doorway, peeked through the side windows. Inside, no one was in the living room. She gazed at the red couch, the stripe-cushioned Mexican wooden chairs, the mirrored wall, and exotic sculptures. The bamboo shades were at half-mast. She tied the cloth belt around her blue dress, spit on her hands, wiped her face and fluffed up her hair that lay natural and free. She placed her hand on her throat and tangled with the necklace that Rosetta had given to her, the medallion of Mary and her grandmother's Star of David. She cradled and kissed it with a prayer.

Ruby wiggled the chipped bronzed door handle. It was unlocked. Before she entered she glanced at her watch. Seven o'clock. Hannah and Steve knew she was coming. But they were nowhere in sight. Steve had offered to pick her up at the airport, but Ruby insisted on riding home alone, picked up by a car service. Needed the time to adjust, sink into the sea level flatland and wide spacious sky that made Florida feel like a continent, not a peninsula. Okay. Now. Ruby whispered to herself. It's now or never.

She picked up her pieces of luggage one by one, opened the door, stepped through the entrance, and called out. "Steve, Hannah. Anybody home?" Ruby waited. The large orange sun illuminated the backyard. The pool turned dark green-blue with strays of orange-gold waves running down the middle, the trees a lost paradise. "Hello?" Ruby called out again.

Somewhere in the distance, a car door closed, keys jingled, footsteps pounded up the walkway, muffled chatter ignited the silence around her. It was them. Ruby's heart beat hard, shaking her belly, her palms moistened, her knees weak. They were here…

About the Author

Marta J. Luzim, MS is a Psychospiritual therapist-healer/intuitive and Creativity Coach in practice for thirty-five years. She is President and Founder of Primal Healing and Art and the 501(c)(3) non-profit organization and production company, Give Her A Voice, Inc. GHAV's first theatrical event was in April, 2011 at Cinema Paradiso in Fort Lauderdale, FL., showing raw, real life stories, dance and film about women who are on the journey to evolve, heal and have a voice from and beyond their abuse, addictions and PTSD from complex trauma.

She has written a column titled Women's View. She wrote and produced a short film called Primal Urgency, seen on Vimeo. Her two plays Breathing Under Water and Vows of Love had public readings. Her Heart of a Woman book can be purchased on Amazon.com. http://amzn.to/RS7RfN

The Calling is Marta's first novel. She is currently working on a memoir. Her lectures, blogs and articles are available on YouTube and c-zines. She can be reached through her websites www.martaluzim.com, and www.giveheravoice.org.

Marta's life has been dedicated to evoke each woman's unique voice to empower love, intimacy and creative vision.

Marta lives in South Florida with her husband Ron of forty three years. Her daughter Lara lives in NY with her soon to be husband, Roman.